stand by me

Book 1

A SouledOut Sisters Novel

neta jackson

THOMAS NELSON
Since 1798

NASHVILLE DALLAS MEXICO CITY RIO DE JANEIRO

Published in Nashville, Tennessee, by Thomas Nelson. Thomas Nelson is a registered trademark of Thomas Nelson, Inc.

The author is represented by the literary agency of Alive Communications, Inc., 7680 Goddard Street, Suite 200, Colorado Springs, CO 80920. www.alivecommunications.com

Thomas Nelson, Inc., titles may be purchased in bulk for educational, business, fund-raising, or sales promotional use. For information, e-mail SpecialMarkets@ThomasNelson.com.

Library of Congress Cataloging-in-Publication Data

Jackson, Neta.
Stand by me : a SouledOut sisters novel / Neta Jackson.
p. cm. -- (A SouledOut sisters novel ; bk. 1)
ISBN 978-1-59554-864-1 (trade paper)
1. Christian women--Fiction. 2. Chicago (Ill.)--Fiction. I. Title.
PS3560.A2415S73 2012
813'.54--dc23

2011048495

Printed in the United States of America
12 13 14 15 16 17 QG 6 5 4 3 2 1

To the Dumpster-divers
we know and love . . .
it's been an education

stand by me

Also by Neta Jackson

The Yada Yada Prayer Group Series

The Yada Yada Prayer Group

The Yada Yada Prayer Group Gets Down

The Yada Yada Prayer Group Gets Real

The Yada Yada Prayer Group Gets Tough

The Yada Yada Prayer Group Gets Caught

The Yada Yada Prayer Group Gets Rolling

The Yada Yada Prayer Group Gets Decked Out

The Yada Yada House of Hope Series

Where Do I Go?

Who Do I Talk To?

Who Do I Lean On?

Who Is My Shelter?

Prologue

Midwest Music Festival, Central Illinois

Kat Davies ducked into the billowing exhibition tent staked down in a large pasture in central Illinois like a grounded Goodyear blimp. She'd been at the Midwest Music Fest three days already—didn't know it was a *Christian* festival until she got here—and needed a little respite from the music pulsing morning till night on the Jazz Stage, Gospel Stage, Alternative Stage, Rock Stage, Folk Stage, and a few more she'd forgotten.

Besides, she'd be heading back to Phoenix in two days, and sooner or later she needed to figure out how to tell her parents she'd "given her heart to Jesus" after the Resurrection Band concert last night. Maybe this tent had a quiet corner where she could think. Or pray. Not that she had a clue how to do *that*.

Kat had a good idea how they'd react. Her mother would

flutter and say something like, "Don't take it too seriously, Kathryn, dear. Getting religion is just something everyone does for a year or two." And her father? If he didn't blow his stack at what he'd call "another one of your little distractions," he'd give her a lecture about keeping her priorities straight: Finish premed at the University of Arizona. Go to medical school. Do her internship at a prestigious hospital. Follow in the Davies tradition. Make her family tree of prominent physicians proud.

Except . . . she'd walked out of her biochemistry class at UA one day and realized she didn't *want* to become a doctor. She'd tutored ESL kids the summer after high school and realized she *liked* working with kids. ("Well, you can be a pediatrician like your uncle Bernard, darling," her mother had said.) And the student action group on the UA campus sponsoring workshops on "Living Green" and "Sustainable Foods" had really gotten her blood pumping. (Another one of her "distractions," according to her father.)

Was it too late to pursue something else? Her parents were already bragging to friends and coworkers that their Kathryn had received her letter of acceptance into medical school a few months ago. Feeling squeezed till she couldn't breathe, she'd jumped at the chance to attend a music fest in Illinois with a carload of other students—friends of friends—just to get away from the pressure for a while.

What she hadn't expected was to find so many teenagers and twentysomethings excited about Jesus. *Jesus!* Not the go-to-church-at-Christmas-and-Easter Jesus, the only Jesus she'd known growing up as the daughter of a wealthy Phoenix physician and socialite mother. That Jesus, frankly, had a hard time competing with Santa Claus and the Easter Bunny.

But these people talked about a Jesus who cared about poor people. A Jesus who created the world and told humans to take care of it. A Jesus who might not be blond and blue-eyed after all. A Jesus who said, "Love your neighbor"—and that neighbor might be black or brown or speak Spanish or Chinese. A Jesus who said, "All have sinned," and "You must be born again." The Son of God, who'd died to take away the sins of the world.

That Jesus.

That's the Jesus she'd asked to be Lord of her life, even though she wasn't exactly sure what that meant. But she desperately longed for something—Someone—to help her figure out who she was and what she should do with her life. The guitar player in the band who'd challenged the arm-waving music fans last night to be Christ-followers had said, "Jesus came to give you life—life more abundantly! But first you must give your life to Him."

That's what she wanted. Abundant life! A life sold out to something she could believe in. To give herself to one hundred percent. So she'd prayed the sinner's prayer with a woman in a denim skirt whose name she never learned, and a "peace like a river" flooded her spirit.

Last night, anyway.

But by the light of day, she was still heading in a direction—medical school—that she didn't want to go.

Big fans circulated the air in the large tent, though mostly it just moved the stifling July heat around. Thick, curly strands of her long, dark hair had slipped out of the clip on the back of her head and stuck in wet tendrils on her skin. Redoing the clip to get the damp hair off her neck and face, she wandered the aisles, idly picking up brochures about Compassion International, Habitat for Humanity, and YWAM. *Huh.* What if she just dropped out of premed and did something like this Youth With A Mission thing. Far from Phoenix and the Davies Family Tradition. Go to Haiti or India or—

"Nice boots," giggled a female voice nearby.

Kat glanced up from the brochure. A cute brunette with a shaggy pixie cut grinned at her from behind a booth that said Find Your Calling at CCU! Kat self-consciously looked down at the Arizona-chic cowboy boots peeking out beneath her designer jeans and flushed. Ever since she'd arrived at the festival, she felt as if she'd walked into a time warp—girls in tank tops and peasant skirts, with pierced nostrils, guys wearing ponytails, tattoos, shredded jeans, and T-shirts proclaiming Jesus Freak. Kat had felt as conspicuous as a mink coat in a secondhand store.

"Thanks. I think."

The young woman, dressed in khaki capris and a feminine lemon-yellow tee, laughed. "This your first time to the Fest? Where're you from?"

Kat felt strangely relieved to be talking to someone else who didn't look like a throwback to the seventies. "Phoenix. First time."

"Wow. You came a long way."

"You?"

"Detroit. But during the year I'm a student at CCU in Chicago. I get a huge discount off my festival fee if I sit at this booth a couple hours a day during the Fest." The girl grinned again and extended her hand across the stacks of informational literature. "I'm Brygitta Walczak."

Kat shook her hand. "Kathryn Davies. But my friends call me Kat. With a K."

"Like 'kitty kat'? That's cute. And . . . blue eyes with all that dark, curly hair? Bet the guys love that."

Ignoring the remark, Kat glanced up at the banner above the booth. "What does CCU stand for?"

"Chicago Crista University. Usually we just call it Crista U. Located on the west side of Chicago. I'll be a senior next year. Christian ed major."

"Christian ed? What's that?"

"You're kidding." Brygitta eyed her curiously. "*Mm*. You're not kidding. Uh, are you a Christian?"

Kat allowed a wry smile. "For about twelve hours."

The pixie-haired girl's mouth dropped open, and then her amber eyes lit up. "That is so cool! Hey . . . want a Coke or something? I've got a cooler back here with some soft drinks. Wanna sit? I'd love some company."

Brygitta dragged a folding chair from an unmanned booth nearby, and Kat found herself swapping life stories with her new friend. Unlike Kat, who had no siblings, Brygitta came from a large Polish family, had been raised in the Catholic Church, "went Protestant" at a Youth for Christ rally in high school, planned to get a master's degree at Crista U, and wanted to be a missionary overseas or a director of Christian education somewhere.

"Sorry I'm late, Bree," said a male voice. "Uh-oh. *Two* gorgeous females. You've cloned yourself. I'm really in trouble now."

Kat looked up. A young man about their same age grinned at them across the booth. He was maybe six feet, with short, sandy-brown hair combed forward over a nicely tanned face, wire-rim sunglasses shading his eyes. No obvious tattoos or body piercings. Just cargo shorts and a T-shirt that said CCU Soccer.

Brygitta jumped up. "Oh, hi, Nick. This is Kat Davies. She's from the University of Arizona, first time at the Fest. Nick Taylor is my relief. He's a seminary student at Crista—well, headed that way, anyway."

Nick slid off his shades and flashed a smile, hazel eyes teasing. "So, Miss Blue Eyes. Has Brygitta talked you into coming to CCU yet?"

Kat laughed and started to shake her head . . . and then stopped as her eyes caught the logo on the banner across the booth. *Find Your Calling at CCU!*

Transfer to Crista University?

Why not?

Chapter 1

Chicago, three years later

T*he earrings.* A slight panic rose in her chest as Avis searched the jewelry box a second time. Where were the ruby earrings Peter had given to her as a wedding present? They went perfectly with the wine-colored moiré silk dress lying on the bed, and she'd already told Peter she was going to wear them.

Avis Douglass sucked in a deep breath and blew it out slowly. *Think, Avis, think.* They couldn't be lost! She'd only worn them a few times since their wedding six years ago. The deep red brought out a rosy glow in her dark chocolate skin. But . . . ruby earrings weren't exactly de rigueur for an elementary school principal in her fifties. She'd had a few kids at Bethune Elementary—just a few, but still—who wouldn't have thought twice about ripping them out of her ears.

Besides, she liked to save them for special occasions. Like this weekend.

Their sixth anniversary.

A smile tickled her lips, and Avis sank into the upholstered rocker beside the queen bed, forgetting the earring hunt for a moment. *Six years. Amazing.* Second marriage for her. First for Peter. Old college friend of Conrad's who'd never married. Looked her up after Conrad died of pancreatic cancer, and one thing led to another . . .

She closed her eyes and rested her head on the back of the rocker, careful not to disturb the twists piled on top of her head after her visit to Adele's Hair and Nails that morning. Peter would be home soon—he often put in five or six hours at the office, even on Saturday—but she still had time to get dressed. The tiny smile broadened. Her man had turned out to be a class-A husband—well, mostly—in spite of "baching it" for several decades. She was proud of the way he'd built Software Symphony from a grassroots startup to the thriving business it was today, in spite of the obstacles he'd had to climb over as an African-American male. He treated his employees well—black *and* white—giving them opportunity to advance, even get more training if needed. He took his involvement seriously as a board member of Manna House, and under his guidance the women's shelter had operated in the black for the past few years.

But those things made him a good man. What made Peter a good *husband* was not only that he was crazy about her—she wanted to giggle like a girl every time he called her "my queen"—but his unflappable steadiness. A man she could count on. His thoughtfulness about little things and helpfulness around the house went a long way too. Avis chuckled. At least he'd learned to fold his own laundry and do the dishes while he was baching all those years!

In fact, the only time they'd ever had a serious disagreement was over the girls.

Her girls. He didn't have any kids.

Not that they'd had any problems with Charette, her oldest, who was married and living in Ohio. Or Natasha, the youngest, still single, working in D.C. as an advocate with the Center for Law and Social Policy. No, their only tension had been all the drama her middle daughter, Rochelle, dumped into their laps. Like last Valentine's Day . . .

"Can't believe it's almost one o'clock!" Avis giggled as Peter unlocked the front door and they slipped into the darkness of their third-floor condo. "Makes me feel like a teenager tiptoeing home after curfew."

Peter took her warm winter coat and threw it over the back of a chair. "Except now I get to spend the night." He chuckled. "Come here, beautiful." He pulled her close, and she felt his warm lips pressing gently on hers.

She wove her arms around his neck, breathing in the faint, cool smell of his aftershave. The evening still glowed in his eyes. He'd brought her a dozen red roses and then taken her to dinner and dancing in Uptown. On the way home they'd stopped at a vantage point where they could see the lake, shimmering in the clear February night. Moonlight had tickled the water out beyond the icy buildup along the Lake Michigan shoreline.

Breathtaking, even in winter. But thank God for the car heater! The outside temperature hovered around zero.

Avis wiggled out of his embrace and headed for the bedroom. Using the matches she kept in her bedside table drawer, she lit several candles around the room—but when she turned around, she burst out laughing. Peter was leaning against the door frame, arms folded, one of the long-stemmed red roses held between his teeth.

"You're nuts, you know that." Still laughing, she slid the ruby earrings out of her ears and turned her back to him. "Here, help me with this dress." The red silk dress was one of his favorites. But instead of unzipping the dress, he slid his arms around her again from the back and nuzzled her neck.

Blaaaaaatt!!

The loud door buzzer in the other room made them both jump. Avis gasped. "Who could that be at this hour!" She started for the intercom beside the front door.

Peter spit a sharp retort under his breath and then called after her, "Whoever it is, tell them to butt out and come back tomorrow."

The buzzer rang again, loud and insistent. Somebody had a lot of nerve—at one o'clock in the morning! Avis pressed the Talk button. "Who is it?"

"Mom? Mom, it's me! And Conny! Please, let us come up!"

Rochelle! Avis pressed the button that released the door down in the lobby, her heart suddenly beating faster. What was Rochelle doing out this late at night? With six-year-old Conny at that! The girl must've lost her mind!

"Don't tell me . . ." Peter's voice behind her was flat. More than flat. Annoyed.

Avis opened the door, stepped into the hallway, and peered

over the banister. She could hear Rochelle's and Conny's footsteps thumping up the carpeted stairs of the three-flat, and then their heads appeared as they trudged up the last flight. Conny, bundled in a hooded parka, dragged behind his mother, pulled by her grip around his wrist.

"Rochelle! What in the world—?! Conny, come here, baby." Avis bent down and wrapped her arms around her grandson. "It's all right, sweetie, Grammy's here." She slid the hood of the parka back and kissed the top of his loose, curly hair.

Rochelle brushed past her into their front room. Avis followed with Conny and shut the door.

Peter had turned the living room light on and stood facing them, arms crossed, frowning. "There better be a good explanation for this, Rochelle. Do you have any idea what time it is?"

Rochelle ignored him and turned to her mother. "I'm sorry, Mom. I—I lost my apartment and . . . and just didn't know where else to go. I came by earlier, but you weren't here. Where were you guys? You never stay out this late!"

Avis saw Peter shake his head in disgust. "We were out, Rochelle," she said evenly. "You should have called. We had our cell." Taking off Conny's coat, she helped the little boy lie down on the black leather couch. "What do you mean, you lost your apartment?"

Rochelle flopped down in the matching leather armchair. "I *told* you a couple weeks ago I lost my job. I've been looking, honest I have, but it's a zoo out there! Everybody's cutting back, letting people go, not hiring." She hunched forward, elbows on her knees, her thick black hair full and wavy around the honey brown skin of her face, not quite looking at her mother. "We just need a place to stay until I figure out what to do. Or . . . or if I could borrow some money for the rent, I'm sure I could get my apartment ba—"

"No." Peter's sharp retort left Rochelle's mouth open.

Avis winced. *Oh, Peter, let her finish.* This wasn't just about Rochelle, but Conny too.

Rochelle jumped up, eyes flashing. "I'm not talking to you, Peter Douglass! I'm talking to my mother." She turned to Avis. "Mom, *please*. I need some money for my meds. I'll pay you back as soon as I—"

"I said no!" Peter took three strides and stood between Rochelle and Avis. "This begging has got to stop, Rochelle. This is your third apartment. We gave you money for first and last month's rent. And you have a Medicaid card for the meds. We can't keep bailing you out."

"Peter—" Avis started.

"I lost the bloody card!" Rochelle's voice rose. "Or someone stole it . . . I don't know. But it takes weeks to get another one, and I need the meds *now*. You know that." Again she turned imploring eyes on her mother. "At least let us stay here till I find another apartment."

Avis cast a pleading look in Peter's direction. Rochelle did need her antiretroviral drugs—three times a day—to treat the HIV she'd contracted from her philandering husband. *Ex*-husband now. Dexter not only had played around but had become abusive. Avis shuddered. The past five years had been a series of crises getting Rochelle and Conny out of that mess, into a shelter, into a treatment program, finding an apartment, then a series of jobs that never seemed to work out . . . and now this.

Peter just stood there, arms crossed, shaking his head. "It's not going to happen, Rochelle."

With a screech the girl darted around her stepfather and ran toward the hall. Avis thought she was running for the bathroom and started to follow, but Rochelle ran past the bathroom, into the master bedroom, and slammed the door. Hurrying down the hall after her, Avis heard the lock turn.

"Rochelle. Rochelle, open the door."

"I'm not leaving!" she yelled. "I don't have any place to go!" Loud sobs erupted behind the locked door.

Avis could feel Peter's presence behind her. Turning, she put a hand on his chest and pushed him firmly back down the hall and into the front room, out of earshot. "Peter. It's one o'clock in the morning! We can't turn them out now. Think of Conny." *Think of Rochelle too.* No way did she want her daughter—still young, vulnerable, not well—out on Chicago streets at this time of night.

"And let her think her tantrum is working? No way."

Avis was firm. "Peter. Let them stay the night. Just for the night. We can talk about what to do in the morning."

Her husband threw up his hands. "All *right*. All right. Just for the night. But we take them to Manna House in the morning. They know her situation. They know better than we do what resources are available." Peter's shoulders slumped slightly, as if giving up. "Maybe they have room at the House of Hope. That's more long-term than the shelter, and she can keep Conny with her. Why don't you call Gabby Fairbanks in the morning?"

Avis nodded, relieved. "Good idea. At least get her on the waiting list." She wasn't sure if she was grateful to Peter for backing off or angry at him for being such a stubborn lump. Still angry, she decided, and headed back down the hall.

"Rochelle?" She knocked softly. "Please open the door. You and Conny can stay the night. I'll make up the studio couch in Peter's office. But it's late. We all need to get to bed." She knocked again. "Rochelle?"

She waited. After a few long moments the lock turned and the door opened. Rochelle, red-eyed and tight-lipped, nodded but slipped past her mother and into the bathroom. Avis heard the water running in the sink . . .

Avis sighed, staring at her newly manicured nails. She'd called Gabby Fairbanks at the House of Hope the next morning—Manna House's "second-stage housing" for homeless moms with children—but all Gabby could do was put them on the waiting list. "And we've got two other moms ahead of her," Gabby had said. "So sorry, Avis. It might be several months."

They'd offered to keep Conny for a few days, but Rochelle wouldn't hear of it. "It's both of us or neither," she'd huffed. So they'd taken them to Manna House. But when Avis called the shelter the next day, they said she'd checked out.

Disappeared was more like it. They didn't hear from her for days. Days that turned into weeks. And when Avis tried to call her cell, all she got was *"This phone is no longer in service."*

"Guess she had someplace to go after all," Peter had pointed out. "We can't be jerked around by her tantrums, Avis. She's a smart girl. She'll figure it out."

Avis sighed again. Not a day went by that she didn't think about her daughter and grandson. Conny especially. Rochelle's little boy had started kindergarten this year. Avis wished she'd helped them find an apartment here in Rogers Park so he could attend Bethune Elementary where "Grammy Avis" could keep a watchful eye on him. But no, Rochelle had found an apartment on the South Side and enrolled him down there. But if she'd lost that apartment . . . was she taking him to school every day?

And Rochelle used to bring him for a sleepover a couple times a month. Sweet times. But . . . they hadn't heard from Rochelle for over two months now, not since that Valentine's Day fiasco—

Avis's eyes flew open with a start. That was the last time she'd worn the ruby earrings. *Oh no. No, no, no.* Rochelle wouldn't have . . . would she? But her wild-eyed daughter had been in this very room that night, right after she'd taken off the expensive earrings.

Snatching up the jewelry box, Avis dumped the contents out on the bed, pawing through them desperately. She had to find those earrings! Surely she'd just misplaced them. She even dumped out her top dresser drawer, thinking they might have dropped in there by mistake.

No ruby earrings.

She heard the front door open. "Avis? I'm home!"

Avis quickly threw her lingerie back in the drawer and slid it into the dresser just as the bedroom door opened and Peter poked his head in.

"Hey, beautiful. I picked up the mail. Got something with

a South African postmark." He dangled the envelope just out of her reach for two seconds before handing it to her. "Hey, you gonna wear that red dress again? Nice. Do I have time for a shower?"

Without waiting for an answer, her husband disappeared down the hallway toward the bathroom.

Avis glanced at the return address on the envelope. *Nonyameko Sisulu-Smith, University of KwaZulu-Natal, Durbin, SA.* It'd been awhile since she'd heard from Nony! But no time to read it now. Stuffing the envelope in her purse, she snatched the dress off the bed and hung it back in the closet. She couldn't wear the red dress, not without the ruby earrings. She needed more time to look for them. Surveying her options, she finally pulled out a black satin crepe two-piece pantsuit with flared legs and flattering cowl neckline. She'd add a royal blue pashmina scarf and blue onyx earrings and tell Peter to wear his black suit and blue tie.

But as Avis slipped the silky top over her head, a sense of dread sank into her belly, and she had to sit down on the bed, hands covering her face. How could she suspect her own daughter?! But if Rochelle *had* taken the ruby earrings and pawned them, it might explain why she'd been avoiding them lately.

Avis shuddered. She should have tried harder to contact Rochelle. Maybe it wasn't a tantrum but guilt that kept her away. *Tomorrow . . .* she'd leave another message on Rochelle's cell, ask to meet her someplace so they could talk, use wanting to see Conny as an excuse to find out how they were doing, what was going on. Surely Rochelle knew it was important for Conny to have regular contact with his grandparents.

As for tonight, if Peter asked why she wasn't wearing the rubies, she'd just have to tell him she'd misplaced them somehow. *Which could very well be true . . . right, Lord?* No way could she let Peter guess her suspicions, or this could turn out to be the worst anniversary ever.

Chapter 2

Peter had said he wanted to do something special for their anniversary—and a dinner reservation at the top of the John Hancock Building was definitely a delightful surprise. The maître d' led them to a table right by the floor-to-ceiling windows in the Hancock's Signature Room with a panoramic view of Chicago's skyline. April's drizzle had spilled over to the first Saturday of May, but as dusk settled over the city, the clouds began to retreat and a scrap of moon peeked through. The lights sparking through the mist from every stately building along Lake Michigan looked like a field of diamonds.

Avis gave up her coat at the coat check but was glad for the blue pashmina that could double as a shawl, as the air in the restaurant was a bit too cool for her taste. Peter had seemed surprised when he got out of the shower and saw the change of outfits, but she'd hurriedly confessed she couldn't find the ruby earrings, had probably put them in a "safe place"—so safe she couldn't remember where—and assured him they'd turn up when she had more time to look. He'd given her a puzzled look but said nothing more about it.

She'd wrapped herself in her own thoughts as Peter drove south on the Outer Drive, Lake Michigan on their left, deepening into twilight's indigo blue. On their right, stately high-rises sailed past, lighted windows winking cheerily, but she barely noticed. *Oh Jesus, where are Rochelle and Conny tonight? Are they safe? Warm? Please, Lord, watch over them.* She'd fingered the cell phone in her coat pocket, tempted to try Rochelle's number right then, not wait till tomorrow.

"You okay, honey?" Peter had asked, concern in his voice. "You're not coming down with another cold from all those peewee germ-carriers at school, are you?"

She'd given him a reassuring smile. "I'm fine. Just tired is all. It was a busy week." Busy wasn't the word. More like Crisis City. Three teachers were out because of the flu. The school had gone into a temporary lockdown on Thursday because a fifth grader had brought a realistic-looking water gun to school in his backpack. Then an order for supplies had been delivered by mistake to a school in Georgia, leaving the Bethune school office without a working copy machine all week. Not to mention the school board was once again threatening school closures. The last time CPS closed schools for budget reasons, Bethune Elementary had received an influx of jilted students, cramming every classroom to capacity.

"I know. You work too hard, baby. You could quit, you know. How many years have you put in at that school? They should give you full retirement right now! But even if they didn't, we'd make it. Recession or not, we'd figure out a way."

When she hadn't responded, he'd let it drop.

Help me here, Lord. I know the Word says to praise You in all circumstances, but I'm having a hard time getting my praise on right now. She needed to put aside her worry about Rochelle and focus on her husband tonight. This was their evening.

Now, as their server filled the water glasses, Avis noticed they were the only African-Americans in the restaurant. Not exactly a local hot spot for the general population. Opening the menu, she raised an eyebrow. Delectable entrées—and prices—dripped from the menu. "Are you sure, honey?" she murmured. "It's a bit, um, pricey."

Peter's dark eyes twinkled. "I think my queen is worth a splurge now and then, don't you? Besides, I'd say we have something to celebrate—six whole years of marriage and we're still on speaking terms."

That sparked a laugh and she felt the tension in her shoulders begin to relax.

She chose the South African lobster tail. He ordered the roasted chicken that came with creamy grits and king oyster mushrooms. "*Mm-hm*. You can take a man out of the South, but you can't take the South out of the man," she teased. She didn't remind him of his brief sojourn as a "vegetarian" when they'd been courting, hoping to lose those pounds he'd gained eating out as a bachelor all those years. It hadn't lasted too long once he tasted her cooking, though he still had to avoid too much sugar and carbs as a borderline diabetic.

Which meant he passed on dessert—though she had to slap his hand when he kept sticking his fork in her dark chocolate mousse cake. They lingered over coffee, making small talk, enjoying the magical view. Peter made a tent with his fingers, gazing out over the city. "Six years . . . God's been good to us. Real good, Avis. And I'm grateful. We both have good jobs, make a decent living. But sometimes I wonder . . ."

His voice trailed off. Avis waited until he spoke again.

"I mean, do we just keep on doing what we're doing until we retire? Or do we look ahead, ask ourselves, what would we really like to do *before* we retire, while we've still got our health and a little energy." He frowned slightly. "Can't take it for granted, you know."

"Do? What do you mean?"

He threw out his hands and laughed. "I don't know! Travel maybe. Or put our experience to use doing something else, something different. It'd be fun to brainstorm. What's something you've always wanted to do, Avis? Maybe a dream you had when you were a little girl, but life just went a different way."

"I always wanted to be a teacher." She smiled, remembering playing "school" with every stuffed animal she could round up from the time she was five. "Guess I'm living my dream."

Peter snorted. "Lucky you. I thought it'd be cool to be an astronaut, ever since John Glenn orbited the earth when I was a teenager, but *that* obviously didn't happen—and I don't think NASA would have me now that I'm pushing sixty." He leaned forward suddenly and took Avis's hand. "Okay, you're living your dream as far as your job goes—but isn't there somewhere you've always wanted to travel to? Hawaii? China? Alaska?"

"Alaska? You're kidding. Too cold." She shivered just thinking about it. Then she smiled mischievously. "But, *mm*, Hawaii would be nice . . . or maybe South Africa. Nony's always begging the sisters in the Yada Yada Prayer Group to come visit."

Peter looked thoughtful. "That's an idea. Speaking of Nony, any news about how Mark is doing? What'd she say in her letter today?"

Letter! Avis felt a twinge of guilt. She'd been so distracted by the missing earrings and worry about Rochelle that she hadn't even opened the card from the Sisulu-Smiths. Just stuck it in her purse to read later. "Uh, haven't read it yet, but it's in here, I think . . ." Avis rummaged in her roomy leather bag and pulled out the square envelope. Using her table knife to slit the top of the envelope, she pulled out the card.

"How sweet. She remembered our anniversary!" The front of the card was a pen-and-ink drawing representing an African man and woman in traditional dress dancing in each other's arms as a circle of angels surrounded them. The clothes of the man, woman, and angels were overlaid with a bright wash of red, yellow, and green. "*Mm,* it's beautiful."

"Let me see it." Peter reached for the card. A folded note fell out as he opened the card and read the inside aloud. "'Angels celebrate your everlasting love . . . Happy Anniversary.' And it's signed Nonyameko and Mark."

He handed the folded note to Avis. "It's probably for you— Oh, look at this." He turned the card to the back and showed it to her. In tiny script it said, "An original watercolor by the Women's AIDS Initiative." "Isn't the Women's AIDS Initiative the program that Nony started?"

"*Mm-hm.* She's trying to help single and widowed women start small businesses so they don't have to turn to sex to support themselves. Also to help women with AIDS, since many times the man abandons them, not wanting to take responsibility." Avis looked at the card again. "These cards must be one of their enterprises."

Nonyameko . . . A wave of homesickness for her South African friend washed over Avis. Married to Mark Smith, an African-American professor of history at Northwestern University, Nony had been one of her Yada Yada Prayer Group sisters for several years. But the prayer group all knew Nony's heart burned with a desire to help her South African sisters who were suffering from AIDS in devastating numbers.

Nony was the one who took it personally when Rochelle was diagnosed with HIV, as if she were her own daughter. That, maybe more than anything, had fanned Nony's passion to *do something* for women like Rochelle back in her home country. Except . . . Mark had been on track for tenure at the university and balked at moving the family halfway across the world.

Avis shuddered as memories flooded into her mind. The senseless attack on Mark by a white supremacist group he'd routed from the campus . . . months of rehabilitation for the brain injury that took the sight from one eye and left his speech and day-to-day functioning impaired, even though slowly improving . . . the need to take an indefinite sabbatical from teaching—

"More coffee, ma'am?"

Avis's eyes flew open to see their server poised over her cup with a fresh pot of coffee. She nodded, even as her thoughts tumbled backward. "Only God could take that tragedy and turn it into something good," she murmured as the server left.

"Tragedy?"

She smiled at her husband's puzzled look. "Just thinking about Nony and Mark. How Mark's injury finally opened the door for Nony to follow her dream." She waved the hand-painted card. "And now look."

Peter grimaced. "Yeah, well, I hope we don't have to suffer a tragedy like that to shake *us* out of our ruts . . . Hey, what's her letter say? If it's not private, read it to me."

Avis unfolded the note. "It's to both of us. 'Dear Avis and Peter . . . Many blessings on your anniversary. I wish Mark and I could be with you to celebrate. But maybe we can take a rain check—'" Avis glanced up. "Maybe they're planning to come back for a visit!"

Peter shrugged. "Maybe so. Go on, read."

She searched for her place. "All right . . . 'Mark and I would like to talk to the two of you about something. As you can see from the card, we have been able to start a few small businesses with some talented girls—greeting cards, rug and basket weaving—but to be honest, we need advice and practical help from someone more experienced in business than we are. We are wondering if the two of you would consider coming to South Africa for an extended visit. Whatever time you could spend would be a gift—three months? Six months? A year would be even better—'"

Avis heard a gasp and looked up. Peter's eyes had widened, and they seemed to dance in his face. "I can't believe this!" he said. "That's it, honey! We were just talking about doing something new, something different. And here's Nony, out of the blue, dropping an opportunity into our laps."

"No, *you've* been talking about doing something new and different, not me."

But his eyes had strayed to the expansive view out the large windows, as if he hadn't heard, fingers absently drumming on the tablecloth. "I'd love to do something like that—a trip with a purpose. I could help Nony and Mark draw up some basic business plans that could apply to a number of small businesses. Marketing—that's the key . . ."

Avis felt her head whirling. Peter was jumping on this too fast. Yes, she'd just teased about taking a trip to South Africa—but for three months? Or six? No, no . . . maybe a two-week visit in the summer.

She skimmed the rest of the letter. *We could also use your teaching skills, Avis. Many of our girls need help with basic education—math, language, typing, even health and hygiene. We'd love to arrange for some classes but need a teacher. You—*

"So what else did she say?" Peter's attention had turned back to her.

Avis kept her eyes on the sheet of paper, not wanting to look at her husband. She licked her lips and read the last paragraph. "'The boys are growing like weeds and doing well in school. Marcus is trying to decide where to go to university next term. Praise God Michael won't leave home for a few years yet! Both boys love playing soccer—'"

For some reason Avis's eyes teared up. She didn't resist when Peter gently took the letter to read the rest for himself. "*Hm*. See you skipped over the part where you fit into this proposal," he said. She could feel his eyes on her as she fished in her purse for a tissue and blew her nose. Silence hung between them as she picked up her coffee—now lukewarm—and sipped it.

"Tell me what you're thinking, honey. To me, this practically feels like a word from the Lord. We were just talking about planning ahead, doing something new—and now this!" Avis could still hear the excitement bubbling in his voice.

She had to slow this train down fast. "Peter, I know. But it's not that easy to just pick up and go to South Africa for . . . what did she say? An *extended* visit? It's . . . it's not just our jobs, though in this economy you don't just throw out a good job and think you can get another"—she snapped her fingers—"just like that."

He said nothing. She played with the cloth napkin in her lap. "It's . . . it's also other responsibilities. Family, and . . . and—"

"Family? We've got an empty nest, girl!"

Now her eyes did lock on his. She took a deep breath and let it out slowly. "Just because *you* don't have any children, Peter Douglass, doesn't mean we don't have family responsibilities. I'm . . . worried about Rochelle. And Conny. We haven't heard from her in over two months. *Almost three months!* She—"

"Rochelle." He practically spit out the name. "I knew it. She's got you just where she wants you, Avis, worried sick. Don't you get it? She's just mad because we didn't bail her out the last time she mismanaged her money, and she's making us pay. It's nothing but a tantrum, I guarantee it."

Avis shook her head. "Maybe. Maybe not. But . . . I can't just leave the country for months, not knowing if my grandbaby is all right. Or Rochelle either."

"So." Peter's voice was tight. "Just how long are we going to let Rochelle dictate what we do with our lives? Tell me, Avis. How long?"

Chapter 3

The 92 Foster Avenue bus pulled to the curb as the automated female voice chirped to life. "Magnolia. This is Magnolia. Next stop, Broadway. Transfer at Broadway for the Red Line."

"That'll be us, guys." Kat Davies slipped her backpack over one shoulder and stood up, grabbing for the nearest pole as the bus lurched forward once more. Her companions—two other young women and one guy—also vacated their seats and made their way to the back door of the bus as it headed toward the next intersection.

"Twenty-two stops," muttered one of the girls, bumping up behind Kat. "Can't believe this bus stopped *twenty-two times* before we got to our stop. Isn't there a faster way to get to this church you like so well?"

Kat laughed. "Can't believe you bothered to count every single stop. It'll be worth it, I promise." Pixie-haired Brygitta Walczak was her roommate at Crista University. Both were graduate students, Kat completing her master's degree in education, Brygitta in Christian ed.

At the next stop the doors wheezed open and Kat and Brygitta hustled down the steps. Behind her Kat heard the other girl ask one of the passengers, "How do we transfer to the El from here?"

"Livie! I *know* how to get to the El! Come on!" Kat wagged her head as the other two CCU students—Olivia Lindberg, a sociology major, and Nick Taylor, a seminary student—joined her and Brygitta on the sidewalk. It was *so* tempting to stick Livie into a "dumb blonde" pigeonhole sometimes, the way she kept asking obvious questions. Livie was an undergrad, three years younger than the graduate students, but the four had ended up in CCU's Urban Experience program and developed a Four Musketeers mentality on their assigned excursions into Chicago. "All for one and one for all!" they joked, though Kat suspected it covered up some mutual insecurity as they navigated unfamiliar "urban experiences," such as the Manna House Women's Shelter in Uptown and what was left of the notorious Cabrini Green public housing site. Manna House had been pretty cool—but Cabrini Green . . . Kat shuddered every time she thought about it. She couldn't imagine living there, ever. Yet at one time fifteen thousand of Chicago's poor had been crammed into the string of crime-ridden high-rises.

But the Urban Experience advisor had also given participants a list of urban churches to visit, at least three by the end of the school year. Definitely more inspiring. Stuck at the university during spring break, Kat and Nick had visited SouledOut Community Church in Rogers Park, Chicago's northernmost neighborhood along Lake Michigan, and they'd insisted that Brygitta and Olivia come with them for a second visit. "It's definitely cool! Like no church you've ever attended before," Kat enthused.

Her roommate had been dubious. "But are they, like, you know, evangelical?"

"They're *Christian*, Brygitta. Doesn't the name 'SouledOut' say anything to you? Just . . . come and see for yourself."

"Will we be the only white people?" Olivia had wanted to know.

"I told you, Livie. It's multicultural. Black *and* white, and a few other somethings too. You'll be fine."

At least Kat hoped Livie would be fine. The sociology major was trying hard to adjust to the big city, but it was obvious she hadn't strayed far from her small-town Minnesota roots before. Kat had to give the girl credit for signing up for the Urban Experience program at CCU. But there were times she wanted to smack her.

Like now. They were halfway across the intersection when Kat realized Olivia was still standing back on the curb. "Livie, come on! We gotta cross here!"

"But the Wait light is blinking!"

Arrgh. Kat ran back, grabbed Olivia's hand, and pulled her across Foster Avenue just before traffic got the green light, then flounced ahead to walk with Nick.

"Livie's just nervous in the city," Nick murmured in Kat's ear. "Go easy on her . . . Hey, your hair smells nice. What is that—coconut?"

Kat gave him the eye. Nick was a tease—okay, a borderline

flirt—but it was just play between friends. She hoped. Nick wanted to be a *pastor,* of all things. No way did she want to end up a pastor's wife. But . . . his compliment tipped the corners of her mouth. Her dark curly hair, thick and long, was her best feature. That, and her ice-blue eyes. It was nice of His Maleness to notice.

"Hey, guys, wait a sec!" Brygitta's voice turned them around. She and Olivia were looking up and down the street they'd just crossed. "Isn't there a grocery store somewhere near here? I didn't get any breakfast and I'm going to be famished if I have to wait clear till church is over."

Kat glanced impatiently at her watch. She'd *told* her roomie to eat something before they left. They had a whole stash of energy bars in their room. But . . . it was only eight thirty. SouledOut's service didn't start until nine thirty. She looked at Nick and he shrugged. "Okay. Guess we have time. I think there's a Dominick's a few streets over. Saw it from the El last time. It's only a few blocks out of our way."

The foursome changed course and walked east on Foster Avenue. Sure enough, the big chain grocery took up an entire block along Sheridan Road. As they wandered through the produce section, Kat noticed a couple of the employees loading up boxes on a cart with lettuce, broccoli, and other vegetables—taking them out of the cases where they'd been displayed and wheeling them through a pair of swinging doors into the back rooms. Curious, Kat followed, peeking through the plastic windows in the doors and watching as the carts were wheeled through another set of doors leading outside.

Outside? What . . . ?

Goodness. The stuff was being thrown out!

Kat tugged on Nick's jacket sleeve. "Meet me outside when you guys get done," she hissed. "Out back." She pointed in the direction of the swinging doors, then spun around and hurried past the checkout lanes, out the automatic doors, and scurried as fast as she could around to the back of the store.

Sure enough, the two employees were dumping the boxes, produce and all, into a Dumpster.

Kat blinked. A few minutes ago shoppers could have still bought that stuff and taken it home to eat. Now it was . . . what? Out of date? Gotten rid of to make room for fresher stuff? Doomed to go to the garbage dump?

This was outrageous! The stores ought to at least give it to a local homeless shelter or something.

Food. Nothing got Kat's dander up like the thoughtless way people just bought "whatever" at the store, never thinking about the horrific way chickens were caged to maximize egg production, or the chemicals used to make those tomatoes red. And the waste! All that plastic packaging. And now this! Dumping good food!

As soon as the coast was clear, Kat lifted the lid of the closest Dumpster and peeked inside. At least six or seven boxes of produce were in there!

"Kat! What in the world are you doing?"

Kat jumped at the sound of Brygitta's voice, banging her head on the Dumpster lid she was holding. Brygitta and Olivia were staring at her openmouthed, and Nick was grinning with amusement.

"Look at this!" She poked her head back into the Dumpster. "Good food. C'mon, help me get this box out of here."

"Oh, Kat! That's stealing!" Olivia sounded truly panicked.

"Is not. It's been thrown away." Kat tugged at the closest box with her free hand. "Somebody help me here."

"What do you think you're going to do with it?" Brygitta demanded.

"I don't know . . . take it to the church with us. They'll know what to do with it."

Nick joined her at the Dumpster, lugging out the box of lettuce and broccoli. "Hold the lid open!" he called to Brygitta and Olivia. "I can reach that other one."

Five minutes later Nick and Kat were crossing the street at a brisk pace, laughing, each carrying a box, heading for the Red Line El station one block up and one block over. "Ha!" Kat snickered, glancing over her shoulder at Olivia and Brygitta, walking ten paces behind them. "They're pretending they don't know us."

Chapter 4

Avis and Peter rode home in silence, and they might as well have had a bundling board between them in bed that night. She wet her pillow with silent tears in the darkness, knowing the evening had not ended with the hoped-for tenderness and sexual joy of other anniversaries.

Avis slipped out of bed early the next morning, while the sun seemed to be making up its mind whether to come up or not. Stuffing her feet into a pair of cozy slippers and wrapping an afghan around her shoulders, she curled up in a corner of their soft leather couch with her Bible. She needed some quiet time with God—desperately needed some time alone with God!—because she was scheduled to be the worship leader at SouledOut Community Church that morning, and she was no more prepared in her spirit to lead worship than to hand in her resignation at Bethune Elementary Monday morning.

Oh God! she cried out from her heart. *I really bungled our anniversary this time—*

Avis stopped. What was she doing? Jumping right into her problems, crying on God's shoulder without even acknowledging His presence. Who was she to barge right into the throne room of God and demand that He fix the mess she'd made of things last night?

Oh God! she started again. But the praise that usually began her prayers just wasn't there.

She stared at the well-worn Bible in her lap. If Nonyameko were in her shoes—and hadn't her friend been in shoes much more painful than Avis's right now?—she'd turn to the Psalms and let the psalmist's words be her prayer.

Avis opened her Bible to the Psalms. Many verses were already underlined, words of praise or comfort that had spoken to her spirit in times past. She turned to Psalm 8, a favorite, and began to whisper the words aloud, making them personal as Nony so often had done . . .

"'O Lord, my Lord, how majestic is your name in all the earth!'" *Yes, yes, this is what I need to do. Turn my eyes on almighty God to put my worries in perspective.* "'You have set your glory above the heavens. From the lips of children and infants you have ordained praise because of your enemies, to silence the foe and the avenger!'"

That verse was already underlined in heavy red. Avis remembered the first time those words had spoken to her, when her first husband had died of cancer, leaving her a widow too soon. If the simple praises of little children could silence the enemy, then her praises were that powerful too. *Take that, Satan!* No way could the Prince of Darkness—the evil one who wanted to steal her joy, her peace, even her anniversary—do his nasty work in an atmosphere of praise to the Lord God of heaven.

She prayed the rest of the psalm and continued right on into Psalm 9, no longer whispering. "'I will praise you, O Lord, with all my heart. I will tell of all your wonders. I will be glad and rejoice in you. I will sing praise to your name, O Most High!'"

Tears of joy spilled down her cheeks as morning sunlight finally peeked into the windows of their third-floor apartment. *This* was what she needed to do when they gathered for worship at SouledOut that morning—to praise the Lord with all her heart, to simply rejoice *in God*. Yes, she *could* lead worship this morning, because it was about God, not about her. Maybe others were walking in similar shoes, coming to church after a ragged week, things undone, wrongful things said, worries clogging their hearts . . . but the praises of little children—*and us big babies too*—could silence the lies of the enemy.

Avis was about to close her Bible when her eyes fell on Psalm 5. "'Give ear to my words, O Lord, consider my sighing . . .'" *Hm*. Not exactly a psalm of praise. But it seemed like an invitation to open her heart. Praying again with the psalmist, she murmured the words aloud: "'Listen to my cry for help, my King and my God, for to you I pray. In the morning, O Lord, you hear my voice. In the morning I lay my requests before you and wait in expectation . . .'"

She closed the Bible and held it tight to her chest, as if pressing the words into her heart. "Thank You, Lord!" she whispered, squeezing her eyes shut. "I needed this reassurance that I can lay my worries in Your lap—even a silly thing like my lost earrings—and I can wait in expectation, because I know

You are working all things together for our good . . ." For the next few minutes she poured out her pain over the situation with Rochelle and Conny, regret over the way their anniversary had ended the night before, and not knowing what to do about Nony's outrageous request to come to South Africa for an "extended visit."

"You on the phone, Avis?" Peter's sleepy voice startled her eyes open as he shuffled into the living room in his robe and slippers. "Oh. Sorry. Didn't know you were praying. Just heard you talking." He turned to leave.

"Don't go. It's all right." Avis patted the couch beside her. "Come sit down?"

Peter hesitated and then sank onto the other end of the couch. "Coffee ready by any chance?"

"No. Sorry. I needed some time to pray, wasn't thinking about coffee. But . . ." She reached out a slim brown hand and touched his. "I want to say I'm really sorry about last night."

Peter frowned slightly. "Yeah, kind of a bum end to our evening. But . . . guess I overreacted, and I'm sorry about that."

A strange peace settled into Avis's spirit, and suddenly she knew what she needed to do. "Peter, I don't want to throw cold water on your idea of looking forward, of maybe doing something new with our time—whether it's this invitation from Nony or something else. It took me off guard, I guess. So I'm willing to talk about it and pray about it together. We can trust God to show us what He wants us to do, can't we?"

She felt his fingers gently close around hers. She went on. "I'll send an e-mail to Nony, let her know we got their beautiful anniversary card and the amazing invitation, but we need some time to think and pray about all the implications. At the same time, I do have a request."

Peter scooted over on the couch and put his arm around her, pulling her close. "What's that, baby?" he murmured into her hair.

She relaxed into his side, tucking her feet up on the couch. "I'm really concerned about Rochelle and Conny. I don't want it to be 'either-or.' I need to find out where she is, if she's okay, how Conny is doing, resume some regular contact. Then . . . well, then it'll be easier to think about other things." She twisted in his embrace so she could see his face. "Will you help me?"

Peter was quiet a long moment, then he stifled a yawn. "Sure, baby. Whatever you want . . . especially if I can get some coffee in the next ten minutes. I'm still asleep."

"Oh, you!" Avis reared back and punched him in the shoulder. "If you're sleep-talking, maybe I should ask for a new car or that trip to Hawaii before you wake up!"

Chapter 5

It was a good thing the elevated commuter train wasn't crowded on a Sunday morning. Both Kat and Nick took up a double seat across from each other to accommodate the bulky cardboard boxes of lettuce and broccoli.

Brygitta leaned forward from the seat where she and Olivia sat just behind Kat. "I can't believe you guys are actually going to take those boxes into the church."

Kat just grinned and waggled her fingers over her shoulder. It was no use trying to convince Brygitta. Her roomie was probably imagining a brick edifice with a pipe organ or something. Once they got there, she'd see that it wasn't a big deal.

Besides, Kat didn't really care what Brygitta thought. She felt kind of proud that she'd rescued this produce from oblivion. Hopefully several families were going to eat some fresh food who might not have otherwise.

Metallic brakes squealed as the train pulled into the Loyola station, sitting high above the street below. A young Latino couple with a baby got on and made their way to the back of the car.

"That's the fourth stop," Brygitta piped up behind Kat. "How many more till we get to Howard Street?"

Honestly. But humoring her friend, Kat grabbed a pole and swung out of her aisle seat to study the map posted above the windows. "Um . . . three more. It's the end of the Red Line, anyway. Everybody gets off." She sat down again as the train jerked forward and turned sideways to talk to her two friends, though Olivia had her nose buried in a textbook. "Have you guys decided what you're going to do this summer?"

Brygitta groaned. "Oh, Kat, I don't know. I should just go home when the semester's over in a few weeks and get a jump-start looking for a summer job. But I signed up for summer mini-term, thought it'd be a good way to get Christian Ethics out of the way so I can graduate next January, which means all the jobs will be taken by the first of June. Besides . . ." She rolled her eyes heavenward. "Can't really stand the thought of another summer in Detroit. Living at home with Mom, Dad, Grandma, three obnoxious younger brothers . . . need I elaborate?"

Kat laughed. "Nope."

"At least you're graduating in a couple weeks . . . Hey, can I come home with you? I've never been to Phoenix. What's the summer job situation like?"

Kat shrugged. "Same as everywhere, I guess. Haven't had to deal with it. My father always finds something for me to do in his practice, but—"

Olivia's head jerked up from the book she was reading. "Practice? Is he a lawyer or something?"

"A doctor," Brygitta hooted. "Cardiologist, right, Kat?"

Kat nodded. Not that she wanted to talk about it. Her father was still upset that she'd dropped premed and transferred to CCU. "I'm signed up for mini-term too. I—"

"Why? I thought you were graduating." Olivia's pale blue eyes were uncomprehending.

So I don't have to go home yet, was on the tip of Kat's tongue. But she said, "I need more Spanish so I can qualify for my ESL certificate. And I've been thinking . . ." Her eyes drifted to the back sides of the apartment buildings they were passing, mesmerized by the crosshatch of back porches with wooden railings and open stairs zigzagging from the top floor to the ground. *Had* she been thinking? Or was this a bubble of an idea that'd been floating in her subconscious and only now just popped?

"Thinking what?" Brygitta prompted.

"About staying here in Chicago for the summer." There. Saying it aloud gave strength to the idea. "I mean, if I stay *here*, I could start looking for a job now, not wait till I get back to Phoenix. And . . . it'd be fun. More time to explore the city. I hear there are lots of ethnic festivals, stuff like that, all summer long."

Nick leaned out of his seat across the aisle. "Really, Kat? I've been thinking the same thing. I'm taking a class for mini-term too. But if I stayed in Chicago for the rest of the summer, I could get a head start looking for a church position that would satisfy my practicum and let me graduate in January—"

"Howard Street," announced the disembodied voice from a speaker. "Howard Street is next. End of the line. Everyone must exit the train. Transfer to the Yellow Line or Purple Line at Howard."

The train eased to a stop beside the wide platform. Another train going the opposite direction pulled in along the other side. Once again there was a scramble to grab backpacks and purses, as well as the two large boxes Kat and Nick juggled as they squeezed out the sliding doors. Leading the way, Nick headed down the stairs to ground level, through the station, and out onto Howard Street.

"Which way?" Olivia pressed her back against the station wall to avoid the crunch of people exiting the station.

"Just follow us, you goose . . . Watch that bus turning in." Kat and Nick walked swiftly up the sidewalk along the busy street, Brygitta and Olivia close on their heels. A block later they turned into a large parking lot surrounded by stores, including a large Dominick's store that anchored the mall at the far end.

"Where's the church?"

Kat refused to be annoyed by Olivia's anxious questions. "Right over there. Told you it was in a mall."

As they crossed the parking lot, they could see the sign painted in lively red letters across the wide expanse of windows:

SOULEDOUT COMMUNITY CHURCH

And beneath in smaller letters, but still large enough to be read from several yards away:

ALL WELCOME

A tickle of excitement quickened Kat's steps. Cars and minivans were pulling into the parking spaces near the wide storefront, and people of all colors piled out—brown, white, tan—the kids running, parents hollering at them to slow down, teenagers huddling together outside with their iPods. The young Latino couple with the baby Kat had seen on the train also disappeared through the double glass doors.

"Welcome!" boomed a deep voice as they came in. A middle-aged black couple stood just inside the doors, greeting people as they entered. The man held out his hand. "I'm Sherman Meeks, this is my wife, Debra. Your first time at SouledOut?"

Kat couldn't exactly shake hands while holding the box. "Hi. I—uh, some of us were here once before. Um . . . Mr. Meeks? Is there someplace I can put this box? It's food. To give away."

"Food?" The man blinked, as if he didn't understand the word.

"Oh, honey, our potluck isn't until next Sunday," his wife said kindly. "It's always the second Sunday of the month . . . Oh! Good morning, Edesa. How's Gracie?" Debra Meeks turned to a pretty black woman breezing in the door, holding the hand of a dark-haired little girl.

"*Buenos Dias,* Sister Debra! Gracie, give *Señora* Meeks a hug."

Spanish-speaking? The woman didn't *look* Spanish—

"Told you so," hissed Brygitta, leaning close to Kat's ear. "Why don't you guys just . . . just go dump those boxes somewhere and let's go in."

Kat ignored her. She turned back to Mr. Meeks. "Do you have a kitchen here? We could just put these boxes in there for now."

"Of course, of course." Mr. Meeks pointed toward a set of double doors on the far side of the room. "Just go through there. You'll see it on the left."

"You guys find a seat, save a couple for us, okay?" Kat

whispered to Brygitta and Olivia. "We'll be right back." She and Nick threaded their way through the knots of people clustered behind the rows of chairs in the large room, through the double doors, and into the small kitchen on the left of the hallway.

Kat stopped. Nick's box bumped into her.

Someone else was in the kitchen.

The woman turned. She was older, but it was hard to tell her age. Her skin was flawless. Creamy dark chocolate. Not a wrinkle anywhere. Shiny black hair swept up on top of her head into a cluster of twists. Plum lipstick, a touch of color on her cheekbones. A plum-colored suit, very feminine. Gold hoop earrings. She'd been fixing a cup of tea.

"Can I help you?" Her voice was rich. Dignified. Kat was mesmerized.

When Kat didn't answer, Nick spoke up. "Hi. I'm Nick. This is, uh, Kathryn. We, um, brought these vegetables in case some folks here could use them. Free for the taking."

The woman took a step or two and peeked into the boxes they were holding. "Vegetables? Where'd they come from?"

Uh-oh. Kat quickly found her voice. "Dominick's Food Store. They were going to get thrown out, so they, uh, gave them to us."

The woman lifted an eyebrow. "Were *going* to get thrown out? Or had *already* been thrown out?"

Kat glanced at Nick. He was turning red around the ears. She sighed. This lady was no slouch. Might as well be straight up. "I saw them take them out of the display cases to throw away. We grabbed them just minutes after they'd been for sale in the store. I'm sure they're still good."

"I see." The woman studied them a long moment. Kat was

suddenly conscious of their jeans and gym shoes, a stark contrast to her careful grooming. "Why bring it here?" the woman asked.

"Oh, well, we were coming to church anyway, and we found this food on our way here, so . . ." Kat didn't know what else to say.

"Ah." The woman's face seemed to relax. "Well, I don't know what we're going to do with it. Maybe you can put it out on the coffee table after the service. But . . . just put the boxes on the counter for now. If you came to worship, let's go worship."

"Let's go worship" . . . odd thing to say. But Kat and Nick hurriedly set the boxes down on the metal counter and followed the woman back into the main room. Brygitta waved at them from the next to last row of chairs, and they squeezed into the empty seats beside their friends just as Kat heard the same woman's voice, louder now, but resonant and full: "Good morning, church! Let's all stand as we prepare our hearts, our minds, and our bodies to worship our Lord and Savior, Jesus Christ, this morning!"

Kat's head snapped up. The woman in the plum suit was standing at the microphone on the low platform at the front. *Oh good grief. She's the worship leader!*

Chapter 6

The whole room rustled as people got out of their chairs, and the keyboard offered a few quiet chords. Kat felt a poke in her side as she and her friends stood up too. "Bet we made a real good first impression on that lady," Nick murmured.

Kat just rolled her eyes at him.

The worship leader opened her Bible. "Listen to the Word of the Lord from Psalm 8: 'O Lord, our Lord! How majestic is your name in all the earth! You have set your glory above the heavens! From the lips of children and infants you have ordained praise . . .'"

Kat saw Brygitta quickly turn pages in her own Bible to follow along, but Kat closed her eyes, letting the words flow over her, into her.

"'When I consider the work of your fingers, the moon and the stars, which you have set in place, who are we—mere men, women, and children—that you should care for us? . . .'"

At least this psalm was somewhat familiar, even though Kat hadn't started to read the Bible seriously until three years ago.

"'You made us ruler over the works of your hands; you put everything under our feet: all flocks and herds, and the beasts of the field, the birds of the air, and the fish of the sea . . .'"

Now Kat squirmed. Where was that woman going with this? Seemed like some people used the biblical mandate in Genesis to "have dominion" over the earth as an excuse to exploit it. *"Rape it" would be a better phrase*, she seethed. This psalm could be taken the same way—that phrase, "under our feet," was practically an invitation to trample over God's creation.

Kat's thoughts were pulled back as the worship leader finished with a ringing, "'O Lord, our Lord, how majestic is your name in all the earth!'"

"Amen!" several people responded, hands lifted high. "Glory!"

The room quieted. The worship leader's face was wet with tears. "I don't know about you, brothers and sisters, but God spoke to me through this psalm this morning. I was being pulled down by concerns pressing in from several sides all at once—"

"Lord, Lord! Know what you're sayin'!" someone said from the back of the room.

"My praise was all locked up," the woman at the mike continued. "Lead worship this morning? Are you kidding, Lord?"

A laugh tittered through the congregation. "Keep it real, Avis!" a wiry black woman called out. "Keep it real!"

"But as I read this psalm, I was reminded that coming to church isn't about me. It's about God! It doesn't matter if I've had a good week or a bad week! We're here to give praise to the Lord of all creation! The King of kings! The Name above every name! And as we focus on Him, our concerns will take on perspective. Of course God cares about the problems we face! And He's going to work them out, people. Whatever's weighing on your heart right now. That's His job. *Our* job is to come before Him with awe and adoration and thanksgiving! Because Satan—that dirty trickster—can't mess with us when our hearts are full of praise!"

By now, cries of "Praise God!" "Glory!" and "Hallelujah!" were ringing from every end of the room. Kat stole a glance at Brygitta and Olivia, who looked a bit like cornered mice.

But at that moment the praise band—a keyboard, electric guitar, drum set, bass, and saxophone, as well as several singers—launched into a lively song, one the CCU students sang in chapel services at the university, though not quite like this. Kat's former thoughts faded as she felt herself swept in with the rest of the voices around her: "Lord, we lift your name on high . . ."

Two hours later, after an hour of singing, clapping, and praising, followed by a thoughtful teaching by one of the pastors—a tall, rail-thin white man they called Pastor Clark, who seemed well past retirement age and rather frail—Olivia leaned over and pulled Kat's sleeve. "I didn't know the service would go so long. I've got to get back to school and study. Finals are coming up, you know!"

"Shh!" Kat hushed. "They're welcoming visitors."

". . . stand and tell us your name and where you're from?" The woman in the plum suit had come back to the mike. A few people stood up—somebody's parents, an older white couple from Indiana . . . a black teenager who'd brought her cousin . . . a man who spoke in halting English and said he'd just been walking by and heard the music, so he came in.

The congregation clapped and called out, "Welcome!" after each introduction.

"Anyone else?" The attractive black woman at the mike looked directly at Kat.

Kat popped up and waved the others up too. "My name is Kathryn Davies—most people call me Kat—and this is Nick Taylor, Brygitta Walczak, and Olivia Lindberg. We're all students at Crista University and"—*might as well say it now*—"we brought a couple boxes of still-good lettuce and broccoli that we'll put out after the service. Free for the taking!"

She heard a quiet groan from Brygitta as the four of them sat down again. "I can't believe you did that."

Fine. So Brygitta was embarrassed. How else was she supposed to let people know the food was available? There was a table in the back, they could just put it there.

"Did we miss anyone? If not, we want to invite our visitors to join us at the coffee table right after the—"

"Hold on, Avis, now." The wiry black woman Kat had noticed before scurried to the front and took the microphone from her. "We got us an announcement you don't know about, so . . . no, no, don't you go sittin' down. You stay up here. And where's your man? Peter Douglass! Get yourself up here."

Kat craned her neck. A distinguished-looking, middle-aged

black man with touches of gray in his close-cropped hair was pushed up to the front to some general laughter—which turned to clapping when he put his arm around the waist of the woman in the plum-colored suit and gave her a teasing squeeze.

"That's right, that's right, you give that lady a *big* hug, 'cause we fixin' to celebrate Avis and Peter's sixth wedding anniversary, right here at SouledOut Community Church, right now. Hey, Jodi and Stu? You comin' out with that thang?"

At that, the double doors leading to the back rooms pushed open, and two white women came out carrying a large decorated sheet cake between them. The wiry woman with the mike started to sing, "Happy anniversary to youuu . . ." which was immediately picked up by the rest of the congregation as the cake was carried carefully to the front, presented to the embarrassed couple, and shown to the congregation. The end of the song was swallowed up in a round of applause, laughter, and catcalls to "Kiss her! Kiss her!"—which the woman's husband did by wrapping both arms around her, tilting her backward, and planting a big smooch on her lips.

Brygitta and Olivia sat bug-eyed and openmouthed, and Kat couldn't help grinning. She'd never seen anything like this in *church*. All around them the room was practically convulsing with laughter and clapping. But somehow the self-appointed emcee with the mike managed to be heard over the hubbub. "Now don't nobody leave till you've had some cake an' coffee an' given this fine couple a blessin'. Pastor Clark an' Pastor Cobbs, you two wanna give the first blessin'?"

An African-American man—shorter and stockier than the other pastor and younger by a decade or two—came forward and laid a hand on the Avis woman's shoulder, the other hand lifted in blessing over the couple as the first pastor offered a simple prayer: "Lord, we thank You for Avis and Peter Douglass, for the blessing they are to our congregation here at SouledOut Community Church. Pour out an extra measure of Your blessing on them in the coming year, on their children and grandchildren—"

The second pastor jumped in. "And we thank You, Jesus, for giving them a second chance at love! Bless them as they come in and go out. Bless them abundantly in ways they might never expect, because You are a *good* God, and they can trust You to look out for them, whatever the future holds."

Kat wasn't quite sure when the prayer ended, because other people jumped in with "Amen!" and "Yes, Lord!" But pretty soon the anniversary couple was ushered to the back to cut the cake and receive congratulations.

Kat nudged Nick. "Come on. Let's get the boxes and put them out while everyone's around the table back there."

Nick grimaced as if he had second thoughts about the plan, but leaving their two friends to fend for themselves, he followed Kat into the kitchen, where they found the boxes of produce pushed into a corner, and walked them out to the coffee table.

The wiry black woman, her hair worn in sculpted braids, seemed to be in charge of the table. "Excuse me," Kat said, trying to get her attention, "can we put this—"

"Florida!" Someone else got to her first. "Cut a piece for First Lady Rose an' I'll take it to her. She's up front prayin' with somebody an' we don't want it to be all gone before they're done."

Kat waited until the piece of cake for "First Lady Rose"—whoever that was—had been whisked away, and then she tried again. "Uh, the lady over there"—she pointed to the couple getting congratulations a few feet away—"said maybe we could put these boxes of food here so people can help themselves." The coffee table would've been the perfect spot, except now it was covered by the large sheet cake, plates, plastic forks, and napkins.

The woman named Florida stared at her. Then at the boxes. "Where this stuff from?" She reached in and plucked out a head of broccoli. "Looks a mite yellow on the tips."

Kat flushed. "Well, maybe a little. But it's still good. I'm sure some people could make use of—"

"Well, girl, I know you mean well, but you can't put it *here*. We're a little busy having us a celebration this mornin', know what I'm sayin'? 'Sides, not sure why you think anybody's gonna want—"

"It's all right, Florida. They asked me about it before church." To Kat's relief, the worship leader lady—Avis Douglass, they said her name was—left her husband's side and approached them. "Of course, I didn't know you'd planned all this!" The woman swept her hand toward the decorated sheet cake, which was rapidly disappearing as kids and teenagers snitched extra pieces.

"Whatchu think you doin', Carla! You kids get on outta here. I *know* that's your third piece!" Florida hustled back to the table, flapping her apron at the gaggle of kids, who ran off giggling.

Avis Douglass turned back to Kat and Nick. "But she's right, there's no room on the table for the, uh, produce you brought. Let's see . . ." She looked around the room. "Why don't you put the boxes on a couple of chairs right by the door, where people will see it as they go out. But I ought to warn you. What doesn't get taken will probably get thrown out—unless you want to take the leftovers with you."

Kat saw Brygitta and Olivia beckoning urgently. "Uh, no, my friends need to get back to school. So . . . well, we'll just put it by the door like you said. Thanks."

Drafting Brygitta's and Olivia's help, the students dragged a line of four chairs together, set the boxes on them, and opened the top flaps. "Do you think we should make a sign?" Kat murmured, thinking out loud.

"No! You made an announcement, for pity's sake. Everyone will *know*. Now come on." Brygitta flounced out the door, Olivia on her heels.

Kat hesitated. "Just . . . give me a sec," she said to Nick and walked quickly back toward the coffee-and-cake table. The crowd around the anniversary couple had thinned. She waited until the last two people congratulating Avis and Peter Douglass had finished gushing and then stuck her hand out. "Just wanted to say Happy Anniversary to both of you. Also . . . I really enjoyed the service this morning. Thank you for, you know, helping us worship."

Peter Douglass shook her hand. "Thank you, young lady. Glad you came today."

Out of the corner of her eye, Kat saw her friends once again beckoning impatiently. "Well, I'd like to come back again and"—an idea flashed in her head like a neon sign—"I'd really love to talk to you. Maybe next time?" On impulse, she gave Avis Douglass a quick hug and then fled toward the door.

Chapter 7

Startled by the enthusiastic hug, Avis groped for her husband's arm to regain her balance.

"Who was *that*?" Amusement colored Peter's voice as they watched the girl with the dark wavy hair flounce out the front doors with her comrades. The whole room was emptying and Florida was starting to clean up the coffee table.

Avis shrugged. "They introduced themselves at the end of the service. From Crista University I think they said." For the life of her she couldn't remember the girl's name, even though she'd been told in the kitchen before service, and the girl had introduced herself and her friends at the end as well. Wait . . . did she call herself "Cat"? That couldn't be right.

"Avis!" Florida cut into her thoughts. "You two wanna take the rest of this cake home? Otherwise I'll serve it up at Yada Yada tonight since we meetin' at my house . . . oh. You comin'? Or you guys got anniversary plans?"

Yada Yada tonight? Avis closed her eyes for a brief moment.

She'd almost forgotten that the prayer group had changed—again—to first and third Sundays. She'd been hoping she and Peter could do some sleuthing and make contact with Rochelle and Conny this afternoon. On the other hand, if they didn't find her right away, they were going to need a lot of prayer—big time.

"Celebrated our anniversary last night," Peter stage-whispered to Florida behind his hand. "Can't afford to take Her Royal Highness here out on the town *two* nights in a row." He laughed. "But I will take that cake—"

"Oh no you don't." Avis pinched his waist, which had developed a bit of flab in the last few years. "At least not the whole thing. Wrap up *one* piece for the man, Florida, and take the rest home for Yada Yada. And yes, I'll try to be there tonight. Will call you if I can't."

"I heard that." Jodi Baxter, one of her Yada Yada sisters, joined them, licking icing off her fingers. "Good grief, since when would you let a little thing like an anniversary—or a wedding, for that matter!—keep you away from Yada Yada? We'd be lost without our fearless leader, Avis!"

"*Humph*. That right there would be a good reason to stay home, in case you all need a reminder that Jesus is your leader, not me."

Jodi laughed, tucking a stray lock of wispy brown hair behind her ear. "Yeah, but I can still call you boss lady, since I'm just a lowly teacher at Bethune, and you, my dear friend, are Ze Princi*pal*!"

Avis wagged a finger. "Careful, or Ze Princi*pal* will assign Lowly Teacher to lunchroom duty." The moment the tease was out, she wished she hadn't said it. It was sometimes awkward juggling the different hats she had to wear around Jodi—professionally, as her boss at Bethune Elementary where Jodi taught third grade, and then personally, as prayer group sisters and friends who shared intimately with one another at Yada Yada.

But seeing that Florida was busy wrapping a couple pieces of cake in a paper napkin for Peter, Avis pulled her friend aside. "Seriously, Jodi, if I don't get to Yada Yada tonight, it's because . . . well, we haven't heard from Rochelle for over two months, and if I can get in touch with her, I'm going to try to see her. I'm . . . real worried about her and Conny. So ask the sisters to pray for us, okay?"

"Oh, Avis, I'm sorry. I didn't realize it'd been that long since you'd seen your daughter. Of course we'll pray. And I'll touch base with you at school tomorrow, okay?—Uh-oh. Denny's out there in the car already. I better go." Jodi gave Avis a warm hug and scurried toward the front doors—then stopped by the boxes on the chairs. "What's this stuff?" she called back.

"Dumpster food!" Florida hollered. "Help yourself if you're desperate. An' what you don't take, I'm gonna throw out!"

Avis and Peter got some Thai takeout on the way home. She'd stopped cooking a big Sunday dinner when the girls left home, and Peter had been in the habit of eating out on Sunday all those years he'd been "baching," so they usually went out to lunch with friends or got takeout after church.

Avis was just as glad, especially today. She wasn't really

hungry after their decadent meal on top of the Hancock last night, and besides, she was eager to get started looking for Rochelle.

While Peter changed clothes, she spooned out the pad Thai and beef with pea pods from their white cardboard containers onto two plates and fished a couple pairs of chopsticks from a kitchen drawer. When her husband came to the table, he eyed the chopsticks suspiciously. "If you don't mind, honey, just give me a fork. I'll do the chopstick thing when we actually eat out in a Thai restaurant, okay?"

Peter said a brief blessing over the food and dug in. Avis toyed with her chopsticks until he'd almost cleaned his plate, then said, "I'd like to try to contact Rochelle this afternoon—before the workweek starts. Any ideas where we should start?" She knew she was asking a lot. Peter liked to take a nap on Sunday afternoon and then watch a basketball game on TV, especially if the Bulls were playing.

Peter sat back in his chair and pursed his lips, which he often did when he was thinking. "Well, first things first. Have you tried her cell? Left her a message?"

"I *did* that for a couple weeks back in February, practically every day! But she never returned any of my calls, so I stopped. You said don't chase her, and she'd call me. But . . . she hasn't." Avis blinked back the hot tears that suddenly threatened.

He patted her hand. "I know. I know, honey. So I think it'd be okay to try again now, since several weeks have gone by. She's got pride, Avis. Probably hoping you'll call and make the first move now that she's simmered down. But if she doesn't answer, leave a message, see if she calls back."

Peter took his plate to the sink, rinsed it, and stuck it in the dishwasher. "You okay with that, honey?" Getting a nod from her, he headed for his favorite chair in the living room with the Sunday paper.

All right. It made sense. Avis put her own dishes in the dishwasher, then took her cell phone into the bedroom, propping herself with several pillows on their queen bed. But she hesitated. *Lord, You said the Good Shepherd left the ninety-nine sheep who were safely in the fold, and He went out looking for the one lost sheep. Can You make that two, Lord? Rochelle is lost, and Conny too. And I don't know how to find them.*

She hit the speed-dial number for Rochelle and held her breath while it rang. Once . . . twice . . . then an irritating squeal and computerized message. *"This phone number is not currently in service."*

What? Maybe she'd dialed the wrong number . . . no, she had Rochelle's number on speed dial, same as always. Still, she tried the number again and got the same message. Unwilling to give up, the third time she typed in the number, digit by digit. Same message.

Avis felt like throwing the phone across the room. Not in service? What did that mean? Now she couldn't even leave a message!

Avis marched into the living room, ready to say, *So what now, Peter?* But Peter was asleep in the recliner, snoring softly. Watching the slow rise and fall of his chest and his slippered feet resting on the footrest, her resolve melted. The man was tired. He'd put in a six-day week running his business. It wasn't his fault that Rochelle hadn't paid her phone bill. She'd asked him for advice because she wanted finding Rochelle to be his priority too. But . . . he was asleep. And she wasn't helpless.

Avis made herself a cup of lemon tea with honey, sipping the hot liquid as she leaned against the kitchen counter. *So, what next, Lord?*

But the voice she heard in her head was her father's. Something Buck Thomas had said when she'd phoned him as a new mom, panicked because she'd lost Charette in the Marshall Field's store at Christmas. *"Go back to the place where you last saw her, Avis. Start there. Don't go running off in a dozen different directions."*

Okay, so where was the last place she'd seen Rochelle and Conny?

The Manna House Women's Shelter. She'd taken her daughter and grandson there the day after Valentine's Day. But they hadn't stayed more than a day . . . Still, it was a place to start.

Grabbing her address book from the shelf near the kitchen phone, Avis looked up the number under M . . . and dialed. The phone rang five or six times before someone answered. "Manna House."

"May I speak to Mabel Turner, please?" If anyone would know where Rochelle was, it would be the director.

"Sorry. She ain't here on Sundays. Be back in the office tomorrow morning."

Avis shut her eyes and pressed her fingers to her forehead. Of course. But surely someone on the staff was there. "Is there someone on staff I could speak to?"

"Hold on." The phone went dead. Avis waited a full minute before a voicc camc on again.

"Hello? Nancy Cox speaking."

Nancy? She didn't know anyone on staff named Nancy. "I'm . . . my name is Avis Douglass. I was hoping to speak to someone on staff who might know if my daughter, Rochelle Johnson, has been on your bed list recently."

"Oh. You probably need to talk to Mabel Turner. She'll be in tomorrow. I'm just day staff on weekends. Rochelle Johnson? I don't recognize that name, but that doesn't mean much. She could've been here during the week. Even on a weekend there're always some new faces, and I don't always learn all the names. But Ms. Turner has a list of everybody."

"All right. Thank you." Avis pushed the Off button on her phone.

Now what, Lord? She was back to square one.

Or was she? Why not try Rochelle's last apartment? She said she'd been kicked out for nonpayment of rent—but what if she meant she *might* get kicked out? What if she was still there?

But she'd have to drive to the South Side. No home phone. Rochelle only had a cell.

Avis quickly changed out of the plum-colored suit into a pair of jeans, gym shoes, and a white cotton pullover sweater. Grabbing her car keys and a light jacket, she paused in the living room where Peter was still dead to the world. Should she wake him? Ask him to come with her? . . . No. If Rochelle was still mad at Peter, still saw him as the Big Bad Guy that Mama married, maybe it was better if she went alone.

Scribbling a note that she laid on her husband's lap, Avis quietly slipped out the front door of their apartment and hurried down the stairs. But she only got to the second-floor landing when the door of the apartment below them opened.

"Avis? Oh, good, it's you." Her downstairs neighbor, Louise Candy—a name that always made Avis want to ask where *that* came from—poked her head out. Her dyed blond hair was rolled up in curlers, and a tanning salon tan framed her pale blue eyes. "Just wanted to tell you that Ted and I are going to Costa Rica for the summer—some business deal he's got going there, a real hot property—so we're looking for someone to sublet our condo for three months or so. But even thinking about interviewing strangers to stay in our condo makes me tired. So thought we'd pass the word among friends. Don't want just anyone renting it, you know."

Definitely. Avis didn't want just anyone living downstairs either. They had a quiet building—a three-flat that had gone condo a few years ago—and only the first-floor family had kids, two preschoolers. She and Peter were the only African-Americans in the building, but they got along well enough with the other two condo owners.

"Sounds like a great opportunity. I'll let you know if I hear of someone." Avis gave a quick wave and hurried down the next flight before Louise tried to fill her in on their latest business scheme in Costa Rica.

But as she crossed the narrow residential street and unlocked the door of her Camry, it hit her: if she and Peter did something like he was imagining—go to South Africa or Timbuktu for six months or a year—they'd probably have to sublet their apartment as well.

She shuddered as she started the car and pulled out of the parking space. Put *that* in the minus column.

Chapter 8

Monday at Mary McLeod Bethune Elementary School lived up to its reputation as "Wild Horse Roundup Day." In every classroom Avis peeked into as she navigated the halls, teachers were having to corral kids who were practically bouncing off the walls after a weekend with too much TV, too much sugar, and too little attention from grown-ups. By Tuesday they'd be settling down, but in the meantime the row of chairs in the school office for kids being remanded for detention was full before noon.

After-school detention wasn't an option at the elementary level, so Avis rotated all teachers and support staff to supervise a separate lunchroom, which meant each person had to be on duty only once or twice a month. If more than five kids were assigned to detention on a single day, Avis added herself to help supervise.

Like today.

By the time detention was over—seven disgruntled miscreants dawdling their way through the school lunch of tuna-noodle casserole, followed by a grade-appropriate extra math assignment—Avis had a headache.

And she still hadn't had time to call Manna House.

Closing the door to her office, she sank into the padded desk chair, leaned her head back, and closed her eyes, ignoring the stack of mail the school secretary had put on her desk. Her trip to the South Side yesterday afternoon had been fruitless. She'd found the apartment at the last address she had for Rochelle, but there was no name on the mailbox in the foyer of the apartment building, and no answer when she pressed the buzzer. Not knowing what to do, she'd hung around for a while, hoping someone would come out or go in who might know whether Rochelle still lived there. Two big dudes with tattoos and low-slung jeans were buzzed in by somebody about ten minutes apart, but they just shook their heads. Then a plump woman—she looked Hispanic—came out pulling a wire grocery cart and said, "*Sí*, I think I know who you mean. Pretty woman, skin like caramel candy, lots of hair? And a little *niño* about five or six?" Avis had nodded eagerly. But the woman had shrugged. "Haven't seen them around lately. Maybe they moved."

She'd given up then, but it was already after five. The Yada Yada Prayer Group would've started by then, and would be almost over by the time she drove back to Rogers Park from the South Side. She'd called Florida on her cell, apologized for her absence, and said Jodi could explain.

Peter had been upset that she'd gone to the South Side by herself. "You should've woken me up! That neighborhood's crime statistics are going through the roof!"

Maybe she should feel glad he was concerned about her

safety. But his comment irked her. Wished he felt that upset about Rochelle and Conny living there.

Avis pressed her fingers to her temple. She couldn't let her mind go there. She needed to keep moving forward, take the next step: *call Manna House.* Avis pushed the stack of mail, requisitions to sign, and interschool memos to the side and picked up the phone.

"Mabel Turner, please," she said when the regular receptionist at the shelter answered. Nice girl, recently engaged, she'd heard, to a young man at her Korean church.

"Oh, hello, Mrs. Douglass! Hold on . . ." Avis waited a long minute and then heard, "Mabel Turner speaking."

"Hello, Mabel. This is Avis Douglass. I'm—"

"Avis! What a nice surprise. Didn't see you here last month when SouledOut hosted Sunday Night Praise. Everything all right?"

"Uh . . . yes, fine. I'd just lost my voice, had laryngitis. Hope the service went all right." SouledOut Community Church was one of several churches that sent a small praise team and someone to speak at the shelter once a month on Sunday evenings. With Peter still on the Manna House board, he and Avis often came with the SouledOut team. "But actually, why I'm calling . . . I'm wondering if my daughter Rochelle has been on the bed list at Manna House lately? You may remember, I brought her there several weeks ago, the day after Valentine's Day, but she and her little boy, Conny, only stayed one night, and"—Avis felt her throat tighten—"we haven't heard from her since." She reached for the water bottle she kept on hand.

"I'm sorry, Avis. That's got to be hard."

Avis took several swallows of water, hoping Mabel would say more, but that was it. "So . . . has she been back? I mean, has she been on the bed list since then? I'm worried about her—her health, you know. And Conny. I need to find them."

There was an awkward silence. Then she heard Mabel sigh. "Avis, I'm sorry. The bed list is confidential. I mean, we can't tell people over the phone if someone is here or not. Or whether they've been here. If Rochelle tells you, that's fine. But . . ."

Avis gripped the receiver. She couldn't believe this! Mabel knew her personally, knew Rochelle was her daughter. Valentine's Day hadn't been the first time Rochelle had been an emergency resident at Manna House. So what was this all about?!

"Avis? You still there? I'm sorry, your question about the bed list threw me. Even though I can't tell you names on the bed list, I can tell you I personally haven't seen Rochelle since she was here last. That's not a hundred percent guarantee she hasn't been here, especially if she came and went on a weekend, but I should have said that up front."

A knock at her office door was followed by Jodi Baxter poking her head in. *"Oh. You're busy. I'll come back,"* the younger woman mouthed silently and started to pull back.

But Avis waved her in. "Thanks, Mabel. Guess that's basically what I need to know." *It'll have to do, anyway.* She hung up the phone and turned to the third-grade teacher. "Hi, Jodi. What's up?"

Jodi closed the door behind her and pulled up one of the visitor chairs. "That's my question. You didn't make it to Yada Yada last night. What's up? Was that Mabel Turner?"

Avis nodded. "I was trying to find out if Rochelle and Conny have been back to Manna House in the past couple months, but she said the bed list is 'confidential.'" She grimaced. "I'd think family would qualify for information."

"*Mm.* I see your point—but also hers. Some women don't want other people to know they're at the shelter."

"Thanks for the support." Avis allowed an edge of irritation to slip into her voice but tried to soften it by asking what happened at Yada Yada the previous night.

"It was good. Everybody made it—except you, of course. But I shared that you hadn't heard from Rochelle for a couple months and were looking for her. We prayed for you both." Jodi looked at her quizzically. "So what happened yesterday?"

Avis told her about Rochelle's phone being cut off so she couldn't even leave a message, and the dead end when she went to Rochelle's apartment. "Doesn't sound like she's been back to Manna House either. Mabel did say she hadn't *personally* seen her. Guess that's almost as good as saying she hasn't been on the bed list."

Jodi reached across the large desk and touched Avis's arm. "I can hardly imagine how I'd feel if I hadn't heard from one of my kids for a couple months and didn't know how to contact them. And not knowing whether little Conny is okay either! You must be going nuts, Avis. Can I do anything? Help you look? Something!"

"Thanks, Jodi. I'll let you know if there's anything. *I* don't even know what to do next."

"Guess it's prayer then." Jodi grinned. "Seems to me my friend Avis once told me to *pray first*, not just when all my other options had run out." She took Avis's hand in both of hers and began to pray.

Avis appreciated Jodi's heartfelt prayer, but only after she'd banished the irritating thought, *Does she think I haven't been praying?*

After her "amen," Jodi jumped up. "Oops, gotta get back to my class. My aide is probably wondering why it's taking so long to photocopy the permission slip for our field trip to the Adler Planetarium." But at the door she turned. "Oh, nobody last night has heard from Nony for a while. Have you gotten any news?"

It took Avis two seconds to reroute her thoughts. *Nonyameko's invitation.* But she wasn't quite ready to put that out on the table for her Yada Yada sisters to pray about. Not yet. Because they'd all have an opinion first. Probably get all excited and muddy the decision she and Peter needed to make. But she could mention the card.

"Actually, Peter and I got an anniversary card from Nony and Mark a few days ago. It was made by the Women's AIDS Initiative—one of the businesses they've started. Very artistic. I'll have to bring it to show you."

"Would love to see it—okay, gotta go."

Avis stared at the door as it closed behind Jodi. What was wrong with her? All weekend she'd been getting irritated at the least little comment. Not like her—at least not the way Avis usually thought of herself. *Calm. Confident. Focused. Knowing God's in control.* But now her thoughts and feelings jerked about like Mexican jumping beans. Not surprising on one hand, with Rochelle and Conny missing. But that wasn't the only thing.

Peter wanting to "do something new, different" in the next few years. Nony's invitation to come to South Africa.

Even the missing ruby earrings. Not being able to find them—and not knowing if they were simply misplaced or truly gone—had left her feeling jittery. Anxious.

Breathing, *Lord, I need You!* Avis sighed and pulled the stack of mail toward her. It helped calm her mind to systematically work through the pile—a request from a parent for an early dismissal, another for additional testing for their child, supply requisitions to approve, evaluation forms from teachers, feedback on her school budget for next year—until she picked up the envelope from the Chicago board of education.

Slitting it open, she pulled out the single sheet on CPS letterhead. Skimming through the letter, she read it once, then again more carefully, until the words began to blur. Dropping the letter, she leaned her elbows on the arms of her desk chair, head dropping into her hands. *Oh God, not again. Not now!*

Peter worked late on Monday night, and Avis had a PTA meeting on Tuesday, which included a serious discussion on playground bullying and the importance of parents and teachers working together to put an end to it. On Wednesday evening they went to Pastor Clark's midweek Bible study at SouledOut Community Church, a series on Jesus' teachings about the kingdom of God, "present now, within you," Pastor Clark kept emphasizing.

It was Thursday before she and Peter even had time to sit down together for supper. Avis felt almost too tired to cook, but they both needed a good meal. She thawed some chicken thighs and stuck them in the oven with a rub of seasoned salt, herbs, and smoky-flavored paprika, made a pan of cornbread, and pulled out a bag of green beans from the freezer. Easy. But hearty.

"*Mm*, looks great, honey." Peter rubbed his hands together as she served up their plates. Offering a quick prayer of thanks, he dug into the food, slathering two pieces of hot cornbread with butter and honey.

"You'll never guess what happened today," he said after polishing off the first piece of cornbread. He pointed his fork at her. "Jack Griffin—remember him? He's the guy in Indianapolis with a software business similar to Software Symphony, wanted us to merge our companies about three years ago as a partnership. I wasn't interested at the time—but today, who shows up in person? Jack Griffin! Wants to make me an offer, buy me out! A nice offer, I have to admit." Peter shook his head as he cut into his chicken. "Can't believe it. Right out of the blue, just like that. Something to consider, don't you think, honey?" He forked a man-size bite of chicken into his mouth.

Avis just stared at him. "Why would you do that? *Sell* the business?"

Peter chewed thoughtfully. "It's just something to think about. The economy is still in big trouble—you know that. A lot of people aren't able to make their mortgage payments. All those foreclosures. Gas keeps going up. Unemployment still high. I might be wise to sell before the economy bottoms out."

Avis's mouth went dry. "But . . . what about your employees? They depend on you. Florida's husband, Carl, for instance. What would happen to him if you sell?"

Peter wiped his fingers on his napkin. "That's a good point. Might make it a condition of the sale that current employees would keep their jobs. But . . . honey, don't look so distressed. We don't have to make a decision tonight. I want to think it over, talk to some people, pray with you . . . but I have to admit, when something like this drops into your lap, you wonder if God is telling you something."

Avis shook her head. It was almost too much. "Not sure it is the best time to sell. I need to show you something." She got up and rummaged through the large canvas bag she carried to school each day and returned to the table with a letter. "Been meaning to show you this."

Peter took the envelope and frowned. "School board, eh?" He pulled out the letter and read it. She watched his face. A flicker of interest widened his eyes and smoothed out the frown. She could tell he was reading it a second time, just like she had—though she'd now read it a dozen times since she first opened it.

Finally he looked up. "So they've put Bethune Elementary on the list of possible school closings for next year."

She nodded, her throat tightening. "They've come close a couple times, but praise God, we always squeaked through. Bethune *is* one of the best public schools in the Rogers Park area. I don't see how they can even consider closing it!"

He nodded. "Worried about your job, honey?"

"Not just my job! My teachers . . . the kids . . . everything we've worked hard to develop at Bethune to give these kids a good preparation for middle school and high school. I'm proud of what we've accomplished!" Avis threw out her hands, the food on her plate mostly untouched. "What kind of screwed-up system would shut down a high-performing school rather than shake every tree possible to keep it open? And I find out through a form letter?"

Peter reached across the table and took her hand, holding it quietly for a few moments. Finally he spoke. "Honey, I hear you. I know it would be very hard for you. And tough for everyone—your staff, the kids, the parents. You've done a fantastic job at that school. You have a right to be proud. But . . ." A light seemed to turn on in his eyes. ". . . maybe God's saying something to us through everything that's happening. Nony's letter. A prospective buyer for Software Symphony. The possibility that Bethune Elementary might be closed next year . . . Maybe God's showing us this *is* the time to consider taking that mission trip to South Africa!"

Chapter 9

Kat Davies hustled up the stone steps and into the Memorial Student Center, which housed the student union, student newspaper, a game and rec room with a mega-size TV, and—her destination—the Chip Off the Block Café, commonly known as "The Chip." Spying Nick in a corner booth, she swung her backpack off and slid into the padded bench seat across from him. "Hey."

"Hey, yourself." The tall seminary student had his hands around a large paper cup with a straw poking through its plastic lid. "You gonna get something? Try the chocolate-caramel shake." Nick waggled the paper cup. "Guaranteed to make you fall in love."

She made a face. "No thanks. I'm good." Yuck. All that sugar. She fished her water bottle out of her backpack. "Have you seen Brygitta?"

"Yeah, she said she'd meet us here—and speaking of pixie-haired gremlins . . ."

"Hi, guys." Brygitta slid into the booth beside Nick, dropping an armful of books on the table while clinging to an identical large paper cup with lid and straw. "Oh, Kat. *Water?* You *have* to try their new chocolate-caramel shake. It is sooo good." Kat's roommate sucked on her straw happily. "Where's Livie?"

Nick slurped the last of his milk shake. "I left her a message. Didn't hear back, so I don't know."

"You guys talking about me?" Olivia arrived out of breath, blond wisps falling out of the clip where she'd bunched her hair on the back of her head.

"Yeah, we're dissin' you." Kat laughed, masking a twinge of envy as she scooted over to make room for the younger girl. Olivia had "classic" features that looked good even when she was a mess. Lucky guy who'd wake up to *her.* Kat self-consciously pulled a long strand of her own dark, curly hair taut and wrapped it around her finger.

Olivia slid into the booth beside Kat. "Sorry. I stopped to get coffee. So, Nick, what did you mean in your message, 'Let's talk summer'?"

"Just that." Nick pushed his empty cup aside. "What are we going to do this summer? None of us has made concrete plans yet, and I, for one—and Kat, for two—are thinking about staying in Chicago instead of going home. Big plus for me—I could start looking for a summer job now instead of waiting till mini-term is over in June."

Brygitta nodded. "Same here. Kat's been talking to me ever since Sunday, and I think . . . I'm in. Just working up the courage to tell my family I'm not coming home."

"Just do it, Bree," Nick snorted. "You're over twenty-one, for heaven's sake."

Brygitta rolled her eyes. "Ha. I'll let *you* talk to my father. Have you ever won an argument with a Polish tatu? When you're the only girl in a family with three brothers? And don't get me started on my grandmother. She's got my whole life planned already."

Kat laughed with the others—but inside she winced. Brygitta wasn't the only one who needed courage to talk to her father. Dr. Ken Davies was going to have a royal fit when she told him she wasn't coming home to Phoenix this summer.

Olivia frowned. "So why do we need to talk about this—the four of us, I mean. It might be good for some, but maybe not everyone. Isn't it an individual decision?"

"Of course, Livie," Kat soothed. "If you decide to go home this summer, that's fine. But we were thinking, if the *four* of us stayed and split the rent for an apartment, our expenses would go way down. And it'd be fun to hang out together in Chicago for the summer. Definitely taking our 'urban experience' to another level—actually living in the city instead of doing hit-and-runs from campus."

Olivia was quiet for several long moments, toying with a saltshaker. "I don't know . . . Mom and my younger sister are home alone. I think they need me to come home."

"Alone? Where's your dad?" Brygitta blurted.

Kat shot her a look. But Olivia shrugged. "Left us a long time ago. I was ten."

Kat's heart melted. "Oh, Olivia. I'm so sorry. I . . . we didn't know."

Olivia shrugged again. "No big deal. I'm over it." The slender blonde gave them a shy smile. "I'm glad you guys want to include me. I've never had friends like you before. It *would* be fun—if you guys don't get all crazy. Let me think about it."

Kat reached over and gave her a squeeze. "Oh, Livie. I'm glad you're going to think about it. But . . . no pressure, okay?"

Olivia nodded and busied herself with her cup of coffee.

"So what's next?" Brygitta asked. "We need to find an apartment—"

"And jobs," Nick put in.

"—but, like . . . where do we even start looking?" Brygitta went on. "Chicago's a big city!"

"What did you guys think about SouledOut last Sunday?" Kat said. "We've already met some people at that church. Maybe they could help us find a place."

Brygitta laughed. "You *know* what I think about it. That service was looong!"

Nick shrugged. "Didn't really feel that way to me. I liked the way everyone got so involved. At my home church the choir's up on stage doing a performance for an audience. But here . . . everyone was singing, clapping, saying 'amen' to the preacher. Kinda cool." He grinned and leaned back, arms spread out along the top of the vinyl seat.

Kat nodded. "Same here. Have to confess, most of the churches I've tried don't do a whole lot for me. But . . . SouledOut is different. I felt excited to be there. Like we were, you know, really worshiping God."

Brygitta leaned an elbow on the table and rested her chin

in her hand. "*Hm*. Hadn't really thought about it like that. Just not what I'm used to, I guess."

"Well, me either. But . . ." Kat's thoughts drifted to the lady in the plum-colored suit who'd led worship last Sunday. How she'd said, *"Let's go worship!"* Not *"Let's go to church"* or *"The service is starting."* But *"Let's go worship!"* Like being invited to join in a big celebration at the White House—no, much better. Being invited into the throne room of heaven, to celebrate the King of kings! Lord of all creation!—

A pair of fingers snapped in her face. "Kat? Kat? Are you in there?" Nick waved his hand in front of her eyes. "I think we lost you."

Kat grinned sheepishly. "Sorry. I was thinking about SouledOut. I'd like to go again on Sunday, if any of you—"

"I will," Olivia said. "I think I need to give it another chance. At least my last exam will be over and I won't be so distracted."

Kat blinked in surprise. "That's great, Livie!" Maybe she'd misjudged the girl.

Nick raised his hand. "Make that three."

Brygitta rolled her eyes. "Oh, all right. Four."

Kat closed her laptop and stretched. *Done!* Felt so good to finish her last term paper—and it was only Thursday. Paper wasn't due until Monday. She'd have the weekend to do some rewriting and proofing before turning it in. She glanced at her watch. A little after ten. Brygitta hadn't come in—probably still at the library, which was open till midnight on weeknights. Maybe she should go over to the Memorial Center and hang out for an hour, do something to relax.

Ducking into their small bathroom, she ran a wide-bristle brush through her thick mane of dark waves, touched up her blush and lipstick, and smiled approvingly in the mirror. A lot of women paid big bucks to get the effect of her natural curl. It softened her nose, which was a bit too big for her taste, even though Brygitta told her it gave her a "noble" look. Yeah, like Julius Caesar.

The "Flight of the Bumblebees" ringtone ended her beauty inspection. Snatching her cell phone off the desk, she looked at the caller ID. *Drat.* Her father. She didn't want to have "the summer talk" right now! She should have called *him*, taken the initiative. She hesitated. Could let it go to voice mail—but she'd still have to respond to his call.

Might as well get this over with.

She pressed Talk. "Hey, Dad! We must be on the same wavelength! I was just going to call you."

"Hi, sugar. Didn't want to call too late—but I've got some good news. You won't have to look for a job this summer. My receptionist is taking maternity leave in June and I need a bright young woman to fill in." He chuckled in her ear. "Talk about great timing, eh? For both of us!"

"Oh, Dad, that would be great—except that's what I was going to call you about. I might not be coming back to Phoenix this summer—"

"What do you mean, 'might not'?"

Kat wanted to kick herself. She shouldn't have said "might not." Left too much wiggle room. "Well, it's exciting, actually.

I've been involved in this Urban Experience program here at CCU, and some of us in the class have been talking about staying in Chicago for the summer and—"

"Kathryn. What are you talking about? Is this some kind of payback, just because your mother and I won't be able to make it to your graduation? I thought you understood our situation."

She almost shot back, *"Understand? I understand that taking a cruise with the Jeffersons is more important than seeing your only daughter get her master's degree."* But then, they hadn't made it to her undergrad graduation either—not after she'd dropped premed at the University of Arizona and transferred to Crista U for her senior year. She hadn't protested then either. They were disappointed, and frankly, it was easier *not* having them come. But still . . .

"No, Dad," she said patiently. "Not payback. I understand, really. It's just . . . if I'm going to teach in a city school, I need more experience with the culture and people here." She thought fast. "I'm hoping to get a tutoring job with kids, or maybe—"

"Why not here in Phoenix?" her father snapped. "I just don't understand some of the decisions you're making, Kathryn. If you'd followed through on your premed studies, you'd almost be ready for an internship by now—"

"Dad, please—"

But her father went on as if he hadn't heard. "—and I could have put in a good word for you at any number of hospitals here in Phoenix. What does a teacher make? Peanuts. And even if we're just talking about a summer job, I'm certain no *tutoring* job"—she didn't miss the scorn in his voice—"could match the salary I'm offering you to fill in at my office."

Kat grimaced. This wasn't going well. She took a deep breath. "Dad, I really appreciate it. I do. But this is something I'd really like to do. Look, I'm supposed to meet up with some friends in a few minutes. I'll call Mom this weekend for Mother's Day and we can talk about it some more, okay? Love you both! Bye!"

Deliberately leaving her phone behind, Kat grabbed her purse and flew out of her dorm room. Maybe she needed one of those decadent chocolate-caramel milk shakes after all.

The four friends piled off the Foster Avenue bus Sunday morning, but instead of heading directly for the Red Line El station, they detoured to the Dominick's grocery store again.

"Are you sure they said there's a potluck this Sunday? Maybe it's a special Mother's Day thing." Olivia trotted to keep up with Kat. "I mean, what can we buy ready-made that would be potlucky?"

"Yes, I'm sure they said potluck on the second Sunday, and nobody said anything about it being special for Mother's Day. We can get one of those veggie trays they make up in the deli. It'll be perfect."

"Or brownies. Or cookies. Or a pie," Nick said hopefully, but Kat whacked his arm with the back of her hand.

Mother's Day balloons, potted flowers, and signs abounded in the large grocery store, making Kat feel guilty that she hadn't followed up on her promise to call home this weekend. Well, she'd call this afternoon. After all, it'd been too early in Arizona to call this morning before they left.

"I still don't think we need to bring anything," Brygitta said. "They know we're students. And church folks always bring extra for visitors and guests at these potlucks."

"Exactly. They don't think students would think to bring anything. Which is why we're going to." *And maybe redeem the first impression we made last time*, Kat thought.

But she couldn't help wondering what other good stuff had been thrown out in the store Dumpsters that morning. It wouldn't hurt to just look, would it? While Brygitta and Olivia argued over whether to get a veggie tray or fruit tray, Kat slipped outside and around to the back of the store. No one in sight. Lifting up the lid of the first Dumpster, she was met with a putrid smell of rotting . . . something. She let the lid fall back with a bang, which made her jump. She cast an anxious eye at the double doors, but they stayed closed.

Waiting another minute or two, she lifted the lid of the next Dumpster. Oooh . . . what was that? She squinted into the dim interior. As things came into focus, her eyes bugged at the six-packs of fancy fruit juices, still in their plastic shrink-wrap. Lots of them. Holding up the lid with one hand and leaning over the edge, she snagged a six-pack with her other hand and pulled it out into the light. "Sell by May . . ." She squinted at the fine print on the plastic bottles. "Good grief! That's only yesterday! These are still good!"

Glancing around to be sure she was still alone, Kat slung off her backpack, stuffed the six-pack inside, then strained to reach another . . . and another . . . and another, until she had four of the juice packs zipped inside her bag, all that would fit. Heavy as it was, she couldn't get it on her back again, so she just lugged it by the top strap and headed for the front of the store—where she ran into Nick, Brygitta, and Olivia coming out the automatic doors with a plastic grocery bag.

Brygitta rolled her eyes. "Kat. You didn't."

Kat tossed her head. "Did. But don't worry, I promise not to embarrass you. It's one-hundred-percent fruit juice, just one day past sale date, perfectly good. We can just put it out on the table with the rest of the potluck stuff. Who's to know we didn't buy it? Nick, will you help me get this backpack on?"

"Forget it, I'll carry it," he said, just as a loud rumbling a block over caught their attention.

"Oh no, the El! We missed it!" Olivia cried.

"I think that one's going south." Kat began to run. "Maybe we can catch the northbound if we hurry!"

Chapter 10

Avis slipped the navy blue rayon dress over her head and let it fall softly just below her knees. Delicate silver filigrees decorated the scoop neck and three-quarter-length sleeves, complimenting the silver buckle on the navy belt. She'd already gotten two phone calls that morning wishing her Happy Mother's Day. The first, from her youngest daughter, Natasha, in D.C., had gotten her out of bed. "Oh! Sorry, Mom! I keep forgetting about the time difference!" The second, from her oldest daughter in Ohio, was cut short by Charette's nine-year-old twins clamoring for a chance to talk to "Grammy." They were growing so fast. She and Peter should really go see them sometime this summer.

No call from Rochelle. She closed her eyes a brief second, took a deep breath, and blew it out slowly. She couldn't let that cloud her whole day. She had a lot to be thankful for.

Peter poked his head into the bedroom as Avis slid the post of a silver hoop into the nearly invisible hole in her earlobe.

"You ready, honey? I put your dish for the potluck in the car already."

"*Mm-hm*. Thanks. Just need to get my coat." She turned around for him, showing off the dress. "Look okay?"

"*Mm*, very nice. Gonna turn a few heads at church, I'd say."

"Oh, stop." Avis felt her face flush at his compliment. "You're the only one whose head I want to turn." She reached for her Sunday purse, making sure she had her wallet, hand cream, cell phone, tissues—

"By the way, did you ever find the ruby earrings?"

He said it casually—too casually—and she tensed, but slowly shook her head. "I've looked through everything. I . . ." Her eyes suddenly misted and she reached for the tissue box on her vanity table.

"Hey, hey, baby. I didn't mean to upset you." Peter came to her side and gently massaged the back of her neck as she dabbed at her eyes. "It's just so odd. You're not the type to misplace things. But maybe I can help you look this afternoon. Do you remember when you last wore them?"

Avis pulled away. She didn't want his touch right then. But it was a direct question. "Valentine's Day, I think . . ." *I know.*

"*Huh.*" He frowned as if pondering for a moment, started to say something, and then seemed to reconsider. "Well. That's a start, anyhow. But we better get going now. I'd like to get there a few minutes early to pray with the pastors—something the elders decided would be good to do before Sunday service."

Avis nodded, blew her nose, and busied herself getting her coat. But a sense of dread settled into her stomach as they locked the front door and headed down the stairs of the three-flat. If

Peter thought about it very long, he was going to end up at the same place she had when reviewing the events of last Valentine's Day.

The same day Rochelle had shown up at their place, sobbing, upset, and as irrational as a jilted lover, barricading herself in their bedroom.

At the front door of SouledOut Community Church, Jodi Baxter's son Josh, his wife, Edesa, and their two-year-old adopted daughter, Gracie, were handing out red and white carnations to all the women and girls in honor of Mother's Day. Red if your mother was still alive, white if your mother had passed. Avis accepted a white carnation and a kiss from little Gracie and gave a hug to Edesa. "Happy Mother's Day yourself, dear sister," she whispered in the young woman's ear. Such a sweet family.

Clutching the white carnation, she found her way to her usual seat in the second row of chairs arranged in a semicircle. Avis always chose a seat on the far right aisle if possible, so she had room to worship—body, soul, and spirit—without bonking someone else on the head or stepping on their toes. And—*Thank You, Jesus*—she wasn't scheduled to lead worship this Sunday. It had been a stressful week, and she was grateful for a few minutes to just sit and pray by herself before worship began.

Make that a few seconds.

"Avis! We missed you at Yada Yada last Sunday. Jodi said you were looking for your daughter. Did you find her?"

She looked up into the angular face of Leslie "Stu" Stuart, the willowy social worker who lived upstairs in the Baxters' two-flat. Single and just turned forty, Stu still wore her faded blond hair long and straight—a style Avis wasn't sure was appropriate for a middle-aged woman. But so be it. Stu was Stu, still wearing short skirts and tall leather boots. She held a red carnation.

"Thanks, Stu." Avis smiled wanly. "No, haven't located her yet. Keep praying."

Stu crouched beside Avis's folding chair—*padded* folding chairs, at least, thanks to Stu's single-minded Chair Fund fund-raising a few years back—and lowered her voice. "Maybe I can help. I could put out her name through some of the social service agencies, see if she's applied for any kind of assistance lately." The praise band was sounding the notes of the call to worship. "Think about it. I'll talk to you later."

Stu gave her a quick hug and slipped into another row just as Peter appeared, squeezing past Avis's knees and sinking into the seat next to her. He leaned toward her ear and murmured, "Pastor Clark doesn't look good to me. We spent most of our time praying for him. The man should really take a sabbatical."

Avis glanced toward where the two pastors were sitting in the front row on the left side of the room. Pastor Hubert Clark, in his early seventies, had been the pastor of Uptown Community Church, the mostly white church that had merged with New Morning Christian—mostly African-American—and their pastor, Joe Cobbs, to form SouledOut Community Church. The two men, as different in personality and preaching styles as day and night, had somehow managed to work together as a team in surprising ways, each complementing the other's strengths. They'd had a scare a couple years ago, though, when Pastor Clark had a heart attack, but the man was nothing if not determined to die with his boots on. Avis wasn't the only one who appreciated the older man's gentle wisdom and pastor's heart.

"Don't think you can convince him to take a sabbatical," she whispered back, as that week's worship leader—a young man named Justin Barnes—invited the congregation to stand. "He's only preaching once a month now, isn't he?"

But Justin diverted their attention. "Good morning, church! It's a beautiful day in the neighborhood—I grew up on Mister Rogers, you know." That got a laugh, because Justin wasn't the only one who teased Pastor Clark that he *had* to be the TV icon's twin brother. "But even that spring sunshine out there can't compare to the beautiful day *in here*, because we're going to get *down* and get *ready* to have us some church. Amen?"

"Amen!" and "Say it, brother!" rang out from the rows of chairs, along with laughter and clapping, even as the double glass doors from outside opened and Avis noticed the four students from Crista University slip in and stand uncertainly in the back—trying to find some empty seats no doubt. All of them had taken red carnations.

She was surprised to see them back. The church was often visited by groups of students from this or that Christian college, sent by well-meaning professors to get a "taste" of Chicago's cultural diversity. They usually came once and then moved on to the next "experience." But what was it with college students these days? They still dressed in scruffy jeans like teenagers.

And some were graduate students! The young man with the sandy-brown hair and wire-rim sunglasses was a seminary student, if she remembered correctly. Didn't young adults ever put on some good clothes for church? The wear-any-old-thing mentality seemed vaguely disrespectful to her.

Avis shook off the thought. She was showing her age, brought up in another era when her mother scrubbed and braided and dressed Avis and her sisters in their best frilly dresses, Mary Jane shoes, and hair bows. Besides, she was here to worship the *Lord*, not worry about a bunch of curious white college students.

Closing her eyes, she let the words of the first worship song, taken from Psalm 42, sink into her spirit.

"As the deer pants for streams of water, so my soul longs after You . . ."

Oh yes, Lord! Her spirit felt so dry and thirsty lately. Avis raised her arms upward, wrapping herself in the words of the psalm. *Thirsty . . . thirsty . . . so thirsty, Lord . . .*

After the children were dismissed to their Sunday school classes, Pastor Joe Cobbs took a text from Matthew 5, challenging people to consider what Jesus meant when He said we were to be "the salt of the earth" and "the light of the world."

"Can anyone give me a definition of who Salt People and Light People are?"

"I thought Jesus said *He* was the Light of the world!" protested Pastor Clark from the front row. The room tittered.

Everyone suspected Pastor Cobbs had told him to say that to provoke discussion.

A teenager took the bait. "Yeah, but if we let our light shine—living the way the Bible says—people will see Jesus."

"That's right, that's right," several murmured.

"Light People bring clarity, not confusion," someone in the back piped up.

"Good, good," said Pastor Cobbs. "What about Salt People?"

"When Salt People show up, the 'flavor' of the situation improves!" another suggested. That got a laugh.

As the lively sermon continued, Avis wrote in the back of her Bible, "When Salt People show up, the 'flavor' of the situation improves," and "Light People bring clarity, not confusion." She wanted to think about that. Her marriage could use a little more "salt" and "light" right now.

After getting everyone on their feet to sing "This Little Light of Mine," the young worship leader invited everyone to stay for the Second Sunday Potluck after the service. "Any other commercials?" he deadpanned. "Announcements?"

There were the usual: Youth group at six, making plans for their Memorial Day outing. Elder David Brown and his family were moving next week and could use some help loading the truck. A key ring had been found, could be claimed in the church office.

Then one of the visitors, the girl with all that dark hair, bounced up and waved her hand. "Hi! I'm Kat. We"—she indicated her three friends—"were here last Sunday from Crista University. And we're looking for an apartment in this area that we could rent for the summer. Or we'd be willing to house-sit if you know anyone going out of town. We'd be glad to take care of pets and plants and stuff." She grinned. "If anyone knows any leads, let us know, okay?" She sat down.

Avis felt a flicker of annoyance. They wanted to move into the neighborhood? Which meant they were planning to hang around awhile. But . . . why this neighborhood? Were they intending to show up at SouledOut all summer?

So what, Avis? she scolded herself. Wasn't her concern. It was just . . . they seemed so full of themselves. The girl, "Cat," anyway. What kind of name was that? Sounded like a pole dancer.

But she forgot about the Crista students as chairs were moved out of the way and tables set up, and she joined the flock of women bustling in and out of the kitchen with steaming hot dishes. Soon the serving tables were loaded with beans and rice and macaroni and cheese—Avis's standard potluck offering—as well as fried chicken, greens and ham hocks, pasta salads, large pitchers of lemonade, and pans of chocolate cake, brownies, and chocolate chip cookies. To her surprise, the student visitors set out a neat veggie tray—the kind grocery stores make up in the deli—and a plastic tub of sour cream dip. And the "Cat" girl unzipped her backpack and set out several six-packs of fruit-juice blends, which were immediately snapped up by the younger set.

Well, at least they were pulling their share.

Once the stacks of paper plates, plasticware, and Styrofoam cups arrived, Pastor Cobbs boomed a prayer of thanks over the food, including his standard, ". . . and remove all impurities from the food we are about to partake . . . Amen!"

As usual, the kids jostled each other to be first in line, until

Florida Hickman swooped down on them like an eagle after its prey. "You kids! Where's you manners? Let the parents with little kids go first—an' the pastors an' elders and they spouses. And if you're a visitor to SouledOut, come on now, get in line. These kids can wait."

Avis would have just as soon held back a bit, but with Florida directing traffic, she and Peter got their food and found seats at a long table with Debra and Sherman Meeks and Jodi and Denny Baxter. Peter, Denny, and Debra, along with David Brown, were the current elder board, each serving a staggered two-year term. Peter had just been elected at the beginning of the year, and she was proud of him serving in that capacity.

But a disturbing thought flickered across her mind, even as the table talk bounced from bemoaning the Chicago Bulls' losing season to whether the economy would ever recover. *How can Peter think about taking an extended trip when he's just agreed to serve a two-year term as an elder?* She shook her head. She and Peter were just dancing around this issue. They really needed to talk—

"Okay if we sit here?"

Avis blinked. Two of the Crista students—the "Cat" girl and the timid blonde—stood by two empty chairs across the table, holding their plates of food hopefully.

Chapter 11

Of course!" Sherman Meeks jumped up and even pulled out the chairs for the two young women. "By all means. We need some youth at this table of old folks."

"Speak for yourself, Meeks." Denny Baxter feigned a wounded look. "A few of us here aren't over the hill *yet*."

"Don't mind him." Jodi extended her hand. "I'm Jodi Baxter. This is my husband, Denny. And please remind us of your names . . . ?"

"Kathryn Davies." The talkative girl beamed and shook Jodi's hand. "Though most people just call me Kat. Kat with a K. And this is Olivia Lindberg. We're both from Crista University. I'm in the graduate school. Education."

"Undergrad," squeaked the younger of the two. "Sociology."

"Would you like something to drink?" Denny offered. Neither girl had a cup. "I'd be glad to get you some lemonade. They've made enough to float a Carnival cruise."

Kat—*With a K*, Avis reminded herself—shook her head. "Uh, no, unless there's something else besides Styrofoam cups."

The three couples just looked at her.

Olivia spoke up. "Kat doesn't do Styrofoam. Bad for the environment, you know. But . . . I'd love some lemonade. Thanks."

"O-*kay*." Denny smothered an amused smile and disappeared toward the kitchen.

"Mrs. Douglass, right?" Kat smiled at Avis, crunching on a raw baby carrot. Avis noticed that the girl hadn't taken any fried chicken, only beans and rice and the macaroni and cheese. "You were the worship leader last week. I was hoping you would lead worship again this Sunday. Did the guy today sub for you because it's Mother's Day? Or is there a rotation?"

Girl, Avis thought, *if you stick around awhile and observe, you'll learn the answers without having to ask so many questions.*

Peter filled in the momentary silence. "We have several worship leaders, some of them newer than others. A way to grow people in their gifts. But I know that's unusual. The church I grew up in always had the same person leading worship."

Denny Baxter returned with two plastic glasses from the kitchen filled with lemonade.

"Thanks! That's so nice of you," Kat said. "We'll be glad to wash them. Do you save the plastic forks too? We'd be glad to wash them too, if you like. Right, Livie?"

The other girl nodded but seemed slightly embarrassed.

Avis caught Jodi Baxter smirking at her. Jodi had tried once before to get the church to wash and reuse the plasticware they used at potlucks, but most of the women had rolled their eyes and protested, "What? Wash the *plastic*? That's why we use it, so we can just toss everything!"

"So you girls are looking for an apartment to rent?" Debra Meeks asked sweetly. Avis noticed the slight emphasis on *girls*.

"*Uh-huh*. And Nick too," Kat said. "We'd like at least three bedrooms, so we three girls don't all end up in the same room."

"*Mm*. Things sure have changed since I was a girl," Debra murmured.

Avis smiled. At least Debra shared her surprise that these Christian college students were planning on sharing a co-ed apartment.

"Avis, honey, didn't you tell me that the couple downstairs want to sublease their apartment this summer? Do you know how much they're asking?"

Avis stared at her husband. *No, no, no, Peter. You didn't just say that out loud.*

But Kat was already on it. "Really, Mr. Douglass? That is so *awesome*. Can you find out how much they're asking?"

"Oh, uh, it's probably much too expensive for students," Avis said quickly. "Our building is condo, so they've got a mortgage."

Kat tossed her mane of wavy hair, eyes dancing. "Maybe not. After all, there're four of us to share the rent. Would you give them my phone number, Mr. Douglass?" She fished in her bag for a small notebook and pen, scribbled a number, tore out the page, and handed it to Peter. "Oh!" She jumped up from the table, still grinning. "I gotta go tell Nick and Brygitta we've got a nibble!"

Avis let Peter have it the moment they were in the car. "Peter Douglass. I can't believe you told those students about the Candys' apartment like that! They might not want a bunch of students living in their condo. It's not like we even know these kids!"

"What are you talking about? Didn't Louise Candy tell you to let them know if we heard of anyone needing an apartment? Students might be just the thing! And if not, no big deal, the Candys can always say no. And maybe you're right—they might be asking more than these students can pay. Let them figure it out."

Avis pressed her lips together and rode in silence until they turned into their block. "That's . . . not the only thing. We live in the building too. We've got a condo association. Don't the other owners have some say about who lives there? It's only three apartments, after all."

Peter shot a quick glance at her and then concentrated on backing into a parking space in front of their building. Once he'd turned off the motor, he faced her again. "I can't believe I'm hearing right. My Avis, principal of Bethune Elementary School, champion of young people, reigning monarch and peacemaker of the motley crew known as the Yada Yada Prayer Group—*that* Avis doesn't want four students from a Christian university to live in our building for three months. *What*, my dear, is your problem?"

Avis turned her head away from him and contemplated the front of their building. The empty cement urns on the sides of the steps could use some geraniums and vinca vines to spruce up the entrance. All danger of frost was past. Maybe she should plant some marigolds or petunias along the front of the bushes. No one else in the building seemed inclined to plant flowers.

"Avis?"

She turned back to her husband and sighed. "You're right. We should let the Candys know about the students. I don't know . . . it's just, they annoy me for some reason. Not sure what it is. Their big ideas. Their big egos. A bunch of idealistic white do-gooders. Especially that one girl, Kat."

Peter chuckled. "It's not like you haven't had to dodge some white-girl attitudes from some of your prayer group sisters. Naming no names, of course."

Avis had to smile. "True. But the Yadas have been through some serious stuff together and hung in there. Makes a big difference. *Anyway* . . ." She opened her car door and climbed out. "Forget what I said about the Crista students. Go ahead and tell the Candys about them if you want."

Which he did, stopping to knock on the Candys' door while Avis continued up the next flight to the third floor. Hanging up her coat, she changed into comfortable black slacks and a white cotton sweater. Before storing her purse on its shelf in the closet, she took out her cell phone. Should she try Rochelle's number again? Probably an exercise in futility, but . . .

Pressing the speed-dial number for Rochelle, she almost flipped the phone closed when the voice mail message came on, then suddenly realized it was saying, "*. . . can't answer the phone right now. You know what to do at the beep. Thanks.*"

The phone was back on! And that was Rochelle's voice on

the message. Quickly Avis said, "Hi, honey. This is Mom. Just wanted to wish you a Happy Mother's Day. I'm missing you and Conny terribly and want to know how you are. Please call. Please? Talk to you soon." The end-of-message beep cut off her last word.

Peter came into the bedroom, loosening his gray-and-blue tie. "Louise Candy sounded very interested in the students. They knew it'd be hard to find someone to sublease for just a few months, so they'd already started putting up notices at Loyola and Northwestern . . ." He stopped. "Are you okay? What happened?"

"I got through to Rochelle's voice mail." Avis's voice came out in a croak. "Left her a message to call."

"That's wonderful, sweetheart. I'm glad. Real glad. Shows that she's okay, right?"

Avis shook her head. "I don't know. I guess." It *was* Rochelle's voice, and the phone was back on, after all. A thread of hope. "But now what?"

"Wait a few days. See if she calls back." He shrugged off his sport coat and threw it on the bed. "Let me get out of this suit and then I'll help you look for those ruby earrings like I promised."

"I . . . don't think it will help." Avis surprised herself. But it was time to bring her worries into the light. *Light People bring clarity, not confusion.*

"Why not?" Peter stood in his socks, holding the dress slacks he'd just taken off. "I might think of looking places you haven't. You know, two heads better than one?"

"That's not what I mean. But . . . put your pants on. I can't talk serious talk with your bare legs and stocking feet staring at me." A giggle escaped in spite of herself. "In fact, I'm going to go make some coffee."

A few minutes later Peter came into the kitchen dressed in old tan Dockers and a black and red Bulls T-shirt. She handed him a cup of coffee with a splash of milk and two teaspoons of sugar as he pulled out a chair from the kitchen table. "Okay, what's this serious talk about?"

She sat down with her own cup of black coffee. "The last time I wore the ruby earrings was Valentine's Day. And remember what happened that night when we got home?" She reviewed the stormy evening, how Rochelle had come crying to their door, how she'd locked herself in their bedroom in a fit of temper when they said she and Conny couldn't stay with them. "I was undressing when she came, don't think I'd even had time to put the earrings away. And I've looked everywhere for them!" She swallowed the lump in her throat. "What I'm worried about is . . . what if Rochelle took the earrings that night and pawned them or . . . or something. And that's the reason she hasn't contacted us, afraid we've figured it out. And maybe that's why she left Manna House after just one night, because she knew she could get some cash and make it for a while."

There. It was out. It felt good to tell Peter that this possibility occurred to her first, rather than have him get suspicious and accuse Rochelle. This was right. She should have done it sooner.

"Mercy me." Peter shook his head. "Rochelle has her problems, but . . . stealing? From her own mother? Hard to believe."

Avis wanted to hug him.

"But . . . you don't know this for sure. You're just guessing, right?"

She nodded.

"Well. Then we've got to hold it as a 'maybe.' Not jump to conclusions. But it's possible. So I'll take your word for it that it's not much use to keep looking for them."

"I'm so sorry, Peter." Avis reached across the small table and touched his hand. Strong brown hands. "They were your wedding gift to me. A precious gift."

He took her hand in his. "Don't worry about it, baby. I insured them. In fact, might be better if they are stolen rather than just lost. Not sure I could make a good case with the adjuster for 'My wife misplaced them.'" He lifted his cup. "Any more coffee?"

The earrings were insured? *Better* if they were stolen? For a brief moment she was tempted to pour the rest of the coffee on his head.

Avis kept her cell phone on all the time, even during staff meeting Monday morning, just in case Rochelle called.

The letter from the school board had said "Confidential" in big black letters across the top, so she wasn't at liberty to tell the staff that their jobs might be on the line if the school closed. Some might get offered jobs elsewhere in the public school system as students were diverted to other schools. But another job for her? Not likely. Not unless another principal retired. And what kind of mess would she inherit if she did?

Fortunately, this Monday started the week off on a good foot, as most kids seemed glad to get back into a routine after the weekend, and no one got sent to the office for detention. Which meant that Avis actually got to eat a quiet lunch in her office, using the time for some end-of-school-year planning and prayers for her teachers and students. When her cell phone rang, though, she practically dumped the contents of her purse trying to get to it—but it was only Peter calling to ask what she thought about talking to the pastors sometime that week about the invitation from South Africa.

"Uhhh . . . don't you think we need to talk some more first?"

"Well, sure. But we do need to make some decisions. I've got this offer to buy the business on the table. So let's talk tonight, okay? Then maybe we can ask Pastor Clark and Pastor Joe if we could meet with them after Bible study on Wednesday night, since we'll all be there anyway. Oh, gotta go. My other line is ringing. Love you." Peter clicked off.

Stuffing things back in her purse, Avis realized Nonyameko's letter was still among the contents. Opening the pretty anniversary card, she read the note again:

> . . . As you can see from the card, we have been able to start a few small businesses with some talented girls—greeting cards, rug and basket weaving—but to be honest, we need advice and practical help from someone more experienced in business than we are. We are wondering if the two of you would consider coming to South Africa for an extended visit. Whatever time you could spend would be a gift—three months? Six months? A year would be even better. We could also use your teaching

> skills, Avis. Many of our girls need help with basic education—math, language, typing, even health and hygiene. We'd love to arrange for some classes but need a teacher. You'd be a wonderful encouragement to these young women . . .

She stared at the card a long time. The struggling economy . . . the unexpected offer to buy out Software Symphony . . . the threat of more school closings, including Bethune Elementary . . . Maybe God *was* lining things up, preparing them for a change of direction.

All right, Lord, I'm listening. Forgive me for my reluctance to consider this invitation. It's just that it's so big! And then there's Rochelle and Conny. I really need to know that they're—

"Mrs. Douglass?" The knock on the door and the secretary poking her head in happened simultaneously. "We've got a situation. One of the fifth-grade boys was caught showing a handgun to another classmate out in the schoolyard. A real gun. But no ammunition, thank God!"

Avis flew out of the office right on the secretary's heels.

Chapter 12

Kat felt giddy all the way home on the El from the morning service at SouledOut. Just like that, a possible apartment to rent for the summer! It was an answer to prayer—and she hadn't even prayed about it yet! Which was something to think about. Did God answer prayers even before you prayed?

Nick was a little more guarded. "Don't get your hopes too high, Kitty Kat. We don't know how much they're asking. And"—he lowered his voice so that their conversation didn't carry to the two girls sitting on the other side of the aisle, though the rattle and squeals of the commuter train made that unlikely—"far as I know, Livie hasn't made a decision yet whether to stay here this summer. Dividing the rent three ways versus four could make a big difference."

"What a wet blanket you are!" Kat shoved him with her elbow. "And you want to be a pastor? Where's your faith, Reverend!"

He turned his face and stared out the window.

"Aw, come on, Nick. I didn't mean to hurt your feelings. Sorry. It's just . . . isn't it kind of a confirmation that this is what we're supposed to be doing? I mean, it beats looking in the paper and making sixty-dozen-eleven phone calls or driving all around the city looking at rat-hole apartments. And wouldn't it be cool to get an apartment in the same building as someone from the SouledOut church? That Douglass couple, no less."

Her friend nodded. "Yeah, gotta admit, it'd be nice if it worked out. Just . . . slow down a little bit, Kat. Wait till you call and get more information. That's all I'm saying."

"Uh, can't call. Mr. Douglass didn't give me their number, or even their name. But I gave him my number and he said he'd speak to them."

"Ah." Nick raised an eyebrow at her. "So we have to wait for them to call? Ha. That's gonna drive you nuts, isn't it, Kat girl."

"Nooo." She tossed her head. But it gave her pause. What if the people didn't call? "Well, if we don't hear from them in a day or two, we could call the Douglasses and ask if they've spoken to them."

"You've got the Douglasses' number?"

Rats. She hadn't done that either. "They're probably in the phone directory. Or we can call the church."

"*Or* we could look in the paper or contact the college housing office for a few more options instead of putting all our eggs in this one basket."

"Whatever."

But even back in her dorm room, sprawled on her bed trying to study for upcoming finals, Kat had a feeling about this.

Something was *right* about it. The fact that they'd put out the word at this church they'd found, and *bam!* Right away someone had mentioned a possibility. A sublease for the summer. Probably furnished to boot! How perfect was that? And it would put them in the same neighborhood as SouledOut—a church they already felt attracted to—giving them a church home. Wasn't that another confirmation that God was going to make this happen?

Absently twisting a long strand of thick hair around her finger, Kat added another plus. The apartment was in the same building as an older couple she'd met at church. Her mother would like that. He was an elder and she was a worship leader. Double pluses. Though her parents probably imagined a large brick church with choir robes, an impressive podium, and a lot of pomp and ceremony—like the one in Phoenix where the Davies family name was on the membership rolls, though they rarely attended.

She didn't have to mention that the church met in a mall, or that the "older couple" was black—not sure what her parents would think about that. They'd surely tell her they weren't *racist*, but if they had qualms about her living right in the city, they might not be too keen on a racially mixed neighborhood. Not when their whole world was a lily-white subdivision out in the suburbs of Phoenix.

But living in the same building as the Douglasses would be cool. Kat had felt attracted to Avis Douglass the first time she'd led worship. The woman was such a . . . a diva! Kat had never seen anyone worship quite like her. As if God was right there—"in the house" as someone had said—and she was in awe of His majesty. Joy seemed to bubble out of her pores, and she danced and lifted her arms as if she were the only one in the room. Kat would love to get to know her better, to discover what made this woman tick.

Might not be easy, though. Even though Kat had tried to be superfriendly, the woman seemed kind of . . . distant. Like she was being held at arm's length. In fact, thinking back on it, Mrs. Douglass hadn't seemed all that keen on the idea of them renting the apartment in their building when her husband brought it up.

For the first time she felt a tiny wrinkle in the Perfect Plan.

The door opened and Brygitta barged in, dumping an armload of books on the other bed. "Kat! Have you eaten supper yet? I'm famished. Some of us are going for pizza."

"Supper? What time is it?" Kat checked her watch. Yikes, ten after six . . . 5:10 in Phoenix. "No, you guys go on. I still gotta call my mom for Mother's Day." Her mom would soon be gone to her Sunday evening women's book club, and *then* her name would be mud for sure.

The call came during her final exam in Adolescent Psychology on Monday afternoon. Most of her professors had assigned either a final paper or a take-home exam. But this professor gave his final exam in class, though he encouraged the use of laptops to answer the essay questions, in lieu of the old-fashioned "blue books" that were handwritten. "Of course it's easier to cheat with a laptop," he'd drawled, "but if you're in a master's program at a Christian university and decide to cheat, you've got bigger problems than the grade you get on an exam."

Kat was on the third essay question using her laptop when her phone vibrated in her jean jacket pocket. She slipped it out unobtrusively and stared at the caller ID. She didn't recognize the name—*Candy?*—but it was a 773 area code, same as SouledOut. *Oh God, oh God, please let them leave a message.*

The moment the professor called time, she hit the Print button that sent her exam to the queue in the professor's printer, stuffed her laptop into her backpack, and darted into the hallway, pressing the phone to her ear as she listened to the message.

"Hi. This is Louise Candy. I was given this number by our upstairs neighbor and understand you are looking for an apartment for the summer. Please call me at . . ." And the female voice rattled off a number.

Rats. She didn't have time to call back now. Bree had proofread the research paper she'd written last week and made a bunch of corrections she still had to incorporate—and the paper was due before five o'clock. *Arrgh.* Whatever made her take Classroom Counseling Strategies, anyway?

But the moment she dropped off the paper in her professor's office at 4:40, Kat found a quiet bench out on the commons, listened to the message again, and then hit Reply.

The phone rang. And rang five more times before voice mail picked up. *"You've reached the Candys. Leave a message."* Swallowing her disappointment, Kat left her name and number, said yes, they were definitely interested in subleasing the apartment, and she would call back later.

Turning up the collar of her jean jacket as a chilly, late afternoon wind blew through campus, she called Brygitta's cell phone. "Where are you? The lady called back . . . you know, the one subleasing their apartment! . . . No, she called during one of my exams . . . Yes, of course I called her back! But all I got was voice mail. I'll try later . . . What are you doing for supper? . . . The dining hall? Ugh. But I guess I can do salad." Kat shuddered. The university dining hall, even with its buffet-style food stations, still didn't get it when it came to food ecology and justice issues.

But she smiled as she flipped her phone shut and gathered up her backpack. Having their own apartment and being able to cook the stuff *she* believed in eating was going to be totally awesome.

Both Kat and Brygitta had take-home exams due the next day, so after supper in the dining hall they holed up in the room they shared in Graduate Housing and put a Do Not Disturb sign on their door. But when the Candy lady hadn't called back by nine o'clock, Kat said, "I'm calling."

This time the phone picked up on the second ring. "Candy residence."

Kat pushed the Speaker button and frantically waved Brygitta over. "Mrs. Candy? This is Kat Davies at Crista University, returning your call. About subleasing your apartment?" Grinning, Brygitta bounced over to Kat's bed and they put their heads together—short pixie cut to wavy waterfall—listening.

"Oh yes. Our neighbor upstairs, Peter Douglass, told us you and some other graduate students might be interested in subleasing for the summer. That might work out for us, as we're going to Costa Rica for a few months and don't really want to leave our condo empty for that long. A business venture, very exciting, we . . ."

Kat rolled her eyes at Brygitta as the woman kept talking. *Costa Rica. Very nice. Lucky you. But we don't care where you're going, lady, just tell us about the apartment!*

As the woman finally took a breath, Kat jumped in. "Can you tell us what you're asking?"

"A thousand ten per month. Worth every penny—"

Brygitta nearly fell off the bed. *"A thousand TEN?"* she mouthed at Kat.

"—the apartment is completely furnished, of course," Mrs. Candy went on. "Two bedrooms plus a study with a fold-out futon, utilities included, quiet street. Parking is crowded but, well, that's living in the city, right? Uh, how many did you say would live here?"

"Uh, at least three, hopefully four. Three women, one man. We're all students here at CCU. We can provide references if you'd like. We also attend the same church as your neighbors, the Douglasses."

Brygitta hit her on the shoulder. "Shameless name dropping, you hussy," she whisper-hissed.

"Ah, well, that's good. We're not church people ourselves, but we don't want any loud parties or drugs or drinking or anything like that."

Kat stifled a laugh. "No, no, you don't have to worry. We're all very responsible. In fact, Nick Taylor is in seminary, studying to be a pastor."

Brygitta bounced off the bed and hopped around the room, mimicking Kat silently. *"Nick is in seminary, studying to be a PASTOR!"*

Kat waved her down, trying not to laugh. "Um, would it be possible for us to see the apartment? That way you could meet us, and we could talk about the available dates and expectations." Kat thought fast. "Would you be available Sunday afternoon? We'll be in the neighborhood for church in the morning and could come over if that would work for you."

She grabbed a pen and scribbled as Louise Candy gave her the address. "Thank you very much. See you at one o'clock on Sunday. I'm sure we can find it."

Kat punched the End button on her phone and screeched. "Eeee! Brygitta! I think this is going to work out! Can you believe it? Falling into our lap like this? I gotta call Nick and Livie!"

"Yeah, but . . . a thousand *ten* a month? That's outrageous."

"Not if we divide it four ways. That's only two-fifty and some change each. We pay more than that here."

"Yeah, but—"

Kat shoved the paper at Brygitta. "Hey, can you Google this address and find where it is in relation to SouledOut while I call the others? Hopefully we can walk there."

Brygitta took the paper. "Uh, Kat? You just wrote the address on your take-home exam. With a ballpoint pen."

Chapter 13

Avis dragged herself home late that evening. Even though they'd acted quickly, returning all students to their classrooms and keeping them there until security had had a chance to sweep the school, news of the pistol on the playground had spread like poison ivy at summer camp. So not only did she have to meet with the police and the boy's mother—a single mom who lived with her brother—but she also had to field calls from frantic parents until almost seven o'clock. As it turned out, the handgun belonged to the boy's uncle and had never been used, but since handguns were illegal within Chicago city limits, the gun had been confiscated and the uncle had been given a citation to appear in court. The charge: possession of an illegal weapon and endangering a child.

Peter was sympathetic. He even picked up the phone and ordered takeout from Jamaican Jerk, a tiny restaurant on Howard Street popular with the locals, so she didn't have to cook. "Guess now's not a good time to talk about Nony's invitation," he admitted. She rolled her eyes at him and locked herself in the bathroom, drawing a deep bubble bath and soaking in it for half an hour, letting the hot water draw the tension out of her muscles.

When she finally reappeared swathed in a comfy caftan and a head wrap, the food had arrived and she realized she was famished. Diving into the oxtail and beans, jerk chicken wings, and sweet potato fries, she felt energy seep back into her bones. Finally, leaning back in her chair and sucking on a chicken-wing bone, she relented. "It's all right, Peter. We can talk about Nony's invitation."

He arched an eyebrow at her, as if not quite sure she was serious.

"Actually, as I was praying at school today, I realized your idea of talking to the pastors is a good thing—you know, get their thoughts and prayers to help us decide what's the right thing to do." She picked up another sweet potato fry and tried to read his expression. "Or . . . were you thinking we would make a decision and then kind of just announce it to them?"

He made a face. "Well, I wouldn't have said it quite that crassly. But I was hoping we would come to some agreement on a direction and present it to them for their wisdom and counsel."

She toyed with another sweet potato fry. "I can see that. It's just . . . I don't know how to think about the future with so many things hanging fire. We don't know for sure whether Bethune will be closed next year or not. And we still haven't heard from Rochelle." Her composure broke a little. "I'm . . . I'm really worried about Conny, Peter. Whatever's going on with Rochelle can't be good for him."

"I know. I'm worried about Conny too." Peter laid down his fork and stared at his plate for a long minute. Then he sighed. "I need to be honest with you, Avis. Things aren't going that well at Software Symphony. With the economy the way it is, people aren't buying upgrades for their computers or investing in new applications. Sales have slowed way down, and we're barely breaking even. I may need to lay off some of my employees soon if things don't turn around. Which makes Griffin's offer to buy me out seem like a godsend."

"Oh, Peter." How had she missed the worry lines around his eyes?

"To tell you the truth, I'm inclined to pick up the phone and tell Griffin I'll accept his offer before he changes his mind. Because I don't think the economy is ever going to fully recover."

By the time Wednesday evening rolled around, Avis didn't feel much like going out again to Bible study. Repercussions from the pistol incident—suspending the student for two weeks, calling a special meeting for concerned parents Tuesday evening, making a full report to the school board—had taken up most of the last three days. And now she was getting pressure from some of the teachers and staff to install a metal detector at the doors of the school. Something she absolutely did *not* want to do. This was an elementary school, for heaven's sake!

But she and Peter had asked to meet with the pastors after Bible study, so she grabbed a quick bite at home and then drove her Camry to the Howard Street shopping center, since Peter was coming straight from work. Rolling the windows down, she realized that May temperatures had moved into the seventies that day for the first time, and she'd basically missed it.

Attendance at midweek Bible study was small compared to Sunday morning—mostly singles and couples without children since it was a school night. She gave a quick glance at the people filling the circle of chairs. Two were Yada Yada sisters: Estelle Bentley and her husband, Harry—another couple who'd gotten married in their fifties—and Jodi Baxter. The Meeks, Fairbanks, and several others were also there. Pastor Clark was already seated, talking earnestly with Harry Bentley. She noticed that the thin, lanky pastor did look paler than usual.

No Peter yet.

Estelle—a good-sized black woman but well proportioned—wrapped Avis in a big hug. "Sister Avis, are you all right? Sister Jodi told me what happened at school this week. Lord, have mercy! Do you need Harry to patrol the hallways? He does security, you know."

Avis smiled wearily. "Thanks, Estelle. We want to dial down the hysteria, not pump it up. But thanks for offering your man. I'm sure he doesn't need more to do."

Estelle raised her eyes heavenward. "*I* need him to have more to do. Can't stand to have a man under my feet all day. Thank God for that security job he's got part-time."

Chuckling, Avis chose a seat. It wasn't as if Estelle was home all day herself. The woman still worked part-time as a cook at the Manna House Women's Shelter in the Wrigleyville neighborhood, where several SouledOut members were either on the board, on staff, or volunteered.

Jodi plonked herself in the seat next to her. "Surprised to see you here after all that's gone down at school this week. You okay?"

Avis just squeezed Jodi's hand and nodded. As much as she loved her friend and third-grade teacher, she just didn't feel like talking any more about the drama at school. "Where's Denny?"

"Oh, you know. Boys' wrestling match tonight at West Rogers High. Says the athletic director should be there for the boys. Ha. I know Denny. He can't stand to *not* be at a game or match or what have you."

Peter slid into the seat on the other side of her just as Pastor Clark announced the topic for that evening would be "Our Identity in Christ."

"Sorry I'm late," Peter whispered. "Phone kept ringing up to the last minute."

She squeezed his hand. "We just started. But better shut off your cell phone."

The study was a good one, though Avis felt her identity as a child of God wasn't an area where she struggled. But she could tell that Gabby and Philip Fairbanks, who were working to repair their marriage, were listening intently and looking up every scripture. Well, praise God. If they kept Jesus at the center of their relationship, they might make it. *"A cord of three strands is not easily broken . . ."* Maybe she'd share that verse from Ecclesiastes with Gabby to encourage her.

As soon as the study was over, Avis and Peter followed Pastor Clark back to the pastors' office. Joe Cobbs had been preparing for his Sunday sermon during the Bible study, but he jumped to his feet and welcomed them when they knocked on the door. As they settled into the chairs he offered, Pastor Cobbs raised his eyebrows at them. "So what's this about? You guys finally deciding to get married?"

That got a laugh. He knew good and well Pastor Clark had married them at Uptown a few months before the two churches had merged.

"I think it took the first time." Peter grinned, but Avis could tell he was nervous by the way he leaned forward in his chair, forearms on his thighs, rubbing his hands together. "We want to talk to both of you about some decisions we need to make, but—"

"It's complicated," Avis said, then wished she could take it back. *Good grief.* She knew better than to finish her husband's sentences.

But Peter just said, "Honey, do you have that invitation from the Sisulu-Smiths? Why don't you read it for the pastors."

Avis pulled the envelope with the South African postmark out of her purse and read the note from Nonyameko. Both pastors knew the Sisulu-Smiths, who had been members of Pastor Cobbs's church before the two churches merged, and then members of SouledOut. They had stayed close to the couple when the tragic beating had almost taken Mark's life, and their move a year later to South Africa had been a loss for the whole church.

"Wow." Pastor Cobbs shook his head when Avis had finished reading the letter. "That's an amazing invitation from Nony and Mark. Are you two seriously considering going to South Africa? I'm jealous."

"Well . . ." Peter glanced at Avis. "There's more." She listened as her husband admitted the restlessness he'd been feeling, realizing the two of them had some good years left and maybe they should choose how to spend them, rather than just drift along the same old paths. He noted the falling sales at Software Symphony, and then the amazing offer of a buyout. And finally, the confidential notice Avis had received from the school board about possible school closures, including Bethune Elementary—right after getting this invitation.

Hearing it all laid out like that, Avis had a strange sensation. What was happening in their lives bore a striking parallel to what had happened to the Sisulu-Smiths. Nony and Mark had struggled for years with different visions of what they should be doing. Then a tragedy, loss, uncertainty—and pieces of their life had been taken away. But in the end it had opened the door for something new.

Was that what God was doing?

Both pastors listened in silence and sat quietly for several moments after Peter was done, as though considering all they'd heard. Finally Pastor Cobbs spoke. "I appreciate your willingness to include your pastors as you two face this decision. I'm certainly willing to pray with you as you consider the implications." He smiled wryly. "Can't say I'm excited about losing one of my elders and one of our best worship leaders though."

Pastor Clark had said nothing so far. He sat hunched over, a bit like a scarecrow losing its perch, rubbing his bony chin. When he did speak, he addressed her. "Sister Avis, you said, 'It's complicated.' Is there something more you'd like to share with us?"

A lump caught in Avis's throat. It was as if the older man

could see into her heart. She nodded gratefully. "There's one thing that makes it hard for me to even consider such a life-changing invitation right now—which has caused some stress between Peter and me." She took a deep breath, keeping her eyes on Pastor Clark's kind face for courage. "My daughter Rochelle and our grandson, Conny. They're missing. We haven't heard from them for, well, it's three months now."

"Rochelle . . . She was diagnosed with HIV, wasn't she? I remember she shared once here at SouledOut. A brave girl."

"Yes. Infected by her philandering husband." Avis spit it out, fresh anger rising in her throat. "We got a restraining order against him because he was getting abusive. She was doing all right for a while, being monitored at a clinic, taking her meds. But then . . . things just started falling apart. And now . . . we've lost touch."

Out of the corner of her eye, Avis saw Peter shift in his chair, as if a bit edgy at the turn the conversation was taking. Both pastors expressed concern, agreeing it was definitely a priority to make sure her daughter and grandson were safe and in a good place. "If there's anything we can do to help you find Rochelle, please let us know," Pastor Clark said.

"Absolutely." Pastor Cobbs tented his fingers thoughtfully. Avis noticed that the flecks of gray in his close-cropped hair added a distinguishing touch, even though the pastor was several years younger than Peter. "But it does seem that God is doing *something* new. I don't have a clear sense of what you *ought* to do, but I think I speak for both Pastor Clark and myself, we want to pray with you and stand with you as God reveals what your next steps should be."

After promising to keep them posted and spending time praying together, Avis and Peter walked out to the parking lot. She wondered if he was disappointed. The pastors had been open and supportive, but they had given no clear direction. Well, they could talk when they got home. They'd driven separately, and Avis walked toward her car. "See you at home. You need something to eat."

"Yeah, thanks, I'm starving." Peter pulled out his cell phone and turned it on. "*Huh*, got a message . . ." He started for his car, phone to his ear. But as Avis unlocked her door, she glanced toward his car and saw him frowning in the stark illumination of one of the parking lot lights. Suddenly he came striding toward her, clearly upset.

"Here. Listen to this." He punched a couple buttons and thrust the phone at her.

She pressed his phone to her ear. *"Peter. Jack Griffin here. I've been crunching some of the numbers you gave me, and, well, we've got a few problems with doing the buyout. Call me when you can and we'll talk."*

Eyes widening, Avis stared at her husband. With sudden force he slammed his hand on the hood of her car. "See? Should've told Griffin yes when the door was wide open! What are we going to do if this falls through?"

Chapter 14

Kat stopped at the wide entrance of The Chip and did a 360 of the booths ringing the student center café. The café was crowded this Friday afternoon with families in town for graduation tomorrow. Spying a hand waving at her from a booth in the corner, she managed the obstacle course around several knots of young siblings and grinning parents of soon-to-be graduates. "Whew!" She scooched into the vinyl seat, shoving her backpack into a corner. "I'm surprised you got a booth, Ms. Vargas."

The dark-eyed woman smiled. "No problem. I just told a few of my students it was their booth or their grade."

Kat laughed. She'd had Ms. Vargas for Spanish her first year here at CCU as a transfer student and enjoyed her sense of humor—one reason she'd signed up for the Urban Experience program, where the lively middle-aged woman served as advisor.

"So." Sipping from a tall, frosty glass of iced something, Ms.

Vargas eyed Kat. "What's this about? You wanted to see me. *Como esta?*"

Kat laughed. "I'm good! For one thing, finals are over. I graduate tomorrow. Just picked up my cap and gown." She patted her bulging backpack. "Although I'm staying for mini-term, taking a refresher Spanish course. Seemed like a good idea when I signed up for it, because I'd love to teach ESL. But right now? The thought of another class fries my brain!"

Ms. Vargas opened her mouth as if to say something, but Kat rushed on. "Anyway, what I wanted to tell you is that I'm staying in the city this summer! You inspired me to not just do the tourist thing in Chicago, but to actually get involved. Not just me, but Nick Taylor and Brygitta Walczak too. And maybe Livie Lindberg. We're looking at an apartment this weekend—practically fell into our laps! You see . . ." And Kat rattled on about visiting SouledOut Community Church as part of their "urban experience" and how they found out about an apartment to sublease for the summer. She finally paused for a swig of her water bottle. "This will give us the opportunity to, you know, get involved in the church this summer. Maybe work with kids. I'd like to find a job tutoring if I can."

Ms. Vargas let a few quiet moments pass before responding. "And?"

Kat blinked uncertainly. "And . . . what?"

"What are you hoping to learn from this experience, Kat?"

"Well, uh . . ." Kat wasn't sure what Ms. Vargas was driving at. "I'm sure we'll learn a lot. Getting to know people in the neighborhood. Finding out what we can do at the church. It's pretty different from the Phoenix suburb where I grew up, and SouledOut . . . well, it's pretty exciting. So diverse. Really energetic. You must've been there, since it was on your list of recommended churches to visit."

Ms. Vargas nodded. "Yes, I have a friend who's a member there. Edesa Baxter. You'll probably meet her if you do attend SouledOut this summer. I knew her as Edesa Reyes, originally from Honduras. We . . . Never mind, that's neither here nor there." The UE advisor leaned forward, her dark eyes locking on Kat's. "Kat, let me say something. You are a vivacious, idealistic young woman. Brimming with enthusiasm for your latest passion, whether it's a new theory of teaching, or being green, or . . . or eating vegan, or whatever it is you call it."

Kat shook her head. "I'm not exactly vegan. More like—"

"Whatever. Let me finish. I—" An insistent beeping suddenly distracted the UE advisor. She fumbled at her watch and pushed a button. "Uh-oh. I totally forgot I have a meeting with a student and parent in five minutes. *Lo siento* . . . I'm sorry."

The woman slid out of the booth but paused. "So I'll just say this, Kat. Talk less. Listen more." Then she grinned. "And come talk to me at the end of the summer. *Adiós, mi amiga!*" With a laugh, Ms. Vargas disappeared among the warm bodies still crowding into the café.

Talk less. Listen more. Huh. Ms. Vargas's comment made Kat feel like a sixth grader again. Her middle school teachers were always telling her to shut up and sit down. In fact, going over the brief chat with the UE advisor, Kat felt her face flush hot. Sure, she'd done most of the talking in the café, but the prof had asked her what was up, hadn't she? She thought Ms. Vargas would be excited that four of her students were taking the whole "urban experience" thing seriously. But all she had to say was, "Talk less, listen more"?

Kat wished she hadn't bothered letting the UE advisor know what they were doing this summer. She hadn't seemed all that impressed.

Well. So be it. If Ms. Vargas thought she talked too much, she'd keep her mouth shut. Though if she left the talking to Nick or Brygitta or, heaven forbid, *Olivia*, they wouldn't even have an apartment to check out this weekend. After all, she was the one who let the people at SouledOut know they were looking for a place to live in the city this summer. And at least she wasn't like Olivia, always asking anxious questions or stating the obvious.

Kat generally avoided her friends that evening and the next morning. Wasn't hard. Graduation on Saturday was by ticket only for family and friends, and Brygitta and Nick had both been given tickets by other graduating friends whose families couldn't come for one reason or another. "See you there! We'll cheer when they call your name, Kat!" Brygitta promised.

But Kat was having second thoughts about attending graduation at all. What was the point? Her parents hadn't come. She'd get her diploma whether she did or didn't attend. And to be honest, the party atmosphere and hoopla on campus was annoying. All these undergrads had come to CCU to get a Christian education, but most of them basically ignored the big city around them except to shop in the Loop or go out for Gino's Pizza. Now they were graduating. They'd get their diploma and go back to their lives in small-town America without ever having to deal with "the big city." Even the Urban Experience program was extracurricular, not required. A big mistake, in Kat's humble opinion.

Besides, it was a gorgeous spring day—temps climbing toward the seventies and a blue, blue sky. And, good grief, miniterm started on Monday, which didn't give much of a break. Kat didn't feel like sitting for hours in the auditorium while alphabetical lines of undergrad and graduate students crossed the stage. She felt like getting out of there. *Doing* something. Maybe she'd . . .

Eyes gleaming with her sudden idea, Kat went back to her dorm room, dumped books and notebooks out of her backpack, and repacked it with a fresh water bottle, granola bars, a windbreaker . . . and the Google map Brygitta had made of the address they were going to visit tomorrow.

Getting off the El at the Howard Street station, Kat deliberately walked to the shopping center where SouledOut Community Church was located, intending to follow the map from there to see how long it would take to walk on Sunday. It wasn't necessary. She was sure they could make it by one o'clock after church. According to the map, the address was only a mile or so away.

She hadn't expected anyone to be at the church—after all, it was Saturday, almost noon—so she was surprised to see a rental moving truck parked alongside the walkway in front of the church "storefront" and a good-size group of people inside: teenagers and young adults, along with some kids and parent-types. And as usual—for SouledOut, anyway—it was a mixed crowd of blacks, whites, and everything in between.

Not like campus, where "minorities" were still a minority.

What was going on? The moving truck . . . oh yes. There'd been an announcement last Sunday that one of the families was moving. Away? Or just in the neighborhood? A glance at the back of the truck showed that it was empty. So the move must be done already, and they were feeding the work crew who'd showed up to help.

Watching from the parking lot, she felt a little left out. She briefly considered going inside. They'd probably welcome her. But she hesitated. She hadn't helped with the move, so maybe it was a little presumptuous to show up at lunchtime.

Kat pulled out the map they'd printed out. Go down Clark street, turn on Pratt, head toward the lake, then go south a few blocks, turn again . . . okay, maybe it was a mile and a half. But it was a gorgeous day and she was up for it.

Clark Street was a trip. She'd never seen so many different tiny restaurants and grocery stores—mostly Mexican food—and little carts on the street corners selling hot ears of corn, an assortment of tamales, and a drink called *arroz con leche*—to name a few. A bustling fruit market. Shops with *quinceañera* and prom dresses. Even a western-wear store with cowboy boots, hats, and belts with big silver buckles. Kat bought one of the ices from a cart with a big orange and white umbrella, using her smattering of classroom Spanish. She felt giddy. Staying in this neighborhood was going to be so fun!

Turning east on Pratt, then making a few more turns onto residential streets containing a mix of big old houses, two-flats, three-flats, and six-unit apartment buildings, Kat consulted her map, looked up . . . and realized she'd arrived. There it was. A brick three-flat. Well maintained. In fact, flower beds in front of the bushes that lined either side of the cement steps looked as if they'd been freshly dug, and rows of pink and purple petunias—or were those pansies?—nodded in the noonday sun. The big stone urns on either side of the steps were filled with red geraniums and some long vines.

Kat grinned inside. Nice, very nice. Glancing about and seeing no one nearby, she ventured up the steps and into the small foyer. Three mailboxes. Three sets of buttons. Three names. "First floor, Logan. Second, Candy. Third, Douglass," she murmured. She didn't really want to run into the Candy lady, since they didn't have an appointment until tomorrow, but for a brief moment she was tempted to push the button that said Douglass. Were they home? It'd be fun to see their apartment. It would give her an idea of what the Candys' apartment was like. But she hesitated. Probably a bad idea to show up without—

The outside door to the foyer opened and Kat turned quickly, feeling caught. But it was a young black woman, no one she recognized. Pretty, skin on the creamy side, lots of hair. Seeing Kat, the woman stopped, as if startled. They stared at each other. Funny, Kat thought, the girl's hair was almost like her own, full and long and wavy. Darker, though. Black with brown and gold highlights.

The stranger's eyes flickered. "Who are you? You here to see someone?"

"Uh, no. Not exactly. I have an appointment to see an apartment here tomorrow. I was checking to be sure I had the right address." *And what business is it of yours?* she felt like adding.

"Who's moving? I didn't know someone was moving."

"Do you live here?" Maybe she was the first-floor people.

The young woman ignored her question. "Who's moving?" she repeated. Her eyes darted from Kat to the door and back again. She seemed awfully nervous.

"Not exactly moving. Second floor. They're going on a business trip. I—several of us—are subleasing their apartment for the summer."

"Oh." The woman seemed visibly relieved. "Okay. 'Scuse me, I need to leave something." She moved to the mailboxes, took a pencil and folded piece of paper out of her shoulder bag, scribbled something at the bottom of what looked like a note, then stuck it through the slot in one of the boxes. Pulling the outside door open again, the young woman hustled down the steps and was gone.

As the door wheezed shut, Kat edged back toward the mailboxes and peered at the name on the one in question. *Douglass.*

Curious, Kat went outside to the sidewalk and looked both ways. Halfway down the block she could see the woman running, hair flying.

Kat stared after her. What in the world was *that* about?

Chapter 15

Avis popped open the trunk of her Camry and lifted out several plastic grocery bags but had to set them on the curb to close the trunk. She wished Peter were home to give her a hand, but he had a board meeting at the Manna House Women's Shelter, then was going back to the office—*another* Saturday—and wouldn't be home till suppertime. If only they lived on the first floor! As it was, she'd have to make at least two trips up to the third floor.

But she had to smile as she relayed the grocery bags up the steps and into the foyer. The petunias, phlox, and alyssum she'd planted that morning in the beds on either side of the steps looked so cheerful! Ditto the geraniums and trailing vines in the cement pots. Even if it did mean she got a late start to the grocery store and had to wait in a checkout line ten people deep.

Unlocking the inner door to the stairwell, she propped it open with her foot and grabbed two bulging bags in each hand . . . and hesitated. Had the mail come? Well, she'd check when she came down for the second load.

The phone was ringing when she got inside their third-floor apartment. Dumping the bags on the kitchen table, she caught the caller ID. *Software Symphony.* "Hi, Peter. I'm here, just got back with the groceries."

"Oh, okay. I called awhile ago, didn't get an answer."

"I had my cell."

"I know, but didn't want to talk while you were out. Got a minute?"

"Uhh . . . I've still got more groceries down in the foyer. Some frozen stuff. I better not leave them. Can I call you back?"

There was a slight pause. "Sure. Talk to you in a few minutes."

Avis winced. Peter didn't sound good. *Oh, Lord, what now?* He'd been moody ever since that call from Jack Griffin last Wednesday, even though the two men had had a long phone call the next day, and the offer wasn't completely off the table.

She was halfway down the carpeted stairway when she met Louise Candy coming up, mail in her teeth, Avis's grocery bags hanging from each hand. "Um, hi," her neighbor said, voice muffled. The middle-aged white woman with the garish fake tan set the bags on the landing and rescued the letters from her mouth. "Saw your groceries on my way in, thought I'd bring them up."

A bit taken aback, Avis nodded. "You didn't have to do that. But thanks. Nice of you." She'd wanted to pick up the mail . . . but guessed it could wait till later. She needed to get the frozen stuff into the freezer and call Peter back anyway. Picking up the bags, she turned to go back up the stairs.

"By the way," Louise called after her, "thanks for finding someone to sublet our condo. You know, those students from that Christian college or seminary or whatever. We figure if you and your husband recommend them, they gotta be all right."

"I—" Avis pinched her mouth. She wanted to say it was Peter, not her, and they couldn't exactly recommend them, but that might come out wrong. Still, she needed to say something to correct the assumptions. "Actually, we only just met them ourselves. They were visiting our church and asked about a place to rent for the summer. Please make your own determination if they're suitable. We don't have anything invested in them renting from you." All of which was true.

"Oh, sure. I know. I talked to one of the girls on the phone, Kat Somebody—funny name, isn't it?—and they're coming by tomorrow afternoon. Sure would be nice if it worked out, though, 'cause now they want Ted in Costa Rica right after Memorial Day, and I'd like to be able to go with him."

"Oh. Well, hope it works out."

Avis started once more up the stairs with the grocery bags, but Louise called after her again. "Hey. The flowers out front look nice. Did you do that?"

Avis kept going. "*Uh-huh*. Glad you like it." And finally made it inside her door.

She felt a little guilty about Louise Candy as she made room in the freezer for the Styrofoam tray of chicken breasts, a bag of precooked shrimp, and two bags of frozen green beans. They'd been building neighbors for, what, going on two years now, and they had never done much more than chit-chat in the hallway, except for the rare condo meetings when they needed to make decisions about the building, like replacing the roof or getting the furnace cleaned before winter. Same with the family on first. They all had their own lives, like cars in different lanes on the expressway, not even having to stop at the same stoplight.

Still, the woman seemed to be reaching out. Avis decided she'd make more of an effort to get to know Louise when the Candys got back from Costa Rica, invite her up for coffee or something.

If she and Peter weren't in South Africa or somewhere by then.

Peter! He was waiting for her to call back. Punching Redial, she cradled the kitchen phone between her shoulder and her ear as it rang, figuring she could put away the rest of the groceries as they talked.

"Avis. Glad you called back. But I've got a Com Ed guy here I need to talk to in a few minutes. Will you be home for a while?"

"Peter. Just tell me what's going on. Then we can talk more later, okay?"

She heard him sigh on the other end. "Okay. It's Carl Hickman. He had an accident today in the mailroom. Tripped over something or slipped—we're still investigating—and hit his head on the corner of a counter. Split it wide open. Knocked him out for about five minutes, and there was a lot of blood. But when the paramedics came, he was in a lot of pain, seems like he injured his neck too."

"Oh no, not Carl!" Carl Hickman was Florida's husband. One of Peter's top employees, rising from the ranks of mail clerk up to general manager. "Where is he? What hospital? Does Florida know?"

"They took him to St. Francis, and yeah, she's up there with him now. But, Avis . . ." She heard her husband suck in a deep breath and blow it out. "It's not just Carl. If he's out for a long time, I don't know what I'm going to do. I don't have anyone who can replace him, no one with his experience, and— Oh. I gotta talk to this inspector Com Ed sent out. Something about the electrical wiring. See you when I get home."

The phone went dead. Avis realized she was standing in the middle of the kitchen still holding the same package of pasta she'd taken out of the grocery bag when she first called Peter back.

She dropped the package on the table and went hunting for her purse and jacket. This wasn't just any employee. It was Carl Hickman. She needed to get up to the hospital to be with Florida.

A gentle rain had settled in when Avis drove her car out of the hospital parking garage two hours later. Her newly planted flowers would love it, anyway. And the news wasn't all bad about Carl. The gash in his head had required twenty-four stitches, but the doctor said head wounds tended to bleed a lot but weren't necessarily serious. They were more concerned about the neck spasm that prevented Carl from turning his head even a little, and they wanted to keep him overnight to check for possible concussion as well.

As for Florida, once she knew Carl wasn't going straight to heaven, she began fussing. What was she going to do with him underfoot, lying around the house? He better get better quick and get back to work. Avis had to chuckle at her friend. Those two had been through hell and high water and made it to the other side—with Jesus, no less—so she was sure they'd make it through this.

She parked the Camry out front—they only had one space in the three-car garage in back, and Peter's Lexus was newer than her car, so they figured it was safer there—and dashed through the rain into the foyer. Oh, the mail. She dug out her keys and unlocked their box, but it was empty. Peter must be home.

Her husband was sitting in his recliner, eyes closed. "Hi, baby," she said, unloading her purse and damp jacket on a chair. "You okay?"

He reached out a hand and she took it, leaning over to kiss him on the forehead. But he pulled her down until she was half sitting on the arm of the recliner and half in his lap. Relaxing into his embrace, she snuggled her head on his shoulder.

"Got your message," he murmured. "Glad you went up to see Carl. How's he doing? Florida all right?"

"*Mm-hm*. Hopefully Carl will be too. But you didn't answer my question. Are you okay?"

He sighed. "Yeah. I guess. It's just . . . strange. I hadn't even verbalized this thought in my head until today, when Carl got hurt. But in the back of my mind, guess I've been thinking that if the sale of the business falls through, well, one alternative would be to keep the business, put Carl in charge for a few months, and just take a leave. Still do the mission trip thing. Isn't Mark Smith doing some teaching at KwaZulu-Natal University in Durban? I'm sure they have Internet and cell phone connections. I could keep in touch with what's going on at Software Symphony if needed. But . . . now this."

Avis didn't respond, but her mind tumbled. What was with Peter? It was as if he'd decided he was going to do this mission trip thing no matter what!

Okay, Avis, don't get bent out of shape, she told herself. *He admitted it was an idea in the back of his mind that he hadn't really put into words until now. And he's telling me—"confessing," as it were.*

Her spirit softened. "Honey, we really have to trust God with this. We're still asking God what we should do. If we're supposed to go to South Africa, God's going to make it possible, right? And right now our concern is for Carl. His family can't afford for him to be off work, though I know you'll do right by him while he's laid up."

He sighed again. "Sure, sure. But . . . I just don't know how I'm going to manage if he's out very long. Carl's a key player, been with me the longest."

"Well, let's not imagine the worst. Our heavenly Father knows . . ." And Avis slid right into a prayer, asking God for healing for Carl, comfort for Florida and the rest of the Hickman family, wisdom for Peter, and guidance for both of them in the decisions facing their future. ". . . In the *mighty* name of Jesus. Amen."

She didn't know about Peter, but she felt better giving it all to God. Tilting her head back, she kissed Peter on the cheek, catching a faint whiff of his aftershave, and pushed herself off his lap—an awkward dance since she had to wiggle off the recliner sideways as well. "Guess I'll start some supper . . . Oh. Did you get the mail?"

"*Mm*. On the lamp table."

Avis picked up the clump of mail and sorted through it. A business magazine, Com Ed bill, pack of local coupons, junk mail addressed to "Resident," two catalogs . . . wait. What was this? A sheet of lined school paper folded in thirds was stuck between the two catalogs, half crumpled. School paper? She smoothed it out and opened the folds. *"Mom . . ."*

Rochelle's handwriting. Suddenly light headed, she groped for the closest chair and sat down.

"Avis? What is it?"

She licked her lips. "Rochelle . . . she left us a note."

Peter put the recliner's footrest down with a thump and was at her side. Leaning over her shoulder, they silently read the handwriting together.

> Mom, thanks for the Mother's Day message. Sorry I couldn't answer. Phone on the fritz. Just want you to know Conny and I are okay. Maybe we can meet up somewhere. Conny asks about you. Love, R.
>
> P.S. Flowers look nice.

Chapter 16

Avis tossed and turned all night. Half the time her heart was singing. *Thank You, Jesus, that Rochelle and Conny are all right!* And *Thank You, Jesus, Rochelle got in touch with me!* Peter had said, "See? They're all right. She'll come around soon enough." But the rest of the night, she felt like punching the pillow. Rochelle's phone was "on the fritz"? *Humph*. Probably shut off again for nonpayment. And dangling the hope they could meet up somewhere? How was she supposed to do that if there was no way to get in contact with her daughter?

One look in the mirror the following morning—eyes puffy, black silk hair wrap all askew, hair twists sticking out at odd angles and coming undone—and Avis was tempted to stay home from Sunday worship. What she needed was time alone with the Lord, to pour out her heart's concerns about her daughter and grandson, to hear from God how to handle her frustration and seek guidance on what to do next.

Worship . . . worship would be good. But she didn't feel like making small talk with people she only saw once or twice a week. Or getting sucked into pouring out her guts, either, to those perceptive few—her Yada Yada sisters in particular—who would guess right away that something was wrong and would hover around her like a flock of biddy hens.

But Avis had never played hooky from church. Not once in her adult life. Even on trips to see Charette and her family or to attend an education conference, she always found a church to visit. Sunday was the Lord's day, and the Bible said not to neglect meeting together with other believers "as some do," didn't it?

She went to church. But Peter wanted to go early to pray with the elders again, which was the excuse Avis needed to drive her own car and slip in just as worship was starting. And she was glad she'd come when Florida got up to share about Carl's accident. Avis and Peter, the Baxters, and several others gathered around her at the front of the church to pray for his speedy recovery and protection for the family.

Pastor Clark preached that morning, taking his text from Matthew 18, about Jesus' promise that if two agree about anything they ask God for, He would do it. And where two or three gather in His name, Jesus promised to be present among them. "Do we believe this, church? Jesus seemed to be saying that *praying in unity*, agreeing together what we should be praying for, is important. So how do we do that?" Pastor Clark scratched his chin thoughtfully. "*Hm*. I sure would like one of those new BMWs . . . Maybe I'll ask Brother Bentley over there to 'agree' with me and pray about it, too, so I'll be sure to get it!"

Avis saw the retired cop duck his head. Uneasy laughter rippled around the room.

Pastor Clark raised his eyebrows. "Did I step on some toes? Be honest now. But, saints, think about this: the first requirement for praying in unity, for coming to agreement, is that our prayers need to line up with the Word of God!"

Amens bounced from every corner of the room. It was a good message . . . but Avis managed to slip out during the benediction, telling Peter in a whisper that she'd pick up some Chinese takeout for lunch and would meet him at home.

Her cell phone rang while she was waiting at Yuen's Chinese Kitchen on Clark Street for the lunch combination of egg rolls, Szechuan Chicken, and shrimp fried rice.

"Avis Douglass!" Jodi Baxter's voice blasted her ear. Avis quickly lowered the volume. "What's with you today? You came in late and left early—and I didn't even get to hug your neck. Are you okay?"

"Hi, Jodi. Yes, I'm fine. Just . . . needing some space today."

"*Uh-huh*. Either you and Peter had a big fight or you're upset about Rochelle. Which is it?"

"Number 16! Order number 16!" shrilled a voice behind the pick-up counter.

"Look, Jodi, I can't talk now. I'm at Yuen's and they just called my—"

"Wait! Are you coming to Yada Yada tonight? We're meeting at the Garfields'. Tell you what. I'll pick you up and we can drive over together."

"Um . . . sure."

"Okay, I'll pick you up at four thirty."

Avis slipped the phone into her purse and took the paper bag the clerk handed her. *Yada Yada tonight*. Part of her didn't feel like going anywhere . . . but she'd missed the last meeting, and Pastor Clark had just preached about the importance of praying together in the name of Jesus. Yes, maybe that's exactly what she needed to get a breakthrough in the walls she was up against. If she had some alone time this afternoon, she might be ready to share her heart with them and unleash their prayers.

As Avis pulled out of the small parking lot onto Clark Street, she saw the four Crista students walking down the sidewalk, almost to the tiny strip mall she'd just left. Glancing in her side mirror, she saw them head for Yuen's. She shivered. That was close. She was in no mood for the Kat girl's hyper enthusiasm about everything. What were they doing walking this way anyway? The El was—

Ohhh, right. They have an appointment to see the Candys' apartment this afternoon. Suddenly the likelihood of the four students living beneath her for the next few months loomed like an ominous cloud on the horizon. She pushed her speed up. She wanted to get home and lock the door and pretend she wasn't home.

Peter held up a hand when Avis asked if he wanted more shrimp fried rice. "I'm good. Thanks. But think I'll go over to St. Francis to see Carl. You want me to clean up this stuff first?"

"No, it's fine. Go. If you see Florida, tell her I'll be at Yada Yada tonight."

He went for his jacket as she cleared the table, but he stopped back by the kitchen before heading out. "Uh . . . you going to be okay?"

She fluttered a hand at him. "Yes! Shoo! Shoo! The sooner you go, the sooner I can get a few hours' rest before Jodi picks me up." She softened her brusque send-off with a light kiss on his smooth-shaven cheek and accompanied him to the front door.

Laughter from the apartment below floated up the stairwell.

"Sounds like the interview is going well," Peter murmured, giving her a wry grin.

Avis rolled her eyes and shut the door behind him.

Five minutes later she was snuggled in a corner of the living room couch with an afghan, a steaming mug of tea, and her Bible. *Mm. Peace and quiet.* She sipped the hot tea for a few moments, then set it aside and closed her eyes. *Lord . . .*

But the prayers she wanted to pray didn't come. Stuck like peanut butter to the roof of her mouth. How was she supposed to pray? Rochelle's note, which had felt like cool water to her thirst for news of her daughter, now taunted her. She had no way to respond or get back in touch with her! Were she and Conny really okay?

And Peter! He was all hot to chuck life as they knew it and go running off to . . . somewhere. Nony's invitation was probably just a good excuse. Gave his wanderlust a spiritual sheen. But with Carl in the hospital and sales falling, Software Symphony was on rocky ground—not to mention her own job hung in the balance.

She hugged herself, rocking back and forth. *Oh God, I don't know how to pray!*

Praise Me, Avis. Isn't that what you're always telling your Yada Yada sisters? Praise Me in faith, praise Me for what I'm going to do and am already doing, even if you can't see it. Let the joy of the Lord be your strength!

The Voice in Avis's spirit tugged on her heart. What was wrong with her lately? She seemed to be forgetting everything she knew about keeping her eyes focused on Jesus. Instead, she was letting life's choppy waves knock her off balance.

All right, Lord, I get it. We're going to have a little praise party here.

Hefting her big Bible, Avis opened to the Psalms. Bless Nonyameko. Her friend's constant example of praying the scriptures was especially helpful on days like today, when her own prayers felt stuck. Psalm 42 caught her eye and she began to read aloud.

"'As the deer pants for streams of water, so my soul pants for You, O God. My soul thirsts for God, for the living God! My tears have been my food day and night . . .'" *Oh! So true!* She continued to read aloud, the familiar words coming alive and soothing her troubled heart. "'Why are you downcast, O my soul? Why so disturbed within me? Put your hope in God, for I will yet praise—'"

A rapid knocking at the front door startled her.

Knocking? Who would knock? The door was supposed to be locked at the bottom of the stairwell.

Avis threw off the afghan and headed for the door. Maybe Jodi was early. No, wouldn't be. Jodi always rang the buzzer and waited to be buzzed in.

At the door, Avis paused. "Who is it?"

"Mrs. Douglass?" The voice sounded loud and clear, even through the wooden door. "It's us. The students from CCU."

I don't believe this, Avis thought. But it was too late. She'd already announced she was home. She opened the door.

Kat Davies and the other Crista University students—what were their names again?—stood on the carpeted third-floor landing, grinning like kids at Disneyland.

"Hi, Mrs. Douglass!" Kat bounced on her toes as if she couldn't stand still. "We just wanted to tell you that we're going to be your neighbors for the summer! We just signed an agreement with the Candys, and they said we can move in as early as next weekend. We're so excited! Isn't it wonderful?"

Jodi Baxter snickered behind the wheel of the Dodge Caravan as Avis recounted the announcement at her front door.

"As if she were the angel Gabriel, announcing the coming Messiah!" Avis groaned. "What's wrong with me, Jodi? I like young people, don't I? Why does the prospect of these particular students living right under my feet make me feel . . . invaded?"

"I don't know. Hopefully it'll be better than you think. I doubt they'll be throwing any wild parties or turning it into a drug house." Jodi glanced at Avis from the driver's seat. "But that was this afternoon. You were already upset about something this morning. What's going on?"

Avis sighed. Might as well tell Jodi. The younger woman had become a good friend in the years they'd been in the Yada Yada Prayer Group together. They'd made a strange pair at first. Avis thought Jodi was as bland as white bread when she and her husband and their two teenagers had first moved into the city from the 'burbs. But God had taken this "goody-goody white girl" through some tough stuff, and she'd had to go deep. And one thing about Jodi. She was persistent. And loyal.

By the time Jodi parked the minivan a few houses down from the Garfields' one-story brick bungalow, Avis had spilled the whole stew she'd been slopping around in the past few weeks. Rochelle's disappearance since Valentine's Day. The missing earrings. Peter's restlessness. The invitation from Nony and Mark. The offer to buy Peter's business—which might fall through now. Carl's accident. And the note from Rochelle that had shown up in their mailbox yesterday.

The only thing Avis held back was the letter from the Chicago school board. The potential school closings were confidential—and besides, if it happened, it would mean Jodi's job too.

"Sheesh." Jodi turned off the motor but made no move to get out of the minivan. Just sat there shaking her head.

Avis gave her a lopsided smile. "*Uh-huh*. I second that."

"I'm so sorry, Avis. About Rochelle especially. I mean, I knew she hadn't been in touch for a while, but I didn't understand the toll it's taken on you. Forgive me for being so dense."

Avis sighed. "I didn't realize either. I kept thinking she'd stop being mad and call any day. And then suddenly, six weeks had gone by with no word—and I got scared. The note helps a little—but I'm still worried." Her voice choked. "And I really miss Conny. My little sweetheart."

"Oh, Avis." Jodi laid a hand on her arm.

Avis fumbled for a tissue and blew her nose. "Well. Can't sit here all night. Thanks for listening, Jodi. Helps to tell somebody. Besides Peter, that is. He's got his own issues with all this." She opened the door and climbed out of the minivan.

"Uh, just a sec," Jodi called after her. "Gotta make a quick call." Half a minute later she got out, locked the car, and hustled after Avis. "Sorry about that. We better go in."

Avis shrugged, noting the bright clusters of marigolds and chrysanthemums on each side of the door stoop. Ruth Garfield never failed to brighten up the plain brick bungalow with flower beds and window boxes. She'd inspired Avis to do the same to their building.

"We're here!" Jodi called, opening the front door and ushering Avis into the tiny entryway. She stopped and let Avis precede her into the living room—

"SURPRISE!!!!!" A flock of female voices yelled in unison and then launched into an off-key version of "Happy Birthday to Youuuuuu . . ."

Avis gaped at the grinning faces surrounding her. Florida Hickman cocked her forefinger and thumb like a gun and mouthed, *"Gotcha!"* Ruth Garfield, their hostess and everybody's "Jewish mother," was trying to ignore one of her four-year-old twins—the girl, Havah—who was tugging on her arm. Yo-Yo, who could still pass for a teenager in her spiky blond hair, cargo pants, and skinny tops, had Ruth's other twin—the boy, Isaac—in a headlock. Adele Skuggs, wearing a large green T-shirt with Adele's Hair and Nails across the front, pointed at Avis, then to her own hair, and frowned. Message: *Girl, that hair's a mess. Get in my shop tomorrow!* Delores Enriques was singing *"Feliz cumpleaños"* just to confuse everybody. And Estelle Williams—now Estelle Bentley—the group's "Big Mama," and Becky Wallace, pale and lean in comparison, leaned against the living room doorposts as if holding up the tiny house.

As the song ended, Leslie "Stu" Stuart smirked, saying, "Thanks for the call from the car, Jodi. Though giving us more than thirty seconds' notice would've been nice."

Chanda George, spilling out of her too-tight blouse and skirt, giggled and announced in her thick patois, "Never mind dat. Avis, mi tink yuh like de chalklit cake mi made special a-you!"

Avis tried to protest. "It isn't my birthday yet . . . is it?"

Jodi laughed and pushed her into the compact living room. "No, not till Friday, but this is the closest Yada Yada meeting to your birthday, so why not celebrate?"

They made her sit in Ben Garfield's "Daddy Chair"—an overstuffed monstrosity with crocheted doilies on the arms and back—and brought her Chanda's "chalklit cake" and a glass of yummy punch with sherbet floating in it. Avis kept insisting they shouldn't have gone to the trouble, wasn't even her birthday . . . but she drank up the love in the room like lemonade on a hot day.

Jodi presented her with a birthday card she'd made on her computer with Avis's name and its meaning in a flourishing script on the outside page:

Avis ~ "Refuge in Battle"

And on the inside page: "Avis, God has put within you a spirit of refuge—one who listens, who cares, who points us to the One True Refuge, Jesus Christ. You have stood with each one of us through many of life's battles, and we love you." It was signed with all their names.

All except three: Hoshi Takahashi, who was spending the year with International Student Outreach at Boston University.

Nonyameko Sisulu-Smith, now "back home" in South Africa. And Edesa Reyes Baxter, Jodi's Honduran daughter-in-law, who only came occasionally since she'd started a spin-off Yada Yada group at the House of Hope where she and her husband, Josh, were living as support staff for homeless moms with kids.

Avis let the happy chatter swirl around her. *Yada Yada . . . to know and be known intimately.* At least that's what Ruth said the Hebrew word meant. They'd been together, most of them, for seven years this month. These sisters knew her well—and loved her, no matter what. Which made it easy, finally, to share from her heart later that evening, and let these quirky sisters—as different from each other as a drawer full of mismatched socks—pound heaven's ears as they prayed for her.

"So!" Chanda demanded as they finally broke up and were saying their good-byes. "What yuh want Peter get yuh for you birtday?"

Avis just shrugged and smiled. But as she and Jodi drove home, not talking, just relaxing in the warmth of the minivan's heater in the cool spring evening, she knew what she wanted for her birthday.

To find Rochelle and Conny. To wrap her arms around them and bring them home.

Chapter 17

Kat took off the earphones in the language lab and stretched. *Uhhhh.* Mini-term only started yesterday, but already the mountain of homework required for refresher Spanish had fried her brain. And that wasn't counting the three hours of class lecture every morning, every day except Friday. And it was only Tuesday!

She gathered up her books and papers, stuffed them into her backpack, and wearily made her way out of the building. Good thing mini-term was only three weeks long or she might not make it.

But as she made her way across campus to the student center, she took a deep breath of the late afternoon air, smelling of a recent rain, new leaves, and budding flowers. *Mmmm, spring.* That was one thing she enjoyed about the Midwest compared to dry, hot Phoenix—actual seasons. Sure, winter was a lot colder here, but the snow was fun—at least for the first two months—and made her appreciate spring all the more.

And the move into the Rogers Park apartment this weekend was something to look forward to. She'd been surprised after service on Sunday when a guy about her age had introduced himself, said his name was Josh Baxter, and offered to help them move their stuff with the church van if they got the apartment. How cool was that?

The Crista campus had largely emptied out by Sunday evening, and even the student center was practically deserted as Kat headed for the corner booth in The Chip where her friends sprawled in various stages of early mini-term fatigue.

"She arrives! The fair maiden who skipped her own graduation." Nick lifted a large paper cup of soda in a salute. "We thought maybe your professor sent your class to Mexico for language immersion."

Brygitta scooted over and Kat sank down beside her roommate. "Not a bad idea," she moaned. "I'd rather talk to a real person than to that disembodied voice in the language lab. I'm dead. I need food."

"Already done . . . here it comes."

An undergrad student with a once-white dish towel tied around his waist like an apron deposited a huge platter of nachos with melted cheese, chili beans, lettuce, tomatoes, and jalapeños in the center of the booth table. "Sorry for the wait. I'm here by myself tonight." The kid seemed in no hurry to leave. "You guys all staying for mini-term too?"

"Yeah, man. We'll be around." Nick gave him a friendly fist bump.

"Not around much. We'll be living off campus this summer." Kat grinned at the student waiter and lifted a large nacho off the plate and into her mouth, strings of melted cheese dripping from it. *Ohhh, so good.* She felt her spirit rising again—the way she'd felt when they left the Candys' apartment Sunday afternoon.

"All summer? You guys aren't going home after mini-term?" The waiter's eyes glittered. "Man, I'd love to stay in the city for the summer! My hometown in Oklahoma is barely on the map." He made a face. "Their idea of a good time is the chili cook-off at the local VFW."

Kat looked at him with interest. "Hey, would you be—ow! What'd you kick me for, Bree?"

Brygitta gave her a look, but the guy didn't seem to notice. "Where'd you find an apartment? Uh, do you have room for one more? I'd pay my share of the rent . . . well, if I can find a job. Working here at The Chip doesn't pay much—especially now that they've cut my hours."

Nick shook his head. "That's not it, man. We signed an agreement to sublet, and I'm sure the absentee owners wouldn't be happy with us adding a fifth person they'd never met."

The Oklahoma kid shrugged. "Yeah, well. My dad's gonna say he needs me to help with the corn harvest, so it probably wouldn't work anyway. Maybe next year. Well . . . eat up. Anybody want anything else? Refill on sodas?"

"Sure," Nick said, and the student disappeared behind the café counter.

"Kat!" Brygitta hissed. "What were you thinking? You can't just invite someone else to crash in the Candys' apartment. That was the whole point of going to meet them, wasn't it? To let them get to know us, assure them we'll be responsible tenants. I mean, it's full of their stuff, not ours!"

"Okay, okay." Kat shrugged. "I just thought, you know, dividing the rent *five* ways would make it even cheaper. And *you*"—she pointed a finger in Nick's face—"you just want to be the lone guy so you can keep a bedroom all to yourself."

"Who, me?" Nick grinned innocently and stuffed his mouth with a loaded nacho.

They finally cleaned off the plate of nachos and leaned back with their refills of soda and water. "We should talk about Saturday," Kat said. "Josh Baxter—he's about your age, Nick, except he's married and has a little girl—told us to call if we got the apartment and let him know when to show up here with the church van."

"Decent of him," Nick noted. "I was wondering how we were going to get all our stuff up to Rogers Park."

"At least we don't have to furnish the apartment ourselves." Brygitta cupped her chin in her hand and sighed dreamily. "I mean, it's got everything! Dishes, silverware, pots and pans, a TV, DVD player—"

"Yeah, but I remember your parents had to rent a U-Haul trailer to get all your stuff to campus." Kat gave Brygitta a playful shove. "We're going to need every inch of that big van." She looked around the table. "So when can we be packed and ready? Ten? Eleven?"

"Make it noon," Brygitta groaned. "I'm going to need all the time I can get after my class on Friday."

Nick shrugged. "Fine by me."

Kat looked at Olivia. "Livie? Is noon okay for you?"

Olivia cleared her throat. "Um, can we back up a little?" She tipped her head toward the counter, where the undergrad who'd waited on them was making milk shakes for a couple of new customers. "I've been thinking . . . I mean, if that guy over there is seriously interested in staying in Chicago this summer, maybe he should take my place. Would still be four people."

The other three stared at her.

Kat found her voice. "I thought you'd decided to go in with us, Livie. You said you really liked the apartment. You even told Mrs. Candy you'd love to take care of her plants."

Nick frowned. "Livie. You did talk to your mom, didn't you?"

Olivia shrank into her corner. "Well . . . I was planning to—after I saw the apartment, I mean. But . . ."

"Livie!" Kat sputtered, but Nick held up his hand.

"Wait, Kat. Livie, I—we—don't want you to feel coerced into staying here this summer if you feel you need to go home. We want you—but only if *you* want to."

"Nick's right," Brygitta chimed in. "If not, we'll just divide the rent three ways." She eyed Kat. "Right, Kat?"

Three ways! Kat swallowed. That would be pretty tight—and none of them had jobs yet. And she *didn't* want to ask her dad for rent money, though he'd be good for it. No, she wanted to do this on her own terms.

Still . . . they were right. She nodded slowly in agreement.

"Good." Nick leaned forward. "Hey, remember the message on Sunday? You know, when Pastor Clark talked about where-two-or-three-are-gathered-together kind of prayers? Something we haven't done yet is pray about this apartment thing."

"Of course we've been praying!" Brygitta cut in. "At least I have."

"I know. I mean, pray *together* about it. Like Jesus talked about."

"Help us out, Preacher Boy." Kat pointed at Nick's backpack. "Got your Bible in there? Maybe you can show us what you're talking about."

"All right, all right." He dug in his backpack and brought out a beat-up New Testament. "It's Matthew 18, I think . . . yeah, here it is. 'I tell you'—this is Jesus talking—'that if two of you on earth agree about anything you ask for, it will be done for you by my Father in heaven. For where two or three come together in my name, there am I with them.'"

Kat frowned. "*Anything* we ask? It *will* be done?" She shook her head. "I realize I'm kind of new at this, but . . . that's kind of a stretch, isn't it?"

"But Nick has a point," Brygitta said. "We should be praying in unity—or praying for unity—about this."

Nick stuck his Bible into the backpack. "Exactly. Why don't we pray *with* Livie that she'll know what to do and have peace about it? And that the rest of us will have peace about her decision too."

Olivia glanced nervously around the café. "You mean . . . right now? Here?"

Kat shrugged and grinned. "I'm in. Who's going to mind? Apron-Guy over there? He's too busy playing chief cook and dishwasher. Nick, this was your idea. You start."

Kat was brushing her teeth that evening when she heard Brygitta holler, "Who is it?" Kat turned off the water in the bathroom sink and listened. Who was bothering them at this hour? She was tired and wanted to fall into bed.

"Livie!" she heard Brygitta say. "Are you okay?"

Olivia? Kat hurriedly spit out the toothpaste, rinsed her mouth, and flew back into the room. The younger girl stood in the middle of their room, a windbreaker thrown over her pajamas, clutching a sheet of paper.

"Livie! What is it?" Kat pulled their friend down into a three-way huddle on Brygitta's bed.

Olivia groaned. "E-mail from my sister, Elin. She's just finishing eleventh grade." Olivia thrust the paper at Brygitta. "You read it."

"O-*kay.*" Brygitta scanned the e-mail, eyes widening.

"Aloud!" Kat demanded.

"Okay, okay . . . 'Dear Livie, I am so bleeping mad! Mom's got a new boyfriend. Name's Gilly Henderson. He's, like, ten years younger than Mom. *I hate him!* He's here all the time, lying around, drinking and belching. He gives me the creeps—'"

Olivia hugged a pillow to her chest as Brygitta read.

"'—But Mom is all gaga—you know, some man is actually paying attention to her. But he's real mouthy, bosses me around all the time. I haven't told Mom yet, but I am NOT going to stay here with him around. I already asked Aunt Gerty if I could come stay with her and Uncle Ben in Madison as soon as school is out, and she said yes. She met the guy and doesn't like him either. I'm just warning you, Livie—you *don't* want to be in this house this summer, or you'll go nuts! Want me to ask Aunt Gerty if you can come too? How long will you be in Chicago?

Maybe I'll come visit you. It's not that far from Madison, is it? That'd be fun. Love you, your sis, Elin.'"

Brygitta looked up. "Whoa. You didn't know anything about this new boyfriend, Livie?"

Olivia shook her head.

"Arrgh. Sounds like a loser. I'm so sorry, Livie." Brygitta tossed the e-mail on the bed. "Your mom's in Minneapolis, right? So where's Madison? Like Madison, Wisconsin? That's not very far from Chicago—only a few hours, don't you think, Kat?"

But Kat wasn't thinking about Madison, Wisconsin. She picked up Olivia's e-mail and read it again, her thoughts tumbling. This was bad news for Livie and her sister. And yet . . . did she dare say it?

She reached out and touched Olivia's arm hugging the pillow. "Livie, remember how we prayed together a few hours ago, that God would make it clear where you should be this summer? I think you just got your answer."

Chapter 18

Avis pushed aside the pile of paperwork she'd just finished and glanced at the wall clock. Two twenty. School would be out in another forty minutes. Next Monday was Memorial Day—a long holiday weekend coming up. But she still had a meeting at three thirty to talk about the Summer Tutoring and Enrichment Program at Bethune Elementary.

Opening the folder marked STEP, she studied the list of proposed offerings.

Tutoring in Math and English
Mentorships
Art Classes
Sports Clinics
City Culture Day Trips

None of which were funded by the Chicago Board of Education, except for the cost of keeping the building open—lights, air, and janitorial services.

A flutter of excitement, like sugar in the blood, gave her a boost of energy, even though by this time on a Friday she was usually ready for a long weekend nap. Summer sessions abounded at local high schools, middle schools, and park programs. But the summer program at Bethune Elementary had been her brainchild, and last summer had been the maiden voyage. She'd pounded the pavement soliciting donations from local businesses to fund tutors, coaches, supplies, and transportation. Her winning mantra: "STEP is a win-win investment. Keeping kids occupied keeps them off the street."

The letter from the school board two weeks ago had shaken her confidence about running STEP a second time. What if they closed the school halfway through the summer? But just this week, after the spine-strengthening prayers of her Yada Yada sisters, she'd resolved to move forward. "Don't let that ol' devil discouragement gain another inch of territory," Estelle Bentley had told her. "He's defeated already. Just doesn't know it yet."

Remembering Estelle's comment, Avis smiled as she pulled a few more files to take to the meeting. The Yada Yada Prayer Group had sparked a few unusual weddings in their seven short years. Estelle Williams's and Harry Bentley's was the most recent—a match that had to be made in heaven, because no matchmaker on earth would have put those two together! Both had been around the block a few times and had a few gray hairs to show for it. Harry was an ex-cop—"ex" because he'd had to take early retirement after blowing the whistle on some rogue cops—and he'd fallen hard for the Manna House cook at a shelter Fun Night. *Their* surprise wedding had taken place on a Sunday morning at SouledOut, right in the middle of the worship service.

She and Peter, though, both in their fifties, had been the first over-the-hill wedding, jumping the broom at what used to be Uptown Community Church before the merger into SouledOut. The Friendship Quilt the Yada Yadas had made for that occasion hung on the wall of their bedroom.

On the other end of the age spectrum, Jodi and Denny Baxter's college son, Josh, had fallen for Edesa Reyes, one of their Yada Yada sisters, even though the pretty Honduran girl was a few years older. Now *that* was a wedding for the books. They'd tied the knot at the homeless shelter, no less! Edesa and Josh had both been volunteering at Manna House when a crack mother, found dead of an overdose, left a note saying if anything happened to her, she wanted Edesa to raise her baby. Just engaged, Josh felt called to move their wedding date up so baby Gracie could have a daddy too—just like Joseph of old had been told by the angel of the Lord to go ahead, marry the virgin Mary and be daddy to baby Jesus. And a Christmas wedding at that.

Speaking of babies . . . Ruth and Ben Garfield were already married but childless when Yada Yada started—and then Ruth delivered *twins* just before her fiftieth birthday!

Avis shook her head, laughing silently. Nothing boring about the Yada Yadas.

Hmm. Wonder who's next? They had several singles in Yada Yada: Yo-Yo, Stu, Becky, and Hoshi—though Hoshi had moved to Boston. Even Chanda and Adele.

Mm. Probably won't be Adele. She'd rule the roost like a

drill sergeant, same as she did at her beauty salon . . . which reminded her. She needed to make an appointment to get her hair done tomorrow morning, since Peter was taking her out for her birthday in the evening.

The last school bell rang just as Avis got off the phone with Adele's Hair and Nails. As she often did, she walked out into the hallway and stood near the double doors leading outside, saying good-bye to the children, calling most by name, telling some to slow down, have a good holiday, walk don't run, see you next Tuesday!

Waiting until the hallways cleared and the handicap buses had loaded and left, Avis went back to her office, gathered up her notebook and relevant folders, and stopped by the main office to tell the school secretary the STEP meeting would be in the teachers' lounge—except the secretary was nowhere to be seen. Didn't she work at least until four?

Walking briskly down the hall, Avis pulled on the door to the teachers' lounge, but it was stuck—or locked. She knocked. "Who is it?" came a muffled voice.

"Avis Douglass! Why is this door locked?" She was going to have a word or two with whoever locked this door. People were still coming!

The door clicked and opened. Denny Baxter, Jodi's husband, whom she'd recruited to run a sports clinic twice a week, stood aside. "Sorry about that," he said. "Come on in, Madame Principal."

Avis walked in . . . and was met with a loud chorus: *"Happy birthday!"* Then the group launched into, "For she's a jolly good fellow, for she's a jolly good fellow . . ."

A decorated bakery cake sat on the conference table, fresh coffee dripped in the coffee corner, and the AWOL school secretary presented her with a large bouquet of Stargazer lilies.

Avis was tongue-tied for a few awkward moments but managed a smile for the small group of teachers, parents, and university students needing practicum credits who would be her STEP staff this summer. "I . . . I don't know what to say. Thank you. Thank you, everyone." But she caught Jodi Baxter's eye standing over by the coffeepot and mouthed, *"You're behind this."*

Jodi shrugged and mouthed back, *"So? It IS your birthday today."*

Adele Skuggs shut off the beehive hair dryer and waved Avis back into the chair at Adele's Hair and Nails the next morning for the process of getting her twists redone. Avis watched in the mirror as Adele wove the artificial hair into Avis's thick, kinky hair, braiding it near the roots and then twisting the rest.

"Good thing I told Peter not to take me out for my birthday until tonight. At least now I'll have my hair done."

"*Mm-hm*. Hold still, girl. I've got to do the rest of these. I don't want to hurt you." Adele fussed for three hours with the black twists all over Avis's head until they lined up in neat little squares, then used mousse and sprayed it with sheen to make them lie down and shine. Whisking off the black plastic cape, she gave Avis a hand mirror to check the sides and the back.

Avis nodded, pleased, as she held the mirror this way and that. *Nice*. The twists gave her a youthful look, and with her smooth skin, free of any premature wrinkles, she could pass for ten years younger than her fifty-five years. Maybe she'd get a manicure and pedicure too, if Adele's girl could squeeze her in. Just thinking about soaking her tired feet in the bubbling hot water and getting her calves and feet massaged with lotion made her want to purr.

By the time Avis got home, the nails on her fingers and toes a rich burgundy with a feathery white filigree on each index finger and big toe, it was midafternoon. But the SouledOut van was parked in front of her building, taking up her usual parking space. What was the church van doing here?

Just then Josh Baxter and the seminary student from Crista University—Nick Something—hustled out the front door and down the steps, heading for the van. "Oh, hey, Mrs. Douglass!" Josh hollered with a wave. "Just one more load and we're done. Give us a minute and you can have this parking space."

The two young men, who seemed similar in age, grabbed the last few bundles and bags from the back of the van and disappeared once more into the building.

Avis tapped her freshly manicured nails on the steering wheel as her car idled. So. The four students were moving in. And Josh Baxter, bless his overly friendly soul, had gotten permission to use the church van to help them out.

Looked as if the students were threading their way into the fabric of SouledOut Community Church.

It would definitely be an adjustment on the home front. Both of her neighbors moved in totally different social circles. But these students wanted to be part of SouledOut, which put them in *her* life circle in more ways than one.

She sighed. *Sorry for fussing, Lord. It'll probably be fine. I just have so much on my plate right now. I don't feel like I have the energy to relate to new neighbors.*

Josh Baxter came trotting out the door again, waved at her with a big grin, and climbed into the fifteen-passenger van that was used mostly for youth activities. As it pulled out, she pulled in and parked, gathered up her purse and umbrella—which she didn't need after all, in spite of the iffy-looking clouds earlier that morning—and went inside.

Using her mailbox key, she fished out the mail and riffled through it . . . nothing from Rochelle. Only then did she realize she'd been unconsciously hoping that Rochelle would come by and leave another note, or mail her a card, or . . . something. Yesterday had been her birthday, after all.

Don't go there, Avis, she told herself. Letting herself into the carpeted stairwell, she climbed the stairs noiselessly, though she could hear youthful voices, thumps, and laughter coming from the open door on the second floor. Pausing on the stairs just before the second-floor landing, Avis listened. The voices were distant, coming from another part of the Candys' apartment, so she quickly moved past the landing and up to her own door on third.

There'd be plenty of time to say welcome to the neighborhood. Maybe tomorrow. Right now, she needed to call Peter and ask what time they were going out, so she'd know when to be ready. It'd been three weeks since they'd gone out for their anniversary, which had ended rather badly, and she wanted tonight to be different.

After all, her husband had had a stressful week. Carl Hickman had been released from the hospital but started having neck spasms, which put him back in again. So Peter was without a manager, doubling his own workload. And from what she could gather, Jack Griffin was now "looking at his options"—which meant Software Symphony was only one card in the buyer's deck, not the ace.

They both could use a pleasant evening—dinner and dancing? No stress. Just enjoy each other. Enjoy the moment.

She'd just donned her favorite silk lounging pants and top after a leisurely bubble bath and was putting on her makeup when she heard knocking at the front door. *I don't believe this.* She was hardly presentable, but . . . what did she care? Had to be one of the kids downstairs.

Kathryn Davies beamed at her when she opened the door. Her thick mane of brown wavy hair had been pulled back and wound into a large, lumpy knot on her neck, and she was dressed in sweatpants and an oversize T-shirt. "Hi, Mrs. Douglass! We're all moved in. Didn't take long with Josh Baxter's help. What a nice guy he is. Oh! What I came up for is, we're making some vegetarian spaghetti and it's kind of messy, but we don't want to use Mrs. Candy's nice cloth napkins, but we can't find any paper ones." She paused for a breath. "Do you have any paper towels we can borrow? Ha. Guess *borrow* is the wrong word, since I'm sure you wouldn't want them back with spaghetti sauce all over them."

Avis waited to see if the girl was through, then smiled. "Of course. I've got an extra roll you can have." She headed for the kitchen, realizing that Kathryn followed her into the apartment. Rummaging in the small pantry, she found the roll of paper towels and walked back into the living room.

Kathryn had picked up one of the framed photos on the lamp table and was staring at it. She looked up at Avis, eyes wide. "Is this your daughter? I didn't know who she was!"

Avis felt her skin prickle. "What do you mean? You *saw* her?" The photo Kat was holding was Rochelle and Conny, taken last Christmas at a JCPenny Portrait Studio. "When?"

Kathryn nodded. "Last weekend. I, uh, well . . . I came by on Saturday just to make sure we could find the address, even though our appointment with Mrs. Candy wasn't until Sunday. And this girl—the one in the picture—came into the foyer and put something in your mailbox. And . . . then she left." Kathryn smiled big and pointed at the photo. "Really cute kid. Your grandson? I didn't realize the girl was your daughter. Do they live around here?"

Avis just stared at Kathryn, her emotions ricocheting in all directions. She wanted to cry out, *Did she look okay? Was her hair done? Has she been eating? How did she act? Did she have her son with her? What was she wearing? Tell me everything!*

At the same time, she didn't want this white, pampered, eager-beaver grad student to know anything was wrong. Didn't want her to know she hadn't seen Rochelle in over three months. What business was it of hers?

Avis forced a calm smile. "Yes. My daughter and grandson. They live in Chicago. Oh. Here are your paper towels. You don't need to return the roll. Keep it. And, I'm sorry, but I need to finish getting ready because my husband is picking me up soon. Glad you're getting settled." She started for the door, which still stood open. "See you tomorrow at church?"

Chapter 19

"Perfect birthday," Avis murmured to Peter as she slipped into bed later that evening. And it was. They hadn't talked about missing daughters, business buyouts, school closings, trips to the far corners of the world, or starry-eyed white kids from the 'burbs moving into their building. Just enjoyed their shrimp and steak, a celebratory bottle of wine, small talk, and laughter. And in a burst of energy—or foolishness—showed they could still cut the rug to some good ol' Motown tunes.

She cuddled close to Peter's bare torso as he slipped an arm around her and pulled her into an embrace. "Though, *uhhh*, a few of my muscles may be protesting by morning."

Her husband chuckled. "You were still the most gorgeous chick on the dance floor, sweetheart."

She lifted her head from the pillow and looked at him. "I did *not* hear you call me a 'chick.' And if I did, I ought to slap you upside the head."

"Okay, okay." He was still laughing. "The most gorgeous

woman there tonight. I saw the other men looking. Jealous as all get-out that you were with *me* instead of them."

"Oh, stop. I just turned fifty-five. Nobody's looking at me like that anymore."

"*Humph*. I know what I know and know what I saw—and *none* of those oversexed, underdressed, painted-up *chicks* in that restaurant could hold a candle to the beautiful woman I had on my arm tonight." He pulled her closer and nibbled on her ear.

"*Mm-hm*," she murmured. "I can tell a line when I hear one. If you think it'll get you somewhere"—she reached up and traced his face with a finger, first an eyebrow, then his nose, then along his trim mustache and warm lips—"you know me too well."

"*Mm*, baby—"

A sudden, deafening, electronic screech pierced the floor from the apartment below. Both Peter and Avis bolted upright in bed.

"W-what is *that*?" Avis quavered.

The screeching died as quickly as it started, but was followed by the electronic twang of a guitar, still audible through the floor. And then they heard a distant male voice crooning something about, "You are everything that I live for . . ."

"I don't believe this!" Avis vaulted out of bed, flipped on the bedside lamp, and looked around for a weapon. A broom handle, that's what she needed. But with no broom in sight, she grabbed one of the high heels she'd worn that night, fell to her knees, and pounded the heel against the bare floor not covered by the small bedside rug. *Bam, bam, bam!*

The singing stopped.

Beside her the bed was shaking. Still on her knees, she lifted her head and peeked over the side of the bed. Peter had the pillow over his head to muffle the sound, but his whole body was shaking with laughter.

Avis was still steaming the next morning as she poured Peter's coffee. "I knew it! College kids. They think this is still a dorm where everyone stays up until three in the morning. You need to speak to them, Pe—"

A knock on their front door diverted her attention.

"Ouch! Watch the coffee, Avis!" Peter jumped up from his chair as her aim missed his cup and hot coffee splashed in his lap. "Rats. Now I'll have to change my slacks."

The knocking continued.

"You get it," Peter said. "I can't go to the door with wet pants."

Avis meekly handed him a hand towel. "I'm sorry. Are you okay?"

"Yes, yes, I'm fine. Just get the door." Peter disappeared down the hall and into the bedroom.

Avis set the coffeepot back on its warmer, took several deep breaths to steady her nerves, and marched to the front door. She opened it. The seminary kid—Nick—stood on the landing, looking chagrined.

"Uh . . ." His face reddened. "I'm sorry about last night. I hadn't tested my speakers yet and they . . . well, sorry about the terrible screech. Was it okay after that?"

Avis took another deep breath. Okay? *Okay*? Not at eleven

thirty! She cleared her throat. "We could still hear it, and we were already in bed. I'd . . . appreciate it if you wouldn't do your electronic music after ten. And maybe do it somewhere else besides the bedroom right under ours."

The young man nodded. "Okay. I didn't realize it was so late. Guess we were still all hyped up about moving in and getting settled, I— Oh, hello, Mr. Douglass. I was just apologizing to your wife about last night."

Peter appeared next to Avis's shoulder. "We appreciate that. It was disconcerting, to say the least." Avis noticed that he was using his deep, I'm-serious-here voice. "I'm sure it won't happen again."

"Oh no, sir." The young man rubbed a hand over his short hair, combed forward in a popular style Avis often saw in The Gap fashion ads featuring cool, casual white guys. "Well, guess we'll see you at church." Nick turned and hustled down the stairs.

Avis closed the door. "That went well. Considering you sent *me* to speak to him. Should have been a man-to-man thing."

Peter followed her back into the kitchen. "*Hm*. Don't know about that. You were the one who pounded on the floor with your shoe." He chuckled as he resumed his seat at the kitchen table. "Any more coffee in that pot?"

She retrieved the coffeepot. Behind her she heard him say, "Maybe we should offer them a ride to church, you know, to show we're not still mad—hey!"

Avis loomed over him threateningly with the coffeepot. "We will do no such thing. It would set a terrible precedent. They want to live in the city? Let them figure out how to use public transportation. Or walk. It's almost summer. They'll be fine. If it rains buckets, that's one thing. Otherwise . . ." She waggled the coffeepot over his lap once more, then carefully filled his cup. "Besides, there are four of them and two of us. Wouldn't fit. We'd have to take two cars."

He lifted both hands in surrender. "Okay, okay. I was just saying."

The thunder and lightning cracked so close together, the lights flickered. Avis peeked out the bedroom window where she was packing her "church bag" with her Bible and tambourine. When did this storm sneak up? Weatherman had said "a chance of thunderstorms" later in the afternoon. But rain soon lashed the windows. She'd better wear her rain boots and change into heels at church. And she'd need her raincoat now, even though the temperature was supposed to hike into the high seventies that day.

Peter, already shrouded in his London Fog, stood by the front door. He cocked an eyebrow at her as if waiting for something.

"What?" she said.

"It's raining buckets."

She blew out a breath in resignation. "Oh, all *right*."

The four students were grateful for the ride. When Peter said they'd take two cars, Kat protested. "Oh, don't waste extra gas. We're trying to live green as much as we can. We can squish the four of us in the backseat, right, guys?" Which they did, somehow squishing the youngest one—Olivia—across their knees.

Kat peppered the ride to church with questions. "So how long have you two been at SouledOut? . . . Have you lived long in this neighborhood? . . . I met one daughter. Do you have other kids? . . . Grandkids? . . . What kind of work do you do?"

Avis let Peter answer most of the questions but shot him a warning look when the questions got personal about family. He took the hint and kept his answers simple. Just, "Two other daughters, both grown, a couple other grandkids," avoiding the complicated answer about a second marriage, her daughters, not his.

But when he said, "I own a software business here in Rogers Park, and Avis is the principal of one of the neighborhood elementary schools," Kat fairly screeched.

"Ohmigosh! I just got my master's degree in education! And I'm working on my certificate to teach ESL. I'd *love* to talk to you about your school, Mrs. D."

Avis winced at the careless exclamation—practically taking God's name in vain. And when did she give the girl permission to call her "Mrs. D"? But she was spared having to respond as Peter pulled into the shopping center parking lot and stopped in front of SouledOut's double glass doors. The students piled out, darting quickly inside to escape the heavy rain.

Avis followed a few moments later while Peter parked the Lexus. Florida Hickman pounced on her the moment she got inside. "Sister Avis! Pastor Clark wants to see you. Tol' me to tell you the minute you got here."

"Thanks, Flo." Usually that meant the pastors needed

someone to fill in at the last minute—read a scripture, make announcements, pray. She held on to Florida's shoulder for support while she pulled off her rain boots and wiggled her feet into her heels. "How's Carl doing?"

Florida grunted. "*Huh*. Still has me worried. He had this terrible headache yesterday, got so bad he threw up. Soonest I can get him back in to see the doc is Tuesday, tomorrow being a holiday an' all. Say, speaking of Memorial Day, you two doin' anything? If not, why don'tcha come on over to the house and we'll grill somethin'. If this rain stops, that is. Be good for Carl to have some company."

Avis smiled. "I'm sure Peter would like that. I'll let you know for sure—but guess I better go see what Pastor Clark wants."

She started to leave but Florida grabbed her arm and lowered her voice, cutting her eyes toward the Crista students, who stood in a cluster talking to Josh Baxter and his wife, Edesa. "Uh, saw you pull up. How come you an' Peter totin' around them white college kids?"

Avis allowed a wry smile. "They moved into our building yesterday. It poured buckets this morning. Peter's a softie. Add it up."

Florida snickered. "You watch out, girl. They gonna be all up in your bizness 'fore you know it."

Tell me about it. But Avis just waved a hand at Florida and headed through the double doors at the far end toward the pastors' study. She knocked at the half-open door. "You wanted to see me, Pastor Clark?"

"Oh, good morning, Sister Avis." The older man, all knees and elbows, pushed himself out of his chair to give her a "church hug." The exertion seemed to make him cough, and it was a few moments before he caught his breath. "Sorry about that. Sit, please."

Avis took a seat, crossing her ankles and making sure her dress covered her knees. Pastor Clark looked a little ashen. "Are you all right?"

"Yes, yes." The pastor took several sips of water and smiled. "It's just this up-and-down weather. In fact, that's why I asked to see you. Pastor Cobbs came down with the flu last night, and he was supposed to preach today. So here I am trying to put together a last-minute sermon. And on top of that, Justin called a half hour ago. He's lost his voice and he was supposed to lead worship today. I know it's last minute, but could you . . . ?" He looked at her hopefully.

Lead worship? Oh, she couldn't. When it was her turn to lead worship, she always spent extra time with the Lord, preparing her own heart, reading the Word, listening for promptings from the Holy Spirit. But . . . Pastor Clark looked at his wit's end. Poor man. She couldn't leave him bearing the burden of the service alone. She heard herself say, "Well . . . I'll do my best. I don't feel at all ready. Guess we'll wing it together." And she made herself smile.

Pastor Clark chuckled. "Sometimes that's just the time the Holy Spirit takes over, when we don't feel prepared and ready. Oh . . . here's my sermon topic and the list of songs the praise team is planning to do this morning." He pushed a sheet of paper across the desk and smiled encouragingly. "But don't feel limited to that. Why don't we pray? We both need it!"

A few minutes later, bolstered by the prayers she and Pastor

Clark had prayed for each other, Avis headed for the ladies' restroom, hoping to find an empty stall to give her a private moment to think. How much time did she have before worship started? She glanced at her watch. Less than ten minutes. *Oh Lord, I need Your help here.*

Two little girls darted out as she went into the restroom. Now the room was empty. Gratefully, she locked herself into the handicapped stall. The larger stall would give her a little space to think, to pray, to look for some scriptures.

What had she been reading in her quiet time this morning? She couldn't remember. She'd still been upset about the rude disruption the night before. But sitting on the closed toilet seat cover, she opened her Bible to where she'd left her ribbon marker. Oh yes, Psalm 56. She glanced at the sheet of paper Pastor Clark had given her. His sermon topic was "Fear or Faith?" and several of the songs were on the theme of trusting in God. That would fit, even make a nice call to worship—

She heard the door to the restroom push open and women's voices filled the room. ". . . I hear they just moved into the neighborhood."

"Really? I'm not surprised. Such great young people. They seem so eager to get involved."

Avis didn't move. She recognized the second voice as Mary Brown, whose family had just moved from a rented apartment into a nice condo a half block from the lake. The other voice, she wasn't sure.

"But I heard they're all living in the same apartment," said the first woman. "In the Douglasses' building. Not a very good testimony to the neighbors. I mean, three young women living with a single man? Maybe the Douglasses approve of such an arrangement, but . . . well, that sure wasn't how I was brought up."

Avis's jaw dropped. Why did the woman think she and Peter had anything to do with the "arrangement," one way or the other?

"Oh, I don't think you need to worry. I'm sure it's not a problem. Did you see all four of them talking to Josh Baxter a few minutes ago? I heard him talking about the teen group. Maybe he was recruiting them to help with the youth ministry. They'd be a real asset, I'm sure."

"Well, maybe you're right. The one girl, the one with all that thick wavy hair. She's a real pistol, isn't she. Looks kind of Italian, don't you think?"

"No, no, you're wrong. Her last name is Davies, a very English name, you know." Footsteps moved into the stall next to the one Avis was in, a door closed, locked. "I'm just glad to see more white young people coming to the church—if you know what I mean. Educated young people, too, from a Christian university."

"Yes, yes, I know what you mean." A second stall door closed and locked.

Avis's eyes nearly popped. Holding her breath, she strained to listen.

Mary Brown's voice in the next stall continued, "I know we're supposed to be a diverse church and all that. But seems like the blacks and Latinos far outnumber white folks lately."

A snicker. "You're supposed to say 'people of color.'"

A laugh. "Oh, right."

The conversation paused as toilets flushed, doors opened, and water was turned on in the washbasins. Avis's heart was beating so loudly, she was sure the women at the sinks could hear it. Did they really assume no one else was in the stalls? The handicapped stall was large enough they couldn't see her feet unless they got down on their hands and knees. But still.

Faucets turned off, and Mary Brown's familiar voice spoke again. "And what will happen when Pastor Clark retires? That can't be too far off. He's not that well, you know."

"*Mm*, hadn't thought about that. Pastor Cobbs would be the sole pastor."

The voices lowered but still carried. "Well, we can't let that happen. Nothing against Pastor Cobbs, you understand. I like him well enough. But we need more white people in leadership so things don't, you know, get too far off."

"Too black, you mean."

"Exactly— Oh, we better go. Service is about to start." The outer door was pulled open, the voices faded, and the door slowly wheezed shut.

Avis felt as if her blood had stopped moving. Her mind reeled.

There was no way she could get up front and lead worship this morning! Not after hearing two of her white "sisters" worry about the church becoming "too black."

Chapter 20

Wiggling her fingers and grinning good-bye at the cute two-year-old in Josh Baxter's arms, Kat scurried after her friends into the second-to-back row, which had become their usual "pew." Livie and Bree preferred sitting in back where they didn't feel in the spotlight, but the very last row was reserved for parents with babies and toddlers. Kat would've preferred sitting closer to the front, but at least from the back rows she was able to see who all was there without turning around and staring.

But today her mind was on their brief conversation with Josh Baxter and his wife, Edesa. So *she* was his wife. An interracial marriage. So cool. She'd been surprised at Edesa's Spanish accent though. Kat had assumed she was African-American—glowing warm skin, a head full of tiny black braids caught back with a brightly woven headband, and that megawatt smile. But obviously not. *Wonder where she's from?*

Wait. Didn't Ms. Vargas say she knew someone here at SouledOut named Edesa? It must be her!

The praise team was still tuning up. Kat leaned across Nick and whispered, "So what do you guys think? About Josh and his wife inviting us to come to the cookout with the teen group at the beach tomorrow. It's Memorial Day. No classes."

Livie groaned. "Yeah, but I still got a ton of homework before Tuesday."

"We all do, Livie. But it'd be a good chance to get to know some of the kids. And it'd be fun!"

"I'm not ready to sign on to help with the youth group," Brygitta whispered. "We've only been coming here a month."

"Hey, can we talk about it later?" Nick cut in. "It's time for the service to start."

Kat settled back in her chair. The clock on the wall already said 9:35, but the praise team seemed to be waiting for something. The man at the keyboard—at least midthirties, light brown hair combed over a bald spot, wearing glasses and an open-necked dress shirt—stepped over to Pastor Clark sitting in the front row and whispered something. Both of them glanced toward the double doors on the far side of the room. Were they waiting for the worship leader? No one was up at the main mike. Or maybe they were waiting for Pastor Cobb. Kat hadn't seen him yet this morning, or his wife. They usually sat on the front row with Pastor Clark, regardless of who was preaching.

Then she saw Mr. Douglass leave his seat and slip out through the double doors on the far side that led to the kitchen, office, and classrooms. A few moments later he came back and conferred with Pastor Clark and the keyboard guy. That's when

Kat realized Mrs. Douglass wasn't in her usual seat. Had something happened? She'd been in the car with them on the way to church, but . . . Kat swiveled her head. She didn't see Mrs. D anywhere.

Kat hoped she hadn't gone home. Principal of an elementary school! She never would have guessed. But Kat's thoughts were already racing. Maybe she could get a job there next fall if they needed teacher aides. Or maybe even—

Just then the man at the keyboard played a few opening chords and spoke into his mike. "Good morning, church! Let's stand and sing this song from Psalm 27, letting the words of the psalmist sink deep into our hearts. 'The Lord is my light and my salvation, whom shall I fear? The Lord is the strength of my life; of whom shall I be afraid?'" He beckoned to someone. "Terri, sorry to put you on the spot, honey, but can you come up here and sign these words for us?"

Chairs scraped and a rustle filled the room as everyone stood—and by now Kat knew they wouldn't sit back down again for another thirty minutes. Minimum. She watched curiously as a thirtysomething woman with short brown hair came to the front. (He'd called her "honey." Was she his wife?) She'd never seen anyone do sign language to music before, and the woman's motions were almost . . . lyrical in their beauty. Several people in the congregation did the motions along with her, creating a dance of hands. Kat wanted to do them too, but she felt self-conscious. She still wasn't exactly used to doing anything more than clapping to praise music—and she'd never even done that in her so-called home church growing up.

Kat was so busy watching the sign language for *Lord* and *light* and *strength* and *afraid* that she hadn't noticed Avis Douglass appear. But as the last phrase of the song died away, there she was at the mike with that big Bible she carried around. "The Word of the Lord from Psalm 56," she said in that strong voice of hers. "'Be merciful to me, O God, for people hotly pursue me. All day long they press their attack! My slanderers pursue me all day long. Many are attacking me in their pride . . .'"

Was she the worship leader today? Kinda odd to come in late. She'd gone from "missing" to reading the scripture with a kind of . . . fierceness.

"But—" Mrs. Douglass's tone shifted slightly as she read. Calmer, not as fierce, but still passionate. "'—when I am afraid, I *will* trust in You. In *God* I trust; I *will not* be afraid. What can mere mortals do to me?'" The worship leader shut her Bible and held it against her chest. She was silent for a long moment, her chin tilted up, her eyes closed. The room hushed. Then she spoke. "Say these words with me, church: 'When I am afraid, I will trust in You.'"

"When I am afraid, I will trust in You," a chorus of voices repeated.

"In God I trust, I will not be afraid!"

"In God I trust, I will not be afraid."

Twice more Mrs. Douglass had them repeat the words. "*When* I am afraid, *I will* trust in God! . . . In *God* I trust, I will *not* be afraid!"

The back of Kat's neck prickled as the voices around her rose, speaking the words forcefully. She'd read through the Psalms a couple times in the last few years but had never noticed the power of those two juxtaposed phrases, not like this. A few people around her seemed to be crying. She heard, "Thank ya, Jesus!" from one side of the room and "Yes, yes, I trust You, Lord!" from another, as if the psalm spoke to some real and present fears.

Strange, Kat couldn't remember the last time she'd actually felt afraid—well, maybe on 9/11 when those planes crashed into the Twin Towers. But even that terrifying event had seemed so far away from her life in Arizona. She'd only been sixteen at the time, a junior in high school, didn't know anyone in New York. Mostly she'd just felt bad for the people who suffered so much trauma or lost family and friends in the disaster. But it hadn't touched her personally.

Had she ever really needed to trust God like that? In the face of real fears?

Giving a nod to the praise team, Avis Douglass stepped off the low platform and joined her husband. Kat saw him give her a quick squeeze with his arm as the praise team led into another song of worship. *Sweet.*

When the praise team finally sat down and the children had been excused to their Sunday school classes, there was another empty pause. Kat squirmed. Most Sunday church services moved along *click, click, click*. What was supposed to happen now?

After a few long moments, Pastor Clark stood up and stepped onto the platform. He gripped the slender wooden podium as Mrs. Douglass came back and stood beside him. She laid a hand on his arm and prayed that God would speak through this man of God and that the people would have ears to hear.

As she sat down again, Pastor Clark cleared his throat.

"Thank you, Sister Avis. Good morning, church." *Good mornings* came back in reply. "If you know me at all, brothers and sisters, you've probably already figured out that Hubert Clark is not exactly a spontaneous, seat-of-the-pants kind of person. I like order. I like schedules. I like advance notice."

Friendly chuckles greeted his wry confession.

"So when First Lady Rose called this morning to say Pastor Joe had been up half the night with the flu and I'd need to fill the pulpit for him . . . well, the old, familiar stage fright set in. The cold-sweat, knees-knocking kind of stage fright. Maybe Sister Avis knows what I'm talking about, because our brother Justin, who was scheduled to lead worship today, also called in sick. So I did the same thing to our sister here. Put her on the spot and asked her to lead worship at the last minute."

Murmurs of empathy. Well, that explained that, Kat thought.

"But what better time to talk about fear . . . or faith? It's easy to praise God, to be thankful, to have confidence in God when everything's going smoothly, when we're healthy, when the job's secure, when the money's good. But what about when we haven't yet seen the answer to our prayers? When our job gets terminated? When our kids are rebellious? Or when we're sick or someone we love is in the hospital?"

"That's right, Pastor! That's right." A wiry black woman jumped to her feet, the one whose husband they'd prayed for last Sunday because he'd been injured on the job. "*Mmmm.* Lord, have mercy." The woman sat again, fanning her face with a piece of paper. *Florida.* That was her name, Kat thought.

"But, saints, how many times did Jesus say, 'Fear not! Don't be afraid. It is I.'" Pastor Clark stopped, fumbled for a handkerchief, and coughed a couple times. A man on the front row jumped up and gave him a glass of water. But after a few swallows the pastor went on. "Brothers and sisters, praise itself is an act of faith. Why? When we're able to praise God *before* we see the answers to our prayers, we're saying, Lord, I trust *You* to work this out, according to Your purpose. I'm going to thank You now for what You're going to do."

More *amens* peppered the room.

"And secondly, praising God strengthens *us*! The Bible says, 'The joy of the Lord is our strength!' Say that with me, church. The joy of the Lord—"

"—is our strength!" the congregation echoed.

But even as Kat dutifully said the words along with everyone else, she realized something was wrong. Pastor Clark didn't finish the phrase. Instead he gripped the small wooden podium with both hands, wobbled . . . and suddenly, clutching the left side of his chest, he crumpled to the floor.

A nanosecond of disbelief. Then pandemonium broke out. Some lady screamed. Several people rushed to the low platform. A panicked babble of voices. "Somebody call 911!" "Is there a doctor in the house?!" "Pastor Clark! Pastor Clark! Are you okay?"

Kat lurched out of her seat and pushed herself through the crowd of people in the middle aisle. Was there a doctor in the house? She didn't know. But her father was a cardiologist, and he'd made sure every member of his family knew CPR, knew what to do if someone was having a stroke or heart attack, knew how to treat for shock.

Only vaguely aware that Mrs. Douglass was urging people to pray, Kat elbowed her way through the small knot of people huddled around the fallen pastor and dropped to her knees. The pastor's mouth gaped open, and she heard a gurgle . . . a gasp. Pressing two fingers to the man's scrawny neck, she felt for a pulse. *There . . . no, no, lost it.*

"Give me room!" she snapped. "He needs CPR." For a brief second she considered doing mouth-to-mouth resuscitation but remembered that compression-only was recommended when there was no pulse. The keyboard man was still slapping the pastor's cheeks and calling his name. Pushing the man aside, she straddled the pastor's long, thin body, placed both hands over his heart, and began to pump. *One, two, three, four* . . . Half a second for each one. One hundred chest compressions per minute. . . . *ninety-eight, ninety-nine, one hundred.*

Again. *One, two, three, four* . . .

How many minutes had she been doing this? Damp tendrils of hair fell over her face. Her hands and arms ached. Sweat trickled down her back.

. . . *fifty-three, fifty-four, fifty-five* . . .

Somewhere in the back of her brain she heard a siren.

. . . *sixty-two, sixty-three, sixty-four* . . .

Then shouts. "Let 'em through!" "Thank God they're here!"

Kat kept thrusting the man's chest until hands took her by both shoulders and a voice said, "All right, young lady. You can stop. Paramedics are here."

"No! Keep going!" one of the paramedics barked. She pushed again and again, huffing, sweat trickling into her eyes, vaguely aware of the pastor's shirt being ripped open as patches to a defibrillator and several strip leads were attached to his chest. A paramedic started an IV. Another placed a ventilation bag mask over the pastor's slack mouth.

Finally one of the paramedics took over for her, and Kat let herself be pulled up off her knees. Stumbling off the platform, she sank into a chair. Immediately Brygitta was beside her with a bottle of water. "Good heavens, Kat," she hissed in her ear. "Where'd you learn to do that?"

Kat just shook her head, gulping the water. She was exhausted. The five men in the dark blue pants and jackets were strapping the limp body of the elderly pastor onto a wheeled gurney. Liquid dripped into his arm from a bottle held high by one of the paramedics. SouledOut men pushed chairs out of the way. A path opened up to the door. Kat's eyes followed the gurney as it was wheeled outside to the white fire department ambulance with its red and blue lettering and lights parked at the curb.

The rain had stopped.

People stood at the windows and watched as the gurney was loaded. Some were crying. The ambulance doors slammed shut. The siren wailed and pulled out of the parking lot.

Kat saw the Douglasses and a few others push through the doors and run for their cars. A moment later the black Lexus followed the ambulance. Two other cars did too.

Small groups of people were still praying. Some stood and held hands. Others pulled chairs into a circle. Parents collected their children and ushered them out of the building.

Kat still sat in the chair, elbows on her knees, head in her hands. She felt numb. Her mind was blank. How long she sat there, she didn't know. Finally she felt a hand on her shoulder. "Kat? Maybe we should go." Nick's voice. Gentle. Kind. "We can walk back to the apartment. Rain has stopped. Walking will be good."

He took her hand and helped her up out of the chair. She let him lead her through the jumble of chairs, around groups of people still praying, still crying. Livie and Brygitta were waiting with her jacket and Bible. They pushed out the double doors. But as they walked across the parking lot to Clark Street, Kat looked back at the glass windows with SouledOut Community Church painted in big red letters across them.

What had she done? It was the first time she'd ever used CPR in a real situation. Was Pastor Clark going to make it? Did she do it right? What if—

And for the first time in a long time, Kat was afraid.

Chapter 21

As the automatic door of the ER at St. Francis Hospital slid open, Avis had to practically run to keep up with Peter as he strode up to the desk. "The man they just brought in—Hubert Clark. He collapsed in the middle of church. One of our pastors at SouledOut Community Church. Is he . . . how is he?"

The woman behind the glass window barely looked up from her computer. "And you are . . . ?"

"Peter Douglass. One of the church elders. How is—"

"Sir, you'll need to wait. Just take a seat in the waiting room. I'm sure someone will come out to talk to you directly. Does he have family that should be notified?"

Peter looked at Avis. She shook her head. Pastor Clark didn't have any immediate family. No wife or children. Sisters or brothers? She didn't know.

Peter left their names at the desk and slumped in a chair in the waiting room. But he stood up as the Meeks, Baxters, and David Brown came in. *Good, all the elders are here*, Avis thought. "We called Pastor Cobbs from the car," she said. "I think he's on the way."

Jodi glanced at Avis. "I thought he was sick," she whispered. Avis grimaced.

"Have they told you anything?" David Brown asked.

Peter shook his head.

David was in his forties, maybe five-ten, light brown hair thinning on top, his face pockmarked from a severe case of teenage acne. He and Mary had three children, two boys in middle school and a girl in fifth grade, if Avis remembered correctly, though the girl didn't attend Bethune Elementary.

The men huddled together, talking quietly. Debra Meeks took a seat, shaking her head. Jodi Baxter slipped an arm around Avis. "Are you all right?"

Avis gave an absentminded nod. She was watching the huddle of men. Denny and David were white. Peter and Debra were black. She'd never thought anything about the racial makeup of the elders. Denny Baxter was just . . . Denny. A great guy. A great friend. She didn't know the Browns that well, even though they'd been at Uptown with Pastor Clark before the merge, same as she had. Did David have the same reservations about their racially diverse church as his wife, Mary? She'd have to ask Peter if he'd picked up anything on the elder board.

The automatic door slid open, and Pastor Joe Cobbs and his wife, Rose, came into the ER and headed their way. Beads of sweat dotted the forehead of the short, stocky copastor. Rose shook her head as they joined the group. "Joe shouldn't be here. But he wouldn't listen to me." She looked from face to face. "How is Pastor Clark?"

Peter shook his head. "No word yet."

They talked in quiet voices or just sat. Avis walked back and forth, praying silently. The words of Psalm 56 kept running through her prayer thoughts: *"When I am afraid, I will trust in God . . . I trust in God, why should I be afraid?"*

They'd been at the hospital thirty minutes when a man in a white coat came through the double doors that led to the "inner sanctum" and paused at the reception desk. The woman behind the window nodded in their direction. Almost as one they stood and faced the man.

"You're friends of Mr. Clark?" the doctor asked. His face was a neutral mask Avis couldn't read.

Pastor Cobbs spoke. "I'm Pastor Joe Cobbs. Pastor Clark is my copastor at SouledOut Community Church. He collapsed during the morning service. These are church leaders and friends."

The doctor shook his head. "I'm sorry. Mr. Clark didn't make it. Both the paramedics and the doctors here kept working on him, but . . . the paramedics estimated his heart fully stopped even before they arrived at the church."

Debra Meeks gasped. "Lord, have mercy!"

Peter groaned and reached for Avis. They stood a long moment holding on to one another. Avis, her face pressed against Peter's chest, felt numb. All she could think was, *What now, Lord, what now?*

Denny Baxter, who'd known Pastor Clark longer than any of them, and Joe and Rose Cobbs stayed at the hospital to make arrangements for Hubert's body to be taken to a funeral home.

The rest of them reluctantly went home with the assignment to pass the word along to the rest of the church.

Peter and Avis were silent on the drive back to Rogers Park. Once they'd climbed the stairs to their third-floor apartment, Peter sank into his recliner, shaking his head. "I can't believe he's gone. Just like that."

Avis sat on the arm of the recliner, facing him, stroking his close-cropped hair. "You've been worried about him for a while. We knew he wasn't well."

"Yeah. I know. But . . . still wasn't prepared for him to go so suddenly."

They sat together quietly for several long minutes. Suddenly Peter looked at her quizzically. "What happened to you this morning—before worship, I mean? I get that Pastor Clark asked you to fill in as worship leader at the last minute. He said as much. But where were you when service was supposed to start?"

The sour taste in her mouth returned. She was so tempted to blurt out the whole conversation she'd overheard in the ladies' restroom. By an elder's wife, at that! But she felt a check in her spirit. This wasn't the time. Pastor Clark had just died of a heart attack. Her offended sensibilities felt . . . almost petty in comparison.

"I'll explain later," she murmured, bending forward to kiss her husband on the forehead. "Right now I think we need to make some calls. What letters of the alphabet did we say we'd take?"

They were halfway through the Ks, using both the kitchen phone and Peter's cell, when Avis heard a knock at the front door. "Someone's at the door, Terri. We don't know any details about funeral arrangements yet, but we'll call when we do." The knocks came again. "I'm sorry. I need to go. Bye."

Avis sighed. It had to be one of their new "neighbors" at the door. She opened it.

Nick Taylor stood on the landing, hands shoved in the front pockets of his jeans. "We, uh, heard you were home. Just footsteps," he hastily added. "No problem. But . . . we wanted to know if you have any word about Pastor Clark. Especially Kat. She's pretty upset."

Avis's heart melted a little. The four students were too new to be in the church phone directory. But she should have realized they'd want to know. Especially the girl, after jumping in and giving the pastor CPR.

This wasn't news for standing on the landing. "Come in, Nick." She opened the door wider and led the young man into the living room. She sat down on the couch and motioned for him to join her. "I'm sorry, Nick. We should have told you and your friends right away. Pastor Clark . . ." She shook her head. "He didn't make it. He's home with Jesus now."

Nick's shoulders sagged. He shook his head slowly. "I . . . I can't believe it. We thought surely the CPR would keep him alive until the paramedics showed up. You're sure? He's dead?" Then he looked sheepish. "Of course you're sure. You don't say things like that unless you're sure."

Avis just watched his face. The young man seemed truly distressed.

He sat on the couch for several minutes, his elbows leaning on his knees. Then he looked up at Avis. "Would you mind coming downstairs and telling the girls? I think Kat's going to take this pretty hard. It's the first time she's done CPR in a real situation. That it didn't save him . . ." Nick shook his head. "Maybe you could help her."

"The first time?" Avis was startled. The girl had leaped into the situation as if she'd given CPR a dozen times. Bossy. Confident. No one had stopped her. No one had asked if she knew what she was doing. Probably because most of them didn't know CPR themselves and were glad someone—even someone as young as Kathryn Davies—looked as if she knew what she was doing.

Unwelcome thoughts crowded into her mind. *Had* the girl known what she was doing? If she had, would Pastor Clark still be alive?

No, no. She couldn't let her mind go there. But she wasn't sure she could reassure the girl either.

"I'm sorry, Nick. I'm afraid you'll have to bear the news. We have a lot of calls to make to let people in the church know that Pastor Clark died. But if we hear any more information, we'll be sure to let you know downstairs." She stood up. "Do we have your phone numbers? Here's ours . . ."

Avis grabbed the church phone directory she'd been using and wrote down their names and numbers as Nick read them from his cell phone. Then she gave him their number, hoping it wasn't a mistake to do so. She didn't want a lot of calls from them about every little thing.

Nick seemed reluctant to leave but finally went back downstairs. Avis immediately called the Hickmans, the next number on the list.

The phone was picked up on the first ring. "That you, Avis? What's the word, girl? Me an' Carl 'bout ready to go crazy over here."

"Oh, Florida. Pastor Clark didn't make it. It was a major heart attack. He's gone."

Avis heard the gasp in her ear. Then, "Carl! Carl! Get on the phone!" A second phone picked up, and Avis repeated her sad news.

Carl's voice was gruff. "All right. Was afraid of that when I heard what happened. Uh, Ms. Avis, tell your man to call me. I know he wants to know when I'm comin' back to work, but might be another week or so."

Florida waited until the second phone went dead. "Why bad things happen all at the same time, Avis? First Carl gets hurt at work, now this."

Avis winced. Good question. And her list was even longer. Rochelle still missing—at least not communicating. Bethune Elementary possibly getting shut down. Her own job on the line if that happened. Peter's business hitting bumps in the road. The buyout he'd hoped for now in question.

"I don't know, Flo. Just got to keep trusting, I guess. Uh, about the holiday. I don't think we'll come over to barbecue. We might need to help plan for the funeral."

"Oh, yeah, yeah. I understand. Don't feel much like doin' anything myself. But call me when you get any more news, hear?"

Avis worked her way through the other names on her list, hearing Peter doing the same thing in the study. They needed a better system to get word around, even though Jodi Baxter and Debra Meeks were making calls too.

Avis finally put the phone back in its cradle and wearily massaged the back of her neck. She had to get out of her church clothes. Soak in the tub. Do something to release the tension in her shoulders and back.

But the phone rang before she was even halfway to the bedroom. Caller ID said *Rose Cobbs*.

"Avis? Sister Rose here. Pastor would call you, but once we got home I made him go back to bed. He's running a temp of 102."

Avis murmured something sympathetic as she walked to the bedroom with the phone, slipping off her shoes and wiggling one-handedly out of her dress.

"Funeral is set for next Saturday at ten in the morning. So we need to get word around to the church . . ."

Avis wanted to groan. Making all those calls *again*?

"But the main thing Pastor wanted to call about is . . . could you and Peter meet with him at the church tomorrow? Maybe one o'clock? He's presuming you have the day off since it's a holiday. *Humph.* He's also presuming he'll be the picture of health tomorrow," she added. Avis noted the tinge of irritation. *Men*. Even pastors.

"Uh, meet? Do you know what about? If it's planning for the funeral, we could use more—"

"Not the funeral. He wants to talk to you and Peter about stepping up to the plate in the wake of Pastor Clark's death. He needs you, Avis. You and Peter both. He wants to avoid a leadership crisis."

Chapter 22

Kat lay curled up on the green-and-brown tweed couch, wrapped in one of the Candys' afghans. For the past hour she'd been wrestling with the news Nick had brought down from upstairs. *Pastor Clark is dead . . . Is it my fault? . . . He had a pulse! When I started the CPR, anyway . . . Didn't I push on his chest hard enough? . . . Is the church going to blame me?*

And another set of anxious thoughts wove through the others. *Maybe staying in Chicago this summer wasn't a good idea . . . None of us have jobs yet—and I had a ready-made job back in Phoenix . . . And why did we move into this apartment so soon? We'll have to commute to school every day for the next two weeks!*

She heard Nick's cell phone ring somewhere in the apartment—that annoying "laugh track" ringtone—and then his voice, indistinct, answering. Her housemates had all drifted to different rooms to be alone with their thoughts and feelings after the distressing events of that day. Or do homework. Whatever. Right now she didn't care that she had a Spanish novel to read and fifty vocabulary words to memorize and use correctly in a sentence by Tuesday.

Pulling the afghan over her head, she burrowed deeper into the couch.

But a moment later she felt a hand shake her shoulder. "Kat?" Nick lowered himself to the couch beside her. "That was Mrs. Douglass upstairs. She called to say the funeral will be next Saturday at ten. She had promised to let us know any news."

Kat sat up. "Did she say anything else?" *Like, are people blaming me for what happened?*

Nick shrugged. "Not really. Seemed in kind of a hurry. Said she had a lot of calls to make. Guess she's got to call everybody again." He pushed himself off the couch. "I better go tell Brygitta and Livie too."

Kat frowned as Nick headed down the hall to look for the other girls. With sudden determination, she threw off the afghan, stood up, and hunted for her shoes. She was going to go nuts worrying about this. Best thing to do was just go up to the Douglass apartment and ask.

The door of the third-floor apartment finally opened after she'd knocked three times. Avis Douglass was wearing a casual warm-up suit in blue velour, no earrings, reading glasses perched on her nose, cordless phone in hand. Up close, Kat realized the woman's warm brown skin was smooth and wrinkle free, making her seem younger than fiftysomething. Mrs. Douglass didn't say anything, just arched her eyebrows at Kat as if they were question marks.

"Uh . . . can I talk to you for a minute, Mrs. Douglass? I know you're busy, but I need to ask you something."

The woman seemed to hesitate, and suddenly Kat felt foolish. She should have called first—though that probably wouldn't have worked, since the woman had obviously been on the phone. But just when she'd decided to forget it and run back downstairs, Mrs. Douglass opened the door wider and stepped aside. "Of course. Come in, Kathryn."

Kat walked into the spacious living room—though, actually, it was the same size as the Candys' apartment below but not as cluttered with excess furniture and "stuff." The black leather couch and matching recliner were the primary focus, with a glass-topped coffee table, an area rug of warm tan, rust, and black designs, and bookcases running along one wall. "Nice," she murmured.

Avis Douglass sat on one end of the couch and graciously indicated the other end for Kat. "You wanted to ask me something?" Her voice was composed. Low. Well modulated. Kat felt calmer just being there.

"Yes. I . . . well, this is kind of awkward. But I've been worried all day about what happened to Pastor Clark. So just thought I'd ask straight up."

Mrs. Douglass waited.

Kat sucked in a breath and blew it out. "Did I do something wrong? Doing the CPR, I mean. My dad—he's a cardiologist—is big on everybody knowing how to do CPR, so he taught me. But . . . that was the first time I'd done it in a real emergency." Her heart was thumping in her ears, but she couldn't read the woman's face, so she rushed on. "You told Nick that the doctors are saying Pastor Clark died of a massive heart attack. But I really thought doing the CPR would save him! So when I heard he'd died, I got worried that I'd done something wrong. That people would blame *me*."

Unbidden, tears sprang to her eyes, and Kat quickly brushed them away. No way did she want to appear like a crybaby. Even though she really wanted to ask, *"Do* you *blame me?"*

Mrs. Douglass studied her neatly manicured hands for several long moments. She finally looked up. "No one is blaming you, Kathryn. And you shouldn't blame yourself. I learned CPR a long time ago since I'm responsible for a school full of children and adult staff, but I've never had to use it, so I can't evaluate the effectiveness of your efforts. But . . . I'm sure you did your best. That's all anyone can do. And ultimately, our lives are in God's hands. Only God determines when it's 'our time.' We have to trust God in this, even though we're all in shock to lose Pastor Clark like this. So suddenly."

Kat felt a rush of relief at her words, but this time the tears spilled over.

Mrs. Douglass handed her a box of tissues. "Don't worry. We're all shedding a few tears today." She stood up. "But you'll need to excuse me. I still have a lot of calls to make. You'll be all right?"

After mopping her face, Kat stood up too and nodded. "Thanks. Uh, is there anything I can do? I'd like to do something." Suddenly she brightened. "I could help make calls to people in the church! About the funeral, I mean. Nick said you'd already called people to tell them Pastor Clark had died, and now you have to call again. I'm sure you're tired of being on the phone."

Mrs. Douglass shook her head and murmured, "Thanks anyway." But just then her husband poked his head into the living room. "Avis, can you— Oh. Sorry. I didn't realize anyone was here. But when you have a minute, I need to see you." He waved his cell phone. "Pastor Cobbs wants to talk to us by phone as soon as possible."

"See?" Kat urged. "I know you have other things to do. Let me help make calls. Give me the list, tell me what to say. I'll do it right away."

A few minutes later Kat walked out the door with the SouledOut phone list, the names and numbers marked that still needed to be called, and information about the funeral written on a slip of paper. Even though she'd come up to the third floor heavyhearted, Kat fairly flew down the stairs.

"So." Kat eyed her housemates over a glass of pureed carrot juice the next morning. "We're all going to the youth group picnic at the lake this afternoon, right? It starts at three."

"Is it still on?" Brygitta looked horrified. "I mean, one of their pastors just keeled over in church and died!"

"Oh, I'm sure they've canceled," Olivia said, munching on a piece of raisin toast.

"Wrong. I called Josh Baxter to check. *He* said getting the teens together is even more important since that happened, to give them a chance to talk about it."

"Well, sure. Have a meeting or something. But not a picnic."

Kat shrugged. "All I know is, he said the picnic is still on. Said Pastor Clark wouldn't want them to sit around sogging in their grief. He'd want them to *live*."

Nick leaned back in his chair at the kitchen table. "I like that. Makes me wish Pastor Clark were going to be around longer. I think there are a lot of things I could've learned from him."

Kat smiled fondly. That was so like Nick. "Back to the question. Who's going to the picnic? Livie? Brygitta? Would do us all good to get outside."

Getting a promise that they'd *try* to get stuff done by three would have to do. Kat put some potatoes on to boil for a cold potato salad—they'd done some food shopping at the Rogers Park Fruit Market on Saturday afternoon after moving in—and tackled her Spanish vocabulary. Having a deadline helped to focus her attention, and by two o'clock she was peeling the chilled potatoes and chopping celery and onions for the salad.

At the last minute, Josh Baxter called and said they'd gotten a permit to use the fire ring up at the Lighthouse Beach in Evanston. They'd need a ride. But if they didn't mind riding with a two-year-old, Edesa would pick them up in his parents' minivan while he trucked the teens in the church van.

Kat was excited. She'd been wanting to get to know Edesa Baxter, especially since the young mom's Spanish was so fluent. The Dodge Caravan pulled up in front of the three-flat right at three, and the four college students piled in. Nick sat in front with Edesa, Livie and Brygitta crawled into the third seat, and Kat and her potato salad sat next to two-year-old Gracie's car seat in the middle.

The little girl watched Kat with big, solemn eyes. Kat smiled and waggled her fingers. "Hi. Remember me? My name's Kat."

The round, olive face puckered in a frown. "You not a *cat*. You a *muchacha*!"

Brygitta and Olivia snickered in the rear seat.

Kat caught Edesa smiling at her daughter in the rearview mirror. "Kat is her nickname, *niña*," the young mother tossed back. "You should call her 'Miss Kathryn.'"

The little girl howled with glee. "No-o! She Miss *Gato*! Me-oww."

Now everyone laughed. Kat was tickled. "Miss *Gato* is just fine, Miss Gracie."

As the car headed north along the lake on Sheridan Road, Edesa pointed out various places they were passing. Kat wanted to listen, but Gracie chatted away, peppering Kat with questions. "What's dat?"—pointing to the bowl in Kat's lap. "Is dat your daddy?"—pointing at Nick. "Can you skip?" . . . "See my fairy shoes?"—showing off her miniature gym shoes with Velcro straps. Wondering what made them "fairy shoes," Kat caught tidbits from the front seat about the cemetery that marked the boundary between Chicago and Evanston . . . the stately buildings of Northwestern University . . . the lighthouse in the distance that was their destination . . . and then Edesa turned into a small parking lot overlooking one of the many public beaches running along the Lake Michigan shore.

The church van had already arrived. Josh and half a dozen teenagers were lugging coolers, pans of food, and a portable charcoal grill to the sole picnic shelter in a grassy area. A set of steps led down to the beach, where a couple of the teen guys were setting up a volleyball net. Tucked into a grove of trees above the beach was a fire ring, and Nick joined a crew hauling firewood for an end-of-the-evening bonfire.

Kat deposited the potato salad with the other food, eager

to get acquainted with some of the teens and join the volleyball game. But Gracie pulled away from her mother and grabbed Kat's hand. "Miss *Gato*! Miss *Gato*! See my fairy shoes? They sparkle!" The little girl jumped up and down, making the heels of her shoes light up. Then she pulled Kat down the steps to the beach, a plastic bucket and shovel in her other hand.

Not seeing the girl's mother, Kat took off Gracie's shoes and her own sandals and resigned herself to helping build a "sand mountain." The sky was overcast, but at least the air was warm, somewhere in the seventies. A gentle breeze blew in off the lake, and all threats of rain had disappeared during the night. Playing in the sand was kind of fun. That was a plus moving to Rogers Park—a lot closer to Lake Michigan than the CCU campus.

Shouts of laughter and playful trash talk went back and forth over the net as often as the volleyball. Watching the game, Kat realized she hadn't known Nick was such a powerhouse volleyball player, slam-dunking the ball over the net and high-fiving his teenage teammates.

Kat had just started to work up a good case of feeling left out of the fun when Edesa Baxter ran across the sand and plopped down beside her, out of breath. "Oh, I am so sorry, *mi amiga*. I did not mean to leave Gracie alone with you. The wind blew the napkins all over the grass and I had to chase them! But *gracias*. Now, go! Go! Have some fun."

Kat had a sudden change of mind. "That's all right. I'd like to stay with you and help Gracie finish her mountain." She dug handfuls of wet sand from the shoreline and patted them onto the "mountain." "I think one of my professors at CCU knows you . . . Ms. Vargas? How do you know her?"

Edesa seemed happy to talk. Kat learned that she and Ms. Vargas had both attended a Spanish-speaking church in the city—*Iglesia del Espirito Santo*, or Church of the Holy Spirit—but now that she and Josh were married, they'd decided to make SouledOut their home church. Everything about Edesa came as a surprise to Kat. The vivacious young woman had family back in Honduras, and she'd originally come to the States on a study visa. She and Josh had been volunteers at the Manna House Women's Shelter when a young Latina had died of a drug overdose, leaving a three-month-old baby. Even though they were both still in school at the time, Edesa and Josh had pushed up their wedding date to provide a home for the baby.

"Gracie," murmured Edesa, watching the tiny girl poke her plastic shovel at a bug in the sand. "Our gift from God. Her adoption was finalized two months ago."

Hispanic. Adopted. Kat had presumed the little girl with the loose black curls and latte skin was a mix of black mother, white father. So much for presumptions.

"You said you were in school. What did you study?"

Edesa laughed. "Long story! I changed my major after working at the shelter, decided to get my master's degree in public health. I did my master's thesis on 'A Hierarchy of Food Needs for the Urban Poor.'"

"That's fantastic!" Kat could hardly believe it. A kindred spirit! "I am *so* psyched about the importance of healthy food. In fact, I am *so* glad I met you. I mean . . ." Kat's mind was spinning. ". . . what if we—you and me, I mean—offered a class to neighborhood families about nutrition. Maybe at SouledOut. What do you think?"

"A class?"

"Yes! Maybe four sessions or something. I mean, last week I saw kids on the way to school eating potato chips and candy bars. At seven in the morning! I wanted to snatch it out of their hands. Somebody needs to teach those families about good nutrition!"

Edesa dug her toes into the sand. "*Sí.* But it's not that simple. Nutrition is hardly the first priority for poor families. Not even second or third. They—" Her head jerked up.

Someone was banging loudly on a pot up near the picnic shelter. A moment later Edesa's husband appeared at the top of the steps hollering, "Come and get it!"

"Guess it's time to eat." Edesa smiled at Kat, but her smile had lost some of its dazzle. "A conversation for another time." The young woman swept up little Gracie, collected the pail and shovel, and busied herself brushing sand off the child's legs.

The volleyball game broke up. Kat followed the herd of hollow-legged teens up the steps to the grassy area and picnic shelter, a bit taken aback. What did Edesa mean that nutrition wasn't a top priority for poor families? What in the world could be more important?

Well. The woman might have a master's degree in public health, but Kat could teach her a thing or two about food issues.

Chapter 23

Pastor Cobbs rose from his desk chair as Avis and Peter came into the pastors' study. "Peter. Avis." He shook hands with both of them. "Thank you so much for coming in on a holiday. Please . . . sit."

Avis slipped a tiny bottle of hand sanitizer out of her purse and squeezed a few drops into her hand. She couldn't afford to catch whatever bug the pastor was fighting—not with only a few weeks left of school. At least he didn't look as wasted as he did yesterday at the hospital. "How are you feeling, Pastor?" Her concern was genuine.

"Better, better. Fever's gone. Nausea's gone. Still some congestion here"—he thumped his chest—"but guess that's to be expected. You two all right?"

Peter nodded. "Yes, fine. Well . . . given the circumstances."

Pastor Cobbs sighed heavily. "I know. I'm still in shock. Feeling terrible that I wasn't at the service yesterday morning, but . . . it couldn't be helped." He absently tapped the eraser end of a pencil on the desk, seemingly lost in thought for a few moments. Then he roused himself. "Well. Has everyone been notified of the funeral next Saturday?"

Avis nodded. "I believe so. Sister Jodi and Sister Debra made calls, as well as the two of us. Oh—one of the Crista students helped as well. Kathryn Davies."

"Kathryn Davies . . . Didn't someone say she gave CPR to Pastor Clark until the paramedics arrived?"

"That's right."

"And then helped make phone calls . . . *hm.* Interesting." The pastor tapped the pencil again as seconds ticked by.

Finally Peter cleared his throat. "Pastor, you said you wanted to talk to us."

Pastor Cobbs tossed the pencil aside. "I'm sorry. I'm not exactly functioning on all cylinders today." He took several sips from a bottle of water, then eyed them both. "Pastor Clark's death is a major loss to our congregation—with a lot of implications. We're suddenly faced with a leadership vacuum. Both of you are professionals in the workaday world, so I know you're well aware that *any* change in leadership—especially if unexpected—can easily become a leadership crisis. Even in the best of circumstances, a change in leadership can be a difficult time for a congregation. Bottom line . . . I need you. Both of you. To keep things from unraveling until we come to unity as a congregation about how to go forward."

Avis and Peter glanced at each other. She'd thought First Lady Rose was being a bit melodramatic yesterday when she'd said Pastor wanted to meet with them to avoid a "leadership crisis." But Avis had chalked it up to the stress of the day and assumed Pastor Cobbs would be dividing out some of Pastor Clark's tasks among a number of people. But "to keep things from unraveling" felt more ominous than just being asked to take on a few more responsibilities.

"Uh, say a little more, Pastor," Peter said. "As you know, Avis and I are seriously considering that mission trip to South Africa. Her school year will soon be over, and when Carl Hickman comes back to work, I was hoping—"

"I know. To be blunt, Brother Peter, I'm asking you to set that aside. Not forever, but for now. When you came to talk to Pastor Clark and me about the Sisulu-Smiths' invitation, none of us foresaw this situation. If we were to have that same meeting today, I would say this isn't the time. You are needed here."

The muscles in Peter's jaw tightened. Avis realized her husband was struggling with what probably felt like cold water being poured on his dream. She leaned forward. "Pastor, I'm not sure I understand why you are talking to us. We have a board of elders, good people, all of them—and yes, certainly, Peter is one of the elders. But shouldn't you be consulting with the whole elder board about this situation and how to go forward?" As the words left her mouth, Avis suddenly worried that she'd been too outspoken. Would the pastor be offended that she'd challenged him?

But Pastor Cobbs nodded. "I do plan to meet with the elders—as soon as we can find a time this week when everyone can be there. But I needed to talk to the two of you first, because"—he cleared his throat—"I want to put your names forward to the elders as interim pastors. They would need to give their approval and blessing, of course—but I need your willingness and your permission first."

Avis and Peter were quiet as they left SouledOut an hour later and walked toward Peter's car, each lost in their own thoughts. But instead of driving toward home, Peter headed to Sheridan Road. "I need some air," he said. "Want to walk along the lake a bit?"

Sounded good to Avis—although she would have preferred to go for a walk by herself. She wasn't ready to talk about Pastor Cobbs's startling proposal just yet.

But once they'd parked at Loyola Beach, locked the car, and started hand in hand along the bike path, Peter didn't seem inclined to talk either. Charcoal smoke wafted in the air, carrying the tangy smell of grilled chicken. The grassy park along the beach was full of holiday revelers throwing Frisbees, romping with dogs, laughing around picnic tables, or just lounging in lawn chairs. Bikers dodged pedestrians on the paved path, rarely slowing down, sometimes cursing the occasional trio who insisted on walking three abreast, forcing the bicycles onto the grass.

Avis breathed deeply of the warm air, catching the cadence of disparate languages as they passed other walkers. It was a perfect day for a holiday. Not yet too warm, humidity low, scattered clouds drifting across the sky. The tall buildings of Chicago's Loop rose several miles to the south, but here the trees were in full leaf and the grass was lush and green. The slate-blue expanse of Lake Michigan, so wide it faded into the horizon, was still too chilly to tempt many swimmers, even though lifeguards were on duty.

She'd asked, *"Interim pastors?"* Why her and Peter? Pastor Cobbs thought a married couple would be received more easily to "fill in" on short notice than just one person. Also easier for two to share the pastoral responsibilities than just one person. Both she and Peter already held leadership roles in the church. Both were grounded in the faith. Both were respected in the community.

To Pastor Cobbs it was a slam dunk.

Avis was honored that he felt that way about them. But she and Peter already had full-time jobs. Could they do this? For how long?

Something else bothered her. While the pastor was talking, the conversation she'd overheard in the ladies' restroom—Was it just yesterday? Seemed like a year!—niggled in her head. If she and Peter accepted this role, the pastoral team would be all African-American. In a multicultural church. A few weeks ago she might not have even thought about it—especially for a temporary role. After all, meaningful relationships had developed at SouledOut across color lines and cultures in the past few years, and "differences" seemed to fade as what they shared in common as the family of God deepened and became more important.

But after the chitchat in the ladies' room, obviously not everyone felt that way.

"Avis?" Peter's voice seemed to come from some faraway place.

She shook off her troubled thoughts. *"Mm?"*

An in-line skater plugged into an iPod, eyes hidden by wrap-around sunglasses, zoomed toward them, causing them to jump to either side of the path. Glaring after the skater, Peter gestured toward the wall of large rocks hugging the bank between park and beach. "Let's sit before we get killed, okay?"

Avis joined him on one of the flat-topped boulders, wishing she'd worn jeans instead of her good slacks to meet with the pastor. But the rock was warm and forgiving. She hugged her knees and watched the seagulls screeching at the water's edge, flapping up into the air, then down onto the sand again, pecking here and there.

She heard Peter groan. "I don't know what to do." He wasn't looking at her. Just gazing out over the water. Was he talking to her? Or to God?

But she said, "I don't either."

Another long silence. Then Peter threw up his hands. "I don't understand what God is doing! Why would He put the opportunity in our laps to go on mission for Him, to get out of our ruts and *do* something different, exciting, worthwhile—just to jerk the rug out from under us and ask us to plug holes in the SouledOut dike?"

Avis had no answer. Her questions and train of thought had run along a totally different track than Peter's. Not once had she factored in the "implications" of Pastor Clark's death on the mission trip to South Africa. Though . . . they'd been praying that God would show them what they should do, to make it clear.

Maybe this was His answer.

Jodi Baxter poked her head into Avis's office the next morning before the first bell rang. "Hey."

"Hey, yourself." Avis glanced up from her computer where she'd been scrolling through the e-mails that had piled up over the long weekend. "Ugh. Didn't anybody at the superintendent's office stay home over the holiday weekend? I've got twenty-seven *school-related* e-mails I need to deal with. This morning!"

"Need a hug?" Jodi didn't wait for an answer but came around Avis's desk and wrapped arms around her from behind.

Avis gave a short laugh. "Oh, all right. I know what that means. *You* need a hug." She swung her chair around and eyed her friend. Denim skirt and sweater to match the thirty-degree drop in temperature since yesterday. "Are you okay?"

"Am I okay? Let's see . . . Our pastor just died of a heart attack in the middle of worship. Amanda came home from U of I a week ago, but we've barely seen her because she's already juggling two nanny jobs. And one of my third graders—Sammy Blumenthal, small for his age—is being bullied by one of the bigger boys. Other than that, I'm peachy keen."

Avis gestured at her visitor chair. "Sit. Tell me about the bullying."

Jodi sighed as she sank into the chair. "It's Derrick Blue. He's pushing Sammy down on the playground, tripping him in the hallway, stealing food from his tray at lunch, calling him names, making fun of his yarmulke. I think we may need a meeting with the parents. Although . . . they never show up at parent meetings, so I don't know."

"Names? Like racial slurs?"

Jodi grimaced. "You don't want to know. But I'd rather not let this escalate into a racial issue. At this age they hardly know what those words mean. But I'd also like to nip the bullying in the bud before this kid goes on to middle school."

Avis sighed, pulled a pad of paper toward her, and wrote down the names. "I'll talk to both boys and see how that goes. If necessary, I'll contact the parents. Thanks, Jodi. We can't let this bullying go on. It can have disastrous consequences if allowed to fester."

"Oh. One more thing. Pastor Cobbs called last night asking if Denny and I would put together several folks to plan the funeral service for Pastor Clark. He's trying to track down any family who should be notified and make burial arrangements. Uh, we'd really like you and Peter to help us plan. We already asked Estelle and Harry. They're coming over tomorrow night at seven. Are you guys free?— Oops. There goes the bell." Jodi launched herself out of the chair and headed for the door. "Let me know if you guys can make it, okay?" The door closed behind her.

Avis picked up the phone and dialed Peter's number. She was sure he'd agree. This decision was easy. Plan a service for a beloved pastor. Do it. Then it's done.

It was the other decision that had a thousand loose ends. Stand in for Pastor Clark . . . indefinitely? What did it even mean?

Chapter 24

The Red Line rattled out of the Morse Avenue Station, packed with early morning commuters. Kat grabbed a pole and hung on as the elevated train lurched and picked up speed. The train seemed even more crowded than usual after the holiday weekend.

"Uhhh," groaned Brygitta, squished right behind her. "Adding a forty-five-minute commute to both ends of a school day sucks."

Kat had to agree. Five stops and then they had to transfer to the Foster Avenue bus. But at least both trains and buses ran about every ten minutes at this time in the morning. They should make their nine o'clock classes all right.

The train was too crowded to talk. She couldn't even see Nick and Olivia. Maybe they'd ended up in another car. But she couldn't help smiling to herself, remembering the campfire at Lighthouse Beach the night before. She was glad they'd gone. The campfire ring had been tucked among the trees on a slight slope above the sandy dunes that led down to the beach. Firelight and shadows had danced on the faces of the fifteen or so teenagers, erasing the differences in their skin tones, though the group was fairly evenly mixed between white, black, and Latino. No Asians, though. Odd.

One of the younger boys, maybe fourteen, a white kid with freckles and reddish curly hair—Paul Somebody—had brought a guitar, and he had played while the group sang gospel songs. She'd been surprised how good he was for his age. Edesa had pointed out another boy, a couple of years older, dark brown hair, drop-dead good looks already, and said they were brothers. Last name Fairbanks. Kat had to take her word for it, because the two didn't look anything alike.

Besides Josh and Edesa, the only other youth leader had been the worship leader guy, Justin. He'd been home with laryngitis when Pastor Clark died, and he still didn't have much of a voice, but he'd told the kids he'd needed to be there tonight, needed to be with "his peeps."

"The reason I'm a son of God tonight," he'd croaked, "is because of Pastor Clark. I won't lie to you. I messed up when I was your age, and that wasn't too long ago. Ended up in juvie for five months. Pastor Clark and a couple other guys from SouledOut led a Bible study down there. At first we all made fun of him—this old white dude, skinny as a stick, coulda knocked him over with my little finger. I just hung out at the Bible study for somethin' to do, to break the boredom. But he kept comin' every week, talked to us like regular people. Told me I had lots of potential. Told me God had a purpose for my life, if I was willin' to follow Him."

Justin had gotten a little emotional at that point, but he'd soon recovered. "Pastor Clark prayed with me, an' I think he kept prayin' for me every day—before *and* after I said yes to God. I'm goin' to college now"—the kids around the circle had clapped—"and I'm real sad at his passin', 'cause I sure did want him to be there when I graduated."

The young black man's sharing had seemed to turn on a faucet, and several other kids had shared memories of Pastor Clark—his gawky smile, the jokes he told on himself, and the time he came to youth group and talked about becoming young men and women of character. "He told us character was more important than a high IQ, or top grades, or being popular, or makin' lots of money," said a girl with lots of dark, straight hair and olive skin. "I'll always remember that."

"Yeah," another boy had piped up. "He said character is what you do and who you are when nobody's watchin'. Now *that* spooked me. Know what I'm sayin'?" The other kids had laughed.

As she'd listened, Kat had felt a sense of loss, realizing she'd never get to know the man. Her only interaction with him had been pushing on his chest while he lay dying. Had anyone in her life talked to her about character like that? Seemed like it had been mostly, "Don't waste your time on trivial pursuits," or "Do what you need to do to get ahead," or "You're a Davies, act like it!"

At least the Jesus she'd met at the Midwest Music Fest had shown her a new way. The last shall be first, and all that kind of stuff. Right there in the Bible!

Bree's poke in her back interrupted her thoughts. "Berwyn. That's our stop." Together they pushed their way out of the car, following the back of Nick's head and Olivia's blond ponytail down the stairs and out onto the street.

As they walked the few blocks to the bus stop heading west, Brygitta paused at a row of newspaper boxes lining the sidewalk. "All I want is the classifieds," she said, feeding quarters into one of the boxes and pulling out a *Chicago Tribune*. "I need to start looking for a job. Anybody else want a paper?"

"Classifieds!" Nick scoffed. "Easier to do an Internet search. C'mon, people, this is the twenty-first century."

Brygitta whacked him with the newspaper. "So? I can start looking right now on the bus, and *you* have to wait till you get to your computer."

Kat ignored both of them. Newspaper jobs or Internet searches might land her anywhere in the city! No, she was going to concentrate on the neighborhood near the church, even if she had to go door to door.

Both Olivia and Nick had an afternoon class on Tuesday, so Kat and Brygitta headed back to the apartment on an earlier bus. "By the way, looked like you and Edesa were hitting it off at the picnic. What were you talking about?"

Kat shrugged. "Oh, just getting acquainted. But I did find out she's got a master's degree in public health! And *bam*, I got this neat idea. Maybe the two of us could teach a class on nutrition at SouledOut—advertise it around the neighborhood."

"Really? What did she think about that?"

Good question. Kat wasn't sure. Edesa had made some

comment about nutrition not being very high on the food priority list. "Uh, well, we didn't really get to talk about it. Oh! Here's our stop."

Swinging off at Foster and Broadway, Kat pulled her friend toward Sheridan Road. "Hey. Let's pick up some groceries before we get the El. We need more eggs and a green pepper. My turn to cook supper and I'm going to make a frittata."

Brygitta shrugged. "I guess. But maybe we should grocery shop on Sunday when we're at SouledOut. There's a Dominick's right there in the shopping center."

"Thought Sunday was supposed to be a day of rest," Kat teased.

"*Huh*. You should talk. You only started going to church a couple years ago."

Kat draped an arm around Brygitta's shoulders and laughed as they headed toward the big chain store. "Yeah, but you've been going since you were in the womb, so you should know better."

As they crossed Sheridan, Kat playfully pushed Brygitta toward the front doors on the north corner, stuffing the envelope with their food money into her pocket. "Look, you go on, get some eggs and stuff—oh, some mushrooms too! And maybe a couple cans of tuna and a couple loaves of whole-wheat bread for lunches. I'll come meet you in a few minutes."

Brygitta stuck both fists on her hips. "Kat! No way. You're not going Dumpster-diving again."

Kat laughed. "I just want to look. You never know." She trotted off down the street and around to the back of the store before Brygitta could protest any more. No one seemed to be around. Lifting the lid on one of the Dumpsters, she squinted into the depths. Flattened cardboard, broken glass, old boards, paper trash . . . but no food. Strange. She moved to the next one and lifted the lid. Same thing. Just trash. No food.

"Iffen you lookin' fer somethin' ta eat"—Kat jumped. Where was that voice coming from?—"change-over ain't till Thursday midnight. Purty good pickin's Wednesday night an' Thursday."

Kat peered around the second Dumpster. A street bum—well, he looked like someone who lived on the street to her—in grease-stained trousers, dirty gym shoes with no socks, a wool sweater that had seen better days pulled over a shirt of indeterminate color, and a gray knit hat pulled down to his eyebrows, sat on a piece of cardboard, his back against the brick wall of the big store.

"Oh, uh, thanks." Kat felt slightly embarrassed to have a homeless man who looked as if he could use a good meal telling her when "the pickin's" would be good. She started to leave and then remembered the apple she had in her backpack, left over from her lunch. Slinging the pack off her back, she unzipped it and dug around until she found the apple. "Here." She held it out. "Would you like this?"

The man's eyes, sagging under folds of pale skin, glittered, and his mouth broke into a grin, showing a mouth full of gaps and bad teeth. He nodded, took the apple, and arranged his bite to take advantage of the teeth he did have.

Feeling awkward, she nodded at him and backed away.

But what the old man had said stuck in Kat's mind all the next day. If he *was* old. Hard to tell. But he looked like he'd been out on the street for eons. She wondered what he'd look like if he got cleaned up, shaved, his teeth fixed . . .

When she met her housemates at The Chip for a late lunch, she told them she needed to study in the library until late, so go on home without her, she'd come later. When they parted ways, Olivia worried about her taking the bus and El alone. But Kat just waved them off. "I'll be home before dark, Livie. I promise." She started for the library, then turned and yelled, "Nick, it's your turn to cook! Save some supper for me!"

Well, she did have a lot of homework and the library was as good a place as any. She spent the afternoon translating a passage from a Spanish novel and working on a take-home midterm, then finally headed for the bus at six o'clock. The air was a good ten degrees warmer than yesterday, maybe in the sixties, and Kat got off the bus a couple of stops before Broadway, feeling like stretching her legs with a good walk. The wind off the lake half a mile ahead ruffled her hair, and she loosened the clip that usually held it at the back of her neck and shook it out, frizzy waves falling past her shoulders and lifting in the breeze. Ah, felt good.

Crossing Sheridan Road, she headed directly for the back of the Dominick's store, though she slowed her pace. She wasn't sure she wanted to run into the same homeless guy again. But all she saw were two big semis backed up to the loading docks and men going in and out, pushing dollies piled high with boxes. *Drat*. The place was too busy. Maybe she should wait awhile . . . or come back? No, too far to come back. She'd wait awhile, see what happened.

Walking north on Sheridan to kill time, she saw a paved path leading to a park beyond some high-rise apartment buildings. Wandering through the park, she followed the path through an underpass beneath Lake Shore Drive and came out on one of Chicago's many beaches. And there was the majestic lake, its surface ruffled with whitecaps by the constant wind. Kat grinned, shaking her hair in the wind.

But she shouldn't stay too long. Walking quickly back to the store, she saw first one truck pull out of the alley into the street, and right on its tailgate another one. Maybe the coast was clear. Grinning, she headed once more for the back of the store.

But even before she got to the Dumpsters, Kat saw a slight figure standing on a wooden crate, holding open the lid of the far Dumpster and leaning over the side, head hidden. She hesitated . . . but it was obviously a girl or woman, not the old guy. And there was another Dumpster. She was not going to leave without seeing what "the pickin's" were today.

Kat walked quietly up to the closest Dumpster, set down her backpack, and lifted the lid. *Gold mine!* Plastic-wrapped six-packs of snack yogurts, sell-by date only yesterday . . . a box with tomatoes and green peppers, slightly bruised or overripe . . . a whole box of cauliflower, just a tad brown on the florets . . . a bag of apples, condition unknown. Grinning, Kat dragged out the box, added some of the yogurts, a few heads of cauliflower, and the bag of apples. Squatting down, she unzipped her backpack to stuff as much in as it would hold. She'd carry the rest in the—

"You! What are you doing, stealing food other folks need?!"

Kat was so startled, she nearly lost her balance. But she quickly stood up to face her challenger—and realized she was face-to-face with the young woman she'd seen in the foyer of the three-flat, the same woman in the photo of the apartment upstairs.

Avis Douglass's daughter.

Kat steadied herself. "I . . . I'm not stealing. They just throw this stuff away." *And why are* you *here helping yourself, if it's stealing?* she wanted to add.

The young woman's eyes narrowed. "You're that girl I saw in my mom's building. Moving in, you said. Which means *you* aren't living in the street like some. I bet you've got money. Why don't you just . . . just go in the store and buy what you want, and leave this stuff for folks that really need it?" She flipped a hand toward the store.

Kat's mind raced. What was this about? The young woman had on a pair of jeans, a hoodie with the hood loosely covering her raven-black tresses, and scuffed gym shoes. A bit disheveled, but she was still an attractive young woman, with smooth honey-brown skin and long strands of tightly coiled waves straggling out of the hood around her face.

"And you're Mrs. Douglass's daughter. I saw your picture in her apartment."

The woman tensed, her eyes suddenly fearful.

Kat picked up the box and held it out. "Are you saying you need this? Take it. And here . . ." She set the box down, dumped the food out of her backpack into the box, and straightened. "It's yours."

Kat's words hung in the air as the young woman stared at the box for a long moment. Then she darted forward, grabbed the bag of apples and a six-pack of yogurt, and stuffed them into an already-bulging black plastic trash bag she was carrying. Starting toward the street, she suddenly stopped and turned back. "Don't tell my mother you saw me here."

"But I don't even—"

"Promise me!"

Kat hesitated, and the woman seemed to panic. *"Promise me!"*

"O-*kay,* I promise. Just tell me your name. I'm—"

But the woman turned and fled.

Chapter 25

The nine-year-old slumped in the chair in Avis's office the next day, arms crossed defiantly across his rumpled T-shirt. She watched him for a few moments, not saying anything. Shaggy brown hair that needed a haircut—a wash wouldn't hurt either. Pasty skin. Tall for his age, thick in the neck and shoulders. *They'll snatch this kid up for football in high school and not give two cents whether he's got passing grades or whether he's learned to get along with other people.*

"Derrick. Tell me about your family."

His pale eyes jerked up. This was obviously not what he expected when he'd been called into the principal's office. The eyes narrowed suspiciously. "Why you wanna know?"

"Just getting to know you. Who lives at your house?"

"Just . . . my mom and dad. He drives a truck so he ain't around too much. An' me and my brother."

"Is your brother older or younger?"

"Older. What's it to you?"

Avis decided to ignore the surly tone. "So what kind of things does your family like to do together?"

The boy shifted uncomfortably. The arms uncrossed, and he sat on his hands. "I dunno. Watch TV, I guess." Avis said nothing. He shrugged. "My mom works late, so mostly it's just me an' my brother."

"So your brother takes care of you?"

Derrick scowled. "S'posed to. But he an' his friends are always pushin' me around. So mostly I just stay outta their way."

Avis's spirit sagged. What she had on her hands was a neglected kid with absentee parents and a bully big brother.

"Tell me about your friends."

Another shrug. "My dad don't want me to play with the kids in my neighborhood. Says there's too many gooks an' spics an' nig—uh, blacks."

Avis pressed her lips together. *I'll bet*. So much for calling in the parents. She forced herself to keep her voice friendly. "Do you like Sammy Blumenthal in your class?"

A sneer lifted one side of his mouth. "That beanie-boy? Why would I like *him*?"

"Why not?"

"'Cause he's a wuss. All ya gotta do is look at 'im an' he goes cryin' to the teacher."

"But I understand you do more than just look at him."

The boy hunched and stared at the floor.

Avis watched him sadly. No wonder Derrick picked on other kids. The proverbial pecking order.

Finally she got up from her chair, walked around her desk, and pulled up a second chair next to Derrick. He cringed slightly away from her. She didn't touch him, just sat close. "Derrick, would you like to carry the flag into the auditorium and lead the Pledge of Allegiance when we have our final assembly in a couple weeks?"

Now he stared at her, mouth open. Then the eyes narrowed again. "You messin' with me?"

"No. What do you think?"

Was that a smile at the corners of his mouth? "Well, yeah. Sure. That'd be cool."

"Just one thing. Sammy Blumenthal will be carrying the Illinois flag at the same time. I need to see that you two can get along if this is going to work. If I hear otherwise"—she shrugged—"I'll need to get someone else."

The boy's pasty face seemed to brighten. "Okay. No problem."

"Good." She stood up. "I'll walk you back to Mrs. Baxter's class." And tell Jodi to get Sammy Blumenthal into her office on the sly so she could ask *him*.

Estelle Bentley's bosom heaved as she chuckled. "Avis Douglass, you sure do have an odd way of dealing with school bullies. Puttin' the bully an' the bull-*ee* on flag duty together. Now that takes the cake!"

Her husband, Harry, wagged his shaved head. "Wish we could do somethin' like that with rival gang kids. Woo-eee." He whistled through his teeth.

Jodi Baxter appeared in the archway of the living room carrying a tray with a coffeepot, a pitcher of iced tea, mugs, glasses, milk, and sugar. "Some like it hot, some like it cold," she sing-songed.

"And *nobody* likes it in the pot, nine days old." Denny Baxter took the tray from his wife and set it on the sturdy wooden coffee table. "When Jodi starts reciting Mother Goose, I know it's time for a looong summer vacation. Harry, you want coffee?"

Harry and Estelle Bentley had shown up at the front door of the Baxters' two-flat at the same time as Avis and Peter Wednesday evening and settled into the comfy living room. Seated in an overstuffed chair, Avis drank in the familiar room. Plants in the bay windows overlooking the street, no curtains. A well-used but still serviceable sofa with matching chair, a recliner, and a hassock provided seats for the six of them. At Yada Yada meetings, they had to import dining room chairs.

"Thanks for coming," Jodi said, curling up with her iced tea on one end of the couch next to Harry and Estelle. "Pastor canceled Bible study tonight—obviously, I guess, since Pastor Clark had been teaching it—but I think some people are gathering at the church to pray anyway. But Pastor said to go ahead and meet tonight to plan the funeral. It's all part of the same thing."

"Well, prayin' sounds to me like a good way to start." Estelle didn't wait on ceremony but launched into a heartfelt prayer of praise. "Jesus! *Mmmm*, Lord! Sometimes we don't understand why things happen the way they do, don't understand why things happen *when* they do. We don't understand why You took one of our saints home just now. But one thing we do know. You are a *good God*! Your love is never failing. You have poured out Your love an' grace an' mercy in many ways on SouledOut Community Church, an' we're gonna trust You now to show us the way ahead. So we *thank* You, Jesus! We thank You!"

Avis joined in the praise, realizing she needed to get her own focus straight if she was going to hear from the Holy Spirit about this funeral service. Not focus on her laundry list of problems. Not on her daily sadness that Rochelle still hadn't contacted her again. Not on the big decision facing her and Peter. Just focus on Jesus . . .

Denny Baxter, not one to pray aloud during a free-for-all praise time, finally cleared his throat and brought the prayer time to a close, asking God's guidance in their discussion tonight and His blessing on the funeral service itself, ". . . that You would be glorified in everything we do and say. Amen."

Jodi—true to form, thought Avis—had written down some areas to consider: music, obituary, sharing time, eulogy, repast. "You forgot resolutions from other churches," Estelle put in.

Jodi tucked her long bob behind one ear. "How do we get those?"

"*Humph*. Just let other churches 'round the city an' people who knew Pastor Clark know about his passin' and invite them to send a resolution in his memory. It'll happen. Then we assign someone to read 'em."

"Uh, well, could you do that part, Estelle? Let people know, and then read them at the funeral?"

Avis smiled to herself. Jodi was quick on the uptake: make a suggestion, and you were likely to end up doing it.

"Why don't we call it a memorial service instead of a funeral?" Denny asked.

"Make that a home-going celebration," Estelle countered.

"Yeah, yeah."

"Like that."

The phone rang. Denny went to answer. When he came back, he stood in the archway, hands in his jeans pockets, a perplexed look on his face.

"What?" the other five chorused together.

"That was Pastor Cobbs. He's been going through Pastor Clark's papers at the office, and he found his will—and he does have a brother in Washington State—plus some general instructions. He, uh, doesn't want money spent on a fancy casket. Said to bury him in a pine box, give everything after paying his bills to set up a scholarship to help send SouledOut kids to college."

Avis blinked back sudden tears. Sending kids to college—a lot better use of money than spending thousands on a fancy casket just going into the ground. *Bless that man.*

"A pine box you say?" Harry scratched the grizzled horseshoe beard that rimmed his jaw, which, combined with his shaved dome, always made Avis think the ex-cop's hair was on upside down. "What's that mean? Anybody know where to get a pine box?"

They all looked at each other. Finally Denny spoke. "Well, maybe Josh and I could build one or something. But we've only got two days. I'm going to have to take time off work. Could probably use you, Harry."

Estelle crossed her arms. "*Humph.* Ain't gonna let that saint of God lie in a plain wooden box. If you're gonna make him a casket, I'll sew somethin' to line it with."

Harry grinned. "That's my girl."

After tossing ideas around for another half an hour, the final assignments were made. Denny, Josh, and Harry would work on a casket. Estelle would make a lining, plus gather resolutions to be read during the service. Pastor Cobbs, of course, would give the eulogy. Peter, who'd been fairly quiet all evening, said he'd work on the obituary and get a printed program made. Jodi volunteered to gather a team of women to provide a repast after the service. "And a team of men to do the cleanup," she said, winking.

Avis agreed to work with the praise team on songs and scriptures. "I'll ask Terri Kepler if she'll do sign language for some of the songs—Pastor Clark really loved her signing." Reluctantly, she also agreed to be the worship leader and emcee the service.

"Well, I guess that's it." Jodi looked around the room. "Anybody want to close with—"

"We need to pray all right," Estelle said. "But somethin' in my spirit says Avis an' Peter need some special prayer right now. You two want to say somethin'?"

Avis and Peter looked at each other. She was sure he was thinking the same thing. Should they say anything about Pastor Cobbs's proposal? He'd said they should decide if they were willing before he brought it to the elders—and Denny was one of the elders. And yet, these were four of their closest friends. Who better to help them sort it all out?

She gave a slight nod. Peter spilled it. Everything. The restlessness he'd been feeling . . . the possibility of an exciting mission trip landing in their laps . . . right up to the meeting they'd had with Pastor Cobbs two days ago.

The other two couples listened soberly.

Peter sat on the edge of the recliner, tension rising in his voice. "It's not just that we have a tough decision to make about the pastor's request. Any wisdom you guys have, good, we want to hear it. But . . . to tell you the truth, I'm struggling with what the heck God is doing here. Feel like I'm getting jerked all over the place. I mean, why even send us that invitation from Nony and Mark if God's just going to slam the door in our faces? It felt like it came straight from heaven, an answer to prayer for something good and useful to do with some of our remaining years. And at first it seemed as if God was opening all the doors—the offer of a buyout for the business, even the possibility that Bethune Elementary might end up on the school-closing list. On one hand, bad news—though even that seemed like God was freeing us up."

Avis saw Jodi's eyes widen at that, and she cringed. Not how she wanted Jodi to find out *her* job might be on the line.

"Then my buyer started waffling. Then Carl Hickman got hurt and left me without a plant manager. Then Pastor Clark died." Peter sucked in his breath. "And now, like a sharp U-turn, Pastor Cobbs is saying don't go, you're needed here. Why? I don't get it."

No one spoke, except to make small murmurs of empathy. Then Harry scratched his beard thoughtfully. "Brother, can't say I know what God's doin' here. Have to admit, I've asked that same question 'bout some of the stuff God took me through. Thought I was goin' blind. None of it made any sense at the time. But in the end, I knew, yes, I *knew,* God was with me all the while."

Estelle wagged her head. "*Mm-hm*. Ain't that the truth."

"As for Pastor Cobbs's proposal," Harry said, "I'm thinkin' you an' Avis would make a great interim team to support the pastor during this transition. Can't think of anybody better. As for all that other stuff? All the yays, nays, and in-betweens. Doors open, doors slammin'. Might be God brought up the mission trip thing just to get you used to thinkin' about change, about something new comin' your way." He turned to his wife. "What was it you was tellin' me about a couple days ago, what God said to Queen Esther in the Bible? Why He put her through all that silly beauty queen stuff?"

Estelle nodded. "*Mm-hm*. 'To prepare you for such a time as this.'"

Chapter 26

"I'm back! Bearing gifts!" Kat set the box from the Dumpster on the kitchen table in the apartment. "Did you save any supper for me?"

Nick appeared in the kitchen doorway in his stocking feet. "Yep. There's a bowl of pasta salad in the fridge and some cornbread in that pan over there. What's that stuff you got?"

She grinned and tossed him a head of cauliflower. "Oh, just some pickin's from the Dumpsters behind that grocery store on Sheridan Road." Should she tell him about meeting the Douglasses' daughter, Dumpster-diving just like she'd been? After all, she'd only promised not to tell her mother. But she hesitated. The more people who knew, the more likely Mrs. Douglass might hear about it. And she'd promised . . .

Nick eyed her stash of Dumpster food. "*Three* heads of cauliflower? Looks like they need to be eaten ASAP. Not sure I want to eat it that many days in a row."

Kat shrugged. "I'll give some of it away then." After all, this was peanuts. She'd been tempted to do a little more diving after giving some of her stash to the other girl—but that bit about taking food from people who really needed it had made her feel awkward. Maybe it was true, maybe it wasn't. Sure, people who really needed food should get first dibs. But what if it just went to waste?

She pulled the pasta salad out of the refrigerator. "Looks yummy. Thanks." She filled a plate with cold salad as Nick disappeared, warmed up a couple squares of cornbread in the microwave, and studied the rescued Dumpster food on the table as she ate.

Maybe the Douglasses could use some. As soon as she'd polished off the pasta salad and cornbread, she snagged a plastic grocery bag from under the sink and put in a head of cauliflower, a couple tomatoes, and a fat green pepper, choosing the vegetables with the least amount of bruises and brown tips. Running up the carpeted stairs in the front hallway to the third floor, she knocked on the Douglasses' door. And waited.

No answer. She knocked again. Still no answer.

They must not be home. Oh well. She hung the plastic bag on the doorknob and scurried back down the stairs.

But running into the Douglasses' daughter digging food out of a Dumpster bothered Kat the rest of the week. Why was *she* Dumpster-diving? Was she one of the people who "needed" that food? But why? She didn't look like a homeless person. And Mrs.

Douglass hadn't said anything to indicate her daughter was in dire straits.

But . . . maybe she didn't know.

After all, the girl had made her promise not to tell her mother. And seemed real panicked that she might find out.

That was it. Mrs. Douglass *didn't* know.

But *why* didn't she know? Good grief, her daughter and grandson lived right here in the same city. It made no sense!

By the time Friday night rolled around, Kat still had no answers. Her friends were all kinds of giddy. Two weeks of mini-term down, only one to go! As they rode home on the El, they talked about going out to a movie or something to celebrate. But they barely made it back to the apartment before a thunderstorm rolled in, and by the time they finished supper—Livie's tuna-and-rice casserole and frozen peas—the streets were awash in a heavy spring rain. So much for going out to celebrate.

But Kat wasn't thinking about mini-term or celebrating. As she loaded the dirty supper dishes into the dishwasher, another question had risen to the top of the pile: What about the little boy in the photo? Where was he? Surely—

"Earth to Kat . . . come in, Kat." Brygitta was tapping her on the shoulder. "Mind telling me why you just put the leftover tuna casserole in the dishwasher?" She retrieved the plastic storage container from the dishwasher and waved it in Kat's face.

"Sorry. Wasn't thinking." Kat took the container and stuck it in the refrigerator.

Brygitta leaned against the counter and folded her arms. "Obviously. Want to know Dr. Walczak's diagnosis? You've been studying too hard. Mini-term has scrambled your brain. No studying tonight. Since we can't go out, let's party in. The Candys have a whole library of DVDs. I propose we pick a romantic movie, pop some popcorn, make root beer floats—I found some vanilla ice cream in the freezer that needs to be used up—and veg out. Theoretically speaking. Veggies not allowed."

Kat smiled thinly. "Sounds good. Except . . . did anybody ask if there's going to be a wake or something for Pastor Clark tonight? I've only been to a couple funerals, but seems like there's always a wake or something the day before."

Brygitta tucked some short strands of her pixie cut behind an ear. "Don't think so. Nick was talking to Mr. Douglass out in the hall awhile ago, and he said there's a 'viewing' at ten o'clock tomorrow morning, and the memorial service at eleven, followed by a 'repast.' I think that means lunch."

"What about the burial?"

Brygitta shrugged. "Don't know. C'mon. Let's choose a movie and drag Livie away from whatever term paper she's writing. If we turn it up loud enough, maybe we'll drown out Nick warbling with his guitar. Doesn't he know he can't sing?"

The rain had cleared and the sky was mottled with occasional clouds the next morning. It was already warm by the time the four students left the three-flat and headed to the Howard Street shopping center for Pastor Clark's funeral.

The large meeting room was already packed with people by the time they slipped inside the glass doors of SouledOut

Community Church. Debra and Sherman Meeks greeted them warmly, handing them each a program. "The line for viewing is over there." Debra Meeks pointed to the aisle against the far wall. "If you want to pay your respects to the family, Pastor Clark's brother is seated in the front row."

Kat craned her neck. A balding man in a well-used suit sat stiffly in one of the padded folding chairs. Had to be the brother. He was as sallow and bony as Pastor Clark had been.

The man who usually played keyboard on Sunday morning was playing organ-type background music as people filled in the chairs. Kat noticed that all the men were in dark suits and ties, the women in dresses or pantsuits. She was glad Olivia had encouraged them to "dress up" a little—at least no jeans. They'd had to walk, though, so they did wear flat shoes.

The students joined the line inching its way toward the casket set on a cloth-covered wheeled contraption. Parents lifted children to peer into the casket. The woman who'd surprised the Douglasses with an anniversary cake—her name was a state, Kat remembered . . . oh yes, Florida—stood to the side with a box of tissues for those who needed one.

As they drew closer, Kat poked Nick. "Look," she whispered. "It's a wooden casket. Looks handmade. So simple—yet it's really beautiful."

"Amazing," Nick murmured.

Now *that* was really living—or dying—"green," Kat thought. She was impressed. As far as she could tell, ecology hadn't seemed particularly high on SouledOut's priority list. She wondered who had the idea for a homemade casket. A-plus for them.

The four of them stood at the open casket together. Kat felt a strange flutter as she looked at the pastor's body. It was Pastor Clark all right—thin face, pale sagging skin, wisps of gray hair carefully combed over to one side, scrawny neck and large Adam's apple tucked inside a stiff white shirt and black suit coat, wrinkled hands resting on his chest. And yet . . . it wasn't. Eyelids covered his once-twinkling eyes. The joyful smile was absent. His expression was dead. There was no life.

This was the first funeral Kat had been to since she'd become a Christian. What had she thought at other funerals? That was it. The person was gone. Body in the ground. The end.

But now? If it was true, that Jesus had died so everyone who believed could be forgiven of their sins and live with God in heaven forever and ever . . . then this wasn't the end. But a beginning.

The realization was so powerful that Kat stood unmoving in front of the casket, staring at the body of Pastor Clark. He *was* alive—but not here. He was with Jesus. When she died someday, she would go to be with Jesus too!

But . . . what about her parents? They occasionally showed up at church, mostly because it was the thing to do on certain holidays, but they never talked about Jesus. Never read the Bible. Both parents thought her decision to "follow Jesus" was just a phase—or they hoped it was. Would they go to heaven, too, when they died? What if—

A sudden sob welled up inside her gut. Tears squeezed out of her eyes. Her shoulders shook. A loud moan escaped her mouth. She couldn't help it. Kat stood in front of Pastor Clark's casket and wept.

Florida was beside her in a moment, stuffing tissues into her hand. "It's all right, baby, it's all right. Young man, find a chair for your friend. Go on, go on." She laid a hand on Kat's shoulder. "It's gonna be all right, honey. Them tears gonna wash a whole lot of stuff that needs to come out."

Kat felt Nick's arm around her shoulders, gently pulling her away from the casket. She let him lead her to some empty chairs toward the back, feeling slightly chagrined. But she couldn't stop crying. A moment later Brygitta and Olivia slid into the chairs beside her. Brygitta took her hand. "Kat, are you all right? I didn't realize you felt that way about Pastor Clark. I hardly knew him myself."

Kat shook her head, pressing the tissue to her eyes.

Nick leaned close. "Don't go blaming yourself, Kitty Kat."

"That's right." Olivia reached over and patted Kat's leg. "Remember, it's not your fault."

Again Kat shook her head. They didn't understand. Her tears weren't for Pastor Clark. Or for herself. For the first time in a long, long time, she wished she could go home to Phoenix and talk to her parents. She was afraid . . . afraid for them to die.

The memorial service was beautiful in its simplicity. A single large flower arrangement stood beside the now-closed wooden casket. Before the service began, Pastor Cobbs explained that Pastor Clark had written a "last will and testament" expressing his wish that money not be spent on a fancy casket or lots of flowers. "Our good brothers Denny Baxter, Josh Baxter, and Harry Bentley made this beautiful casket . . ."

Spontaneous clapping interrupted him and the keyboard played a few trills.

Then the pastor went on. "In lieu of flowers, Pastor Clark requested that a scholarship fund be set up to help SouledOut youth go to college. Although Pastor Clark was not a rich man—after all, we don't pay pastors all that much here at SouledOut"—Pastor Cobbs grinned slyly and an appreciative chuckle swept the room—"this good man set aside a significant portion of his own estate to begin this scholarship fund, which we are calling the Hubert Clark Scholarship. Please see Elder Peter Douglass if you'd like to contribute a gift in memory of Pastor Clark."

More clapping and a lot of *amens*. The pastor then beckoned. "Sister Avis?"

Kat kept her eyes on Mrs. Douglass as she took the mike, reading scriptures from underlined passages in Pastor Clark's own Bible between a set of old-fashioned hymns. Wearing a deep blue dress with a soft blue-and-black-patterned scarf draped around the neck and her usual twists caught up in a crown on her head, the woman seemed so smart and professional. How could she be so oblivious to what was happening with her daughter?

Kat shook off the disquieting thought and focused on her hymnbook. Most of the hymns—"Pastor Clark's favorites," Mrs. Douglass explained—were vaguely familiar to Kat, but certain phrases stood out with new meaning:

"Abide with me . . . in life, in death, abide with me."

"Alleluia! Sing to Jesus! . . . Not as orphans are we left in sorrow now . . ."

"Be still, my soul, the hour is hastening on, When we shall be forever with the Lord . . ."

"The Lord is my Shepherd, I'll not want . . . And in God's house forevermore My dwelling place shall be."

Estelle Bentley, Harry the ex-cop's wife—a plus-size, stately black woman who often wore colorful caftans and matching head wraps that looked African in style—read what she called "resolutions" in her deep resonant voice. Kat had never heard anything like them. "*Whereas* Pastor Hubert Clark was a deeply respected member of this community, we at Peaceful Baptist send our condolences to the members of SouledOut Community Church . . ." There were several "*Whereas-es*" in each resolution from various churches, businesses in the area, and individuals.

"Interesting," Bree murmured under her breath. Kat guessed her friends hadn't heard resolutions like these before either.

After the resolutions, Mrs. Douglass invited people to share memories of Pastor Clark. The first one up was Justin, the young college man and juvenile offender who'd shared at the campfire on Memorial Day. A few of the teens followed, and Kat again heard some of the stories they'd told that night. Several adults shared as well—faithful visits in the hospital, bringing communion to the home when someone was sick, his meaty Bible studies on Wednesday nights. Funny stories too, like the time he offered to drive the youth group to a gospel concert on the south side and ended up in Indiana. It felt good to laugh after the tears that had flowed earlier.

Even Pastor Clark's brother stood up, an awkward man in his late seventies, taking the mike to thank everyone "for being Hubert's family" these past years. "I can tell these were happy years for my brother. I only wish . . . wish we had stayed in touch." His eyes got moist and he sat down, but several people reached out to him, murmuring condolences.

A lump caught in Kat's throat as Pastor Cobbs took the mike. Could that happen to her family? Lose touch? Her parents hadn't called her since graduation—of course, they were on that cruise—and frankly, she hadn't tried to call them either. But she couldn't let that happen. Even if it was hard, she'd try harder to stay in touch with her parents.

The program said *Eulogy—Pastor Cobbs*. But the short, sturdy man started to sing. "I have decided . . . to follow Je-sus . . ." The praise team picked it up, and most of the congregation joined in. As the last line died away—"No turning back, no turning back"—the pastor said, "Pastor Clark isn't with us today. He's with Jesus—"

"Glory! Oh, praise Jesus!" the Florida woman called out.

"—but if he *were* here, I know he'd want to ask each and every one of you: Do you love my Jesus? Will you be coming too?"

Pastor Cobbs let those words sit in the silence of the room, even as the guy on keyboard continued to play softly the chorus they'd just sung. And then the pastor said, "None of us knew that last Sunday would be Pastor Clark's last day on earth. He didn't know it either. But he was ready. Are you ready? If today was your last day to live, are you ready to die?"

Chapter 27

Avis poked her head into the church kitchen. Several women were bagging up leftovers from the repast and setting them in the pass-through window that opened into the main room for families to take home. True to her threat, Jodi Baxter had rounded up a crew of men who either had their arms in sudsy water up to their elbows or were whipping dishes into the cabinets as fast as they were dried—including her husband, Denny, his tie loosened, shirtsleeves rolled up, and a big white dish towel tied around his waist.

"Need some help in here?" Avis truly hoped the answer was no, but thought it was the polite thing to ask.

"Ha!" Jodi swept an arm at the dish crew. "Put an athletic coach, an engineer, and a marketing manager in charge of the dishes, and what we have here is the most organized cleanup SouledOut has ever seen!"

Denny Baxter winked at Avis. "You bet. Better skedaddle

or you just might get caught in a cog, get baptized in this soapy water, and—"

Jodi whacked him with a dish towel. "Oh, stop. Avis, we're fine. You go on. Tell Peter the program looked great. That picture of Pastor Clark on the front was perfect!"

Avis smiled and backed out of the kitchen. The picture *was* wonderful—a candid shot of Pastor Clark laughing, surrounded by some of the younger kids, including little Gracie Baxter, who had her arms wrapped around one of his pant legs.

Jodi poked her head out the kitchen door. "Wasn't it fantastic that Sabrina McGill went up for prayer when Pastor Cobbs gave the invitation? I know Precious is thrilled—and I'm sure Gabby Fairbanks is happy too."

Avis smiled. Precious McGill and her teenage daughter, Sabrina, had been some of the first residents at the House of Hope. "Sabrina's graduating this June, right? Pretty amazing for a teen mom with a one-year-old."

Jodi laughed. "That's God for you! Oh—you're next on the list to host Yada Yada tomorrow night. You good?"

Now Avis winced. She'd forgotten it was her turn. It wasn't that she minded hosting her Yada Yada sisters. They all took turns having their every-other-Sunday prayer meeting at different homes. Just . . . not this week. Not with The Big Decision still hanging over her head. Not with the students right downstairs. She had some things to bring up for prayer and didn't want any "surprise visitors" knocking at the door.

"I'm hosting in two weeks," Jodi said. "You want to trade? I don't mind."

Avis nodded in relief. "You, my sister, are the best. I'll host in two weeks, I promise." She gave Jodi a hug and headed back to the main room.

Most of the congregation except the cleanup crew had left. There was no burial to attend. The funeral home staff had loaded the casket into the hearse right after the service and driven to O'Hare Airport. Pastor Clark's brother was paying to take the body back to Washington State for burial, where the Clarks had a family plot.

"Ready?" Peter had her purse and Bible. They waved a few more good-byes and walked out to Peter's Lexus in the parking lot. She'd be glad to get out of her dress and heels and do nothing the rest of the day. It had been a beautiful memorial service, but she felt drained.

When they got to the car, Peter said, "Say, would you be open to going somewhere for coffee? Maybe the No Exit Café over by the tracks. I'd like to talk."

Avis almost laughed. So much for kicking off her heels. She knew better than to suggest they go home and change first. Once in, there was no way she'd want to go out again. She shrugged. "Sure, fine. The No Exit is kind of funky, but . . . okay."

Funky was right. Even funkier than she remembered. A room that looked like a throwback to the sixties, deliberately unfashionable. An odd assortment of chairs, some comfortable, some not. Tables of various sizes. A stage that often featured music artists and even Broadway plays done by local theater groups on evenings and weekends to rave reviews. Avis definitely felt overdressed as she looked around the room at the clientele and staff in various versions of shredded jeans.

But a table in the back corner gave them a modicum of privacy and the coffee was first-rate. She relaxed. This was good. Back home, she'd probably have felt obligated to do a load of laundry or clean the bathroom. Normal Saturday chores that hadn't been done yet—and maybe wouldn't get done at this rate.

She eyed her husband over the rim of her coffee cup. Still a good-looking man for his age. Smart mustache. An impeccable dresser. Rich, dark skin, like Colombian roast coffee. A trim haircut with only a touch of silver sprouting along the sides. But at the moment he was frowning.

"Earth to Peter . . . what are you thinking?"

"Oh. Just about the girl downstairs—Kathryn. She was pretty shook up this morning. Kind of surprised me, since she didn't know Pastor Clark all that well."

"Yes. Surprised me too. Strange girl." Very strange. The plastic bag of slightly moldy vegetables they'd found hanging on their doorknob a few nights ago—from a Dumpster, no doubt—had to be her work. Like a cat bringing a dead mouse and leaving it as a "gift" for her people. Avis had quietly thrown the whole bag out.

She tipped her head at her husband. "Is . . . that what you wanted to talk about?"

"No, no." He was quiet a long moment. "The service today did something to me—in here." Peter tapped his chest. "Made me think about the void Pastor Clark leaves in our congregation—which is kind of funny, when you think of it. He was way past retirement age, an old geezer to be sure. An old *white* geezer at that. Not many preachers I know—white or black—have the kind of personality to share the pulpit. At least, the church I grew up in only had one pastor and he was a one-man show. Feel free to read between the lines."

Avis had to laugh. She definitely could read between the lines.

"But somehow Pastor Clark and Pastor Cobbs did it. Our two churches merged, and they made a team. And now Pastor is asking us to help fill in for the team. I'm beginning to realize what a big deal that is. I mean, it would be so easy for Joe to simply take Pastor Clark's death as a natural opportunity to go back to a one-man pulpit. No disrespect intended. But he's asking for help, to keep the team mind-set alive and well from day one."

Avis nodded slowly. She hadn't looked at it like that, but it rang true. "And . . . ?" She had an idea what was coming.

Her husband shrugged. "I don't know. Somehow, right in the middle of the service, I quit struggling. It just seemed right to say yes to Pastor Cobbs's proposal. If you're willing, I mean. Because it would have to be both of us." He laughed in self-deprecation. "No way could just one person fill those big ol' size fourteen shoes Pastor Clark used to wear!"

Avis and Peter got on the speakerphone and called Pastor Cobbs that afternoon. He was delighted with their decision. "And what about the Sisulu-Smiths' invitation?" he asked bluntly. "Can you be at peace putting that on the shelf indefinitely?"

As Peter responded, Avis realized it hadn't been that hard

for her. She'd been *theoretically* open to the idea all along, but as long as Rochelle and Conny were "missing"—or at least incommunicado—she hadn't been able to fully embrace the idea of leaving the country, even for a few weeks. In fact, Pastor Cobbs's proposal had given her a worthy excuse to lay it aside: they were needed here.

". . . so we'll write Nony and Mark and tell them it's not possible right now," Peter was saying. "But you did use the word *interim*, right? *Until* the church calls another pastor for the team."

Pastor Cobbs chuckled. "I hear you. Yes, temporarily standing in the gap. But I have to be honest, sometimes calling a new pastor can take a year or more. Especially for a church like ours, which is called to embody the diversity within the body of Christ. We need leaders who are not only excited about that vision but see it as essential for the health of the church today." He could be heard chuckling again. "Some *experience* in a multicultural church would be nice too. Brother Hubert and I had to learn on the job."

They talked a bit about various responsibilities, but Pastor Cobbs put a longer discussion on hold. Right now he wanted to call the other elders, let them consider the proposal overnight, and meet before worship to see if this could be a unanimous decision. "You're excused from that meeting, Peter, since you and Avis are the topic under consideration. But the sooner we do this, the better. Lord Jesus!" Without skipping a beat, Pastor Cobbs launched into a prayer. "I thank You for this brother and sister, putting aside their own desires and stepping up to the plate when their church calls . . ."

Avis had been on the schedule to lead worship the next morning—the first day of June—but Justin Barnes had called a few days ago and said he'd gladly take her place since Avis had covered for him the previous Sunday. She was relieved, since she'd also led worship for the memorial service.

Jodi Baxter pulled her aside as she and Peter arrived at SouledOut a few minutes before nine thirty. "Denny told me Pastor Cobbs shared the proposal with the elders this morning," she whispered. "Just want you to know we both support you one hundred percent. Whatever else happens."

Avis gave her a funny look. "What do you mean?"

"Nothing. It's going to be fine." With a quick hug Jodi headed for the front door to steal her granddaughter, Gracie, who was just coming in with Josh and Edesa.

A few minutes later Justin was giving the call to worship from the mike, and the praise team had everyone on their feet with songs of praise and worship. As the words flowed through her spirit, Avis found herself praying for young Sabrina, already a single mom, with so many challenges ahead—but now she had Jesus. *Oh Lord, give her wisdom! Guide her along the way.* And praying for her daughters—Charette and her family in Ohio, the twins growing so fast . . . Natasha working in a government office in Washington, D.C., . . . and Rochelle.

Oh God, where's Rochelle? Bring her back to me, please. Jesus, please protect little Conny. I don't know where they are, don't know why Rochelle hasn't contacted me. My heart is so sore, Lord . . .

The pain she usually hid beneath the busyness of every day

suddenly triggered tears she couldn't hold back. But at the same time, the words of the song they were singing—"I'll Praise You in This Storm"—washed over the searing pain with a cool, healing touch. Yes, she *would* lift her hands, for God *is* who He is, no matter what storm she was going through!

"*Thank* You, Jesus! Glory to Your name! *Glory!*"

She felt Peter's arm slip around her waist and hold her. Had she said that out loud? She hadn't really meant to, but her heart was so full. The tears still flowed, but they weren't tears of despair.

The music finally faded and Pastor Cobb took the mike as people sat down with a rustle and scraping of chairs. Avis found a tissue and dabbed at her eyes, grateful she didn't have to lead worship or be up front for any reason.

And then she heard her name.

"Sister Avis and Brother Peter, would you come stand with me, please? And, Rose, honey, would you join us?"

What? What was this about? Avis sent a startled glance toward Pastor Cobbs, but he was smiling and beckoning with his hand. Peter took her hand and she felt herself getting up out of her seat and walking to the front. First Lady Rose had joined her husband—a sweet woman who didn't like the limelight.

Approaching the low platform, Avis hesitated, but Pastor Cobbs said, "Come on now, come up here and stand with us." Which they did, even though both Avis and Peter were taller than the pastor's five-foot-six.

Pastor Cobbs addressed the congregation. "As you all know, we said good-bye to our beloved Pastor Clark yesterday, amen?" *Amens* flooded the room. "And, glory to God, even in death, the man left a legacy. At the end of the service, several new names were written in the Book of Life, amen?" The *amens* got louder, and Avis saw Precious McGill, who'd been a teen mom herself and now was a grandmother in her early thirties, jump up from her seat and throw her arms in the air, the loudest of all. Daughter Sabrina, the cause of all this joy, ducked her head in embarrassment.

"But, brothers and sisters, Pastor Clark's death is also a challenge for SouledOut Community Church." Heads nodded. "Hubert Clark and I were called by God to be copastors of this church, but now God has called him home. Where does that leave us? Where does that leave me? Without a copastor. What is God saying? What is God doing?"

Avis felt her cheeks burning. It was hard standing up in front of the congregation like a mannequin in a store window while the pastor spoke like this. She might have run for her seat if Peter hadn't been holding on to her hand so tightly.

"I'll be honest," Pastor Cobbs went on, "I don't know what God is doing. Our loss is too new, too fresh to see clearly. That's for us as a church to pray about and seek His will in the weeks ahead. But God did speak to my spirit about one thing—and that's my own limitations. You all deserve more than just one man—just *this* one man—can do or be." The pastor, perspiring with the intensity of the moment, mopped his face with a small towel. Then he turned to Avis and Peter. "And so I am recommending that we consider this precious couple, whom you all know, to stand in the gap as interim pastors until God shows us who He is calling to share leadership of this church."

Several people started to clap, but Pastor Cobbs held up his hand. "Let me finish, dear people. Some of you may be wondering, why move so quickly to appoint some interim leadership. Because I don't want this church to get used to seeing me standing up here by myself. In fact, *I* might like it too much." He allowed a wry grin. "I'm just being real. It's not always easy working things out with a partner—all you married folks know what I'm saying, right?"

Laughter mingled with a few rolled eyes and meaningful pokes between spouses.

"As your pastor, I felt we needed to move quickly so that pastoral needs are cared for here at SouledOut while we are waiting on God. I spoke with Avis and Peter earlier this week, and they've given it a lot of thought and prayer. They are willing to be considered, even though it means some sacrifice on their part. The elders are recommending that we have a congregational meeting sometime in the next two weeks to consider appointing Avis and Peter Douglass as interim pastors of SouledOut Community Church."

A number of people, including Jodi and Denny Baxter, clapped enthusiastically. Others said, "Amen!" and "Praise God!" But Avis didn't know what to do. Smile? Stare at the floor? She felt sweat trickle down her face—was it just embarrassment or a hot flash? Whatever it was, she needed to keep her chin up. Forcing herself to look out over the congregation, however, Avis realized not everyone was responding to the pastor's announcement with the same degree of enthusiasm.

Catching a movement with her eye, she saw Mary Brown, the wife of Elder David Brown, look sideways toward someone in the row behind her, a grim expression on her face. The two women's eyes locked, a look passed, knowing nods.

And suddenly the exchange she'd overheard in the ladies' restroom rang in her ears: *"We need more white people in leadership so things don't get too far off."*

"Too black, you mean."

"Exactly."

Avis felt faint. What had they let themselves in for?

Chapter 28

The announcement from Pastor Cobbs recommending the Douglasses as interim pastors took Kat by surprise. Man, that was fast. The memorial service for Pastor Clark was just yesterday—and he wasn't even buried yet. Well, she didn't know about that, but they were saying the brother was flying the body to Washington State, and they'd probably have a service there before the burial. All that rigmarole would surely take a couple more days.

On the other hand, she shouldn't be surprised. The Douglasses were a mature couple, very involved at the church. She knew them as well as she knew anybody at SouledOut—which wasn't very well, but they *were* living in the same building. Mr. D was one of the elders—she was pretty sure about that—and Mrs. D was one of the worship leaders, of course. So why shouldn't the pastor tap them for the job?

Except . . .

She poked Nick as Justin Barnes came back to the mike to

read that morning's scripture. "*Psst*, Nick. Don't you need to graduate from seminary to be a pastor?"

He grunted and whispered back, "Usually."

"Do you think either of the Douglasses have an M-Div?"

Nick sighed. "Don't know. But my guess is no."

Olivia frowned at them both. "Shh!"

Kat glared right back at her, let half a minute go by, and then poked Nick again. "You'll have *your* M-Div in January. Why don't you—"

"Stop," he hissed at her. "I don't want to talk about it."

Whoa. What got his goat?

The rest of the worship service seemed more subdued than usual. Or was it just her? Her mind kept replaying everything that had happened the past week. Including Pastor Cobbs's challenge at the end of the memorial service. *"If today was your last day to live, are you ready to die?"* Three teenagers and a woman with a toddler on her hip had gone up to the front to be prayed for afterward. Were they afraid of dying and going to hell? Funny. That wasn't why she'd decided to become a Christian. She'd been drawn by the desire to *live*, to believe in something—Someone—significant. Following this radical Jesus was a lifestyle choice. She hadn't really thought about heaven or hell.

But Pastor Clark's death had shaken her, made her think about the people in her life who didn't believe in Jesus—like her parents. She'd kind of dismissed their life choices as "their thing." Let them live their lives, let her live hers.

But she was realizing it was more than that.

Kat was glad when Pastor Cobbs gave the benediction and people began migrating to the coffee table, gathering their kids, or forming little huddles to talk. She didn't want to think about her parents anymore. What could she do about it, anyway? They'd made it clear they thought she'd gone off the deep end with this "religious stuff."

She made her way over to the Douglasses, who were being greeted by a small procession of different folks. She stepped in close. "Mr. D, Mrs. D . . . just wanted to congratulate you on being recommended as interim pastors."

Mrs. Douglass gave her a weary smile. "Thank you. Still needs to be approved by the congregation. Whatever happens, we're going to need a lot of prayer." She hesitated a moment and glanced at her husband. Then, "Are you all right, Kathryn? You seemed very upset yesterday."

"Oh." Kat was caught off guard. "Yeah, I'll be all right." She hadn't told anyone what she'd been crying about yesterday. Nick, Livie, and Bree all thought it had to do with Pastor Clark dying in spite of her giving CPR. The thing with her parents was hard to explain . . . but Mrs. D was asking. Maybe she could—

"I'm glad, Kathryn. Will you excuse us? I need to ask Florida how her husband is doing before she leaves. Coming, Peter?" Mrs. Douglass gave her another smile and slipped away.

"In a moment," he called after her. Mr. Douglass laid a fatherly hand on Kat's shoulder. "Kathryn. If you're worried about what happened last Sunday, I want you to know you did a brave thing, stepping in like that and doing CPR. Showed a lot of spunk, a lot of courage. You did good."

"Thanks." His encouraging comment did mean a lot. "But actually," she blurted, "I was upset because of my family. My parents. We're kind of estranged. I mean, they don't get the fact that I've become a Christian."

"I see."

Did he? Kat didn't know how to explain, standing there in the middle of a milling crowd. But a crazy thought popped into her head. The subject of family had come up naturally. Now was her chance. "You and your wife are lucky, you know. To have family right here in the city—you know, your daughter and grandson. What's her name again?"

"Daughter?" Mr. Douglass seemed momentarily flustered. "Oh, you mean Rochelle. Um, yes. It's nice to have some of the family close by . . . Uh, where do your parents live? Do you have siblings?"

"Phoenix. And no, I'm an only. Well, don't mean to keep you. Congrats again, Mr. D." Kat gave a friendly nod and moved away. Was it her imagination, or had Mr. D not wanted to talk about their daughter? Well, didn't matter. She'd gotten what she wanted.

Their daughter's name.

Rochelle.

She found Brygitta. "I'm ready to go. Where're Nick and Livie?"

Brygitta rolled her eyes. "Nick said he needed to leave, had a lot of homework or something. Livie wanted to go with him. I saw you talking to the Douglasses, so I told them to go on, I'd wait for you."

"*Hm*. Was he acting kind of funny?"

"Yeah, kinda." Brygitta pursed her lips. "I think I know why."

Kat gave her a look. "O-*kay*, we need to talk. I have something I want to tell you about anyway. Come on."

Twenty minutes later Kat and Brygitta had commandeered a tiny table at The Common Cup, a coffee shop they'd discovered on Morse Avenue, about halfway between the church and their three-flat.

Kat bit into her toasted whole-wheat bagel smothered with garlic-flavored cream cheese, closing her eyes in pleasure. "*Mmmm*, these bagels are to die for."

Brygitta snickered. "You mean, better than the lentil-carrot-veggie-burger leftovers from last night we'd have to eat if we'd gone home?"

"Oh, come on! They were good. Admit it. And cheaper than meat—which is no small potatoes, since none of us has a job yet."

"Yeah. And mini-term is so intense, I haven't had time to look either." Brygitta bit into her own toasted bagel. "But only five more days and it'll be over. Done!"

"So." Kat licked cream cheese off her fingers. "Tell me what's going on with Nick."

Brygitta shrugged. "Well, don't know for sure. But a week ago—before all this trauma happened—he said, offhand like, that he was going to ask the pastors if he could do his pastoral internship at SouledOut. Made sense to me, since that's where we're attending."

"And?"

"I'm guessing he didn't do it, with Pastor Clark dying suddenly like that and all the shock and everything. And now . . ." Brygitta frowned as she nursed her coffee. "Maybe he's feeling like he missed his chance. With Pastor Cobb appointing *both* of the Douglasses to fill in as interim pastors, there may not be room for an intern."

Kat stared at her friend. "Yikes. You think?" She felt bad that she'd been so oblivious. Nick had once said something to her about maybe trying to get an intern position at SouledOut—but she hadn't given it much thought since then. And he had to do an internship if he wanted to graduate next January. If not SouledOut . . . where?

Some friend she was. They hadn't talked about it or prayed about it with him or anything.

"Now you," Bree prompted. "You said you wanted to tell me something."

Kat sighed. "I do. But you have to promise you'll keep it confidential. I just . . . need to talk it over with somebody."

"I promise! Cross my heart, Girl Scout's honor . . . *What?*"

Kat filled her in on the girl she'd seen in the foyer of the three-flat the day she'd skipped graduation . . . then seeing the picture of the same girl in the Douglasses' apartment . . . and running into her Dumpster-diving behind the Dominick's grocery store. "It's really weird. It's Mr. and Mrs. Douglasses' *daughter.* But she made me promise not to tell her parents I'd seen her there. She was all panicky. And Mr. and Mrs. D don't say much about her, like they don't really know what's going on. I can't figure it out. But . . . something's not right."

"Wow." Brygitta's amber eyes were big.

"What do you think I should do?"

"You can't do anything! You promised."

Kat fiddled with her napkin. "But I did learn her name. It's Rochelle."

"*Mm*. Pretty name."

"Yeah. Pretty girl too. If she wasn't so jittery." Kat stood up. "Guess we better go. I've got stuff to do for class tomorrow too. Have to admit I'm pretty sick of Spanish right now!"

"*Huh!* Tell me about it." Brygitta followed her to the door. "I've got Christian Ethics oozing out of all my pores, like locker room sweat. Ugh."

Kat pulled open the door and stepped into the warm spring air. But a notice taped to the inside of the window of the coffee shop caught her eye. Grabbing Brygitta's arm, she pointed. "Look!"

The two friends stared. The paper said: BARISTA WANTED. APPLY INSIDE.

Kat and Brygitta looked at each other.

"Oh my," Kat breathed. "Except it's just one job. And two of us. Unless—"

"Unless what?"

A slow grin spread across Kat's face. "Unless they'd let us share it. Half-time each. Until one of us finds another job. It'd at least be something. What do you think?"

Brygitta grinned. "Why not? Wouldn't hurt to ask."

Chapter 29

The front door of the Baxters' first-floor apartment stood wide open behind the screen as Avis climbed the steps of the two-flat, arriving a few minutes early for the five o'clock Yada Yada Prayer Group. At that precise moment the other door facing the porch—leading to the second-floor apartment—burst open and Leslie "Stu" Stuart bounced out.

"Avis!" The willowy social worker grinned. "Hey, I didn't get a chance to say congrats about you and Peter filling in as interim pastors at SouledOut. Are you good with that? With your job and everything, I mean? Oh. Here come Ruth and Delores. Hi, you two!"

Stu pulled open the screen door to the Baxters' apartment and held it as Avis and the other two women walked into the small entryway. Ruth Garfield, their own "Jewish mother" who'd finally birthed twins at fifty, and Delores Enriques, a pediatric nurse at the county hospital, joined the other Yada Yadas in the living room. Surveying the chattering women, Avis smiled. The group had changed a bit from when they'd started seven years ago, with a few new faces and a couple others moving on. But walking into a group of Yada Yadas always felt like coming home.

Jodi Baxter bustled into the living room carrying a pitcher of iced tea and a stack of plastic glasses, followed by her daughter-in-law, Edesa, with a steaming teapot and mugs on a tray. "Hot or cold, your choice," Jodi said. "And it's *sweet tea*, made by our own Florida Hickman, Memphis born and bred, so I don't want to hear any snide remarks about how white girls make iced tea."

"Ooh, touchy, aren't you." Stu laughed, took the pitcher, and began pouring glasses of sweet tea.

"Edesa." Avis gave the young woman a hug as soon as she'd set down the tray with the teapot and mugs. "I'm surprised to see you tonight—we don't get to see you much at Yada Yada anymore. How's your prayer group at the House of Hope going?"

"Oh, *mi amiga*. Thank you for asking. Even though we are having a good time at the House of Hope, it's . . . different. I miss my Yada Yada sisters, so I have to come from time to time just to soak up all your faces. Besides . . ." Edesa lowered her voice. "Josh is joining some of the men over at Hickmans' tonight to pray with Carl, so it was a good time to come. And Gracie is being entertained by her adoring Auntie Amanda." Her face lit up with a wide smile. "And . . . congratulations, *Pastor* Avis!"

Avis shook her head. This was getting embarrassing. "*Sister* Avis is just fine." Half the Yada Yadas attended SouledOut, so the word was out. But she wasn't officially a pastor yet and wanted to make that clear. The role was temporary, anyway.

When the last woman had arrived—Chanda George, mother

of three, hometown Kingston, Lotto winner, sometime philanthropist, and usually late—Estelle Bentley called everyone to come together and opened the meeting with a prayer. Avis had functioned as leader of the group from its inception, but recently she'd been encouraging Estelle to take over the role, seeing gifts sparking in the middle-aged woman that needed to be fanned into flames.

As usual, they spent the first twenty or thirty minutes in worship, someone starting a song, another offering a prayer of praise and thanksgiving. Back and forth. No prayer requests yet. Long ago Avis had realized they needed this time to set aside the whirlwind of duties, problems, stresses, work, and worries, and get their focus centered on Jesus. Who He is. Creator. Savior. Lord. Healer. Defender. Protector. Friend.

Then they were ready to share their heart burdens with one another and bring their requests to God.

"Florida," said Estelle, "I hear the brothers are praying with Carl tonight. How's he doing since his accident?"

Yes, Estelle's husband would have gotten a call to show up at the Hickmans', because it was Peter who'd called some of the brothers to go pray with Carl that evening, after Florida told them at church that Carl had had another setback. A minor blackout, when he couldn't remember what he'd been doing for the past hour. Still dealing with pain in his neck. Anxious about getting back to work.

"But he's come a long way, thank ya, Jesus, an' we still expectin' full healin'. Just pray for me too, sisters, 'cause sometimes havin' him underfoot makes me want to give him another bop on the head."

Laughter carried into the prayer as Delores prayed for Carl and Florida and for the whole Hickman family.

Adele Skuggs wanted to praise God for some new clients at Adele's Hair and Nails. "Ain't been easy keepin' my shop in the black in this recession. But God is good. Things are lookin' up."

Yo-Yo Spencer, guardian of her two younger brothers, asked prayer for Pete, deployed in Iraq. "An' now Jerry's talking about signin' up when he graduates high school in June. I know I been wantin' to kick both of them outta the house for years. But now I wanta take it back. Think God does reverse prayers?"

When it was Avis's turn, she asked the sisters to pray for the STEP program at Bethune. "We still need more tutors and volunteers, especially since the program begins the very next week after school's out. Pass the word, all right?"

Avis caught Jodi mouthing something at her ". . . *closing Bethune?"* Avis shook her head. Even though that possibility had come out right here in this room when they were planning Pastor Clark's memorial service, it wasn't time for more public knowledge.

"Sista Avis!" Chanda was waving her hands at her. "What mi hearing 'bout naming you pastor at SouledOut? Why mi always de last to hear tings?"

Avis did her best to share what had happened that week. "And keep in mind that the congregation needs to approve. But whatever happens, I do know Peter and I need your prayers, because our plates are already full with his business and my job at Bethune Elementary. But please, don't call me 'Pastor Avis.' I'm just 'Sister' to you and everyone else, like always. Same for Peter."

"What? Sister Peter?" Chanda's eyes went wide.

That broke everyone up. Avis's side ached from laughing. Good. Might keep everybody from taking this whole "interim pastors" thing too seriously.

Edesa spoke up. "I need some wisdom, *mi amigas*. I had an interesting conversation with one of the Crista University students on Memorial Day. She and her friends came to the youth group picnic at Lighthouse Beach. Maybe Josh has asked them to help with the teens, I'm not sure. But this young woman just graduated from CCU with a master's degree in education, seems very smart. Plus she's quite passionate about ecology—'saving the earth's resources' was the phrase she used."

"Got a burr in her pants, you mean, if you talkin' 'bout that Kathryn Davies," Florida put in. Avis tried not to laugh. She couldn't have said it better herself.

"What I want to know," Florida huffed, "is why these white college kids show up in they raggy jeans at church? They tryin' to *identify* with us 'poor' folks or somethin'? Seems downright insultin' to me! And what's with the Dumpster food she think we wanna eat—"

"Flo!" Estelle gave Florida the eye. "Let Edesa finish. She was bringin' somethin' up for prayer. So hush a minute."

"I'm just sayin'." Florida sat back in her corner of the couch, arms crossed.

Edesa frowned thoughtfully. "Florida's got a point. Kathryn got all excited when I told her I had my degree in public health. Said she'd love to teach a class on nutrition for neighborhood families on welfare, wondered if I'd consider doing it together. She's got this thing about food issues—part of her 'living green' mind-set. She said, 'If only poor people understood nutrition!' As if a little class about eating habits would solve all their problems with poor health."

"Tell me about it." Yo-Yo rolled her eyes. "When my mom was all strung out on drugs and me an' the boys didn't know where the next meal was comin' from, we wasn't exactly thinkin' about the four basic food groups."

Edesa smiled. "Exactly. Just having *something* to eat is basic. Getting enough. Getting it regularly . . . you get the idea. Worrying about organic food and balanced nutrition isn't first on the agenda. I'm sure Kathryn is well meaning, but I'm afraid she's long on knowledge and short on experience . . . not that I'm putting down education!" she hastened to add. "I'm the first one in my family to get a college degree, and I'm so grateful I've been able to go to school here."

"That's all right, honey," Adele put in. "We know what you mean. I could hang out my shingle, listenin' to all the troubles people pour out while sittin' in my beauty chairs. And they get a lot of advice too—because I'm *long* on experience."

"*Humph.* Rich you'd be, too, if you charged them what it cost me for marriage counseling with my first two husbands." Ruth made a face. "Did it do any good? Not so you'd notice. Which is why Ben is husband number three."

Again, the room convulsed with laughter.

"Hush now," Estelle scolded, nodding at Edesa to continue.

"Anyway . . ." Edesa threw up her hands. "I am talking too much. Forgive me, *mi amigas*. Please pray for me. I need wisdom to know how to respond about this class idea of hers. If I say no, she might go ahead and try to do something herself. But I don't want to come across as—how do you say it?—a know-it-all. So also pray that her energy and idealism get channeled in the right direction, before she gets hurt—or hurts others."

Avis felt a pang. She was . . . what? Twice as old as Edesa? Probably had been a Christian twice as long too. And yet the lovely young woman from Honduras was asking Yada Yada to pray for the CCU student. What was *wrong* with her? Too concerned about her own daughter, who wasn't much older than those students, to pray for them.

She took a deep breath and blew it out. "Might as well pray for me, too, when you're praying for Kathryn and her friends. As some of you know, they're subletting the apartment right below us in our three-flat and, I confess, I haven't been as friendly as I should. I just get . . . annoyed."

Florida sputtered but eyed the ceiling, as if trying hard to keep her mouth shut.

"Ah. Maybe you are just the person that girl Kathryn needs," Delores said, nodding her head. "An older woman, wise, a mentor . . ."

Avis shook her head. "I appreciate the vote of confidence. But I'm not exactly feeling like a good mother figure. I—" Avis had to press her hand to her mouth for a moment to keep her lips from trembling. "I'm sorry. I know you all have prayed for Rochelle, but I haven't shared very much with you. The fact is, my daughter is currently estranged from me. I haven't talked to her since Valentine's Day. She wanted to move in, hadn't been doing well, but Peter was against it. We took her to Manna House, but she didn't stay . . . and she's been missing ever since."

Along with the ruby earrings, Avis thought, but that didn't feel like essential information right now.

"But what about dat grandson, de Conny boy?" Chanda looked shocked.

Avis shook her head. "Haven't seen him for three and a half months. It's tearing my heart out. I'm afraid I've been so worried about them, the students downstairs have felt like an intrusion in my life."

The room was silent for several moments. Then Estelle said, "Well. That's what we do best here at Yada Yada—pray. When we don't know what else to do. Pray as you will, and I will close when we have prayed for all the requests mentioned tonight."

They prayed for the next half hour. Even without any immediate answers, Avis felt some of her burden lift. It had felt good to be honest about her non-relationship with the students, as well as the estrangement with Rochelle.

Though she hadn't been completely open about everything—like the comments she'd overheard in the restroom a week ago and the "look" Mary Brown had given the other woman after Pastor Cobbs had recommended her and Peter as interim pastors. Had she only imagined that it meant anything? It was such a touchy black-white thing . . . How could she bring up her discomfort without hurting some of the white sisters in this group? Or talking about an elder's wife behind her back?

Lord, I'm going to have to leave it with You for now.

The Yada Yada group disbanded with hugs and good-byes as they stepped out into the late twilight of early June. Warm, mild, no rain—

"Avis?"

Avis felt a touch on her arm and turned to see Delores Enriques's round, kindly face. "Yes?"

"Perdón, mi amiga. But I still feel in my heart that God has a reason to move those students into your building. No coincidences with God, *sí*? You always used to say."

Avis allowed a wry smile. "*Mm*. No coincidences."

"So, I'm thinking, why don't you and Peter just invite them for supper sometime? Not a big deal. Just let them into your life a *little* bit." Delores made a tiny pinch with her thumb and forefinger. "Remember, God can do a *big* miracle with just a few fish and loaves of bread."

Chapter 30

Olivia's blue eyes popped. "I can't believe they hired both of you for the same job!" The four were parked in the Candys' living room, munching on Sunday evening snacks spread out on the coffee table. Chips. Salsa. Hummus. Veggies. Bean dip.

Nick pulled a handful of tortilla chips from the bag. "Yeah. Congrats. Lucky you."

"We weren't even looking. It was just there!" Kat dipped a carrot in the bean dip.

"And we thought, all they can do is say no. But they said yes! They even liked the idea of splitting the job." Brygitta snorted. "Probably because they don't have to pay benefits if it's part-time."

"Hey. Don't blame them. It was our idea."

"I'm grateful, I'm grateful! They know we can't do day shifts till next week, but they're letting us start evenings this week. We go for training tomorrow night."

Olivia groaned. "I haven't even started job hunting. Don't think I'll have any time till mini-term is over."

"Which is only five days away." Brygitta gave her a playful shove. "We'll keep our eyes open for you."

But Kat was watching Nick, absently working his way through the bag of tortilla chips. "Hey. Nick. Stop a minute." She snatched the chip bag away from him. "What's going on? What's with the Eeyore attitude?"

"Nothing." He grabbed. "Give the chips back."

She dangled the bag out of reach. "I'm serious. You've been bummed out all day."

Nick slumped back against the couch and shook his head. "It's nothing. I'm fine."

Kat tossed the bag of chips back to him. "Look. We're your friends. Does this have something to do with you wanting to do your internship at SouledOut?"

He looked at her sharply, and then his eyes fell. "Doesn't matter, does it? The Douglasses are a shoo-in to be interim pastors. Double duty. I doubt they have room for an intern now."

"You don't know that." Kat got up from the hassock where she'd been sitting and sat down on the couch next to Nick. "You ought to at least talk to Pastor Cobbs. He might be able to work out something."

Nick shrugged. "Maybe if I'd done it earlier. Before Pastor Clark died. But now . . . I don't know. Seems kind of presumptuous now that he's gone and they're looking for experienced people to fill in."

"But you said yourself that pastors need seminary training. You probably have more seminary than either of the Douglasses!"

Nick eyed her sideways and shook his head. "Don't think it matters in this case. The Douglasses have been around since the beginning of SouledOut, they're well known, and they've already got leadership roles. Who am I? A new kid from Crista University."

"*Humph*. Still." Kat folded her arms and sat back, leaning against Nick. "You won't know for sure unless you ask. Come on, Nick! Don't give up without a fight."

He pulled away and gave her an incredulous look. "*Fight?* You think it's going to help me to fight the pastor's recommendation of the Douglasses? Get real, Kat."

"Sorry. Poor choice of words. I didn't mean *fight*. I just meant stand up for yourself. At least *ask*."

Nick shrugged. "I don't know. I'll have to think about it."

"We could pray about it too, you know. Aren't you the one who encouraged those where-two-or-three-are-gathered-together kind of prayers?"

"Yeah, yeah, stick it to me." But after a moment Nick nodded. "Sure. I'd appreciate the prayers."

Training at The Common Cup was fun. Kat and Brygitta were shown how to make espressos, cappuccinos, lattes, and a host of other variations, including *cortados* (espresso and steamed milk) and *con pannas* (espresso with whipped cream). The baked goods—scones, muffins, bagels, and pies, to name a few—were brought in fresh daily. The soups and salads were made on the premises.

And then there was the shop's Specialty Ice Cream, starting with vanilla ice cream or frozen yogurt, adding berries or cookies or candy bar bits, and blending the whole customized creation in a special machine. Kat wasn't sure why anyone would want all that candy added to perfectly good frozen yogurt, but she'd probably have to just grin and bear it.

She decided not to ask where they got their coffee on her first day, but she was curious. Was it fair trade coffee?

Kat took the first evening shift—Tuesday—and was secretly glad that her Wednesday evening would be free. Because she definitely wanted to check out the Dumpsters again behind the Dominick's store on Sheridan at the "change-over." She'd arrive later, giving the trucks time to unload and leave, and time for the staff to dump old food. However, it wasn't the salvaged food she was interested in this time as much as hoping she'd run into the Douglasses' daughter again.

But by Wednesday evening she was bushed. Commuting, classes, homework, *and* working were keeping her up until one or two in the morning. Getting off the bus at Foster and Broadway, she considered heading straight for the El rather than checking out the Dumpster scene. It'd been foggy and muggy all day, kind of depressing. She was hungry and tired and needed to do her laundry. And on top of everything else, her feet hurt. Her evening shift at the coffee shop the previous night had been long—four hours, from five to nine, including cleanup—and she'd been on her feet the whole time.

Go home, dummy, she told herself.

Except . . . what if the girl was there and she missed her?

Okay, I'll just drop by the store and check it out. But if she's not there, I won't wait around. I'll just go on home and try again next week.

The back of the store was empty. No trucks. No store staff. No Dumpster-divers. Somewhat relieved, Kat started to leave. Except, here she was. What would it hurt to look in the Dumpsters, see what had been thrown out this time?

Shrugging off her backpack, Kat refastened the clip that held her hair back, positioned an empty wooden crate with several slats missing for a step stool, and lifted the lid of the first Dumpster. It took a few moments for her eyes to adjust to the dim interior. A box of romaine lettuce—probably some good stuff there—and were those cottage cheese cartons? Past due date. *Hm*, better not, it'd been too warm today . . .

But the lettuce. She'd take a few of those. Leaning over the rim, she reached—

"You again!"

The familiar voice made her jerk upright, banging her head—again—on the lid. She turned. There stood the young black woman, glowering at her. And holding tight to her hand, a little boy.

"Uh, hi, Rochelle." Kat climbed down off the wooden crate. She held out her hand. "I'm glad to see you again. My name's Kat."

The little boy giggled.

"Hush," his mother commanded, ignoring Kat's extended hand. "How'd you know my name?"

Kat shrugged. "Your folks have pictures of the kids and grandkids around their house." Which wasn't exactly a direct answer, but it was all she could think of.

"My name's Conny," the little guy piped up. Cute as a button. Big brown eyes. The same honey-brown skin as his mother. Maybe five or six. "Is your name really Cat?"

Rochelle jerked his hand. "You don't need to know nothin' about her. Come on." She turned and started to leave, pulling the little boy by the hand.

"Wait! Rochelle!" Kat ran to catch up. "I haven't said anything to your mom and dad."

Rochelle kept walking. "He's not my dad."

"What?" Kat fell into step beside her. "Peter's not your dad?"

"Stepdad."

"Oh." Kat's mind was spinning. Not her dad. But Avis was her mother. That might explain a few things. "Look. Come back. I know you came for food. I'll help get some for you. There's romaine lettuce back there. I'm sure some of it's still good."

Rochelle stopped. "Romaine? That makes a real good salad . . ." Turning abruptly, she started walking back into the alley behind the store. "Okay."

At the Dumpsters Kat dragged out the box of lettuce and the two of them picked through it, saving out a couple heads of lettuce each and tossing the box back into the Dumpster. In the second Dumpster Kat pulled out some six-packs of juice boxes that Conny grabbed. "Not sure that's so good," she said. "See? It says 'Juice Drink,' which means it's not a hundred percent juice."

"Don't care. I like it!" The little boy sat down on the ground, tearing open the little straw that went with one of the juice boxes and poking it into the top. Soon he was sucking away happily.

Ten minutes in the Dumpsters and they'd rescued several more vegetables, a cantaloupe, and some loaves of bread. "I got enough," Rochelle announced, hefting the plastic bag she'd filled. "Thanks. Come on, Conny."

Again Kat fell into step, lugging her backpack that now held her loot. Two more people, then a third, passed them on their way back to the street. "Guess we got there just in time to get the first pickings," Kat gloated.

Grabbing Conny's hand again, Rochelle started across the street, dodging traffic. Kat had to trot quickly to keep up. "Uh, where are you headed?"

"Bus comin'. We need to get that one."

They'd made it to the corner. A sign said Bus Stop. Kat saw a bus coming toward them, heading the opposite direction from where she needed to go. "Oh. Um, do you live far?"

"I'm staying with my daddy," Conny piped up again.

"Shut up, Conny!" Rochelle hissed. "Don't go blabbing all our business."

"It's all right, Rochelle." Kat hastened to reassure her. "I won't be telling anyone. But I'd really like to see you and Conny again. Could we—"

The bus wheezed to a stop in front of them. "Sheridan and Broadway," a mechanical voice blared as the doors folded open.

"My bus. Gotta go." Rochelle pushed Conny ahead of her as they climbed the steps into the bus. But just before the doors closed, she turned. "Thanks. You're okay."

"Bye, Cat!" yelled the little boy. "Meowww! See ya later!"

The doors closed. Kat saw them moving down the aisle. Then the bus pulled away and they were gone.

The bus had said "151 / Lake Shore Drive / Union Station." Not much of a clue where they lived.

Forgetting her tired feet, Kat pondered the strange encounter all the way home. Conny said he was living with his daddy. What daddy? The photo in the Douglasses' living room was just Rochelle and Conny. Was Rochelle living with "daddy" too? But if so, why was she Dumpster-diving?

Well, why are you Dumpster-diving, Kathryn Davies? she asked herself. *Maybe you're not the only one who doesn't like to see food wasted.*

Still, something didn't add up.

Finally dragging into the foyer of their building, Kat used her mailbox key to check for mail and pulled out a wad of envelopes and flyers. Mostly junk. A few things for the Candys. With e-mail and cell phones, none of the students got much mail.

But riffling through the wad as she climbed to the second floor, Kat saw her name on a square envelope. Her father's handwriting.

A card from home!

Grinning, Kat hustled up the last few stairs to the front door and let herself in. "I'm back," she called out. "And famished. Save any supper for me?" She dumped her backpack on the dining room table and headed into the kitchen to get a knife to open the envelope.

Olivia followed her into the kitchen. "I was worried about you! You should call if you're going to be so late. It's almost eight o'clock!"

Kat found a knife and slit open her card. "Livie. I've got my cell phone. You can call me if you're worried."

Olivia opened the refrigerator and pulled out a plate with a pot lid covering it. "Just some catfish and rice. Hope it warms up okay."

"*Mm.* I'm sure it's fine. I brought some lettuce. I'll make a salad to go with it." As Kat took off the pot lid and stuck the cold plate in the microwave, she saw Olivia's troubled face. "I'm sorry, Livie. You're right. I should've called. Sorry I worried you. But I'm fine. Where's Bree?"

"Working at the coffee shop, remember? It was only Nick and me for supper. But Mrs. Douglass came down a little while ago. She invited us to have supper with them Saturday night."

"Really? Mrs. Douglass?" The faces of Rochelle and little Conny standing in the alley behind the grocery store flashed in her mind, and her uneasy feelings returned.

"Yeah. We told her this was our last week of mini-term, and she said it could be an end-of-school celebration. Though the Chicago public schools don't get out for another week."

Kat nodded. "That'll be nice." She waved the envelope as the microwave beeped. "Got a card from my folks. Do you mind?"

Olivia took the hint and disappeared. Sitting down at the kitchen table with the plate of leftover food, Kat pulled out the card. A Hallmark card that said "Thinking of You." Inside was a nice little ditty and underneath in her father's handwriting she read, "Home from the cruise. Had a great time! Love, Dad."

That was it.

Chapter 31

Sitting at the dining room table staring at the screen on her laptop, Avis heard a key click in the lock and the front door open. "Peter?" she called.

Her husband poked his head into the large alcove that functioned as their dining room. "Nope, just the boogeyman," he said, dumping his briefcase on a chair and loosening his tie. "Anything to eat?"

"I picked up some chicken from Jamaican Jerk on the way home from prayer meeting. Some oxtail and beans too. Help yourself. How was the elders' meeting?"

Avis had gone to the prayer meeting at SouledOut that had replaced the Wednesday night Bible study since Pastor Clark's death, and Peter had met her there, coming straight from work. But Pastor had scheduled an elders' meeting afterward, so she'd come home alone.

Peter just grunted and headed into the kitchen. "What are you doing? You're worse than I am, bringing work home."

"Not work," she called after him. "I'm e-mailing Nony and Mark. They don't even know about Pastor Clark's death, unless someone else told them. But I'm also telling them that we have to put their invitation on hold indefinitely."

"Yeah."

For the next few minutes all Avis heard from the kitchen was Peter fixing himself a plate of food and warming it in the microwave. That "Yeah" sounded kind of glum. When he came back with his plate and sat down at the other end of the table, she closed the lid to her laptop and looked at him over the top of her reading glasses. "Okay. Out with it. What happened at the elders' meeting?"

He shook his head slightly as he picked up a piece of chicken and took a bite. She waited. "Nothing really," he finally said, mouth half full. "I mean, we talked about adding a discipleship class for new Christians, and who could mentor the teens who made a decision after the memorial service. That was good. Pastor asked us to recommend some members to preach on a rotating basis, at least once, maybe twice a month during this interim time." Peter kept eating, talking between bites. "And we talked about the upcoming congregational meeting next week, went over the budget, how we're doing at midyear . . ."

Peter busied himself with his food for the next few minutes.

"And?"

Peter laid down his fork and let out a long sigh. "I don't know, Avis. Just . . . got a funny feeling. We were talking about the meeting next week and how to take the vote on Pastor's recommendation about interim pastors. And David started raising a lot of issues to consider. Setting a time limit on the interim.

Selecting a committee to start the pastoral search process. Even expressed a concern that this appointment was too much to ask of us, since we both have full-time jobs. But . . ."

David Brown. Mary Brown's husband. Avis got a funny feeling too.

Peter frowned. "Just got a feeling that that wasn't what he was really saying. That he was dancing around the fact that he didn't really support the idea of us in that role. Not sure why. I've always gotten along with David all right. Don't always agree with him about church stuff, but that's why we have several elders. We're not close or anything, but we've always been cordial. So maybe I'm just imagining things."

"I don't think so."

Peter stared at her. "What do you mean?"

She hadn't planned on telling Peter what she'd overheard in the ladies' restroom at the church. As long as Peter wasn't picking up any racial undercurrents at the church, she hadn't wanted to fan any embers. But now she felt he deserved to know.

"You're kidding me," he said when she finished. "Mary Brown doesn't want the church to get 'too black'?"

"That's what she said."

"What in the world does she mean by that?"

Avis made a face. "I didn't ask her. I was cornered in the handicapped stall, remember?"

Shaking his head, Peter pushed his plate back. "Dear God. I thought people at SouledOut were beyond this." A moment later he banged his fist on the table. "Tell you one thing, Avis. I didn't sign up for this kind of mess!" He stood up abruptly, grabbed his dishes, and stomped into the kitchen. She heard him dumping his dishes into the dishwasher and a few other thumps and slams before he came back out again.

"Peter. Wait." Avis got up and went to her husband. "I understand you're upset. I've been upset too. But we can't let the Browns dictate how we feel—and they probably don't speak for anybody but themselves." Except maybe that other woman Mary Brown was talking to, but Avis had to let that go. "Let's pray about it, okay? We need to ask God to help us not let this influence our own attitude or what we do."

Peter still looked grim. "I know. You're right. But this job was going to be challenging enough without the race card popping up." He wrapped his arms around her. "Okay, let's pray. *Humph*. Guess that's why Pastor Cobbs wants *both* of us to be interim pastors, so my wife can help keep my feet on the ground."

"Keep you from flying off the handle, you mean." She gave him a playful poke, and then, still standing with their arms around each other, she began to pray. "Lord Jesus, we need You in a special way right now . . ."

Even as she prayed, Avis realized this was the first time she was praying about the conversation she'd overheard, the first time it had occurred to her to pray *for* Mary Brown. Even though she was always the one telling the sisters at Yada Yada to "pray first!" Give the stuff to God, let God work it out rather than fussing about it.

But when she came right down to it, it was easier said than done.

Peter just squeezed her when she finished and said, "Amen." Obviously willing to let her prayers stand in for both of them.

Avis moved back to her laptop. "Oh. I did go downstairs earlier this evening and invite the students to have dinner with us Saturday night."

Peter's eyebrows went up. "Good for you, girl. Kill 'em with kindness, eh?"

She made a face. "Don't rub it in. Nick and the girl Olivia—the only ones who were there—seemed pleased. Said it'd be a good way to celebrate the end of their 'mini-term' or whatever they call it. Guess they've been commuting back to CCU every day."

Peter rubbed his hands together. "Hey, I think it's time we fired up the grill and did some ribs, whaddya say? And you, my queen, make the best mac 'n' cheese in the world. We'll show those kids some real soul food cooking."

With the fifth graders going on a field trip to the Adler Planetarium on Thursday, and a dress rehearsal on Friday for next week's final assembly—including Derrick Blue and Sammy Blumenthal carrying the flags together down the middle aisle, stoically not speaking or looking at each other—Avis hadn't done anything to prepare for the "celebration dinner" by the time Saturday rolled around. After two days sweltering in the high eighties, the weather forecast predicted a thunderstorm or two late in the day. She hoped it would happen early in the afternoon to cool things off and then clear up so they could eat out on the back porch.

Peter went to work Saturday morning but promised he'd be

home in time to grill the ribs. He liked to grill them slow, three hours or more. But when the phone rang just after she'd put the pot of collard greens and smoked neck bones on the stove to simmer and the caller ID said *Software Symphony*, she muttered to herself, "You better not be calling to say you can't get home to do those ribs, Peter Douglass."

But the voice on the other end wasn't Peter. "Hey there, Avis," said a male voice. "Peter made me make this call, said I was an answer to prayer."

It only took a nanosecond to place the voice. "Carl? Is that you? You're at work?"

Florida's husband chuckled in her ear. "Yeah. Ever since the brothers came and prayed for me last Sunday, I been doin' real good. Decided to come over here in person, tell your man I plan to come back to work on Monday. Had to make sure he hadn't given my job to someone else."

"Oh, Carl! That *is* good news. Are you sure? I mean, did your doctor give the okay?"

"Yeah . . . Hey, man, you don't have to grab. Avis, your man wants the phone back. See ya Sunday, I hope. Thanks for all the prayers—"

"Avis?" The next voice in her ear was Peter's. "Isn't this great news? Nearly fell off my chair when he walked into my office. He's looking great. Oh, hold on . . ."

She heard him calling out, "Hey, man, thanks for coming in. See you tomorrow at church." Peter came back on the phone, his voice lighter than she'd heard it all week. "Yeah, I did tell him he's an answer to prayer—in more ways than one. He's looking a lot better, and having him back will take a big load off my shoulders here at work. But . . . there's another thing. To be honest, Avis, the last couple days I've been wrestling with God about whether I can hold this business together and take on more responsibility at church. And that thing with the Browns . . . *huh*. Don't want to touch it with a ten-foot pole. Been thinking about telling the pastor I can't do this. And then—Carl walks in. Says he's ready to get back to work. Not sure what it all means. Is God trying to tell me something? With Carl managing things, I suppose I'd be able to cut back on my time in the office—but I'm still not sure how things are going to shake down at SouledOut."

Avis let this sink in. She'd been having similar thoughts, not so much about the time involved—though that was an issue—but, like Peter, whether she was up to facing a situation that might prove to be divisive. She didn't want to be at the center of that kind of mess. She'd had enough of those racist attitudes when she was first appointed principal of Bethune Elementary. It wouldn't be good for SouledOut either. But . . . was Carl coming back to work, freeing up Peter, an answer for her too?

Chapter 32

The promised thunderstorm still hadn't materialized when the students from the apartment below showed up right at six. "Yay! Mini-term is over!" Brygitta crowed as they came in.

"No more pencils, no more books, no more teachers' dirty looks!" Kathryn and Olivia laughed as they chanted the childhood ditty.

Nick handed Avis a bouquet of mixed flowers, the kind they sell at the grocery store, but they were fresh and colorful. "With all due respect to the principal of Bethune Elementary, who I'm sure doesn't give dirty looks."

Avis had to laugh. "You might be surprised." She smiled warmly as she took the flowers. "Daisies and alstroemeria! Some of my favorites. You didn't need to do that, but thank you. Come on in . . . Peter's out on the back porch hovering over the grill. You can go out there if you'd like."

As Avis rummaged in a cupboard for a vase, she had a

sudden pang. *Flowers. Oh dear.* With the hot weather this week and no rain, the flowers she'd planted out front of the building were probably dead. She should have watered them this morning at least!

"Anything we can do to help?" Kathryn had her thick brunette hair caught back in a fat ponytail, hands stuck in her jeans pockets.

Avis almost said, *"Yes, go water my flowers!"* But it was supposed to rain . . . let the rain do it. So she said, "Sure. You can cut the ends of those stems and arrange the flowers in this vase, if you would. I need to take my mac 'n' cheese out of the oven."

Nick, Olivia, and Brygitta wandered out onto the back porch, but Kathryn hung out in the kitchen with Avis as she took out the casserole and then tasted the greens. *Mm, perfect.* The cornbread needed another ten minutes though.

"Did you hear that Bree and I got a job?" Kathryn said, snipping the ends of the flower stems and sticking them one at a time into the vase. "Over at The Common Cup on Morse Avenue. It's the coolest thing. They wanted a full-time person, but they're letting us share the job."

Avis set out a stack of soak-proof, heavy-duty Styrofoam plates, the kind you need if you're going to serve ribs. "Part-time? That's interesting. Does that give you enough . . . I'm sorry. Not my business."

"No problem. We don't have a lot of expenses since we're sharing the rent for the apartment, so I think we'll be okay. Nick and Olivia still need jobs though. To tell you the truth, I'd rather work part-time this summer anyway, because I'd really like to do some volunteer work too—maybe tutoring or even teaching a class at the church about good nutrition." Kathryn stuck the last flower stem in the vase. "For poor families in the neighborhood, you know. I mentioned it to Edesa Baxter since she's got her MA in public health, but we haven't had a chance to really talk about it. What do you think about something like that, Mrs. D?"

Avis stood stock still, holding the stack of disposable plates, glad Edesa had given them a heads-up about this idea at Yada Yada last week. She recovered quickly. "I think talking to Edesa about it is exactly the right thing to do. Here—" She handed the plates to Kathryn. "Would you take these out to the table on the back porch? We're almost ready."

Kathryn took the plates but frowned at them. "Are these Styrofoam? Um, no offense, Mrs. D, but these are really bad for the environment. They're not biodegradable. Can't recycle them either. Do you have any regular plates? I'll be glad to stay and wash the dishes, if that's the issue."

It was all Avis could do not to let her mouth drop. Of all the nerve! Hadn't this girl ever heard that when you're in Rome, you do as the Romans do? Especially if you're a guest! But again she made a quick choice not to make an issue of it. "Yes, I do have regular plates. The stoneware in that cupboard. We'll need six of them. But we *are* going to use paper napkins with ribs." *If that's all right with you, Miss Opinionated.*

"Ribs?" Kathryn got a funny look on her face, but she opened the cupboard, counted out six plates, and carried them out the back door to the porch.

Avis was so flustered she almost didn't hear the oven timer beeping away. But after muddling around for a few minutes putting paper napkins in a basket and dishing up the greens, she suddenly remembered the cornbread and pulled it out of the oven. Still okay. *Lord, You're going to have to help me here. Because right now I'm ready to sit that girl down and teach her a few manners.*

"Ribs are ready!" Peter called out. "And I'm starving! Let's eat!"

In a few minutes the glass-topped table on the back porch was full of food—a heaping platter of pungent ribs, the creamy macaroni and cheese, the steaming dish of greens, hot cornbread, honey, butter, and a frosty pitcher of sweet iced tea. Avis had planned to use disposable plastic tumblers, but she brought out tall glasses at the last minute. The paper napkins, however, were going to stay.

Peter asked Nick to say a blessing, which the young man did, and Avis was touched that he prayed "for these good people who have been so kind to us." Well, yes. She was going to be kind if it killed her.

"It's nice out here." Olivia settled into a wicker chair with her plate, on which she'd put a dainty serving of everything. "We haven't used our back porch yet. Everything's still covered with tarps or something. You can see quite a bit of sky from up here on the third floor. And I like all the flower boxes on those porches over there."

Avis enjoyed having a place to sit outside too, though the view wasn't anything to rave about. Just the paved alley behind the garage and the garages and back porches of the buildings across the alley that faced the next street over—a mixture of two-story homes, two-flats, and three-flats—though a number of backyard locust trees and flowering magnolias helped "green" the alley. Right now, billowing white thunderheads towered overhead, taking over the blue sky. But Olivia was right—many of the porches across the way already had flower boxes hung on the railings, full of petunias and trailing vinca vines and ivy. Something that would have to wait at the Douglass household until school was out next week.

"You like flowers, Olivia?"

"Oh yes!" The pale blonde was quite pretty when she smiled. Took away the deer-in-the-headlights look she often wore. "When I have my own home someday, I'm going to have hanging baskets in every window. But right now I'm taking care of Mrs. Candy's violets and other indoor plants. I like it."

Peter was serving up the ribs as the others filled their plates at the table. On a whim Avis said, "*Hm*. I could use some help with my flowers. The ones I planted in front of the building, I mean. Seems that I forget to water them when it doesn't rain."

"Oh, I'd be glad to do it!" Olivia beamed, a touch of pink coming into her cheeks. "In fact, I'll confess. I saw that they looked a bit wilted this morning, so I watered everything. I hope that was okay."

Avis chuckled. "Very okay. Thank you, Olivia."

"What? No ribs?" Peter was saying. He'd stuck his barbecue fork into a nice rack of ribs and was offering it to Kathryn.

But Kathryn shook her head. "No thanks. I'm sure they're good. But I don't eat red meat. I'll be fine."

"I'll take that," Nick said, holding out his plate. "Everything looks great."

By the time they were all served and sitting in the wicker porch chairs, Avis noticed that Kathryn had only taken some cornbread and macaroni and cheese. Good grief. What was wrong with the greens? . . . Oh, right. The smoked neck bones. Avis supposed that was on her no-no list too. It was all she could do to keep from rolling her eyes.

But Nick was obviously enjoying the food. "You make your own sauce, Mr. Douglass? You wouldn't consider sharing your recipe, would you? . . . *Hm.* Didn't think so." Nick grinned as Peter slyly shook his head. "But let me tell you, I don't get to eat like this living with three women!"

Everyone laughed, though Avis realized that Kathryn had disappeared into the kitchen, reappearing a few moments later with a glass of water.

Avis made a concerted effort to keep the conversation light, asking about hometowns—Brygitta was from Detroit, Olivia from Minneapolis, Nick from Portland, Oregon, Kathryn from Phoenix—and areas of study. She was surprised to learn that Olivia had another year before getting her BA in sociology. The girl seemed too timid to go into social work. Maybe she'd do something else—research?

"Yeah, I don't graduate until January," Nick was saying. "I, uh, still need to do an internship, and I have a couple more classes to complete for my master's in divinity."

"He was actually hoping to do an internship at SouledOut," Kathryn piped up. "But—"

"Kat. Don't." Nick glared at her.

"But—"

"Kat." There was a warning note in Nick's voice.

A sudden gust of wind blew some of the paper napkins out of the basket, and Avis felt a drop in the temperature. "Uh-oh. I think that thunderstorm is finally here. We better move all this food inside."

The next ten minutes were a bit hurry-scurry, as everyone grabbed dirty dishes and the bowls and platters of food. Fat raindrops started to spatter on the porch railing just as the sky lit up with a lightning flash, followed several moments later by a loud crack of thunder that made everyone jump. But they managed to get everything inside before the heavens really let loose with sheets of rain blowing over the porch.

"Whew. That came on fast." Kat started scraping the plates over the food disposal in the sink as Avis stuck two Bakers Square pies in the oven.

Nick grinned. "Yeah. I like it. Not like Portland rain, which is mostly a wet mist that just hangs around for days. Uh, what can I do to help?"

"I'm washing dishes. You can dry." Kat had already run a sink full of sudsy water and now ran hot water into the second sink for rinsing.

"Kathryn, we have a dishwasher." Avis pointed. "Just rinse the plates and load them in there."

"I don't mind. It saves water if we just wash them." Kathryn plunged the stack of dishes under the suds.

"Actually, it doesn't, Kathryn. Our dishwasher is a new Energy Saver and uses less water than you've already drawn in the sink there. But since you've already started, go ahead this time."

"Oh." Kathryn hesitated. "Uh, well, electricity then."

Focus on the positives, Avis told herself as she put leftovers away and got out pie plates and dessert forks. *At least the girl is helpful.*

When the dishes were done, Avis took the pies out to the dining room table, followed by Nick and Kathryn carrying the pie plates and forks. In the living room Peter was showing Brygitta and Olivia his Software Symphony website on a laptop. "You should come see this, Nick." Brygitta waved him over. "You know more about computer software than we do. It's really cool."

But Kathryn stopped by the family pictures clustered on a bookshelf between the dining room and living room. "Are these your other daughters?" She picked up a photo.

Avis glanced up from the blueberry pie she was cutting. "Yes, that's Charette, my . . . our oldest. That's her husband, Tom, and their twins, Tabitha and Toby. They live in Cincinnati."

"And this?"

"Our youngest, Natasha. She lives and works in Washington, D.C."

Kathryn picked up the photo of Rochelle and Conny. "So Rochelle is your middle daughter and lives here in Chicago, right? She's beautiful. Surprised she's not married."

Avis was taken aback. Where did this nosy girl get off *presuming* Rochelle was single? Probably assumed she wasn't married when she had Conny. Well, she'd correct that. "She was married to Conny's father," Avis said, tight-lipped. "But the man was abusive. She had to leave for safety's sake. So, yes, she's a single mom now."

"Abusive?"

The look on Kathryn's face seemed horrified. Avis raised her eyebrows. "Yes. It happens, Kathryn, even in the best of families. Most of us have situations, either in our immediate families or extended families, that are less than perfect—"

"Yes, I know," Kathryn murmured. "About that less-than-perfect part."

Avis blinked. Was the girl dealing with some pain in her own family? She usually came across so confident, so . . . together. Avis's irritation softened. "Yes, well, fortunately God is still in the redemption business, so we keep praying for Rochelle's ex. But at least Rochelle and Conny are safe from him now."

Setting the photo down, Kathryn was strangely quiet as the others came to the table. Avis served up the warm pies. "Blueberry or apple?" She put a thin sliver of both on Peter's plate. The occasional dessert didn't hurt. "Anybody for à la mode? Peter, will you do the honors?"

Several plates were slid toward Peter and his ice cream scoop.

"Uh, no thanks," Kathryn said. "Actually, I need to go." She abruptly headed for the front door. "Please excuse me. Something I forgot. Thanks for having us, Mrs. D. Bye, Mr. D!" And she was gone.

"Kat?" Nick got up and started to follow, but Brygitta pulled him back into his chair with a shake of her head.

Peter sent Avis a questioning look. She gave a slight shrug. What was *that* about?

Chapter 33

Grabbing a waterproof windbreaker from her bedroom, Kat hurried on down the stairs and out the front door of the three-flat. The heavy thunderstorm had passed, leaving only a drizzle behind. But she needed to walk. Not talk. Her friends would leave the Douglasses soon and want to know why she left—and she couldn't tell them! She'd confided to Brygitta about meeting Rochelle at the Dumpsters, but that was before Conny showed up and spilled the beans. And again she'd promised not to say anything to the Douglasses.

Tucking her thick hair into the hood of the windbreaker, Kat walked quickly down the tree-lined street, the freshly washed leaves softening the concrete and bricks of the urban neighborhood.

Oh God, what am I supposed to do?! Mrs. Douglass said Rochelle's ex was abusive—and she assumed Rochelle and Conny were safe from him. But Conny said he was living with his dad! Was he in danger?

The residential blocks gave way to Sheridan Road, a busy north-south street. Crossing with the light, Kat kept walking for another block and found herself at a dead-end cul-de-sac facing Lake Michigan, a park off to the left, and a sign saying Pratt Avenue Beach. Ahead of her, a concrete fishing pier jutted out into the lake.

Cutting through the park, Kat headed out onto the pier, deserted after the rain. The choppy lake looked gray and ominous, throwing foamy waves against the sandy beach. She'd have to come back and find this pier again when the weather was nicer—though the lake had a wildness right now that reflected the churning in her own spirit.

How important was her promise to not tell? Rochelle had been adamant about not wanting her mother to know Kat had seen her. Which probably meant the Douglasses hadn't actually seen their daughter recently and maybe didn't even know where their daughter was living. So if she told Mr. and Mrs. D, would that help anything? Could they do something about it?

On the other hand, if Rochelle found out that she told, she'd definitely be upset. Maybe undo everything Kat had done so far to build a little trust between them. The girl was so skittish! How easy it would be for Rochelle to disappear out of Kat's life as quickly as she'd appeared.

Hardly noticing that she was getting fairly soaked from the mist and spray, Kat turned at the end and walked back along the pier. Because of the heavy cloud cover, nightfall was overtaking the city early. But her thoughts were racing. What were her options? If she didn't tell Mrs. Douglass what she knew, then—short of not doing anything—it seemed like she had only one option.

She had to find Rochelle and talk to *her.*

Kat fidgeted all through the worship service on Sunday. Nick had been exasperated because she'd walked out on the Douglasses' supper party and wouldn't tell him why. "Look, I've just got something on my mind," she'd said. "Can't you just leave it at that?"

"*Uh-huh.* Fine talk coming from the girl who told *me*, 'We're your friends! You can tell us what's bothering you!'" He'd left her alone the rest of the evening.

To Brygitta she'd just murmured, "It's that whole Rochelle thing I told you about. Just pray about it, will you? And don't say anything."

Olivia had fussed at her like a mother hen, sure that Kat would catch her death of cold when she came in dripping wet. She'd run a hot bath and made Kat get into dry clothes—which was kind of humorous, given that Livie was the "little sister" of the group.

Now, sitting in the next-to-last row at SouledOut, Kat glanced often at the Douglasses, sitting in the second row on the far right side, their usual place. It was all she could do not to run up there and tell Mrs. D that she'd seen her daughter not once, but three times now, had talked to her, and had seen Conny too. That their grandson was staying with his father, and if they were worried, they should get him away quick! But she felt frozen. What had happened between them and Rochelle?

Last night out on the pier, finding Rochelle and pleading with her to get Conny out of his father's house had seemed like a good idea. But how? When? The only place she knew to look for her was at the Dumpsters behind the Dominick's on Sheridan Road—but mini-term was over and she wasn't commuting between CCU and Rogers Park anymore. She'd have to make a special trip. Was she scheduled to work Wednesday night? Even if she wasn't, it was a crapshoot whether Rochelle would even be there.

Pastor Cobbs got up to preach, but Kat barely listened. The Douglasses had seemed like such a together couple when she first met them. The kind of parents she wished she had—a school principal and local businessman, down-to-earth professions, people who would understand her changing her major to education, her desire to teach kids. Also solid Christians who wouldn't make fun of a daughter's new faith. In fact, watching Mrs. D worship had touched something deep inside Kat, something she hadn't really experienced as a new Christian. Mrs. Douglass seemed to have a very real, very deep, *personal* relationship with God.

And yet . . . Kat had had a hard time getting to know her, even though she and Mr. D lived right upstairs. A distance she couldn't quite break through. Why did she think they could be friends? Mrs. Douglass seemed out of touch with *her* daughter too.

Was it any different than the distance she felt from her own parents? Her father's letter—if you could call it that—was tucked in her backpack. Not a word asking how she was or what she was doing. Did they know her *at all*? Did they even care?

Her thoughts were interrupted by the sax player, a tall black guy with just a tinge of a Jamaican accent who'd been leading worship that morning and came to the mike again after the pastor sat down. "This song by LeToya Luckett may talk to you as it did to me, when I was going t'ru a rough time. Seemed to have mi name, Oscar Frost, written all over it." He turned to the music group and snapped his fingers, "One . . . two . . ."

Kat listened as the praise team sang, "When life closes in, praise . . ." Others in the congregation joined in, but Kat just listened. The song had her name written all over it too. Talking about when things didn't make sense . . . when there seemed to be no way . . . when the pain wouldn't end . . . praise anyway! Give it everything you've got! Lift up your voice and praise God!

A glance toward the right front showed Avis Douglass lifting her voice, lifting her hands, and practically shouting her praise. But even from the back, Kat could see tears running down her face.

Was she crying because of her daughter? If so, how did she do it? How did she praise through her pain?

Kat wasn't there. Didn't know how to get there either.

It wasn't like her parents were abusive or alcoholics or anything, just . . . not there for her. Most people would say, "*What are you complaining about? Count your blessings! You've grown up with money, college, opportunities. You're a privileged kid.*"

Still . . . the empty hole inside hurt. Hurt a lot, if she let it.

After the song the pastor reminded everyone about the upcoming congregational meeting Wednesday night to discuss interim leadership and other issues related to Pastor Clark's sudden graduation to Glory. "Nonmembers are welcome to attend this meeting and give input, but anything requiring a vote will be limited to members. Are there any other announcements or prayer requests before we close?"

To Kat's surprise, Brygitta popped up. "Just want to thank God that Kat Davies and I found a job at The Common Cup over on Morse Avenue. It's a full-time job but we're sharing it, each half time. But Olivia Lindberg and Nick Taylor still need to find summer jobs if anyone has any leads. Thank you!"

Olivia and Nick both looked a bit embarrassed, but the pastor took it in stride, even including a prayer for those who needed jobs in his benediction. And then chairs scraped as people mingled and moved toward the coffee table. Kat sighed and stood up. She should just get a grip. *Good grief.* She did have a lot of blessings—good friends, a place to live, this church, even a new job! She should—

"Sister Kathryn! How are you, *mi amiga*?" Edesa Baxter leaned over a chair and gave Kat a hug. "So happy to hear you found a job! Congratulations! But . . . pouring coffee? Didn't you tell me you wanted to find a job as a tutor?"

Kat nodded. "Well, yes. Eventually. But Bree and I just stumbled on this job. It practically fell into our laps. So we decided to split it—half time each. Figured a half-time job was better than no job at all."

Edesa lifted her eyebrows under the tight corkscrew ringlets that fell over her forehead. "So you are still free half time?" Her smile widened until her dark eyes crinkled. "Then you should see Sister Avis! She runs a summer program at the elementary school. It is called STEP—Summer Tutoring and Enrichment Program. It starts next week, I believe. I'm pretty sure they can always use more tutors. Except . . . it doesn't pay. All volunteer staff. But if you're interested, you can ask Jodi Baxter or her husband, Denny, about it. They volunteer in the program."

Kat's heart had started beating faster the moment she heard the word "tutoring." A summer program at Mrs. Douglass's school? That would be perfect!

Only after Edesa had given her another hug and flitted away to talk to someone else did it occur to Kat that she should've asked if Edesa had thought any more about teaching a class in nutrition this summer.

Oh well. One thing at a time. She'd check out the STEP possibility first. Hopefully she'd be able to work something around her work hours at the coffee shop.

Sacked out on the living room couch with Bree watching a Hercule Poirot Mystery that evening—it felt *so* good not to have any homework hanging over their heads—Kat heard somebody's cell phone ring. She listened. "Dance of the Sugarplum Fairy" ringtone. "Livie's phone," she muttered and turned back to the TV. But a moment later they heard a screech and Olivia dashed into the room, cell phone in one hand, watering can in the other.

"I can't believe it!" Her mouth was a round O. "That was Amanda Baxter—you know, Jodi and Denny Baxter's daughter from church. She's home from U of I. After what you said in church this morning, Bree, she called to say she knows about a nanny job up in Wilmette. This family had called her, but she already has *two* nanny jobs for the summer and had to say no.

But she said she called them this afternoon and they still need someone if I'm interested." Olivia looked from one to the other, blue eyes wide. "What do you think? Should I do it?"

Bree laughed out loud. "Ha-ha. See, Kat, I took lessons from you about speaking up, letting people know what we need. And look! A job for Livie. Wahoo!"

Kat turned down the volume with the TV remote—though Poirot was just about to do his reveal-all summation to the gathered souls in the drawing room. "That's really cool, Livie. If you like babysitting. But Wilmette? Isn't that a suburb up north? How would you get there?"

Olivia shrugged. "The El I guess. Amanda said it goes that far." She made a face. "I don't really like to ride the El by myself, but . . . I guess people do it." She plopped down on the couch. "Would you guys pray with me about it? I mean, it's already an answer to prayer, but guess I need some prayer for wisdom. And courage."

Giving up on the final scene with the funny Belgium detective—Kat was sure the nephew had done it—she turned the TV off so the three of them could pray. But as they held hands with Livie and prayed about the nanny job, she wished desperately that she could ask her friends to pray for her. She needed wisdom too! And courage.

But right now she felt alone with her secret.

The next few days seemed to drag, even though Kat's evening shifts at the coffee shop were busy. She'd hoped to catch Mrs.

Douglass and ask her if they still needed tutors for the STEP program this summer, but it was the last week of school at Bethune Elementary and by the time the principal got home, Kat was at work.

On Wednesday Livie asked Bree if she'd go with her on the El to talk to the family in Wilmette, to help her figure out how to navigate, so Bree traded with Kat for the evening shift—which worked out perfectly for Kat. As soon as she got off work at five o'clock, she headed for the Morse Avenue El station and took the southbound Red Line. If everything worked out, she might even get back in time to go to that meeting at the church.

But . . . what was she going to say to Rochelle? Would she even be there? As the train swayed and jerked between stations, her thoughts became jerky prayers. *Oh God, help me here . . . I feel caught in the middle . . . I don't really understand why Rochelle doesn't want to talk to her mom . . . Am I getting myself involved in a big mess? . . . Am I doing the right thing?*

The day had turned hot and sticky. Getting off at the Berwyn stop, she walked quickly to Sheridan Road and down the two blocks to the Dominick's grocery store. Around to the back. A semi was unloading. Boxes of food were wheeled in. Store personnel came in and out, dumping stuff in the Dumpsters.

Man, how she'd love to see what the pickin's were tonight!

But no Rochelle.

Maybe it was still too early. But it was too hot to hang around outside. Kat went inside and wandered around the air-conditioned store, her mouth salivating at the heaping displays of vegetables and fruits in the produce section. Every fifteen minutes she walked outside and checked the back of the store.

Still no Rochelle.

But by six thirty the truck was gone. And by seven o'clock the double doors leading into the storerooms no longer swung open. Two men—street people by the look of them—showed up in the alley and started digging in the Dumpsters. She might as well check to see what was what before everything was gone.

But she had no sooner lifted a Dumpster lid and spied a box of overripe bananas than she heard a voice right behind her. "I was hoping I'd find you here."

She whirled. "Rochelle!"

The young woman was dressed in a black tank top, khaki capris, and gym shoes with no socks. A cloth bag hung over her shoulder. Nice threads, though a bit rumpled, as if she'd worn them for several days. Her black hair seemed wilder than usual, thick and long and curly. Her honey-brown skin glowed with perspiration in the heat.

"You were looking for me?" Kat couldn't have been more surprised.

"Yes. I need you to do something for me."

"You need . . . well, sure. If I can."

Rochelle jerked her head for Kat to follow and they walked away from the two men digging in the Dumpsters. Eyes darting, as if to make sure no one was watching them, Rochelle dug in the cloth bag and pulled out a small square box wrapped in brown paper and tied with a red ribbon. "Could you sneak this into my mom's bedroom and put it on her dresser? It's, um, a belated birthday present, and I . . . want to surprise her."

"Oh, Rochelle! Why don't you just come to the house and give it to her! She would be so happy to see you—"

"I can't. Just do it, will you? But she can't see you do it."

Kat shook her head. "I don't understand. I'm not sure I could sneak into her bedroom. Why don't I just leave it outside her door at the top of the stairs? She wouldn't know—"

"No!" Rochelle's eyes flickered with panic. "That's not safe. It might get stolen. It's . . . it's special, and you have to put it somewhere she'll find it, but somewhere safe." She thrust the box into Kat's hands. "Please. It's important." She turned and walked quickly away.

"Rochelle! Wait! I need to talk to you about—"

"Meet me here next week!" she tossed over her shoulder and started to run.

And was gone.

Chapter 34

A smile snuck past Avis's fatigue as she climbed the stairs to their third-floor apartment late Wednesday afternoon. Only two more days of school—and Friday was just an hour to pick up report cards and satisfy the school board that it was a "school day." Oh, the excitement she used to feel as a kid on that final day. School's out, school's out!

She started to laugh, remembering the silly pop song her brother used to belt out this time every year. *"Can't wait for summer to throw away my books . . ."* The middle part was a muddle, something about "fishing hooks" and "girls in their bathing suits." Ha. But she could still hear her brother belting out the last line: *"Can't wait for summer, for good ol' summertime!"*

Ah, those were the days. She'd been nine years old when the sixties rolled in. Summer meant playing hopscotch on the sidewalk outside their walk-up in Philly. Screaming and jumping in water spraying from a fire hydrant. Begging the boys to let her play baseball with them in the vacant lot. Innocent summer fun . . .

And then the world went crazy. The president was shot. Civil rights marches spread from city to city. Images on the TV burned themselves into her brain—snarling police dogs, fire hoses used on people, the Ku Klux Klan in their scary white hoods. Her daddy made her stay inside.

And then it got worse. Martin Luther King was shot. Hot and hopeless, people rioted in city after city, burning down their own neighborhoods.

Those were days she'd like to forget . . . like to think were behind them.

Shaking off the ugly memories, she let herself in the front door—and found Peter sprawled on the couch, watching the news on TV. "You're home early. Everything okay?" He usually worked late on Wednesdays and went straight to the church for midweek Bible study. Except it was the congregational meeting tonight.

"Yeah, yeah, I'm fine. Just thought I'd come home early so we could, you know, go to the meeting together. I even picked up some Chinese on the way home so we wouldn't have to cook."

"Brownie points for you, because I'm beat." Avis kicked off her low heels and curled up on the couch next to her husband. "*Mm.* Wish we could just stay home tonight. Watch a movie. Play Scrabble. Soak my feet."

Peter snorted. "Don't tempt me. Not exactly looking forward to this meeting tonight. But can't let the kids downstairs show us up, can we?"

"What do you mean?"

"Nick and the little blonde—Olivia—were leaving just as I came in. She was all excited, said she just got hired as a nanny up in Wilmette starting tomorrow. They were walking up to Howard Street so they'd be on time for the meeting."

"Just the two of them?"

"Uh-huh. They said Brygitta has to work at the coffee shop tonight, and they didn't seem to know where Kathryn was."

Avis shook her head. "That Kathryn—she's a strange one. Wonder why she left so abruptly Saturday night."

"I have no idea. Maybe you should just ask her . . . Okay, okay, I see that look! But I was proud of you, Avis. You were a gracious hostess that evening, even though she stuck up her nose at our cooking." He chuckled. "Nick, now, he couldn't get enough of it! Or her, for that matter."

"Her, who?"

"Kathryn. Nick's sweet on her. Didn't you notice how he watches her out of the corner of his eye? And when she left, he was ready to chase after her."

"*Humph*. Could just be looking out for her like a big brother. She's an only child, you know. She needs a big brother."

"*Huh*. Those weren't big brother looks. I'm a guy. I know these things."

Avis laughed. "Then he'd better think twice, or he'll be eating Dumpster food and veggie burgers the rest of his life."

Peter scratched his chin thoughtfully. "He's a nice kid. In fact . . . I've been thinking about offering him a job at Software Symphony for the summer. Would have to crunch some figures with our accountant, and it'd only be part-time, but we could use some help in the mail room. Sales picked up by a whisker last week. Maybe this economic slump is starting to turn around."

"That'd be nice," Avis murmured. She could feel her eyelids drooping. Oh, how she'd like to just stretch out here and fall asleep.

Peter pushed himself off the couch. "Put your feet up for five more minutes. I know how to serve up food out of those little white cardboard boxes. And then, guess we better go face the giants."

The turnout was pretty good for a Wednesday night. Avis and Peter arrived at five to seven on purpose—not too early, to avoid getting into chatty conversations before the meeting, but not late, either. Avis hesitated before moving to her usual seat in the second row on the far right aisle. Did she want to be so close to the front tonight when at least part of the meeting would be about them? On the other hand, she didn't really want to be looking at other people, trying to second-guess their expressions.

She and Peter sat in their usual seats.

Pastor Cobbs, looking a lot healthier this week, started the meeting right at seven, even though people were still coming in. Calling Matt Kepler to the keyboard, the pastor started off with the hymn "How Firm a Foundation." Even though the hymn was an old one and familiar, Avis closed her eyes and heard the words as if for the first time.

How firm a foundation, ye saints of the Lord,
Is laid for your faith in His excellent Word! . . .

And then the second verse . . .

Fear not, I am with thee, oh, be not dismayed,
For I am thy God, and will still give thee aid;
I'll strengthen thee, help thee, and cause thee to stand,
Upheld by My gracious, omnipotent hand.

"Thank You, Jesus," she whispered as the hymn came to a close. She needed that assurance tonight, that God's Word was her foundation, and His Word promised that God would never leave or forsake them, no matter what happened in this meeting tonight. Would never leave or forsake Rochelle and Conny either.

"Praise God, church!" Pastor Cobbs seemed buoyant and confident as he gripped either side of the small wooden podium. "I'm glad so many of you came tonight, as we seek God's face about the future of SouledOut Community Church. We have several issues to attend to in the wake of the loss of our beloved Pastor Clark—one of which, certainly, is the question of calling someone to take Pastor Clark's place as copastor of this congregation. For that we will need a pastoral search committee, and I'm suggesting that names can be submitted this evening in writing to the elders for that purpose . . . yes, Brother Meeks?"

Sherman Meeks stood, polite and humble as usual. "Thank you, Pastor. It's true that you and Pastor Clark started this church as copastors, and it's been a blessing. But have you considered—should we as a church consider—whether God is simply putting the mantle on you to be our pastor without calling another?" And he sat down.

A murmur rippled through the people gathered in the chairs, some heads nodding, others shaking, many whispering. "Sure would save some money in the budget," someone cracked on the other side of the room. A few people laughed nervously. A few others said, "Amen."

Pastor Cobbs pursed his lips a long moment before speaking. "As I shared on Sunday, I feel this church benefits from a plurality of leadership, because of the nature of this church. We are not a homogeneous church. We have a diversity of races, cultures, colors, ages—which is God's blessing, amen?"

More *amens* peppered the room.

"So I believe we would do well to continue with a plurality of leadership, even though we can't represent every one of our Heinz 57 varieties."

More chuckles.

"Pastor?" Another hand shot up.

"Yes, Elder David."

Now Avis did turn her head. David Brown stood up, thick glasses hiding his eyes. "I agree with you, Pastor, about needing a plurality of leadership, given our, um, mixed membership." He swept a hand to indicate the people in the room. "But just to be clear . . . what you're saying is, the copastor we would be looking for should be, uh, Caucasian—to be an integrated team like you and Pastor Clark."

More murmurings. Avis felt her neck and shoulders tensing. Pastor Clark held up his hand and waited until the room quieted. "If God sends us a white pastor with a heart for unity amid our diversity, praise God. But no, I didn't say that specifically. God might send us an Hispanic pastor, or Asian . . . I don't want to limit what God wants to do."

"But to be realistic," David Brown continued, "our congregation is mostly blacks and whites. And since you already represent the African-Americans here—"

"Excuse me, Brother David. A correction." Denny Baxter stood up, looking for all the world like a former football player, square jaw on a thick neck, All-American good looks, graying hair, dimples in his cheeks. "I'm not African-American, but Pastor Cobbs represents *me*. I believe both he and Pastor Clark were pastors for all of us."

Clapping erupted around the room. Avis didn't move. Out of the corner of her eye she saw the door open and Kathryn Davies slip into the room, finding a seat beside Nick and Olivia toward the back.

Pastor Cobbs cleared his throat. He'd lost his buoyant look. "Thank you, Brother Denny. That is certainly my heart. Brother David, I'm not sure what your point is. Can you clarify what you're trying to say?"

David Brown stood his ground. "All I'm saying is, if in the long run we want to hire a pastor to represent the diversity among us, I'm a bit confused at the present proposal for interim leadership . . ."

"Here we go," Peter muttered. He gripped her hand.

Chapter 35

David Brown's voice was Mr. Congeniality. "With all due respect to the Douglasses, who are five-star members here at SouledOut—"

Avis winced. *Doesn't he realize how sarcastic that sounds?*

"—that would make our interim leadership team unbalanced racially. Three black leaders. Surely there are some white folks in the congregation who could fill Pastor Clark's shoes until we find a more permanent pastor—sorry—copastor, I mean."

Some heads were nodding. Pastor Cobbs seemed to be weighing his next words carefully. "Well, this *is* a meeting for congregational input. We could certainly put some more names on the ballot if you'd like. But I wanted to avoid making this a popularity contest or a bidding war—which is why I proposed only one set of names to share the position."

"Absolutely. But it might be a relief to the Douglasses to know this isn't riding on their shoulders alone. They are busy people, we all know, and already carry a lot of responsibility . . ."

Irritation crawled up Avis's spine. How dare he pretend to speak for them—without even talking to them about it?

". . . but right here in our congregation, we have a young man who will soon graduate from seminary, who needs an internship in a local church to finish his studies. I'd like to nominate Nick Taylor for our interim leadership team." Smiling broadly, David Brown swept a hand toward where Nick sat with Kathryn and Olivia.

Nick's head jerked up, startled. "What? Oh no, that's not—"

Kathryn waved her hand. "I second the motion!" Then she turned to Nick. "You *do* need an internship, Nick. And you said you'd love to do it here."

"Excuse me." Sherman Meeks stood again. "With all due respect to the young man, he's only been here a couple of months and he isn't a member, whereas the Douglasses are seasoned members, with a lot of experience in this church."

"An' nonmembers can't second the motion or vote neither." Florida Hickman eyed Kathryn deliberately. The girl reddened.

"Sisters and brothers!" Pastor Cobbs's voice took a sharp tone. "We are out of order here! These are not decisions to argue about or to make lightly." He seemed to study the congregation, his eyes sweeping to and fro. Then he closed his eyes and lifted a hand. "I would like everyone to be quiet and just pray for a few minutes. We need to wait on the Lord."

Shaken, Avis squeezed her eyes shut. Hadn't the elders agreed among themselves with putting the pastor's proposal for interim leadership to the congregation? Why was David Brown challenging it now? Challenging her and Peter, to be blunt about it.

Unfortunately, she had a good idea. His wife. Mary had been talking to him, telling him to speak up before it was too late and the church ended up "too black." And Kathryn just added to the confusion! Though . . . she was probably just sticking up for her friend, jumping in half-baked, not realizing how it impacted them.

Lord, help us. Avis's jumbled thoughts became half prayers. *Lord, am I willing to give up the idea of being an interim pastor? Well, yes . . . I was happy being just a worship leader before this even came up! So why do I feel resentful about David Brown's challenge? Oh God! Help me not to give in to resentment. Help me not to make Mary and David Brown my enemies. You said to love our enemies, Lord. Help me to—*

"We wait for You, Lord, to show us the way. Amen." Pastor Cobbs's voice broke into her thought-prayers. "Brothers and sisters, it's clear to me that we are not in a position to move forward tonight. And that's all right. To move forward in unity takes time. So I'd like to resume this congregational meeting in two weeks, same time, to consider two things: our interim leadership, and nominations for a pastoral search committee. If you have names to suggest for either, please send them to me or one of the elders personally by the end of next week, so the elders and I can consider them and present a slate to all of you. Are there any announcements or other business that we should attend to right now? If not, Elder Debra Meeks, would you close us out in prayer?"

Avis and Peter slipped out from the meeting as quickly as they could. Peter was tight-lipped all the way home. Parking the

Lexus in the garage, he finally slammed a hand on the steering wheel. "Fine. Let them put this boy in Pastor Clark's place. He's got the main thing going for him—he's *white*."

Avis was startled out of her own struggling thoughts. "Peter! It's not Nick's fault. You said yourself he's a nice kid. You were impressed with him. David Brown is just . . . just *using* him to get at us. Or maybe not us personally . . . I don't know. Whatever's going on, it's not Nick's fault."

Peter snorted. "Yeah, well . . ." He got out of the car, slammed the door, and stalked up the outdoor back stairs of the three-flat.

Avis followed. Peter had already flopped down in front of the TV news when she came in the back door. But she had no sooner put on some water to boil, hoping to brew some herbal tea to calm their nerves, when she heard a knock at the door. The TV volume jacked up louder. *Hm.* Peter obviously wasn't going to get the door.

Nick Taylor stood in the hallway. "Mrs. Douglass, I—"

"Come in, Nick . . . Peter?" she called over her shoulder. "It's Nick."

Nick stepped just inside the door and Peter, put on the spot, turned the TV down and appeared at her side. "Nick," he acknowledged.

"Mr. and Mrs. Douglass . . ." Nick took off his baseball cap, twisting it in his hands. "I want you to know I had nothing to do with Mr. Brown putting my name out there. I think the two of you would make a wonderful interim pastoral team, and if I were a member, I'd vote for you. Twice!"

Peter let a wry grin slip. "Yeah, that's what good Chicagoans do. Vote early and often." He glanced at Avis, chewed his lip a moment, and then sighed. "It's all right, Nick. It'll all work out. Actually, I remember you said something last Saturday night about needing to do a pastoral internship to complete your studies. You're hoping to do that at SouledOut?"

Nick looked distressed. "That was before Pastor Clark died. I'd thought about asking the pastors about it—but then everything changed. And I know this church needs more than an intern now, especially someone who has no experience yet—like me. So I gave up that idea. I don't know how Mr. Brown found out."

Peter nodded. "Don't worry about it, son. Thanks for coming up." He stuck out his hand. "Don't know how God's going to work this all out, but . . ."

Nick shook Peter's hand, then Avis's hand, and scurried back downstairs. Avis closed the door and raised her eyebrows at Peter.

"Okay, okay." He made a face. "You're right. It's not his fault. Just . . . makes it complicated, is all."

Complicated . . . That was the truth. Avis had no idea what was going to happen next at SouledOut.

Avis pushed the uncertainty to the back of her mind the next few days so she could focus on ending school well in spite of muggy temperatures pushing into the nineties. The end-of-year assembly to which parents had been invited took place the following afternoon, and she had to smile as her "tame the bully"

strategy unfolded before her eyes. Derrick Blue, chin up, grinning, wearing a white shirt and bolo tie, his usually shaggy hair slicked and combed to the side, marched down one aisle of the auditorium carrying the American flag, and little Sammy Blumenthal—white shirt, bow tie, yarmulke clipped to his hair—marched down the other carrying the Illinois flag.

Neither of Derrick's parents showed up though. *Lord, give Derrick a glimpse of his worth in spite of his family situation*, she breathed. She made sure to congratulate him and tell him how handsome he looked all dressed up.

Avis stayed late at school Thursday night as teachers turned in final grades and report cards, and she was back early Friday morning to make sure the hour-long "day" moved like clockwork. And it would have, too, except that a deafening clap of thunder drowned out the final bell at ten o'clock and rain poured from the sky. Antsy students eager to leave were diverted into the auditorium where parents could pick them up; students riding buses were held until a break in the rain, and in general the whole process took twice as long.

And no one came to pick up Derrick Blue, even though the thunderstorm passed and the sun poked out. But Sammy Blumenthal plucked at his daddy's coat sleeve and whispered in his ear. Mr. Blumenthal—bearded, wearing a black widebrim hat, the fringe of a prayer shawl peeking out from beneath his black coat—spoke to Avis in a solemn voice. "We can take the young man home. If there's no one there, he can play with Sammy until someone gets home. Is that all right?"

Avis nodded. "I'll call his mother at work and let her know. Give me your phone number in case she wants to contact you."

Much preferable to making Derrick stay at the school until three that afternoon.

It was nearly eleven by the time Avis got back to her office. She stopped and spoke to the school secretary about locking up, and the woman cut her eyes at Avis's door, which was slightly ajar. *"Someone to see you,"* she mouthed.

Avis smiled her thanks for the heads-up.

Pushing the door open, at first she didn't see anyone. No one sitting in the guest chair in front of her desk. Then she saw the person—a young woman—standing behind her desk at the window, back to her, looking out, somewhat silhouetted in the bright sunlight streaming in through the blinds.

Avis's heart leaped. Full, dark hair, rippling in frizzy waves past the young woman's shoulders and down her back.

She gasped. "Rochelle, honey!"

The person turned. Avis's shock turned to confusion. The girl had white skin and blue eyes—not her Rochelle's dark eyes and honey-brown complexion. How could she have been fooled like that? "Oh. It's you. What are you doing here, Kathryn?"

Kathryn Davies seemed flustered. "I'm sorry. You thought I was—"

"My mistake. The bright sun and shadows . . . never mind." Avis strode to her desk chair and indicated the chair on the other side of the desk. "You came to see me about something?"

Kathryn moved away from the window and sat in the chair. "Um, yes. I came to ask if you still need tutors for your STEP program. I'm only working part-time, so I'd have some time to volunteer."

"Yes, well . . . will you excuse me a moment? I'll get the

information." Avis left her office, closed the door behind her, and stepped into the empty hallway. Leaning against the wall, she fought back tears. For those few seconds in time, she'd thought Rochelle had come back, had wanted to see her, had come to make things right between them.

But it was only Kathryn Davies. *Kathryn Davies!* Who seemed to show up whether Avis wanted her to or not. She'd never realized how similar their dark hair was, only slightly different in color. Kathryn usually wore hers bunched up or pulled back. But today it was down. And silhouetted against the brightness of the window . . .

Or had she unconsciously sensed a similarity between Kathryn and Rochelle that she'd resented? Kathryn living under her feet, popping in and out of her life, when it should be Rochelle.

Oh God, she moaned. *What kind of cruel joke is this?*

Chapter 36

Kat fidgeted as she waited for Mrs. Douglass to return. *Did she really think I was her daughter at first?* Weird. She eyed her backpack resting on the floor by her feet. The small box wrapped in brown paper and red ribbon that Rochelle had given her was still in there. Should she leave it on Mrs. Douglass's desk? What a golden opportunity! She'd be sure to get it then.

Kat reached for the backpack—and then stopped. Even if she were able to sneak it onto the desk, Mrs. Douglass would know who put it there. Who was the last person in her office? *Duh.*

Wish I'd thought of doing this earlier. If she'd left the box and slipped out without Mrs. Douglass seeing her, that would've been perfect! Then she wouldn't have to figure out how to sneak into the woman's bedroom. *That* was not going to be easy.

But too late now. Still, what was taking the principal so long?

Just then the office door opened and Mrs. Douglass returned. "I'm sorry to keep you waiting, Kathryn. Here's the information about STEP." She handed Kat a packet of papers before sitting down at her desk. "And, yes, we can always use more tutors. The tutoring program runs from nine till twelve each morning, afternoon sports three afternoons a week, and field trips the other two afternoons. At least that's the plan. It all depends on volunteers and resources contributed by the business community." She eyed Kat across the desk. "Have you done tutoring before?"

Kat nodded eagerly. "Yes, back in high school I tutored in a summer program. It was one of the things that made me change my major from premed to education. And I had to do a certain number of hours tutoring other students at CCU as part of my master's requirements."

"What subjects?"

"Oh, most anything. I had to take a lot of science and math for premed at the University of Arizona, so that's what I tutored at CCU." Kat beamed. Hopefully Mrs. D was impressed with her résumé.

"And your work schedule at The Common Cup?"

"Well, it changes from week to week. But I'll ask for afternoons and evenings. If I get assigned to mornings, maybe Brygitta would trade with me."

Mrs. Douglass nodded and seemed to be thinking about it. "Well, if you're free Monday morning, show up here at nine for our volunteer training day. We start the actual program on Tuesday." She stood and held out her hand across the desk. "Thanks for coming in, Kathryn. We need all the help we can get."

It felt funny to shake hands, as if they'd never met before, but Kat shook the principal's hand, picked up her backpack, and headed for the front doors of the school. Guess the woman had to keep things "professional" at school. At the far end of the wide hallway, a janitor was busy mopping the floor, erasing the week's collection of footprints and dirt.

Elation quickened Kat's steps as she headed back to the three-flat. Her summer was coming together. A half-time job, half-time tutoring. Perfect! Should she call home and tell her parents? She'd promised herself to call at least once a week and it was almost the weekend. But imagining the phone call, the elation seeped out of her spirit like air from a pinhole. Her father would tell her she was foolish to settle for a half-time job. At a coffee bar at that. And her mother would probably want to know if the children she'd be tutoring were clean and disease free.

No, better send an e-mail.

Walking quickly along the damp sidewalks, her loose hair continuing to frizz in the rising humidity after the storm, Kat put her mind to the puzzle she had to solve: how to get Rochelle's birthday gift to her mom without Mrs. D knowing who put it there.

Saturday was sunny, warm, and clear—but Kat had to work the afternoon shift at The Common Cup. When she'd left the apartment, Nick, Bree, and Livie were talking about taking the El downtown to see Millennium Park. *Bummer!* At least working in her dad's office, she'd had weekends off . . . No, she wasn't going to go there. Wasn't this job a gift from God?

Keeping busy helped. Most of the orders that day were for iced coffees, flavored iced teas, cold juices, and yogurt parfaits. Kat put on a smile and cheerfully greeted customers, trying to learn the names of regulars. Checking the schedule for next week, she was pleased to see that she was scheduled for two afternoons, two evenings, and only one morning—which maybe she could trade.

But when Bree showed up at five o'clock to take the evening shift, Kat groused, "Don't wanna hear how much fun you had."

"We didn't go." Bree tied the apron Kat had just taken off around her own waist. "Decided to go tomorrow when we could all go. Besides, Livie wanted to shop for some craft supplies to use with her new charges. Something besides video games."

"Oh, you! I wasted a whole afternoon feeling sorry for myself!" Giving Bree a quick hug, Kat headed out the door. Maybe she'd go for a good brisk walk along the lakefront just to enjoy the beautiful evening before heading home. She was glad she'd worn her gym shoes to work—made it easier to be on her feet all afternoon.

But what Bree said was true. As soon as Kat got back to the apartment, Livie told her they'd decided to pack a lunch and head for Millennium Park right after worship the next day. "Oh . . . my sister e-mailed me today. Elin says she's really homesick for me." Her smile faded a bit. "I don't know, Kat. Maybe I should have gone to Madison, stayed with Aunt Gerty and Uncle Ben like she did—"

"Livie. Don't second-guess yourself. Staying in Chicago is

good! Why don't you invite Elin to come visit you here? It'd be fun."

Olivia shrugged. "Maybe. Guess I could ask her."

A thunderstorm rolled through the city as they got up the next morning, but had passed by the time the four friends walked to church, and the sky was starting to clear by the time the service was over. Kat and Livie grabbed their lunch out of the refrigerator in the church kitchen and headed for the front doors where Nick and Brygitta were already waiting. And then Kat saw Edesa Baxter, bouncing Gracie on her hip, talking to that curly redhead who was program director or something at Manna House.

"Livie, give me a minute, okay?" Kat handed her backpack with their lunch to Olivia and sidled over to where Edesa and the other woman were talking.

"Miss *Gato*!" Gracie squealed and held out her arms to Kat. Kat took the little girl in her arms.

"Buenos tardes, Kathryn!" Edesa flashed her wonderful smile. "Have you met Gabby Fairbanks?—oh." The redhead had already waved good-bye and hustled away. "Too late."

"It's you I wanted to see. Do you have a second?"

"Of course. Right, *niña*? Here . . . go find *Papá*." She took Gracie from Kat's arms, set her down, and shooed her away. "Shall we sit?"

Kat pulled up a chair. "I only have a minute. But I wanted to ask if you'd thought any more about teaching a nutrition class together here at the church. I think we'd make a great team."

Edesa's face grew thoughtful. Finally she said, "Kat, we need more than a minute to talk about this. I appreciate your eagerness to teach good nutrition to families in the neighborhood—but that would be like taking a scripture verse out of its context and trying to make it say something the context doesn't support. Do you see what I'm saying?"

"Um, not really."

"How can I explain? It's just that . . . nutrition is fine-tuning the whole area of people getting adequate food. There are things that have to happen first—getting something to eat—anything!—on a regular basis. Getting enough to eat. Getting food that tastes good so that kids will eat it . . . and so on. It's like Maslow's hierarchy of basic needs—you've studied that, I'm sure."

Kat nodded. Out of the corner of her eye, she saw Brygitta beckoning to her with a frustrated look on her face.

"Then you know a person isn't really interested in talking about self-respect or creativity or other areas of self-actualization until truly basic needs have been met—like food, shelter, safety. It's much the same when addressing the very real needs of adequate food for people with limited means. Nutrition would need to be taught within a broader context addressing even more basic needs."

"Oh." Kat saw Brygitta rolling her eyes. "Okay. I just thought . . . well, maybe we can talk more another time. Uh, thanks, Edesa." She walked quickly to where her friends were waiting. "Sorry about that. I didn't mean to take so long. Come on, let's go."

The afternoon at Millennium Park was fun—though on the way downtown on the El, Kat felt frustrated by her brief talk with

Edesa. Did she mean you can't even *talk* about eating good food until you've taken care of all the other humongous social issues? That seemed dumb. Maybe she'd figure out some way to do something on her own . . . maybe work it into her tutoring at the STEP program.

The flowers in Millennium Park were in full bloom, like walking through an English country garden. The "Bean"—the futuristic Cloud Gate sculpture that looked to Kat like a huge stainless steel kidney bean resting on the plaza—dominated the park, and it was fun to see the Chicago skyline reflected in it. They ate their packed lunch on the lawn of the pavilion, an outdoor stage hosting concerts through the summer. "Let's get a schedule of concerts," Nick said. "It'd be fun to come down here at night."

But the most fun was Crown Fountain, a pair of fifty-foot towers sitting at each end of a shallow wading pool with enormous video images of real faces spitting water into the pool. The faces changed and their mouths "spit" water at intervals, and kids were having a ball splashing and squealing as the water hit the pool.

"Come on!" Kat tossed her sandals onto a stone bench along with her backpack. "Let's get wet!" It had to be eighty degrees at least. The water would feel good.

"I'll watch your stuff!" Olivia yelled after them.

Kat and Bree and Nick cavorted like juveniles themselves in the shallow pool, chasing each other from one end to the other.

"Time out!" Bree gasped finally. "I'll go relieve Livie." She headed for the bench.

Kat started to follow, but Nick grabbed her. "Oh no you

don't. You're not wet enough." Laughing, he dragged her under the latest stream of water pouring from the closest tower.

Kat screeched and struggled—but not too hard—realizing Nick's arms around her felt . . . warm and wonderful. She grabbed him back and they both got soaked before finally making their way back to the stone bench, laughing and gasping.

Olivia shook her head. "You two are nuts. We should go so you two can get some dry clothes."

Yeah, Kat thought, toweling off her hair with the sweatshirt in her backpack. *The weekend's almost over and I still have to figure out how to get Rochelle's gift to her mom.*

Chapter 37

When the four friends arrived back at the three-flat around five o'clock, the perfect opportunity presented itself. Kat had just gotten out of the shower and changed into dry capris and a tank top when she heard the door buzzer ringing in the apartment upstairs and footsteps and voices tromping past their apartment on the way to the third floor. Then the buzzer again and more voices. And then a knock at their door.

Edesa Baxter stood on the landing holding a large, flat bakery cake. "Shh," she said. "May I come in?"

"Of course!" Kat opened the door wider and Edesa set the cake on their dining room table. "What's up?"

Edesa giggled happily. "It's Estelle Bentley's birthday next week, and our Yada Yada Prayer Group is meeting at Avis's apartment tonight. You know who Estelle is, don't you? From SouledOut? Sister Estelle won't suspect a thing since we're a week early, but we don't want this cake to show up yet. Would you . . . would you be willing to bring it up when I call you on your cell phone?"

Who could miss Estelle Bentley? An imposing presence, the attractive middle-aged black woman, and her husband, the ex-cop. Kat grinned. "Absolutely. Your . . . what group?"

"The Yada Yada Prayer Group. Some of us from SouledOut belong to this group, but there are women from other churches too. We meet every other week in different homes. Just happens to be here at Avis's tonight—but God is good, *si*? You live just below to help us with our surprise!" She gave Kat a hug. "Thank you so much, Sister Kathryn. I better go—but can you give me your cell number? I will call you."

When she was gone, Brygitta, Olivia, and Kat crowded around the sheet cake. It had been decorated with purple icing swirled to look like balls of yarn and knitting needles in gold icing, along with "God has knit us together, Estelle!" in purple and gold.

"She must be a knitter," Bree murmured.

"You think?" Kat gave her a teasing shove. But her mind was racing. It sounded like a large group of women up there—and she was supposed to bring the cake up. Maybe Mrs. Douglass would be so distracted, she could sneak Rochelle's gift box into the bedroom—if Mr. D wasn't holed up in there. But it seemed like her best chance. Even better if Bree helped—surely it wouldn't hurt to tell her that Mrs. Douglass's daughter wanted to slip a gift into her mom's bedroom.

"You carry the cake," Kat told Brygitta once she'd filled her in. "I'll look for an opportunity to sneak the gift into her bedroom."

They heard singing upstairs. Laughter. More singing. Forty-five minutes later a text arrived on Kat's cell. All it said was "Now."

Kat and Bree carefully mounted the stairs to the third floor with the cake. Kat tapped lightly on the door. It opened immediately, and as they walked in with the cake, the roomful of women shouted, "Surprise!" And someone began singing, "Happy birthday to youuuu . . ."

Estelle, dressed in a royal blue caftan and matching head wrap—Kat had heard she sewed her clothes herself—clapped her hands and laughed. A few moments later Mrs. Douglass and another woman Kat had never seen before disappeared into the kitchen—probably for plates and ice cream or whatever. *Now!*

She guessed the master bedroom was at the end of the hall, similar to the master bedroom in their apartment, but Kat stepped into the bathroom first in case anyone was watching her. A moment later she peeked out toward the living room. No one was looking. Slipping down the hall, she pushed open the bedroom door, already slightly ajar.

Glancing quickly around, she took in the room. Queen bed with a royal blue duvet and baby-blue-and-cream flowered bed skirt, matching pillow covers plumped up against the wooden headboard. Two dressers—one, tall and masculine on the far side of the bedroom, the other on the near side, wider, lower, with a mirror held by a wooden "scroll." That must be Mrs. D's.

Quickly Kat slipped the box out of the roomy pocket of the hoodie she'd put on just for this purpose and set it on the dresser. No, she'd half hide it behind the photo of her and Mr. D on one side . . . there.

Now to get out—quick!

No one in the hall . . . no one looking this way from the living room . . . but just in case, Kat slipped back into the bathroom, flushed the toilet, ran the water in the sink, and came out again.

Uh-oh. The women in the living room were sharing prayer requests while eating their cake. Awkward. She hesitated in the hallway, wondering what to do.

"Any word from your daughter?" Jodi Baxter was saying.

Mrs. Douglass, sitting with her back to Kat, shook her head. "No. Just that one note in our mailbox. I . . . It's been four months now, still don't know where they are. Please keep praying, sisters. And pray for Peter and me too. Once we find Rochelle and Conny, he and I need to come to more agreement about how much to help them. It's been . . . difficult."

"Tell me about it." Estelle wagged her head. "Grown kids comin' back home? When your own marriage is just a few years old? *Mmmm* . . . Well! No time like the present to pray." The "birthday girl" set her cake aside and took the hands of the women on either side of her. Hands joined, heads bowed . . .

Now. She tried to slip unobtrusively around the group toward the door situated between the living room and dining alcove, but Edesa caught her eye and left her seat, meeting Kat at the door. "There you are," she whispered as voices prayed aloud in the circle. "Wondered where you'd disappeared to. Brygitta left before we could offer her some cake. Would you like to take some downstairs for the four of you? Our thanks for helping with our birthday surprise tonight."

Kat jerked a thumb back down the hall. "Had to use the restroom . . . uh, maybe later for the cake." She really needed to get out of there before Mrs. D realized she was still there. With a quick wave she was out the door and padding down the carpeted stairs to the apartment below.

Kat was grinning. Mission accomplished!

Kat left early the next morning so she could walk with Olivia as far as the Morse Avenue El Station. "Have fun doing your Mary Poppins thing!" She waved as Livie disappeared into the lower area to buy her ticket. They'd all offered to take turns walking Olivia to the El in the morning until she got used to taking public transportation, though she had to walk home by herself since they couldn't be certain which train she'd catch in the evening. So far, so good.

The day had started out cool and was only supposed to hit the low seventies. Kat was glad for the walk to Bethune Elementary, just a half mile through typical Rogers Park residential blocks, each a mixture of big old frame houses with verandas and brick two-flats and three-flats. Walking gave her time to think.

The prayer group that met at the Douglasses' last night—*What did they call it? Yada Yada? Odd*—was something else. She'd been so fixated on getting Rochelle's birthday gift to her mom that she hadn't really thought about it till now. The group was mixed, just like SouledOut. White. Black. Hispanic. And . . . whatever you called someone like Edesa Baxter, who was black but from Central America. Sounded like the women shared a lot of personal stuff and then prayed about it.

Kat felt an ache in her spirit. She wished she could share things with other women like that and pray about them. She and her apartment-mates had prayed together a few times about stuff—the move, needing jobs—but not on a regular basis. And even though she'd tried to read through the Bible a couple times, she'd gotten stuck in all those stupid genealogies and prophetic rantings and ended up mostly reading the Psalms and the Gospels. When she read the Bible at all, that is, which was usually only two or three times a week.

Something was wrong with this picture. She'd decided to become a Christian at that summer music fest and had made some pretty major decisions because of it—like transferring to Crista University—and she really wanted to follow the teachings of Jesus. But . . . what exactly did it mean to have a *personal* relationship with God? When Mrs. Douglass and others at SouledOut worshiped, it was like they were communicating with Someone they knew intimately and loved deeply. Was that why Kat couldn't "get into it" herself? That she didn't really "know" God? Did she *love* Him?

She liked the worship at SouledOut, but if she was honest, it was mostly like observing a cultural experience she admired. Only a few times had she actually felt as if she was worshiping.

The elementary school loomed up ahead, taking up a whole block. She was early . . . so Kat slowed down, still thinking about last night. She'd heard Mrs. Douglass say it'd been four months since she'd seen her daughter and grandson, and they couldn't find her. So they *didn't* know where she was, or that Conny was living with his dad! And something must've gone wrong in Camelot, because Mrs. D had asked for prayer that she and her husband could agree on how much to help Rochelle—and Rochelle had been very adamant when his name came up: *"He's not my dad!"*

Whatever it was, it must've been a big family blowup.

But Rochelle was obviously hurting. Looking scared. Anxious. Dumpster-diving because she had to, not because she wanted to. And though Kat didn't know for sure, she guessed Conny was living only with his dad, not his mom. Why?

Kat's heart sank. Maybe Rochelle didn't have a place to live. Maybe that was why Conny was staying with his dad, even though—

Oh! If Mrs. Douglass had any idea what the real situation was, she'd be frantic!

Kat stopped in the middle of the school parking lot. A new thought pierced her mind as if she'd been struck by lightning.

She had to think of a way to get Rochelle and her mom back together again.

At first Kat had a hard time focusing as Mrs. Douglass welcomed the volunteers, wondering if the woman had found Rochelle's gift on the dresser. She didn't say anything—but why would she? She wouldn't know Kat had anything to do with it.

But her interest was piqued as everyone introduced themselves. Several college students from Northwestern and Loyola, a few parents, even a few people she knew, like Jodi and Denny Baxter—Jodi was tutoring reading and English as a Second

Language, and Denny was doing afternoon sports—and Estelle Bentley, the "birthday girl," who was responsible for putting out breakfast and making sack lunches, but said she had to leave in time to cook lunch at the Manna House Women's Shelter.

Breakfast? Kat scanned the daily schedule Mrs. Douglass handed out. First thing when the kids arrived, they got milk, cereal, and juice, ". . . because a good many arrive without having breakfast," Mrs. D explained. Then story time, divided by age groups . . . tutoring in various subjects in groups no larger than three or four . . . supervised games in the gym or on the playground . . . and finally a choice between computer time or drama. Those who stayed for afternoon sports or field trips got a sack lunch.

"We have twenty-seven children signed up so far, but once the program is going, I'm sure we'll have an influx from neighborhood kids who see what's going on and want to get in on it, or parents who suddenly realize their kids don't have anyone watching out for them. So if you know any more volunteers"—Mrs. Douglass opened her arms wide—"we can use them all."

Estelle's husband, the ex-cop, showed up midmorning to talk about safety and security issues, and he handed out legal forms to fill out, as everyone had to pass a background check in order to work with children in the Chicago schools.

Registration forms, parental release forms, field trip forms for parents to sign . . . Kat's head was swimming by the time she headed out the door with the other volunteers. She barely had enough time to get home, grab an apple for her lunch, and get to the coffee shop to relieve Bree for the second half of their shift.

But she was looking forward to tomorrow. She'd been assigned to tutor math and science, and she had volunteered to assist with the drama group.

Only one thing nagged at her spirit. Last week Rochelle had said to meet her again, same time, same place, probably to make sure Kat had been able to deliver the gift to her mom. That would be good news—mission accomplished. But between now and then, could she think of a way to persuade Rochelle to end this estrangement with her folks?

She was still thinking about this after her shift at the coffee shop as she turned into their street. How she wished she could share the whole thing with Nick and Bree and Livie and pray about it together! But . . . had she even prayed about it herself?

Lord, she breathed, using her key to let herself into the stairwell of their apartment, *please help me think of a way to get Rochelle and her mom back together again—*

She stopped on the first landing. Maybe that prayer was kind of presumptuous. It depended on God, didn't it? Not just her?

Lord, please bring Rochelle and her mom back together again—and if You can use me somehow, please show me what to do.

Feeling a little better about her prayer, Kat used her key to open the front door and called out, "I'm home! What's for sup—" She stopped midsentence. Olivia was sitting on the couch, her face bruised, scraped, and scrunched in pain as Bree carefully dabbed hydrogen peroxide on her bloody forehead. Nick had his arm around the girl protectively. "Wha—what happened?!" Kat cried.

Seeing Kat, Olivia started to weep. Nick shook his head, his expression dark. "Some punk grabbed Livie's purse as she came down the stairs at the El station, made her fall the last six steps." Olivia's whole body was shaking as she cried, and she leaned into Nick's shoulder. "Police car brought her home. Nothing's broken but . . . she's pretty shook up."

"Oh, Livie." Kat knelt down beside her three friends and took one of Olivia's limp hands. "I'm so sorry, so sorry."

Olivia lifted her head and opened weepy blue eyes, her mascara smudged, her lips trembling. "I w-want to go home, Kat. I . . . I just want to go home!"

Chapter 38

It had been a long day, and Avis's feet hurt. After the morning training session for STEP, she had visited five more local businesses, trying to expand her list of sponsors. Only two of the five had promised to donate actual money, but one of the pizza places on Sheridan had promised to send over two large cheese pizzas each Friday as an alternative to the daily bag lunch. Well, every little bit helped.

Now, sprawled on the couch with her feet up, Avis had just clicked off the news and started thinking about supper when Peter came in the door. "You're home early," she said. "Everything okay?"

"Yeah, yeah, I'm good." He tossed his briefcase on a chair and loosened his tie. "Now that Carl's back, I get to leave at a decent hour. Uh, say . . . I just saw a police car pull away from the front of the building. Any idea what that was about?"

She shook her head. "Didn't hear anything. Maybe

someone else on the block called them and they just parked here. Happens."

"Yeah. Probably. Ahhhh . . ." Peter sank into the leather recliner. "Feels good to get off my feet. Can you toss me the remote?"

Avis waggled the remote in her hand. "Aren't you forgetting something? Like, 'How was your training day for the summer program, sweetie? Do you have enough volunteers? Getting enough sponsors?'"

Peter grinned sheepishly. "Sorry. How was your training day for the summer program, sweetheart? Do you have enough volunteers?"

Avis swung her feet off the couch and tossed the remote into his lap as she got up. "Getting there. We could use a few more *men* . . ." She started down the hall toward the bedroom, then poked her head back into the living room. "Oh. Forgot to tell you that Kathryn Davies from downstairs stopped by the school office on Friday to pick up an application. And she showed up for training today. I hope it works out. Her work schedule might be a problem. She's enthusiastic at least." Heading down the hall again, she called back, "I'm going to change out of these clothes and get into something comfy. Got any suggestions for supper?"

But he'd already turned the TV on and probably didn't hear her.

Mm, the bed looked inviting. She was tempted to crawl under the duvet and forget about supper . . . but instead she reached around to the back of her neck, unclasped the silver and turquoise necklace she'd worn with the white embroidered cotton tunic and black slacks she'd worn that day, and opened her jewelry box to put it away. Absently straightening the framed picture of her and Peter on their honeymoon, she noticed something behind it keeping the frame from sitting back in its place. *What's this?*

Moving the photo, she picked up a small package wrapped in brown paper—like grocery bag paper—and a red ribbon. No name, no tag—but it must be for her since it was on her dresser. Sitting down on the bed, she slid the ribbon off, unwrapped the brown paper, and looked at the box. White, square. She lifted the lid . . . and stared.

Ruby earrings.

Avis's lips parted. *Where did . . . Oh, of course.* Peter had said if they didn't find the earrings, he'd replace them. But these were exactly like the ones he'd given her before. Was that possible? It had been a month and a half since she'd discovered they were missing. He must have waited until he found the exact same earrings again.

Sweet of him.

Well. She was not going to get out that fancy red dress and put it on just to show off these earrings. But she could put them on long enough to thank him. Quickly shedding her work clothes, she pulled on a pair of white capris, toe sandals, and a light pink top and then carefully slid the ruby earrings into the holes in her ears.

But looking at herself in the mirror, Avis had to blink back tears. The ruby earrings were beautiful—but did she even want to wear them? They reminded her of that awful night she'd last worn them . . . Rochelle showing up, crying, desperate, saying she'd been evicted, wanting them to take her in. Peter refusing. Taking her and Conny to the shelter the next day, and then . . . nothing. Weeks of silence. Never returning phone calls. And then on their anniversary, discovering that the ruby earrings were missing . . .

Practically ripping the earrings out of her ears, Avis put them back in the box. She was tempted to just put the box back, pretend she hadn't found it. Obviously Peter had wanted to surprise her, hiding the box, but just barely, wanting her to find it. The earrings had been his wedding gift to her in the first place. And now he was "gifting" her again.

All right, Avis, suck it up and give your husband some sugar for thinking of you.

Blotting the wetness from her cheeks and touching up her lipstick, Avis took a big breath, picked up the box, and walked back out to the living room. Leaning over the recliner, she kissed him on the mouth and smiled into his eyes. "Thank you, honey. I found your surprise."

Peter leaned around her, trying to watch whatever he'd been watching on the TV. "Surprise?"

Uh-huh. Playing dumb. "Yes, surprise." She snatched the remote from his hand and hit the Off button. "*This* surprise." She held out the box, minus its brown paper wrapping and red ribbon.

"Hey, I was watching the news about that earthquake in China . . . What's that?"

Okay, she'd play along. She teased him with the box and then opened the lid. "Thank you, Peter. You didn't have to replace them, but . . . it's very sweet."

Peter's eyebrows went up. Reaching out a finger, he touched the earrings and then looked up at her. "The ruby earrings? But, Avis, I didn't replace them."

Avis just stared at him. Her lips suddenly went dry. "You—you didn't? Then—" The enormity of what Peter had just said began to sink in. "Then how did . . . ? Who . . . ?"

Slowly Avis sank down onto the ottoman. Peter let down the footrest and leaned forward in the recliner. "Well, now we know they weren't just misplaced or lost. Whoever took them has returned them."

"Rochelle," Avis whispered. She licked her dry lips. "She's been here. She put them on my dresser. But how did she get in? And . . . what does it mean?"

She had Peter's attention now. "Something good, I think," he said. "She's reaching out—"

A rapid knock on the front door startled them both. Then an urgent voice. "Mr. Douglass? Mrs. Douglass? Are you home? Something's happened. Please, we need to talk with you."

"That's Nick," Peter said, launching himself out of the recliner and striding quickly to the door. He pulled it open. "Nick! Come in. What's happened?"

"It's Livie . . . Someone snatched her purse at the Morse Avenue El Station and made her fall down the stairs. She got pretty banged up."

"Oh no," Avis murmured, joining her husband.

Nick paced back and forth, nervously running one hand over his short hair. "The police brought her home. She didn't want to go to the ER, mostly scrapes and bruises—but she won't stop crying. Her purse had her ID, her checkbook, everything.

We . . . Would you come down and speak with her? We really don't know what to do."

"Of course. Just give me a minute." Avis walked quickly back to their bedroom, put the box with the earrings on the dresser, picked up her Bible from the bedside table, and returned. She nodded at Peter. "We should both go."

Poor thing, Avis thought as they followed Nick down the stairs. *Timid Olivia, of all people.* But purse snatchers sensed these things, picked on the vulnerable, the nervous ones.

Just as Nick said, Olivia was curled up on the couch, weeping in Brygitta's arms. Her blond bangs had been pushed back, and Avis could see an angry lump swelling on the young woman's forehead. Raw scrapes raked across her nose and cheeks, and she had a couple of bloody scrapes on her knees that looked as if they'd been washed and covered with some kind of ointment. The girl cradled one hand in her lap as if it hurt her. Kathryn sat on the floor nearby, shaking her head.

Avis had a sudden pang of compassion for all of them. Babes in the woods—or babes on the streets, as it were. "Come," she said, beckoning to Peter and Nick, both of whom looked uncomfortable with all this female weeping. Pulling up a hassock, she encouraged all five of them to lay hands—gently—on Olivia. "Oh God," she prayed, "Your daughter Olivia needs the comforting presence of Your Holy Spirit right now. She's been frightened, taken advantage of, and physically hurt. The Enemy wants to keep her afraid, but we are asking for a peace only You can give to fill Olivia's heart and mind right now. She's safe now, her wounds will heal. We *thank* You, Jesus, that it was only her purse that was taken, and not her life. We give You praise and glory for protecting Olivia from anything worse! Thank You, mighty God, thank You!"

Olivia was still weeping.

Leafing through her Bible, Avis stopped at Psalm 56 and then continued her prayer, using the scripture. "Be merciful to Olivia, O God, for an unknown assailant pursued and attacked her. This purse thief attacked her in his pride, thinking he could do this and get away with it, leaving her frightened and hurt. She is afraid—but help her to remember she can trust in You. We praise You, O God, for the promises in Your Word. In You we trust, so we do not need to be afraid! What can mere man do to us? Yes, hurt, steal, frighten—but You are a God of justice *and* compassion. Stop whoever did this and bring him to justice. And pour out Your compassion on Your precious daughter Olivia . . ."

Avis was aware that Olivia gradually stopped shaking, and her sobs quieted. When she finally said, "Amen," the young woman gave her a teary smile. "Thank you," she whispered. "But . . . I don't think I can go back to that job. I—I want to go home. I miss my sister . . . I sh-shouldn't have left her alone this summer . . ." The sobs threatened to start up again.

"Shh, shh, it's going to be all right," Brygitta said, rocking her gently.

Nick beckoned to Avis and Peter. Kathryn followed them into the kitchen. "I can take her home," the young man said in a low voice. "I actually think it's a good idea. Livie wasn't all that sure about staying here this summer anyway. Too bad about the nanny job, but . . . we need to do what's best for Livie. Her younger sister's staying with an aunt and uncle in Madison,

Wisconsin. It's not that far. I'll check out bus or train schedules, and the three of us can chip in on a ticket—"

"Nonsense," Peter said. "Take one of our cars. Madison's only three hours or so from here, you can go and be back in the same day. We'll manage."

Nick's mouth dropped open. "Oh, Mr. Douglass! That would be awesome, but . . . are you sure? I didn't think about driving. Maybe we could rent a car—"

"No need. It's done." Peter reached out, putting a hand on Nick's shoulder. "Just let me know when the two of you are ready to go and we'll get the car keys to you."

"Whoa." Nick shook his head. "I can't believe it, but . . . thank you."

Avis had kept her mouth shut, even though she was more than a little surprised that Peter—her Peter, who rarely let *her* drive his Lexus—would offer one of their cars to this young man, whom they barely knew. He probably meant her Toyota, but she couldn't help an inner smile. If Peter was being generous, she knew better than to squelch it.

"It's my fault, you know."

Avis had almost forgotten Kathryn, but the young woman stood in the middle of the kitchen, arms crossed, staring at the floor.

"Oh, come on, Kat, it's not your—"

"Yes, it is, Nick!" Kathryn's head snapped up and her blue eyes flashed, a vivid contrast to the dark hair bunched on the back of her head with a clip. "I never should've pushed Livie to stay with us in Chicago. I thought the fact that her mom has this creepy boyfriend and her kid sister told Livie she was getting out of there was God saying she should come with us! But . . . we all knew Livie was anxious about living in the city, and we never did talk about whether she should've gone to her aunt's to be with her sister. The kid's still in high school, for crying out loud."

"I know, Kat, but—"

But Kathryn was shaking her head. "I don't know. I don't know. Everything's just . . . wrong." With that, she ran out of the kitchen.

Nick looked at Avis and Peter apologetically. "Sorry. Guess we're all a little shaken. I better go talk to her." He started after Kathryn.

Avis held up her hand to stop him. "You might wait a little while, Nick. If the Holy Spirit is trying to say something to Kathryn, don't get in the way. She is a bit impetuous, you know. Maybe she needs some time to think . . . and pray."

Nick hesitated. "Yeah. Guess you're right." He followed them to the door. "Thanks again."

Peter seemed pensive the rest of the evening. Avis made a quick soup with some leftover chicken, adding chicken broth, rice, lime leaves, coconut milk, and red pepper flakes to spice it up, and served it up on the back porch to enjoy the mild evening. Both were quiet as they ate, Avis mulling over the mystery of the earrings. If Peter hadn't bought her a new pair, then these had to be the ones Rochelle had taken—which now seemed the case. But the only reason Rochelle would have taken—stolen—them was because she was desperate for money. And yet . . . she'd returned them. But how? Avis knew Rochelle didn't have a key to their apartment. No one else did either—well, the Baxters had a spare, in case theirs got lost or stolen. But Jodi wouldn't give it out. Would she?

"Avis?"

Peter's voice interrupted her musings. She looked up from her soup. He'd barely touched his.

"I've been thinking about Nick. I'm going to offer him a part-time job at Software Symphony for the summer."

"You said that a week ago."

"I know. Have to admit Wednesday night's meeting knocked it off the radar for a couple of days. But we crunched numbers today, think we can do it."

Avis nodded. "That's good."

"But that's not all. He's young and inexperienced, but I see the way he's concerned about those girls, takes the initiative to take care of things. Yes, they're all friends, but it's more than that. He's got a pastor's heart. And I've been thinking . . ."

Chapter 39

The clock said eight thirty and she had to be at Bethune Elementary by nine, but Kat hated to leave. She'd wanted to see Livie off, but the girl wasn't completely packed yet, even though she'd had all day yesterday. Brygitta had already left for the coffee shop, doing the Wednesday morning shift, with Kat picking up the afternoon shift.

"Come here, you," she said, pulling the younger girl into a hug, still mindful of Livie's bruises. Fresh tears threatened as they embraced. Kat had to fish for a tissue. "I'm going to miss you, but going to Madison is good. Elin will love having her big sis with her."

Olivia nodded. "Yeah. But I'm sorry, Kat. Sorry I'm messing everything up for you guys. You know, not being here to pay my share of the rent and stuff—"

"Hey, we'll manage. It's just for the summer anyway. And I shouldn't have pushed you so hard to come in with us." Kat had rehearsed what she wanted to say, but it was hard getting the words out. "That was selfish of me. Not really thinking about what was best for you. Will you forgive me?"

"Oh, Kat!" Olivia threw her arms around Kat again and hugged her tight. "Of course. And . . . maybe Elin and I will come down some weekend to visit, okay? Maybe ride those Segways or something!"

Kat laughed. "Now that's daring!" Another glance at the clock. "Gotta go. Wish I could go with you two, but . . . Nick! Where are you? I gotta go and want to say good-bye!"

"He's outside checking the car. Go on. I'll call when I get there."

Grabbing her backpack, Kat hurried down the stairs and out the door. Sure enough, Nick was leaning in the open driver's side door of Mrs. Douglass's Toyota Camry, checking out all the features. "Hey," she said, coming up beside him. "Wish I could go with you. But I gotta do my tutoring thing."

Nick straightened and turned to her, wire rim sunglasses perched on top of his head. "Wish you could too. Would love the company on the way back." A slight pause hung in the air. "Especially your company."

She expected a teasing grin, but his hazel eyes held hers, as if he was serious.

"Yeah, well . . . see you tonight. Be safe." On impulse, she stood on her tiptoes and kissed his cheek. Then quickly walked away.

Kat's face burned. She could still feel his cheek, a bit whiskery, on her lips. The smell of his aftershave. What did she do that for? She wasn't sure, except . . . she wanted Nick to know she cared about him, wanted him to come back safe.

Kat felt a little more comfortable her second day of tutoring. She had two boys and one girl in her math tutoring group. Yusufu Balozi was from Uganda, very polite, and spoke English with an enchanting accent. Towheaded Kevin Green never seemed to understand her instructions the first time, so she found herself repeating things a lot. Cute Latoya Sims had her hair done in two dozen tiny braids with tiny beads at the ends—that must've taken somebody a long time! But all three had one thing in common: they hated long division. She'd have to think of ways to make it fun.

But that afternoon, as she served up lattes and scones, chai tea and muffins at The Common Cup, Kat wasn't thinking about long division. Her heart was already feeling Livie's absence in their second-floor apartment, and her mind was frantically searching for what she was going to say to Rochelle when—if—she met up with Mrs. Douglass's daughter later that day.

And suddenly, right in the middle of putting together an arugula salad with dried cranberries, sunflower seeds, golden raisins, walnuts, feta cheese, and balsamic vinaigrette, the two trains of thought came together with the speed of the Metra Express during rush hour. She stopped right in the middle of tossing homemade croutons into the salad.

Livie had just left. They now had an empty bedroom—well, the study, but it had a foldout futon.

Most likely Rochelle didn't have a place to stay. *What if* . . .

Kat moved through the rest of her shift in a heady fog. The

idea was absolutely crazy. Or brilliant. Or both. So crazy, so brilliant, it had to be God.

And it sure would have to be God's idea if it was ever going to work.

Buying a carrot-raisin muffin to tide her over until she got back to the apartment for supper, Kat headed straight for the El station after work and took the Red Line to the Berwyn El stop. The usual Wednesday evening produce trucks were parked next to the loading docks of the Dominick's grocery store, but this time Kat simply waited, leaning against the store's brick wall.

Thirty minutes went by . . . then an hour. And still no Rochelle.

But she told me to meet her here this week! Kat slid her back down the wall until she was sitting on the ground, and she laid her arms and head on her knees. *Jesus, I'm not a very good pray-er, but if this idea is from You, please help Rochelle to show up. And give me the courage to—*

"Hey. You okay?"

Kat snapped her head up. "Rochelle! You came!" She scrambled to her feet.

"Told you to meet me here, didn't I?" The young woman's hair seemed even wilder than last time, a dark mass of tangled ringlets and waves. Her face seemed thinner, pinched, as if she had lost weight. "Did you get that package to my mom—without her knowing it was from me?"

Kat laughed, feeling giddy. "Yes! You won't believe how it worked out." She told about the Yada Yada Prayer Group meeting at the Douglasses', bringing the cake, Rochelle's mom going into the kitchen for plates, Kat sneaking the package into their bedroom. "She never saw me. I'm sure she has no idea how it got there."

"Did she find it?"

"I'm sure she did—or will soon. It's right on her dresser, tucked behind a photograph but not quite hidden."

Rochelle pondered this. "Okay. Thanks a lot. That means a lot to me." She turned to go.

"Rochelle, wait. I have something important I want to talk to you about. If I'm wrong, you can tell me to shut up and go away. But please listen."

Rochelle just looked at her.

Kat wished they could sit somewhere, order a cup of coffee, have a long chat. But that wasn't going to happen. Not here. Not now. She needed to talk fast.

"Rochelle, I know a place you can stay where you and Conny could be together."

Rochelle's eyes twitched. "How do you know we're not together?"

"Because Conny said he's staying with his dad. And I'm guessing you're not. And I'm also guessing you don't want Conny staying with his dad. You want him to be with you."

Rochelle looked away, her eyes blinking fast. Then she turned back. "Where is this place?"

"With me."

"You!" Rochelle stepped back. "But you live right below my mom's apartment." She started to shake her head. "No, no, you don't understand—"

"I understand one thing. Your mom misses you and Conny

terribly. And I think you and Conny miss her too. Whatever happened between you, it's not worth living like this. Separated from your kid. Digging in those Dumpsters."

Rochelle snorted. "You do."

"That's different. Like you said, I don't have to. It's a choice . . . look. Just think about it. But don't wait a whole week. Can we meet somewhere and talk about it?" Kat thought fast. "I work at The Common Cup. It's real close to the Morse Avenue El station."

"I know where it is."

"I work Saturday morning, early shift, but I get off at ten. Morning rush is over, it'll be pretty quiet. Could you meet me there at ten o'clock? Then we'd have a place to sit and talk."

Rochelle shook her head slowly. "Can't do Saturday. I got Conny all day."

"Bring Conny too! We've got great ice cream. My treat."

Silence hung between them. Kat wasn't sure what Rochelle was thinking. "Uh, do you need money for El fare?"

"I've got money," Rochelle snapped.

"All right. But will you come? Please?"

Again a long silence. Then, "All right. Just to talk. Ten o'clock Saturday." And with a few running steps, Rochelle disappeared around the corner of the store.

Kat was a nervous wreck on the way home on the El. What had she done?! But it was time to break her promise and tell Brygitta and Nick everything. Rochelle would understand that she'd have to ask her apartment-mates if they were going to talk about rooming together.

Nick had just walked in a few minutes before Kat, having safely delivered Olivia to her aunt's home in Madison. And that night over a late supper, she spilled the whole story to her two friends. Brygitta already knew a bit of it, and Nick . . . he was probably the most trustworthy secret-keeper on the planet.

"Sure," Nick said. "I could move into the study on the futon, and she could have the master bedroom. Queen bed ought to be big enough for her and the kid."

Kat felt like kissing him again . . . but she didn't.

"He's six? That's a fun age," Brygitta said. "Could be kinda fun having a kid around."

"Uh, I don't think she has any money for rent."

Brygitta and Nick looked at each other. Nick cleared his throat. "Well, if nobody moved in, we'd be splitting it three ways, so what's the difference? Besides . . ." A slow grin spread over his face. "Haven't told you guys yet—kinda got bumped off the radar with Livie moving out—but Mr. Douglass offered me a part-time job in the mail room at his software business. I start tomorrow."

Kat and Brygitta both shrieked. "Nick! That's fantastic!"

"Yeah. I was feeling so grateful on my way home from Wisconsin, I wrote a song in my head . . . Want to hear it?" He started to get up as if to go get his guitar.

The two girls looked at each other and burst out laughing. Nick's music tended to be on the sappy side, but . . . why not. "Sure," Kat said. "But sit down a minute. Let's, you know, pray together first and thank God for your job. And ask God to soften

Rochelle's heart so she says yes to moving in with us. And that she shows up Saturday."

"Wait a minute." Brygitta frowned. "It's not just about Rochelle moving in with us. Aren't we forgetting the big elephant in the room? The fact that Rochelle and her mom haven't spoken to each other for four months? Seems like we need to pray that *that* wall comes down before any of this is going to happen."

Kat's spirit sank a little. Bree was right. Still . . . was it such a big wall? Hadn't Rochelle sent her mom a birthday gift? Hadn't Mrs. D asked her Yada-Whatever-Group to pray that they would find her? Seemed to her like all Rochelle and her mom needed was a little push and that wall would come tumbling down.

Pushing their plates aside, the three friends held hands around the small kitchen table and started to pray. But Kat was also intensely aware that Nick was gently squeezing her hand, as if sending her a message.

Chapter 40

The next two days seemed to pass in a blur. Every time Kat saw Mrs. Douglass at the school, she ached to tell her about their plan. A place for Rochelle and Conny to live! Close by! But Nick had cautioned her not to say anything yet. It wasn't certain that Rochelle would even show up on Saturday, much less accept their invitation, and that would just be another huge disappointment.

Afraid she'd blurt out something, she did her best to avoid the principal, keeping busy helping Estelle Bentley pass out the individual boxes of cereal, small cartons of milk, and juice boxes as the kids arrived, and corralling the three students she was tutoring as soon as they were done eating. On Thursday she brought a bag of apples to help them visualize simple division problems, but it became a "subtraction" problem when some of the other kids snatched apples and ran off with them, throwing them at each other, and in general creating havoc before the volunteers got them under control.

So much for props. She tried story problems. "What if we had a dog wash here in the school playground to raise money for a field trip to . . . where would you like to go, Yusufu?"

"Disneyland!"

"Uh, someplace here in Chicago."

"Great America!" Latoya squealed.

"Okay. Great America. If we charge three dollars per dog, how many dogs would we have to wash to make ninety dollars?"

All three faces screwed up in concentration. She showed them how to divide ninety by three. "Thirty dogs!" Kevin snorted. "No way! Just go to that machine at the bank and take out ninety dollars. That's what my mother does when she needs money."

Oh, brother. These kids needed some money sense.

That evening she Googled "have fun with long division" and was rewarded with a list of cool websites with math games for kids. Perfect. Friday morning she'd ask for computer time early and get her three rascals working with basic division facts online, complete with bells and whistles when they got the right answer.

While online, she checked her e-mail. Still no answer from either her mom or her dad, even though she'd e-mailed them last weekend, telling them about her new job and volunteering with the Summer Tutoring and Enrichment Program. She'd used the whole title, hoping they'd be impressed. But . . . maybe they didn't check their e-mail that often. Well, she'd give it one more day and then maybe she'd call.

Yusufu, Kevin, and Latoya loved the online math games. At least it was a start. Kat was feeling pretty good about her first week with STEP, but Mrs. Douglass stopped her as Kat was leaving at noon. The principal looked slightly annoyed. "The kids are saying you're going to have a dog wash here at the school to raise money to take them all to Great America. What's this about?"

Kat's mouth fell open. "Oh no, no, that was just a story problem for my math students! Are they . . . oh dear. I was trying to make it personal, so I did phrase it like, 'What if we had a dog wash here at the school . . .' but I didn't mean *really*!"

Mrs. Douglass's mouth twitched at the corners. "Ah. No dog wash. Good. We'll have to make that clear first thing next week—if word doesn't spread this weekend and half the neighborhood doesn't show up Monday with their dogs." And then she chuckled. "Kids do take things literally, Kathryn. Be careful what you say."

Kat nodded meekly. She'd taken Theory and Practice in Classroom Management, but all that theory was a bit different from actually teaching real kids. Especially kids as different from each other as Yusufu, Kevin, and Latoya. Worse, she had a master's degree in education but felt as if she'd made a fool of herself. More than anything, she wanted Mrs. Douglass to respect her skills as a teacher.

Her parents didn't. Obviously they were still miffed that she wasn't doing her hospital residency by now. But just in case, she checked her e-mail again before heading for her afternoon shift at the coffee shop. Still nothing. Okay, she'd call after work, try to catch her mom before they went out for the evening or something.

But there was no answer on the home phone when she

called, using her cell on the walk home. It went right to voice mail, and a digital voice announced that the mailbox was full. Good grief! Didn't her mom ever listen to her messages? Kat glanced at her watch . . . five fifteen Chicago time, only four fifteen in Phoenix. She'd leave a message at her father's office. They usually stayed open till five.

"Doctors Davies, Evans, and Campbell."

Kat recognized her father's middle-aged receptionist. "Uh, hi, Ms. Coalson. It's Kathryn Davies. Is—"

"Oh, hi, Kathryn! We thought you'd be back in the office this summer! How's Chicago?"

"It's good. Uh, I'm trying to reach my folks, didn't get through at home. Can I leave a message for my dad to call me? I know he's probably still got patients."

"Sure thing, hon. Want to give me your number just in case?"

Just in case what? That her father had somehow lost her number? But she repeated it anyway.

Kat's alarm rang at five o'clock. In the other twin bed, Bree groaned and put a pillow over her head. *Ughhhh.* Kat felt like doing the same thing. This was her first day to work the six a.m. Saturday shift. It had sounded good at the time, because it didn't conflict with tutoring at Bethune Elementary during the week. But she'd forgotten how early five o'clock was.

Stumbling into the bathroom, Kat turned on the shower, staring at herself in the bathroom mirror as the water warmed up. Supposed to be another hot day in the eighties. Maybe she should cut off all this hair and wear it short like Brygitta. Except Bree's was straight and pixie-like with those wispy bangs and cute wisps in front of her ears. Hers would just frizz up like a Brillo pad. Well, she'd just wash it and get it off her neck with a clip per usual.

Friday evening had come and gone, and still no call from her parents. Well, darn it, she wasn't going to chase after them. She'd sent an e-mail and left a message for her father. It was their turn. Besides, she had something else on her mind this morning.

Rochelle. Would she show up at ten o'clock like she'd promised? And even if she did, what would they do then? There was still the elephant in the room.

But once she was up and dressed, fortified with a glass of blended vegetable juice, Kat enjoyed the walk to Morse Avenue. Early morning runners and dog walkers were out in force. And once she had her apron on and took up her position behind the counter, she was surprised how many customers she'd served before seven o'clock.

The in-and-outers were mostly gone by nine. Then the sip-and-stay set drifted in, laptop, book, or newspaper in hand, ordered their favorite beverages, and settled down at a table for the next hour, lost in their own media world of choice. Kat was in the process of ringing up a café au lait and a blueberry scone for a middle-aged professor type when the hinges on the door squeaked and she glanced up.

Rochelle had pushed open the door and was beckoning to someone behind her.

Conny.

Quickly handing the man his change, Kat glanced at the clock—twenty to ten—and slipped from behind the counter. "Rochelle! You came." She grinned at the little boy. "Hey, Conny. I'm glad to see *you*."

The boy looked up at her with curious eyes. "Mama says you got ice cream here."

"That's true! You want to pick out your favorite flavor?" She held out her hand and Conny placed his in hers, letting her lead him over to the Swirl Freeze machine.

Rochelle trailed behind them. "Guess we're early. Sorry 'bout that."

"It's okay." More than okay! They were here! "I've got another twenty minutes to work, but you and Conny can order something and I'll be with you as soon as I can." She turned back to the little boy, his eyes big at the display of candy bar chunks, cookie pieces, chocolate chips, fruit, and other delectables that could be mixed into vanilla ice cream and swirled together.

Rochelle chose a table toward the back of the shop, sitting with her back to the door, and Kat brought her the simple cup of tea she ordered and Conny's peanut-butter-chips-chocolate-chip-cookie-dough frozen treat to the table with a strawberry on top. "Enjoy. I'll just be another few minutes."

Going back behind the counter, Kat paid the bill for her guests and realized her heart was pumping so hard she could feel it in her chest. *Rochelle and Conny, sitting right there.* And just a few blocks away . . .

Taking advantage of a momentary lull in customers, Kat stepped into the back room out of sight and hit a speed dial number on her cell phone. "Nick!" she hissed. "Rochelle showed up—with her little boy! Will you do something? It's really, really important . . ." Thirty seconds later she said, "Please, Nick. Don't think about it. Just do it! Gotta go."

Kat was so nervous, she handed the next customer a ten and two ones for change instead of a five and two ones. Fortunately, the girl teased, "Wow, some coffee shop. You not only serve coffee but double my money back."

"Whoops. Sorry about that." Kat made the right change and turned to the next customer, keeping an eye on the clock. 9:50 . . . 9:59 . . . 10:02. Her replacement was late! Bree's shift didn't start till five—they had a split shift today. But seeing her distress, the owner said, "Go on. I'll take over till Rob gets here."

Gratefully, Kat took off her apron, made herself a cup of chai tea, and pulled up a stray chair at Rochelle's table. Conny waved his empty dish. "More, please!"

"No way!" Rochelle snapped. "Here." She pulled out a tablet and a pencil. "Draw something. Miss Kat and I are gonna talk." She lowered her voice and tipped her head in Conny's direction. "Can you be kind of vague? Big ears."

Kat nodded. "Sure. Um . . . I talked to my friends and they're good to go if you are. Anytime. Today if you want."

Rochelle pulled a strand of her abundant hair and wound it around her finger. "Why would they do that? Or you, for that matter?"

Kat hesitated. Why? What could she say? But finally she murmured, "Because last week we had another person. And this week we don't. And me meeting you and Conny where we did—that was kind of unlikely, don't you think? So I think it was

God who put the idea in my head. Everything coming together like that."

"God." Rochelle seemed to ponder that. "Yeah, but . . . it's complicated, you know. And I don't have any money right now."

"I know, but—"

Conny suddenly jerked to attention, his eyes bugging. Jumping out of his chair, he ran toward the front of the coffee shop. *"Grammy!"* he screamed . . . and jumped into the arms of a startled Avis Douglass, who'd just come in the door.

Chapter 41

Avis could hardly breathe as she lifted the little boy, whose arms wrapped themselves tightly around her neck. "Oh, Conny, love!" she whispered in his ear. "Grammy has missed you *so much*!"

"Me too, Grammy!" The little boy pressed his face into her neck—and then he pulled back and looked up at her, a pout on his lips. "Where have you *been*?"

Oh, right here, right here, Conny, her heart cried. *All the time.* But she looked up—and saw Rochelle standing beside a chair toward the back of the coffee shop, watching them, her face a mixture of . . . what? Bewilderment? Distress? Fear? Maybe all of them. But Avis saw something else that made her heart wrench. Her precious daughter seemed bony and thin, her face pinched.

Rochelle wasn't well. *Oh God! Don't let her lose her battle with HIV!*

Hesitating just a moment, Avis put Conny down and

walked slowly toward her daughter. For the first time, she noticed Kathryn Davies sitting at the table also. Was it only twenty minutes ago that she and Peter had been sitting in their living room talking to Nick Taylor when his cell phone had rung? When he flipped the phone shut, she'd hardly been able to believe what he said. "Mrs. Douglass, your daughter Rochelle is at The Common Cup. Kathryn's working there this morning. She says to tell you to come right away. Like now!"

"Rochelle?! Kathryn's sure it's Rochelle?"

"Don't quibble! Go!" Peter had said. Avis hadn't taken time to change out of the sweats and T-shirt she'd put on that morning to work around the house. Had just run down the stairs and out to her car. *Oh God, oh God,* she'd prayed. *Let Rochelle still be there when I arrive.*

And now there she was. The familiar thick head of hair. Her honey-brown skin. Dark brown eyes wide, flickering uncertainly. One hand gripping the back of a chair. As they got close, Kathryn Davies rose and slipped away.

"Look, Mama!" Conny announced triumphantly. "It's Grammy!"

Rochelle licked her lips and swallowed. "Hi, Mom." Her voice was a mere whisper.

Avis let go of Conny's hand. "Oh, Rochelle . . ." Reaching out, she wrapped her arms around her daughter and pulled her into an embrace. "Oh, Rochelle, Rochelle, sweetheart," she whispered into the mass of hair. "I love you so much."

Rochelle's body began to tremble. Her arms went around Avis's waist and held on tight. "Oh, Mom! I'm so sorry about the earrings! I was mad because Peter wouldn't give me any money, was going to sell 'em—but I just couldn't. Oh, Mom . . ." She burst into tears.

"Shh, shh, you don't have to say anything. It's enough that you're here."

Mother and daughter held each other a long time, paying no attention to curious looks from other customers. But eventually Avis felt a tug on her sweatpants. "I have to go potty!" Conny announced.

"Never fails," Rochelle groaned, untangling herself from Avis's arms.

Avis smiled down at her grandson. "Tell you what, kiddo. You go potty and I'll get us something to eat. Sound good?"

It was hard to let them out of her sight as they followed the sign to the restrooms. But Avis went to the counter and ordered a banana muffin and glass of milk for Conny, two cinnamon raisin bagels with cream cheese, tea for Rochelle, and coffee for herself. While she waited for the young man behind the counter to put their order together, Avis glanced around the coffee shop. "Where's Kathryn Davies?" she asked him. "Isn't she working here this morning?"

"Was," he said, slicing the bagels. "She got off at ten. I think I saw her leave. Uh, you want your coffee now? The bagels will take a few minutes to toast."

"Hold everything till the bagels are ready." Avis stepped away from the counter to wait by the window. But outside a familiar figure caught her eye. Kathryn Davies was leaning against the building at the edge of the coffee shop window, back to her, shoulders hunched and arms wrapped around herself, as if . . .

Avis stepped outside. "Kathryn?" she called. "Is something the matter?"

Head bent, the young woman flicked a hand as if brushing her off. But Avis walked up and touched her on the shoulder. "Kathryn?"

As Kathryn slowly turned her head, Avis could see she'd been crying. "What's wrong?" A nudge in Avis's spirit prompted her to reach out and turn the girl toward her. "What's wrong, Kathryn?"

The girl shook her head, brushing tears away, eyes not meeting Avis's. "Nothing. I'm all right."

Avis glanced back inside the coffee shop window. No Rochelle or Conny yet. Turning back to Kathryn, she said gently, "Doesn't look like nothing to me. Might help to talk about it."

Kathryn bit her lip to keep it from trembling but just shook her head.

After a long moment Avis broke the silence. "I want to thank you for letting me know my daughter showed up here and encouraging me to come. It means a lot. We've had some problems, but I think we can make it now."

Kathryn nodded. "I know. I could . . . could tell by that hug you gave your daughter. Made me"—her voice lowered to a whisper—"made me wish I was Rochelle."

"You wish—?" Avis didn't know whether to laugh or cry. "Kathryn Davies, do you have any idea the kinds of challenges Rochelle faces? Or the pain she and I have been through lately?!" Avis gave a short laugh. If Kathryn's comment weren't so ridiculous, it would be funny.

Kathryn shrank back. "I know." Her voice was small. "It's just that . . . I can't remember the last time my mother hugged me like that. Or hugged me at all." And suddenly the tears welled up again and Kathryn's body shook with sobs.

Standing there on the sidewalk, Kathryn's words sank into Avis's spirit. All this time, this well-meaning, annoying, impetuous, irritating young woman had just been needing some basic mother love. *Oh God, how wrong I've been!* Yes, things had been tough the past few months between her and Rochelle. But at least they had a relationship that could be restored. But Kathryn? It sounded like there wasn't much of a relationship at all.

Remorse at the way she'd been holding the girl at arm's length for so long felt almost like a physical pain.

Glancing inside the window, Avis saw that Rochelle and Conny had returned from the bathroom and were looking around for her. She was torn, feeling an urgency to go back inside and drink in the sight of her daughter and grandson, touch them, talk to them, listen to their voices. She had a zillion questions she wanted to ask. A desperate need to fill in the blanks. But . . . there was one thing she needed to do first.

"Kathryn, come here." Reaching out, Avis Douglass pulled Kathryn Davies into her arms, laid her cheek against the girl's hair, and just held her close as the girl cried.

"I thought you left!" Conny stuck his lip out at her when Avis returned to the table with the tray of their drinks and food.

"Oh no, baby. Grammy's not *ever* going to leave my boy."

"What happened to Kat?" Rochelle asked. "She and I were talking before you came."

"She's outside. She said she'd come in after a while to finish whatever you were talking about, but she wanted to give us some time first." Avis looked at her daughter curiously. "What's going on?"

"She didn't tell you?" Rochelle toyed with her bagel. "She, uh, invited me and Conny to move in with her and her friends for the summer."

Big Ears jerked upright in his chair. "You an' *me*, Mama? Yeah! I wanna stay with you again!"

Avis's heart beat a little faster. "Conny isn't staying with you right now?"

Rochelle shifted nervously in her chair. "Not exactly—"

"*Uh-uh.* I hafta stay with Daddy so I can go to school." Conny blew bubbles into his milk with a straw.

Now Avis nearly panicked. "Rochelle! Not with—" She stopped herself. Conny didn't need to hear that his father had a restraining order against him because of physical and mental abuse of his mother. Rochelle had extricated herself from the abusive marriage five years ago. *Why* would she put Conny back into that situation?!

Unless she felt she had no choice.

"Rochelle, where are you living right now? I went by your apartment—"

"I *told* you I got evicted. Didn't you believe me? I—I've just been staying around. With friends. Where I can." Rochelle's voice turned almost fierce. "But Conny needed someplace regular, someplace he could keep going to school—isn't that right, baby?" She leaned over and planted a kiss on the top of Conny's head. But Conny was still busy blowing bubbles with his straw.

Rochelle tipped her head up and looked Avis right in the eye. "Your man didn't want us staying with *you*, so, yeah, I made a deal with Dexter that Conny could stay with him till the end of school. He hasn't ever, you know—not to Conny."

"Oh, Rochelle . . ." Avis's emotions churned in her stomach, a raw mixture of fear for Conny spending even one more day with that man, gut-wrenching sorrow that Rochelle had been virtually homeless for the past four months, and anger at Peter. Yes! Anger at Peter. None of this would have happened if Peter hadn't been so stubborn that night back in February, had been willing for Rochelle and Conny to stay with them until they got on their feet.

Kathryn Davies appeared, eyes dry, though a little red, with a smile for Rochelle. "Is it okay to tell your mom what we were talking about?"

"I kind of did. But maybe you can tell her."

Avis looked from Kathryn to Rochelle and back again. What had Rochelle said? She'd gotten so upset at finding out that Conny was staying with his dad, she'd completely missed it.

Kathryn pulled up a chair. "Well, you know, Mrs. D, that Olivia moved back home this week. Which leaves us with some extra room in our apartment. Well, the Candys' apartment. So anyway, knowing that Rochelle and Conny needed a place to live, we decided—Nick, Brygitta, and me—to ask Rochelle if she'd like to move in with us for the rest of the summer. And she's thinking about it, right, Rochelle?"

Rochelle nodded. But the implication of this announcement

left Avis speechless. Kathryn *knew* about Rochelle's situation? Knew they needed a place to live, maybe even knew Conny was living with his dad, and had been talking about it with Rochelle—how many times?

Be wise, Avis, she told herself. There would be time to find out the answers to the questions swimming in her head. She had to focus on now. Rochelle was *here*. Conny was *here*. And Kathryn and her friends had just made a generous offer.

An offer that might even get Peter's approval.

Bored with blowing milk bubbles, Conny wandered over to the book corner and sat down with some of the kids' books on the lower shelf. Relieved that "Big Ears" was out of earshot, the three of them talked.

Rochelle said she was grateful for the offer of a place she and Conny could stay together, but she didn't have any money right now. It'd been tough finding a job without an address, but now . . . Kathryn said don't worry about it. She could be a "guest" until she found a job. Did she want to move in today? . . . No, because all Conny's stuff was at his dad's—and if Conny didn't come home tonight, there'd be hell to pay before Dexter let Rochelle pick up the boy's things . . . Avis jumped in. What if they went to Dexter's place with a copy of the restraining order—and threatened to call the police if he didn't turn over the boy's things? . . . That was tricky, because Rochelle had voluntarily let the boy stay there . . . But wasn't the reason he was at his dad's so he could go to school? School ended a week ago! Rochelle now had a place to stay, and she had legal custody. It was time for Conny to come back to live with his mom . . . But, Rochelle admitted, she was afraid to confront Dexter alone.

Avis was just about to say she'd go confront Dexter herself, when Conny reappeared at his mother's elbow, frowning big time. "Stop talking and let's *go*." He pulled on her arm. "I wanna go to Grammy's house."

Rochelle cuddled him. "You've been super patient, big boy! But I've got a better idea. Why don't we go see the apartment where you and Mama might stay together?" She looked hopefully at Kathryn. "Is that okay? Could we stop at your place so Conny and I can see the apartment? Maybe meet your friends if they're there?"

Fishing out her car keys, Avis noticed Rochelle's hesitance to "go to Grammy's." On the other hand, checking out the apartment Kathryn and her friends were subletting was a good idea. That would give her time to go up to the third floor and talk to Peter.

Chapter 42

Brygitta and Nick were both home when Kat opened the door. In fact, they were caught red-handed moving Nick's stuff from the master bedroom to the study. Kat made introductions, which felt a little awkward at first. But Conny's eyes bugged out at the sight of Nick's electric guitar leaning against the couch. "Hey! You play in a band or somethin'? Can I try it?" The boy made a beeline for the guitar.

Rochelle grabbed for him. "No, Conny—"

"No, no, it's all right. Sure, little guy. Here, let me plug it in." Nick dropped the laundry basket of "stuff" he'd been carrying, and he and Conny disappeared into the study with the guitar.

Bree rolled her eyes. "Uh-oh. I can see it now. Nick and Conny auditioning for *America's Got Talent*. Screaming fans. TV trucks outside."

Rochelle started to laugh, which turned into a coughing fit. Alarmed, Kat ran to the kitchen and brought back a glass of water. Rochelle rummaged in her bag and gulped down a pill with the water. "Thanks. I'm okay now."

"Would you like to see the room?" Brygitta said. "I'm sorry it's not quite ready yet. Nick's washing the sheets. I insisted. Figured you wouldn't want to sleep in his sheets, although he swears he doesn't have cooties."

A grin touched Rochelle's thin face as she and Kat followed Brygitta down the hall. "Is she always this funny?"

Kat chuckled. *Only when she's nervous*. But she didn't say so.

Rochelle stood in the doorway of the master bedroom, taking it in. The large room was dominated by the queen-size four-poster—stripped of its bedding—but two padded chairs by the window were separated by a lamp table, the floor was carpeted, and the wall opposite the window boasted one long, low dresser with a huge mirror, containing four columns of drawers—his and hers. Olivia had originally chosen the foldout in the study as "cozier," and the Candys' second bedroom had twin beds, which Kat and Bree preferred to sleeping in the same bed, even a queen. Which is why Nick had ended up in the master bedroom.

"Why is the guy giving up this nice room for Conny and me?" Rochelle still hadn't entered the room. Almost as if she felt intimidated by it, Kat thought. "And he's already moved out—before you even knew I was coming."

Kat shrugged. "We all had a feeling you would. Hoped so anyway."

Strange electronic sounds came from the other end of the apartment. Brygitta snickered, but Rochelle didn't seem to notice. She finally stepped into the room, running her hand over the thick bed mattress with the soft pad. "Thank you," she whispered—and turning suddenly, gave Kat a tight hug.

For a brief moment Kat could almost feel the hug Rochelle's mother had given her outside the coffee shop. She'd been taken aback at first, not expecting the hug, feeling embarrassed that Mrs. D had caught her crying. But her arms had been so strong, yet so gentle, so enfolding, that Kat felt herself melting into the hug, never wanting it to end. Even when Mrs. Douglass had gone back inside, Kat had still felt those arms around her, and it'd taken her a long while to stop crying—not from loss anymore but from the sheer comfort of being held by a mother's embrace.

They all turned, hearing a muffled knock at the front door and then a voice calling out, "Hello?"

"My mom," Rochelle said and scurried back down the hall, Kat and Brygitta right behind her. But Rochelle stopped so suddenly as the hallway opened into the living room that the two friends ran into each other.

Both Mr. and Mrs. Douglass stood just inside the door.

The weird electronic sounds stopped. "Grandpa!" Squealing, Conny ran out of the study and wrapped his arms around one of Mr. Douglass's legs. The man reached down and lifted the little boy into his arms. "Hey, buddy. I'm really glad to see you."

No real family resemblance, Kat realized as she watched them over Rochelle's shoulder. Mr. Douglass's complexion was dark, a coffee bean brown, while Conny had his mother's honey-brown color. And their features were different. But even if he wasn't Rochelle's biological dad, maybe Mr. D was the only grandfather the little boy had ever known.

"Say, Conny," Mr. D said. "Would you mind if I stole your mama for a little while? I have something special I want to say to her . . ." He put his hand around the little boy's ear and whispered into it. Then aloud, "What do you think?"

"Okay." Conny wiggled out of the man's arms and ran back toward the study door, where Nick was leaning against the doorjamb. "We're making music!"

Mr. Douglass chuckled. "*Uh-huh*, we heard."

Kat felt kind of silly standing behind Rochelle in the entryway between the hall and living room, so she kind of nudged Conny's mother from behind and the three of them took a few steps into the living room until Kat and Brygitta could slip over toward the dining nook. Mr. and Mrs. Douglass didn't seem to notice them. In fact, Mr. D took a couple steps toward Rochelle. "Rochelle, could we go somewhere to talk? Up to our apartment? Or we could go for a walk, whatever you'd prefer."

Rochelle just stood still for a long moment. Then she said, "Can Mom come too? Maybe go for a walk."

"Of course. That'd be great. The three of us."

Rochelle turned to Kat. "Is it okay to leave Conny here for a little while?"

Kat grinned. "Just try to pry him away from Nick."

"Somebody calling me?" Nick stepped back to the doorway.

"We're going out for a few minutes," Mr. D said. "Are you all right with the boy?"

"Sure."

The two Douglasses and Rochelle started out the door. Then Mr. Douglass turned back and spoke to Nick. "This apartment is the beginning of your internship, my brother. Take good care of the flock." And then he followed his wife and Rochelle out the door and down the stairs.

Kat gave Nick a funny look. "What did he mean by that?"

"Uh . . ." Nick looked sheepish. "Just a sec." He went back into the study. They heard him say, "Hey, Conny. You work on your song for a few minutes, okay? I have to talk to these big girls here."

Bent over the guitar, Conny twanged a few jarring notes. "No problem, dude."

Laughing silently, Kat beckoned Nick and Brygitta into the kitchen where Conny couldn't overhear. "What's going on, 'dude'?" She playfully pushed Nick with her hip. "Then I'll tell you guys what happened at the coffee shop." Well, not everything. Her own reaction to Mrs. D's reunion with her daughter was still a little too raw.

Nick got himself a glass of water from the tap and sat down at the small kitchen table. "Okay. When you called me from the coffee shop, Kat, I was actually upstairs with the Douglasses. I thought maybe Mr. Douglass wanted to ask how I liked the job after two days, or worse, maybe I'd messed up, though Carl Hickman said, 'Good job,' when I left yesterday. So I was kinda flabbergasted when they said they wanted to know if I was still interested in doing my seminary internship at SouledOut—"

"Nick! That's fabulous!" Kat squealed.

"Wait just a second, will ya? It's not a done deal. But they said they'd been praying about the church meeting last week—got the feeling it was pretty stressful for them—and they said God had been talking to them about me." Nick stopped, and he swallowed a couple of times, as if trying to control an emotion that threatened to surface.

Kat reached out and touched his hand. "Are you okay?"

Nick nodded. "I just couldn't believe it. They said if I was still interested in doing my internship at SouledOut, they'd recommend me to Pastor Cobbs and—"

"In place of the Douglasses?!" Brygitta screeched.

Kat's mouth dropped. "They're withdrawing?!"

"Let me finish, will ya?" Nick gave them both exasperated looks. "They're gonna propose that the pastor leave only one of them on the list—they didn't say which one—and add me. But of course, the congregation would have to approve." Nick shrugged. "And then you called, Kat, and Mrs. Douglass ran out."

"Incredible." Kat shook her head thoughtfully. "I mean, *I* want you to do your internship at SouledOut, Nick, but I was thinking *in addition* to the Douglasses. But . . . what did Mr. D mean saying that stuff about 'this apartment is the beginning of your internship'?"

"Hey!" They were interrupted by Conny, who ran into the kitchen right then. "C'mon, Mr. Nick! I thought we was gonna do *music*!" He tugged on Nick's arm, and Nick gave an apologetic grin to Kat and Brygitta and let himself be dragged back to the electric guitar.

"*Huh*. Lucky save." Kat rolled her eyes. "I think we're gonna have to get some toys for the kid. Not sure this new music duo is gonna play well for the folks above and below us—not to mention *us*." She jumped up and opened the refrigerator. "Hey, Bree, why don't we make a big lunch salad with that leftover quinoa, add a bunch of cucumbers and onions and stuff, and have some lunch ready when the Douglasses and Rochelle get back?"

Bree snorted. "*You* make the quinoa salad and *I'll* make peanut butter and jelly sandwiches. We've got a kid living with us now, you know."

Rochelle came back alone and didn't say a lot, just that they'd had a good talk. "Mom and Peter feel good about Conny and me staying here with you guys. In fact, I think they really like it." She grinned with a slight irony. "You know, close but not too close, if you know what I mean."

Over Kat and Bree's lunch—Conny turned up his nose at the quinoa salad but grabbed a peanut butter and jelly sandwich and ran off to "explore"—Rochelle said she and "the parents," as she called them, had decided all four of them should go to her ex's apartment at the regular time she'd normally take Conny back that evening, take the order of protection if they needed it, but tell Dexter she had a place to stay now and was taking Conny. "Peter said Conny should have a chance to say good-bye to his dad, not just not go back. That it's the decent thing to do." She shrugged. "Guess that makes sense. But I don't know—stuff that makes sense to most people doesn't always work with Dex. One way or the other, guess we'll be back tonight. That okay with you guys?"

All three nodded.

Rochelle took a taste of the quinoa salad and raised her eyebrows. "Looks weird, but it's kinda good." She laid down her fork. "Just want you guys to know I'm gonna look for a job as soon as possible. It oughta be easier to find one now that I've got an actual address. That was always the stumper when I filled out applications. No address. And most of the time no phone 'cause I couldn't add minutes to my cell."

Nick and Bree told Rochelle not to worry, she could help with the rent when she got a job. And if they knew what kind of job she was looking for, they'd keep their eye out for her.

"Anything, really. Retail, phones . . . not so much secretarial though. My typing's a little rusty. Would love to find a babysitting job or something where I could keep Conny with me. But that's not likely."

Kat's mind did a double take. Babysitting? Of course! Olivia had quit her nanny job—and Rochelle needed one. Breathlessly, she spilled her idea. "Does anybody know the name of the family Olivia was working for? We could call and— What?"

Rochelle was shaking her head. "I . . . Most families won't hire me."

"Why not? Of course they would!"

Rochelle stared at her plate with its half-eaten sandwich and small serving of salad. "Not when they find out I've got HIV."

Now it was Kat's turn to stare. Nick and Brygitta seemed just as astounded.

"I'm sorry." Rochelle looked miserable. "Mom said I needed to tell you guys. Maybe you won't want me either, now that you know."

Kat looked helplessly at her other housemates. What did she know about HIV? Not much. But there was medicine now, wasn't there? . . . and laws about discriminating against people with HIV in the job market . . . and basic safe practices. They even had them posted in various places at CCU, assuming there were people living with HIV within the college community.

"I know you're wondering how I got HIV." Rochelle's eyes came up and she had that fierce look Kat had seen before. "Well, I'll tell you. My husband. Dex and I got married young, and I've never had sex with anyone but him. That's how my mom and dad raised me. But Dex . . . he gave it to me." She snorted with disgust. "He's a real looker, a ladies' man, had girls running after *him*. But I didn't know about the HIV until after I left him." Tears welled up in her beautiful brown eyes. "See? Even now Dexter is about to ruin something beautiful!" She stood up so suddenly her chair tipped over and fell on the floor with a crash. "I'll . . . I'll get Conny and go. I should've told you . . . I'm sorry."

"Wait!" Nick stood in her way. "Rochelle, you don't have to go. Everything's happened so fast today, we don't blame you that you're just now telling us. It's a lot for one day. But our invitation stands—right, Kat? Bree?"

Kat nodded. Bree did too.

"We want you, Rochelle—you and Conny. Because God's been putting all this together, and we know He'll take care of this too." And in a gesture Kat had never seen before, Nick took both of Rochelle's hands in his, closed his eyes, and began to pray. "Jesus, *thank* You for Rochelle and Conny. Thank You for bringing them here to be with us. We know it was You, Lord, because none of us could have put together this crazy, wonderful plan . . ."

Kat didn't close her eyes. She was staring at Nick, seeing

him as she'd never quite seen him before, and her heart felt as if it were doing flip-flops. What was it Mr. D had said as he'd gone out the door? *"Take care of the flock."*

God had given Nick a pastor's heart. Even here. Now. Could she live with that?

Yes, oh yes.

Chapter 43

Avis wrapped the black silk head wrap around her twists to keep them in place and slid between the sheets, scooting over until she was cuddled against Peter's broad bare back, her arm resting along his side, their bodies like spoons. She lay with her head on the soft pillow, feeling the energy that had kept her going all this startling, astounding day draining out of her body.

She was tired. Exhausted even. But her eyes were wide open, staring into the velvet darkness. "Peter?"

"Mm."

"Isn't it amazing to think that this morning we had no idea where Rochelle and Conny were, and tonight they're sleeping in the room right beneath us?"

"Mm-hm."

Rochelle and Conny . . . safe. Together. Here in this building. *Oh Lord, it's almost too wonderful to comprehend! Thank You, Jesus, thank You. Thank You for protecting them, for bringing them home . . .*

How long had her Yada Yada sisters been praying for Rochelle and Conny? Months. Well, years if she counted everything that had happened since Rochelle had fled her abusive marriage and then discovered Dexter had infected her with HIV.

She really needed to call Jodi and Estelle and Edesa with the good news. Well, she'd see them at worship tomorrow. And she'd call the rest of the sisters tomorrow afternoon to tell them how God had answered their prayers.

And yet . . . she shuddered. Rochelle and Conny's situation had been even worse than she'd imagined. She never once thought Rochelle would risk letting Conny stay with his dad. And it'd been touch-and-go that evening too.

"Peter?"

"Mm."

"You really stood up to Dexter tonight. I was proud of you. And so glad you were there."

Peter turned his head slightly, letting her see part of his profile in the moonlight streaming through the window blinds. "Yeah, well, when Rochelle said Conny had been staying with the man and she'd need to go back to get his stuff, no way was I going to let her face him alone. We know what he's like."

"But you said Conny should go with us too. That surprised me."

"*Humph.* I did it for Conny's sake. Poor kid doesn't understand all the adult reasons his mom and dad are separated. It would just be more confusion if he didn't get to make some transition, say good-bye to his dad. He's been living there for, what? Four months? And I knew showing up without Conny would just set the man off, and we'd have a big scene on our hands."

Avis felt a nervous giggle escape. "We almost had a scene on our hands anyway."

"Yeah, well . . . Dexter wouldn't be Dexter if he didn't try to bully Rochelle, make her feel guilty for taking Conny back."

"I know." She raised up, leaned over his shoulder, and kissed his scratchy cheek. She caught a slight whiff of his leathery aftershave. "Thank you for standing up to him. You were so . . . strong. Told him what's what. No shouting. But no nonsense either." She kissed him again. "My man."

Peter's head sank back onto his pillow and his breathing evened out. Avis cuddled closer, her heart swelling with love for him. And yet, not twelve hours ago she'd been so angry with him! But that was before . . .

"Peter?"

"Mm."

"Thank you for apologizing to Rochelle about last Valentine's Day. I know that meant eating some humble pie."

"Humph."

She thought that was all he was going to say, but after a moment he murmured, "Yeah, I was upset at her barging in on us late at night. I had designs on you that evening, which she completed disrupted." He gave a little snort. "To tell the truth, I didn't *want* to admit she needed us that night. But . . . she was hurting and I was being selfish. So I meant it when I asked her to forgive me."

Suddenly he rolled over to face her in the dim moonlight. "Actually, I need to ask you to forgive me too. I thought the whole thing would blow over in a couple of weeks, and she'd get her act together. When we lost contact, it was more serious than I wanted to admit. I know you've suffered a lot these past few months, and . . . I'm sorry, Avis. Really sorry."

A lump caught in her throat. She couldn't speak. But reaching up she traced his lips and stroked his face. "Forgiven," she finally whispered. "And I know Rochelle forgives you too. Did you hear what she said to Kathryn and the others when we got back here with Conny's stuff?"

"No, what? I was putting the car in the garage, remember?"

"She said, 'You should've seen Dad stand up to Dexter.'"

Now Peter leaned up on one elbow. "She said that? She called me *Dad*?" He chuckled. "How about that." He lay down again, still chuckling.

They were quiet again for several minutes as Avis's mind ran through all that had transpired since that fateful day in February, including the missing ruby earrings.

"Peter?"

"*Mm.*" His eyes were closed.

"I think I know how the earrings got back on my dresser."

"*Hm.* You didn't ask Rochelle?" he murmured, eyes still closed.

"No. The first thing she said to me at the coffee shop was she was sorry about the earrings, but I didn't want to talk earrings right then. But I've been thinking . . ."

Silence.

"It was Kathryn Davies."

"Kathryn?"

"Rochelle said she met Kathryn Dumpster-diving, and they ran into each other several more times. She must have given Kathryn the earrings and told her to put them on my dresser sometime when she was here. Maybe the night they came for dinner? I don't know. But it makes sense, don't you think?"

Silence.

Dumpster-diving. Avis's heart twisted. The first time she'd met Kathryn at SouledOut, the girl had her arms full of food she'd "rescued" from a Dumpster. Florida was offended by it. To Avis, the whole thing had been slightly annoying, one more of Kathryn's idealistic ventures to save the world. And yet . . . her own daughter, her precious Rochelle, had been Dumpster-diving because she was hungry. Because she was homeless. Had no money. No food.

And it was Kathryn who'd found her. God had used Kathryn's Dumpster-diving to bring her daughter back to her. God had used Kathryn . . .

Oh God! Forgive me for judging that girl. Your Word says that all the parts of Your body are important—even the Dumpster-divers, I guess. And that we need each other! I didn't realize it, but You did, my Father. You knew I needed Kathryn, that she was the one You were going to use to bring my daughter home again.

"And Kathryn needs you," a Voice whispered in her spirit.

Avis was startled by the clarity of the words. *Kathryn needs* me, *Lord? She seems like such an independent young woman, totally self-sufficient, with all these big ideas.*

"She needed you this morning."

That morning . . . it was true. Avis could hardly believe what Kathryn had said when she'd discovered the girl crying outside the coffee shop. That she couldn't remember being hugged like that by her own mother—or even hugged at all. Was that possible?

Okay, Lord. I see it now. She needed to learn more about Kathryn's family situation. Stand by her in the same way that the girl had stood by Avis and her family, in spite of how often Avis had pushed her away, kept her distance. Why? Why had Kathryn continued to show up on her doorstep, so to speak?

She was hungry. Hungry for a mother's unconditional love? Yes. But more than that. Kathryn was a fairly new Christian. She'd been reaching out to Avis, needing a woman of God to show her the way. Didn't Scripture say for the older women to teach the younger?

Oh God, I've been so blind! Forgive me, Lord. Forgive me . . .

And then there was Nick. What was it Peter had said? That Nick was sweet on Kathryn? Avis wondered how Kathryn felt about that. Or if she even knew. But if it was true, then Kathryn and Nick needed both her and Peter. So maybe it was a double blessing that Peter had given Nick a job. Maybe he could be a mentor to him . . .

Which he'd already become, in a way. After all, it was Peter who said he felt God was prompting him to support Nick's pastoral internship at SouledOut. Even if it meant that one of them should withdraw from the process of becoming part of the interim pastoral team.

Which one? Her or Peter?

"Peter?"

No answer. Her husband's breathing was deep and regular. But she had an idea what he'd say. That they should take the whole idea to Pastor Cobbs and get his discernment. But Peter was convinced that the young man should intern at SouledOut Community Church. And Avis had to agree. Frankly, she wouldn't mind taking her name off the list. A team of Pastor Cobbs, Peter, and young Nick could be dynamite.

There was only one thing that bothered her.

It was David Brown who'd brought up Nick's internship at the congregational meeting. For less than noble reasons. The man and his wife were closet racists. That was harsh . . . but it was true. So if Nick became an interim pastor, even as an intern, would the Browns have "won"?

"Avis?" The Voice in her spirit almost jolted her upright.

She felt like young Samuel in the Bible. *Are You talking to me, Lord?*

"Don't forget, people misunderstood a lot of things I did while I was on earth. And it looked like the devil had won when they crucified Me. But I was obedient to the Father because it was the right thing to do. All part of God's plan."

Avis almost stopped breathing, not wanting to miss this inner Voice.

"So the only question is, is encouraging Nick's internship the right thing to do? If it is, then let Me take care of the Browns and their misguided prejudices."

The inner Voice faded. The only sound in the room was Peter's deep breathing, almost a gentle snore. A sweet peace filled Avis's spirit as she relaxed against the soft pillow and finally closed her eyes.

"Thank You, Jesus," she breathed, "for Your faithfulness—for standing with me in spite of my failures, my sins, my blind eyes and deaf ears . . ."

And Avis slept.

Reading Group Guide

1. If you've read the *Yada Yada Prayer Group* novels, you've already met Avis Douglass. What surprised you the most as you became more intimately acquainted with her in this first SouledOut Sisters novel?

2. Have you ever felt like Avis's husband Peter: "Do we just keep on doing what we're doing until we retire? Or do we look ahead, ask ourselves, what would we really like to do before we retire, while we've still got our health and a little energy . . . put our experience to use doing something else, something different"? How would you approach such a conversation with your spouse or family members?

3. Is there someone in your life who annoys you, like Kat Davies annoys Avis? Have you thought about *why* this person annoys you? How do you respond? Do you . . . pull away? Avoid him or her? Speak with annoyance or frustration? Simply tolerate him or her? Consider: Might God be prompting you to relate in a different way with this person? Why or why not?

4. Even Avis Douglass—a mature Christian—had her moments of feeling stuck in her prayers! (See pg. 137–138.) When was the last time you felt like that—wanting to pray, feeling desperate, but not knowing just how to pray? Avis heard the still, small voice of the Holy Spirit say: *"Praise Me in faith, praise Me for what I'm going to do and am already doing, even if you can't see it. Let the joy of the Lord be your strength."* Avis prayed Psalm 42 to get unstuck . . . try it. Let the "joy of the Lord" by *your* strength.

5. In Chapter 19, Avis recognized she was holding the CCU students at an emotional distance. *"Sorry for fussing, Lord . . . I just have so much on my plate right now. I don't feel like I have the energy to relate*

to new neighbors." Why is it so hard to relate to "new people" when you have a lot on your plate? Is that an easy excuse? When is it OK to pull away from other people? Is there danger in ignoring someone God may be putting in your path for a reason?

6. A multicultural church can be a blessing—and also has its challenges. What do you think the women talking in the Ladies Room at SouledOut (Ch. 19) meant by worrying that the church might become "too black"? Avis never confronted the women or let them know she'd overheard. Was that the right or wrong thing to do? What would you have done if you'd been in Avis's shoes in that bathroom?

7. Kat had promised Rochelle she wouldn't tell her parents about meeting her on the street. But when she learns that Rochelle's ex had been abusive, and that the Douglasses don't know Conny is staying with his dad, she faces a dilemma. What would you have done? Have you been in a similar situation where you've made a promise but feel like you have to break it? What are the implications?

8. When Kat rushed out of the Douglasses' house after dinner, Nick wanted to go after her but Avis stopped him. What do you think Avis meant by telling Nick not to "get in the way" of the Holy Spirit? In our rush to comfort someone or "fix things," how might we "get in the way" of the Holy Spirit?

9. Kat said she wished she were Rochelle—at least Rochelle and her mother had a relationship that could be restored. Kat barely had a relationship with her mother, couldn't remember when she'd been hugged like that (see pg. 363). Is there a broken relationship in your family that needs restoring? What might you do to take that first step toward reconciliation?

For more Reading Group Guide questions about *Stand by Me*, visit www.ThomasNelson.com/RGG

An excerpt from *The Yada Yada Prayer Group*

The lobby of the Embassy Suites hotel in Chicago's northwest suburbs was packed with women. An intense hum rose and fell, like a tree full of cicadas. "Girl! I didn't know *you* were coming!" . . . "Where's Shirlese? I'm supposed to be roomin' with her." . . . "*Look* at you! That outfit is *fine*!" . . . "Pool? Not after spending forty-five dollars at the salon this morning, honey. Who you kiddin'?"

Avis and I wiggled our Mutt and Jeff selves through the throng of perfumed bodies and presented our reservations at the desk.

"Jodi Baxter? And . . . Avis Johnson. You're in Suite 206." The clerk handed over two plastic key cards. "If you're here for the Chicago Women's Conference"—she added with a knowing smile—"you can pick up your registration packet at that table right over there."

Avis let me forge a path back through the cicada convention to a long table with boxes of packets marked A–D, E–H, all the way to W–Z. As we were handed our packets emblazoned with CWC in curlicue calligraphy, I noticed a bright gold sticker in the right-hand corner of mine with the number 26 written in black marker. I glanced at the packet being given to the woman standing next to me at the A–D box who gave her name as "Adams, Paulette"—but her gold sticker had the number 12.

"What's this?" I asked the plump girl behind the registration table, pointing to the number.

"Oh, that." Miss Helpful smiled sweetly. "They'll explain the numbers at the first session. Don't worry about it . . . Can I help you?" She turned to the next person in line.

Humph. I didn't want to wait till the first session. I was nervous enough surrounded by women who seemed as comfortable in a crowd of strangers as if it were Thanksgiving at Grandma's. I didn't want any "surprises." Avis waved her packet at me over the heads of five women crowding up to the table between us and nodded toward the elevators. We met just as the door to Elevator Two pinged open, and we wheeled our suitcases inside.

"What number did you get?"

"Number?"

"On your packet, right-hand corner, gold sticker."

"Oh." Avis turned over the packet she was clutching in one hand, along with her plastic key card, purse strap, and travel-pack of tissues. "Twenty-six. What's it for?"

I smiled big and relaxed. "I don't know. They'll tell us at the first session." Whatever it was, I was with Avis.

As it turned out, we didn't need our key cards. The door to Suite 206 stood ajar. Avis and I looked at each other and stole inside like the Three Bears coming home after their walk in the woods. The sitting room part of the suite was empty. However, through the French doors leading into the bedroom, we could see "Goldilocks" sitting on the king-size bed painting her toenails while WGCI gospel music blared from the bedside radio.

The stranger looked up. "Oh, hi!" She waved the tiny polish brush in our direction. "Don't mind me. Make yourselves at home."

We stood and stared. The woman was average height, dark-skinned, and lean, with a crown of little black braids sporting a rainbow of beads falling down all around her head. Thirties, maybe forties; it was hard to tell. Her smile revealed a row of perfect teeth, but a scar down the side of her face belied an easy life.

Avis was braver than I was and said what I was thinking. "Uh, are we in the right room? We didn't know we had another roommate."

The woman cocked her head. "Oh! They didn't tell you at registration? Suite 206, right?" She capped the nail polish and bounced off the bed. "Florida Hickman—call me Flo." She stuck out her hand. "Avis and Jodi, right? That's what they tol' me downstairs. Anyway, I was going to room with this sister, see, but she had to cancel, and I didn't want to pay for a whole suite all by myself. Had to sell the kids just to get here as it is." She laughed heartily. Then her smile faded and she cocked her head. "You don't mind, do you? I mean . . . I don't need this whole king-size football field to myself. Unless . . ." Her forehead wrinkled. "You want me to sleep on the foldout couch?"

My good-girl training rushed to my mouth before I knew what I was saying. "Oh no, no, that's okay. We don't mind." *Do we, Avis?* I was afraid to look in Avis's direction.We had pretty much agreed driving out that since it was a suite, we could each have a "room" to ourselves. Avis was definitely not the stay-up-late, sleepover type.

"Oh. Well, sure," Avis said. "It's just that no one told us." I didn't know Avis all that well, but that wasn't enthusiasm in her voice. "I'll sleep on the foldout," she added, wheeling her suitcase over to the luggage stand.

I noticed that she didn't say "we." I stood uncertainly. But our new friend had generously offered the other side of the mammoth bed, so I dragged my suitcase into the bedroom and plopped it on the floor on the other side of Florida's nail salon.

Well, this was going to be interesting. I had thought it would be quite an adventure to get to know Avis as my roommate for the weekend. As members of the same church, this was a chance to get beyond the niceties of Sunday morning and brush our teeth in the same sink. But I hadn't counted on a third party. God knows I wanted to broaden my horizons, but this was moving a little faster than I felt ready for.

As I hung up the dress I hoped would pass for "after five" in the narrow closet, I suddenly had a thought. "Florida, what number is on your registration packet?"

Florida finished her big toe and looked at it critically. "Number? . . . Oh, you mean that gold sticker thing on the front?" She looked over the side of the bed where she'd dumped her things. "Um . . . twenty-six. Why?"

About the Author

Neta Jackson's award-winning Yada books have sold more than 600,000 copies and are spawning prayer groups across the country. She and her husband, Dave, are also an award-winning writing team, best known for the Trailblazer Books—a forty-volume series of historical fiction about great Christian heroes with 1.7 million books slold—and *Hero Tales: A Family Treasury of True Stories from the Lives of Christian Heroes* (vols. 1–4). They live in the Chicago area, where the Yada stories are set.